The MOTHERLINE

Every Woman's Journey to Find Her Female Roots

Formerly titled *Stories from the Motherline*

NAOMI RUTH LOWINSKY, PH.D.

Jeremy P. Tarcher/Perigee

Jeremy P. Tarcher/Perigee Books
are published by
The Putnam Publishing Group
200 Madison Avenue
New York, NY 10016

Chapter 1 was published in a slightly different form in *Psychological Perspectives,* issue 23. Chapter 7 was published in a shorter version in *To Be a Woman,* edited by Connie Zweig.

The author acknowledges permission to quote from the following:
Zdena Berger, from *Tell Me Another Morning.* Copyright © 1959 by Zdena Berger. Reprinted with permission of Harper & Row. Anne Cameron, from *Daughters of Copper Woman.* Copyright © 1986 by Anne Cameron. Reprinted by permission of Press Gang Publishers. Meinrad Craighead, from *The Mother's Songs.* Copyright © 1986 by Meinrad Craighead. Reprinted by permission of Paulist Press. T.S. Eliot, "The Love Song of J. Alfred Prufrock," from *The Collected Poems and Plays 1909–1950.* Reprinted by permission of Harcourt, Brace. Nikki Giovanni, "Mothers," from *My House.* Copyright © 1972 by Nikki Giovanni. Reprinted by permission of William Morrow. Judy Grahn, excerpt from "She Who," from *The Work of a Common Woman.* Copyright © 1978 by Judy Grahn. Reprinted by permission of Crossing Press. Susan Griffin, from *Women and Nature.* Copyright © 1978 by Susan Griffin. Reprinted by permission of HarperCollins. David Grossman, from *See Under: Love.* Copyright © 1989 by David Grossman. Reprinted by permission of Farrar, Straus & Giroux, Inc. Homer, "The Hymn to Demeter," from *The Homeric Hymns: The Charles Boer Translation.* Copyright © 1970 by Charles Boer. Reprinted by permission of Spring Publications. Josephine Humphries, from *Rich in Love.* Copyright © 1987 by Josephine Humphries. Reprinted by permission of Penguin USA. Maxine Kumin, "The Envelope," from *Our Ground Time Here Will Be Brief.* Copyright © 1978 by Maxine Kumin. Reprinted by permission of Penguin USA. Rachel Loden, "Orcas Island." Copyright © 1990 by Rachel Loden. Reprinted by permission of the poet. Toni Morrison, from *Beloved.* Copyright © 1987 by Toni Morrison. Reprinted by permission of Alfred Knopf. Sharon Olds, from *Satan Says.* Copyright © 1980 by Sharon Olds. Reprinted by permission of Pittsburgh Press. Tillie Olsen, from *Tell Me a Riddle.* Copyright © 1956 by Tillie Olsen. Reprinted by permission of Tillie Olsen. May Sarton, "The Invocation to Kali," from *Collected Poems (1930–1973).* Copyright © 1974 by May Sarton. Reprinted by permission of A. M. Heath. Amy Tan, from *The Joy Luck Club.* Copyright © 1989 by Amy Tan. Reprinted by permission of The Putnam Publishing Group.

Library of Congress Cataloging-in-Publication Data

Lowinsky, Naomi Ruth.
    The motherline : every woman's journey to find her female roots /
Naomi Ruth Lowinsky.
        p.   cm.
    Originally published: Stories from the motherline. Los Angeles :
J. P. Tarcher, 1992.
    Includes bibliographical references and index.
    ISBN 0-87477-732-1
    1. Motherhood—Psychological aspects.   2. Mothers and daughters.
3. Feminity (Psychology)   4. Women—Psychology.   I. Title.
HQ759.L648   1993   92-36166 CIP
306.874'3—dc20

Designed by Mauna Eichner

Manufactured in the United States of America
1   2   3   4   5   6   7   8   9   10

This book is printed on acid-free paper.
∞

For the parents of my parents —
Emma and Simon
Clara and Leo

and for their great grandchildren —
Aaron, Tamar, and Shanti
Lisa, Debbie, and Adam

A woman writing
                thinks forward
                                through her daughters,
wanders
        in her mothers,
                        pauses in her travelling
to dream again
                with them
                                of what's been lost,
forgotten, falsely
                laid to rest. . . .

RACHEL LODEN
"ORCAS ISLAND"

CONTENTS

INTRODUCTION   xi

CHAPTER ONE   I
Conceiving the Motherline: *The Source of Our Stories*

CHAPTER TWO   25
Feminism and the Forgotten Feminine:
Mastery versus Mystique

CHAPTER THREE   37
Old Wives' Tales: *Relearning the Mother Tongue*

CHAPTER FOUR   53
Wrestling with the Mother:
Of Love, Rebellion, and Our Personal Shadows

CHAPTER FIVE   73
Stories from the Middle of Our Lives:
The Mother-Daughter Loop

CHAPTER SIX   97
Our Place Among the Generations:
How We Are Shaped by Our Times

CHAPTER SEVEN   115
On My Mother's Side:
The Power of the Grandmother

CHAPTER EIGHT   141
Ghost Stories: *Entering the Realm of the Ancestors*

CHAPTER NINE   167
Ashes to Ashes:
A Mother's Childhood Landscape

CHAPTER TEN   179
The Forbidden Feminine: *Finding Our Spiritual Roots*

EPILOGUE   209
Reclaiming Our Feminine Souls

NOTES   217

BIBLIOGRAPHY   225

Acknowledgments

I t has taken this book as many years and stages to enter the world as it takes a child to grow up. Its development has required the attention, support, and nurturance of all who are closest to me.

My husband has been a loving companion throughout the long labor. He has devoted scores of miles on our Sunday hikes to the dialogue that shaped my ideas. He has traveled with me all over the world to gather stories and images, and his warmth, emotional depth, and intelligence illuminate every chapter.

My children and stepchildren, who have taught me most of what I know about mothering, have been kind to my literary baby, always interested in how I'm doing on the book and believing in its potential.

My mother has told and retold me my Motherline stories. She has read many versions of the manuscript, been generous with her time and her memories, and improved the book immensely by inviting me to visit Germany with her. Without her encouragement the book could not have happened. I am grateful, also, to my three brothers. One helped me translate my grandmother's letter from the German. The other two provided moral support, advice, and encouragement.

Emily Hancock has connected me to my literary Motherline. She was the chair of my doctoral dissertation committee and it was her clear-minded guidance that became the foundation for the book. It was she who referred me to my agent and my editor and I cannot thank her enough for both!

My agent, Felicia Eth, opened the door to the publishing world for me. She saw the book's potential, understood its market, and believed in its importance. She has been an invaluable guide in a complex new landscape, a calming influence when I am anxious, and generous with her time and ideas.

My editor, Connie Zweig, has understood my vision and helped me to realize it beyond my expectations. She has an uncanny ability to see what I am reaching for, sometimes before I can see it myself. I am deeply grateful to her and to Jeremy Tarcher for their support and enthusiasm for this book.

Three close friends, Cathy Minor Valdez, Leah Shelleda Fulton, and Carolyn Pape Cowan, have read many versions of the manuscript, given me regular doses of courage and faith over lunch, and seen me through the trials and tribulations of many years of work.

My mentors in the Jungian world, Betty Meador, Joseph Henderson, and Gareth Hill, provided my soul with the nourishment it needed as I continued on my path. Support for my writing from John Beebe, Virginia Beane Rutter, Susan Bostrom-Wong, and Elizabeth Osterman gave me courage when I needed it. Karen Signell and Peter Rutter gave me good advice about publishing. Lynn Franco, Marilyn Steele, and Meredith Sabini have been friends and advocates at crucial moments. Ellen Siegelman, Sue Elkind, Phil Cowan, Marilyn Steele, and Pat Damery read parts of the manuscript, were moved by it, and gave me new momentum to continue working.

I want to thank my students and colleagues at the Women's Therapy Center and the Pacifica Graduate Institute who have helped me understand the impact of the Motherline. And to those who participated in the research for this book, sharing their lives and their stories, teaching me to see the patterns of the Motherline, I owe my deepest gratitude.

INTRODUCTION

So many of the stories that I write, that we all write, are my mother's stories. Only recently did I fully realize this: that through years of listening to my mother's stories of her life, I have absorbed not only the stories themselves, but something of the manner in which she spoke, something of the urgency that involves the knowledge that her stories — like her life — must be recorded.

ALICE WALKER[1]

B eing a mother is an experience of body and soul which ties one to the source of our life and all life. This is a book for women who have mothers, are mothers, or are considering becoming mothers, and for the men who love them. Telling the stories of women whose maturation has been experienced in the cycle of mothering, this book does not sever mother from daughter, feminism from "the feminine," body from psyche. The path to wholeness requires reclaiming aspects of the feminine self that we have lost and forgotten in our struggle to free ourselves from constricting roles; it requires that a woman make a journey to find her roots in the personal, cultural, and archetypal Motherline.

Mother is the first world we know, the source of our lives and our stories. Embodying the mystery of origin, she connects us to the great web of kin and generation. Yet the voice of her experience is seldom heard in our literature. Psychology, the field that examines human nature, has tended to be child-oriented. And much of the feminist literature has been daughter-identified. We are so full of judgments about what mother ought to be that we can barely see what mother is. This has been shattering to a woman's sense of self and her connection to roots. We have no cultural mirror in which to envision the fullness of female development; we are deprived of images of female wisdom and maturity. Finding our female roots, reclaiming our feminine souls, requires paying attention to our real mothers' lives and experience; listening to our mothers' stories, and our grandmothers' stories, is the beginning of understanding our own. When we hear these stories, we tap into the wisdom of our Motherline.

Being a mother is an experience of body and soul that ties one to the source of one's own life and to all life. In the deepest sense of the word it is a religious experience, for the word *religion* comes from the Latin *religare,* which means to bind back to, to reconnect with. This book will help you reconnect to the story of your origins, your Motherline, your body, and your soul.

I have been gathering material for this book all of my life, much like one gathers material for a patchwork quilt. I've taken the stories of the women of my Motherline, memories of childhood, journal entries, my experience raising children and stepchildren to adulthood, pieces of my master's and doctoral dissertations[2] (both of them studies of mothers), the stories I've heard as a psychotherapist and the stories I've told as an analysand, what I've learned from students and colleagues at the Women's Therapy Center and the Pacifica Graduate Institute, and what I've learned at the C. G. Jung Institute of San Francisco where I am a candidate to become an analyst. I've gathered dreams and poetry and prose, and sewed them all together with journeys I have made to create a pattern that evokes female wholeness. Like most women's sewing projects, it has been worked on, put away while children are being raised and life makes other demands, felt guilty about, and brought back out to be worked on again. As in quilting, the design of the book has been created by combining many separate elements into one pattern.

Although the book contains the voices of many women, its structure is based on my personal life because it is the flesh and blood of our female, subjective experience that I seek to bring to consciousness. Each of our stories is unique and yet there is an underlying Motherline pattern. Other women's stories set up sympathetic vibrations so that we can begin to hear our own.

The process of finding one's Motherline is idiosyncratic and chaotic. It takes most of a lifetime. Every woman must engage in it in her own way and in her own time. The reclamation of feminine soul is not a process that can be readily taught. Rather it is a potentiality that can be evoked by shifting the way we listen to women's voices, and the way we see ourselves, our mothers, and our grandmothers. I hope to facilitate this process.

Each chapter of the book describes reclaiming an aspect of the feminine self. It is not the entire story. There are aspects of female nature, such as the warrior-amazon and the erotic lover, that are not addressed here. This book is a search for female continuity and the sense of wholeness that is gained when we find it.

OF SELF, SOUL, AND SHADOW

What is self and soul? Self has come to have specific meanings in psychology. In self psychology, it is used to mean an inborn potentiality for an authentic and vital identity. Jungians use the word *self* in a similar but larger sense. For them, the self is the "potential for integration of the total personality"; it "contains the seeds of the individual's destiny";[3] it includes the psychological, biological, and spiritual aspects of being human.

There has been much controversy among feminist thinkers about whether the experience of self is gender-specific. There are those who argue that a gendered sense of self is a by-product of culture. Though I agree that the culture may warp and damage the female experience of self, it makes no sense to me to separate one's sense of self entirely from one's body. Female identity is rooted in embodied experiences of menstruation, childbearing, lactation, and menopause, which are filtered through the veils that different cultures throw over them. Clearly a woman's identity consists of much more than her reproductive system, and this is where the feminist critique is invaluable in confronting cultural misogyny. But I believe that we go to the depths of our feminine selves in these primal, physical experiences, common to women of all cultures. Devaluing these depths is a function of our own cultural bias.

The word *soul* is most commonly used in a religious context, and means the part of our being that is connected to the immortal. Some psychological thinkers such as James Hillman use soul in a broader way, to name the experience of seeing the gods or the sacred in all life forms. This book is about women's immortality through our birth-giving capacity. Soul here is not separate from body. It is through our full honoring of bodily experience that we become ensouled. Soul does not separate us from ordinary life. It does not float off into the stratosphere as spirit seems to in the distinction commonly made between spirit and flesh. In colloquial usage one who has soul is one who has acquired depth through suffering, often one who has been oppressed. Soul is born of the kind of suffering that brings us in touch with the mysteries of life.

One way we garner soul is through the integration of what Jungians call the shadow. The shadow is that part of our personality that is cast into darkness by our fears, values, temperament, and cultural prejudice—a part of ourselves we do not know. Traits that we deny and repress in ourselves and dislike intensely in others are usually parts of our shadow. Contemporary women are prone to project aspects of their shadows on their mothers. We cut off our natural energy flow when we disown our envy, rage, competitiveness, pettiness, sensuality. Paradoxically, when these traits are recognized and owned, they tend to soften and get humanized. Learning to suffer our own shortcomings and those of others, even to develop a sense of humor about it all, gives depth and richness to the personality. It is an aspect of maturation and of soul.

Jungian theory describes psychological experience on three levels: the personal, the cultural, and the archetypal. Most current psychology emphasizes the personal and neglects the cultural (leaving that to the anthropologists) and the archetypal (leaving that to the theologians). The problems created by this narrowness in psychological thought are more than academic. Mothers get saddled with cultural baggage or with archetypal expectations. Because the gods are dead, mothers are expected to stand in for them, taking the blame for much that more truly belongs to fate. Because we've lost a historical sense of how culture shifts, we are outraged that our mothers did not raise us according to the standards of our times but had the effrontery to be shaped by the values of their own generation. Thus painful intergenerational rifts and misunderstandings arise. Women whose mothers love them deeply feel estranged and unmothered. Women whose daughters long to know them can find no language of mutuality.

OUR MAMMALIAN MAMA

How do we distinguish between the three levels of experience—personal, cultural, and archetypal? Archetypal psychologist James Hillman sees archetypes as the "roots of the soul."[4] Jungian analyst Joseph Henderson describes the archetype as involving both a primordial image and an instinctual root that "create a pervasive sense of being gripped by an urge and dazzled by an image of compelling power."[5] An archetype can be described as an underlying life pattern with both instinctive and symbolic poles of expression surrounding a core of great emotional charge. The great mother archetype, for example, is a primordial image that expresses our instinctual, mammalian nature. It takes many cultural forms, from images of the Virgin Mary to those of the death-dealing goddess, Kali, in India. But the female form with breasts is recognizable in all cultures. We are all born of woman. Her breasts and her womb permeate all times and all cultures. Every culture translates the mother archetype differently, and every biological, or personal, mother has her own unique psychology and connection to her child.

The personal experience of the mother-daughter relationship is shaped by the individual lives and temperaments of the two women. If, for example, the daughter is the longed-for only child of an older mother who tried for years to get pregnant, her experience of her personal mother will be very different from that of the sixth child of an exhausted mother who considered getting an abortion. The quiet, introverted child of a quiet, introverted mother will have a different experience of self than would the fiery, extroverted child of that same introverted mother.

When a woman becomes a mother she embodies the archetypal mother and becomes the culture bearer who will socialize the child. At the cultural level a child will be schedule or demand fed, bottle or breast fed, told she should be seen but not heard, or encouraged to express her spontaneity, raised by her mother or a nanny or an au pair depending on the culture, historical period, class, and personal circumstances into which she is born. However, all these children need to be held and protected, praised and fed and played with, scolded and limited. Though this is done differently in various cultures, a child needs some manifestation of the mother archetype in her life or she will be severely damaged.

It is confusing to sort out the personal, cultural, and archetypal levels of our experience. Archetypes are mostly seen in their cultural manifestation, and changes in cultural attitude become personal battlegrounds between generations. But there are some areas in which the archetype shines through. For example, it is striking to consider how many cultures make similar sounds for naming the mother: Mama, Mutti, Ama, Ema. The "ma" sound brings the lips together as in reaching for the breast. Thus a linguistic form reveals the physiological nature of the archetype across cultures.

I remember seeing a television report about a gorilla mother who had just given birth in a local zoo. She held her baby close. When she lifted her great gorilla hand to tenderly pat its head, a shiver of archetypal energy burst through me. I knew that gesture. Every human being knows that gesture. The mother archetype in her gorilla form had been revealed to me on the evening news!

The words *male* and *female* refer to our biological natures, while the words *masculine* and *feminine* imply cultural and archetypal meanings as well. Jungians historically have been interested in the archetypal distinctions between the masculine and the feminine, not limiting them to one gender. Whether these concepts are useful or stereotypical has been controversial in both Jungian and feminist circles. The feminist critique is that these are culturally biased concepts. Jungians respond by pointing out that the masculine is not limited to men, or the feminine to women.

The terms *masculine* and *feminine* are vital concepts that are typically truncated by the tendency of cultures to make rigid gender distinctions. These hurt both men and women. There is an enormous overlap in what men and women can do. At all levels, including the physical, we are more alike than we are different. But we can rob ourselves of our deep instinctual roots in life if we deny the power of the differences between the sexes. The feminine experienced by a woman is very different from the feminine experienced by a man, and vice versa. Gender differences have biological roots that go far below the cultural level, below human history: they precede our evolution as a species and take us down to our mammalian beginnings.

All mammals are divided into males and females. Females have breasts and wombs. Males have testes and penises. These sexual differences are meaningful; far from being a curse or a limitation on women's lives, our mammalian experience is what grounds us in our feminine selves. My thinking resonates with that of the new men's movement, of which poet Robert Bly is a central spokesperson. He and others argue for a recognition of the differences between men and women at the instinctual level. It is a relief and a pleasure to hear men honoring their own embodied experience. These differences are, indeed, empowering for both men and women.

A PATTERN OF FEMININE SOUL

This book is arranged in ten chapters, each evoking an aspect of the feminine self and how it can be reclaimed. The sequence describes the journey I made, but it is not a linear path. One could begin from any place in the pattern to find one's way into the Motherline.

We begin with a conceptualization of the Motherline as the source of our stories. In the second chapter we consider the women's movement, which at once frees us and gets in our way as we seek our female roots. In the third chapter we pick up the thread of our Motherline search by going back to our forgotten knowledge of the mother tongue, remembering images we took in with our mother's milk, of the primal female experiences of bearing, bonding, and being in relation to children.

In Chapter 4, we confront the developmental problem of differentiation between mother and daughter, which forces both women to engage in the painful process of sorting out self from other, and acknowledging shadow. The thread of our story is taken up in Chapter 5 by four women who, in telling their stories from the middle of their lives, loop from the past through the present to the future and back, weaving a rich tapestry of contemporary female maturity.

In Chapter 6 we follow the thread of women's lives by looking at generational change and how we are shaped by the times we live in. Chapter 7 explores girlhood memories of a grandmother and how this process links a woman to her past and to her future and transforms the mother-daughter dyad into the ancient, sacred, female trinity: maiden, mother, and crone.

Throughout the book, my own Motherline story unfolds; I am confronted by the ghost of the grandmother I never knew. Her voice comes to me from before my birth and requires me to make a journey into the realm of my ancestors. This takes me to Israel in Chapter 8 to meet female relatives and learn their stories, and to Germany in Chapter 9 to see the landscape of my mother's childhood through the ashes of the Holocaust. My journey is part of a pattern of female development; you will see how many women make this descent into the past to find their roots.

In the end we must seek our spiritual roots in the old female religion. In Chapter 10 we traverse the land from the lost shore temples of the east coast of India to a sacred hill in Glastonbury and discover that the forbidden and taboo aspects of feminine soul are a part of our landscape as well as our dreams and our visions. What we have lost or forgotten of the feminine mysteries is hidden in our everyday lives.

Note: The names of the subjects of my study and most of my family members have been changed to protect their privacy.

CONCEIVING THE MOTHERLINE:

The Source of Our Stories

Like those old pear-shaped Russian dolls that open
at the middle to reveal another and another, down
to the peasized, irreducible minim,
may we carry our mothers forth in our bellies.
May we, borne onward by our daughters, ride
in the Envelope of Almost-Infinity,
that chain letter good for the next twenty-five
thousand days of their lives.

MAXINE KUMIN[1]

T his book is about a worldview that is as old as humankind, a wisdom we have forgotten that we know: the ancient lore of women—the Motherline. Whenever women gather in circles or in pairs, in olden times around the village well, or at the quilting bee, in modern times in support groups, over lunch, or at the children's park, they tell one another stories from the Motherline. These are stories of female experience: physical, psychological, and historical. They are stories about the dramatic changes of a woman's body: developing breasts and pubic hair, bleeding, being sexual, giving birth, suckling, menopause, and growing old. They are stories of the life cycles that link generations of women: mothers who are also daughters; daughters who have become mothers; grandmothers who always remain granddaughters. They are stories that evoke the dead: a mother who died while her child was very young; a child who never made it to adulthood. They are stories that show how times have changed and that show that nothing much changes at all.

We all know these stories. The voices of our mothers and grand-mothers telling stories from the Motherline are among our earliest memories. They flesh out what we know about what it means to be human. Yet little of this worldview surfaces into print or into our collective under-standing of history. Women lament the lack of narratives of women's lives, yet women's stories are all around us. We don't hear them because our per-ception is shaped by a culture that trivializes "women's talk" and devalues the passing down of female lore and wisdom.

CARNAL SELF-KNOWLEDGE

Let me give you some images from my own life to illuminate what I mean by the term *Motherline.* I am walking down a long stretch of beach with my mother and my two daughters. I walk between them, linking gener-ations. It is one of those cool, clear, winter days that bless the northern coast of California. Sea and sky are a vivid blue. There is a light wind, and someone thinks she sees whales out there. I can't remember what we are talking about. But I do remember a surge of feeling that goes beyond words, of overarching connections, of the present moment holding within it the seeds of both past and future, and all of it held in the bodies of these four women of three generations.

Walking between my daughters' younger bodies and my mother's older body evokes the feeling of another walk in another time. This time I am the daughter, nine or ten years old. My mother and grandmother walk with me around a lake sparkling in the morning sun. My grandmother's walk is slower. She was older then than my mother is now. I was younger than my daughters are now. Time swirls and a light mist of tears gathers behind my eyes. My grandmother has been dead for many years. How will it feel to become the age she was when I was nine? How will it feel when I am the grandmother, the mother of mothers, as she was, as my mother has become?

Back on the beach, my daughters are giggling, looking at me, then at each other. I realize I must have sunk into that deep place about which they love to tease me. "Oh, oh. Mommy's having one of her archetypal

Motherline experiences. Watch out Grandma, she's going to be talking about cycles, the moon, and the womb!"

We all laugh. It is a familiar joke in the family that I am always finding meaning in what other mothers think of as embarrassing or difficult: menstrual cycles, women's talk, the cord of connection between women of different generations.

There are so many strands of memory that make up this cord. Just after the birth of my first child, a son, my mother came to be with me. I have a physical memory of how vulnerable I felt, and how ecstatic. I felt opened up and raw from the labor and delivery. My breasts were sore and taut. When my son cried, they overflowed with milk.

The physical experience of giving birth changed my universe. I had had a dream, during the pregnancy, of facing a gate through which I had to pass. There was no choice about it. On the other side of the gate lay darkness. I was afraid. I didn't know if it was the darkness of birth or of death I was facing. I learned that it was both. Huge waves of energy, outside my control, passed through me and opened me up to push an unknown being out of the darkness of my body into the light of his first day. This brought me carnal knowledge of my own animal body, my instinctive nature, my connection to all things.

Before that birth I was quite another person. I had been an intellectual maiden curled up in a chair reading T. S. Eliot and asking Prufrock's question: "Do I dare/ Disturb the universe?" Could I write great poetry? Could I be original? The everyday miracle of birth changed my orientation in life. Like every other mother in the world, I had dared to pass through the dark gate; I had dared to bear new life. A baby was born, with ten tiny fingers and ten tiny toes and a sweet little face. He was asleep now in the garden under the shade of an old elm tree. An intellectual maiden died and a woman, his mother, was emerging into life. I knew in my body the sacred connection of all human life to the female body. I had not disturbed the universe. The universe had moved through me. I was a part of everything that was alive. I had carnal knowledge of my own female nature. It would take me a full generation to find words to express what I knew then.

I felt at once whole and broken, fulfilled and empty, vibrant with life and sorely wounded. My mother visited me and her quiet presence grounded me and soothed me. She brought with her my brother, her youngest child, then two. These two boys have formed a bridge between the generations, between her motherhood and mine. Her waters had broken just a couple of years before mine, and so we were sisters in this mothering business, as well as mother and daughter. I was my mother's first-born child. I was very young—nineteen years old. And she was in her early forties, close to the age I am now, helping me with my first-born, while her baby toddled about and asked questions about "the baby." It was my initiation into womanhood.

ILLUMINATING THE MOTHER IN THE DARK

The Motherline is an idea that has crept up on me during the years since my son was born, years of being tempered and shaped by mothering, of listening to women's stories, as daughter, mother, and granddaughter, as friend and psychotherapist, teacher and researcher. I have come to see a pattern in the many strands of meaning I've been handed. The Motherline is a name for that pattern, for the oneness of body and psyche, for the experience of continuity among women. I think of it as a central organizing principle in the psyche of women, like the stem and the roots of the tree of life, through which a woman is related to the ancient earth of female procreation.

Women who are the mothers of daughters experience an obvious relationship to the Motherline: looking backward to their mothers and forward to their daughters. My own experience of being both mother and daughter has seemed to me to be the central drama of my life. I was profoundly moved to see my younger self in my children's development, and to see my older self in my mother's maturation. Stimulated by the women's movement and its rich theory about women's lives, I looked eagerly for literature that would mirror and amplify my life-cycle experience as both mother and daughter. My search was in vain. I found that most of the literature had been written from the viewpoint of the daughter who, if she was not actively angry with her mother, was not much impressed with her mother's life experience. Some of the most compelling women writers joined in the trivialization of women's reproductive experiences. I could not find among them the wise women who could help me understand the power of my female experiences.

We live in a culture that has left the mother's experience, the mother's perspective, the mother's power, in the shadows. Even psychology, the study of human nature, tends to be oriented to the child's perspective. This may be a necessary compensation for centuries in which normal child development was not understood, and in which children were treated as the personal property of parents, abused "for their own good."

In psychotherapy, which is also child-oriented, we reach down to our early childhoods, re-experience how we were wounded, relive the ways our parents failed us. This gives us the revolutionary capacity to break free of the constricting problems of our childhoods, and to become fully ourselves.

But there is an unfortunate side-effect to this process. It casts a great shadow over the experience of the mother. Even women who are themselves mothers tend to get caught up in the collective undertow that pulls us away from identification with the mother. Kim Chernin writes of the difficulty she has had in remembering that she is both a mother and a daughter:

> After twenty years of being a mother I thought of myself still as a daughter struggling to separate from my mother. I had never stopped to think of myself as belonging to an entire generation of women who had raised children and for whom *we* were the mothers, those awesome and difficult and troublesome beings from whom they in turn were struggling for separation.[2]

Why is it so difficult to know our power as mothers? We live in a world that does not reflect the full female experience. We do not learn about women's lives in history books. Literature gives us mirrors to see ourselves primarily as daughters. We are seen as interesting only until we marry. What mother of a daughter ever gets to take center stage? Even Shakespeare, who gave us so many complex female heroines, gave us daughters to understand, or the mothers of sons. Myra Glazer Schotz, in an essay titled "Mothers and Daughters in Shakespeare," writes of a literary world in which daughters are motherless. "Where is the mother of Jessica?" cries Schotz. Of "Desdemona? Ophelia? What woman carried in her womb Regan, Goneril and Cordelia? What happened to the Duchess of Milan after Miranda was born? Did all of these shadowy, unnamed women die in childbirth?"[3]

It is as though when a daughter becomes a mother she fades from the scene. Her insights, her wisdom, her experience, her voice disappear from the world of literature. She becomes a bad joke in popular culture. She descends into the shadows, indeed becomes a shadow. And her daughters rail against her because she is filled with darkness.

In the ancient mother-daughter myth of Demeter and Kore, the mother mourns the loss of her daughter who has been taken by Hades into the underworld. In our own time the story is reversed. Daughters suffer the loss of mothers to a cultural underworld in which maternal maturity and wisdom are imprisoned, unseen and unheard by the culture at large. I am haunted by two lines in Nikki Giovanni's poem, "Mothers":

> *mommy always sat in the dark*
> *i don't know how i knew that but she did*[4]

Our mothers have been sitting in the dark. Often they choose this obscurity because their female vision of life is one that they themselves devalue. We daughters are left feeling motherless because our mothers have no words to express the depth of their experiences, and no feminine authority with which to value their lives.

ELEUSINIAN EMOTIONS

This underworld in which our mothers sit is filled with the ghosts of lost human meanings. An essay on the feminine principle by C. G. Jung gave me glimmerings of what we have lost. In it Jung considers the psychological meaning of the ancient Eleusinian mystery religion, practiced for thousands of years before the Christian era, in which the mother-daughter relationship was celebrated as an expression of the central human mystery. Jung found words to describe this difficult-to-articulate female experience:

> We could therefore say that every mother contains her daughter in herself and every daughter her mother, and that every woman extends backwards into her mother and forwards into her daughter. This participation and intermingling give rise to that peculiar uncertainty as regards time: a woman lives earlier as a mother, later as a daughter. The conscious experience of these ties produces the feeling that her life is spread out over generations—the first step towards the immediate experience and conviction of being outside time, which brings with it a feeling of immortality. The individual's life is elevated into a type, indeed it becomes the archetype of woman's fate in general. This leads to a restoration . . . of the lives of the ancestors, who now, through the bridge of the momentary individual, pass down the generations of the future. An experience of this kind gives the individual a place and a meaning in the life of the generations,

so that all unnecessary obstacles are cleared out of the way of the life-
stream that is to flow through her. At the same time the individual
is rescued from her isolation and restored to wholeness.[5]

Jung goes on to lament that modern women live in a culture "which
no longer knows the kind of wholesome experience afforded by Eleusinian
emotions." No one knows exactly what happened in the Eleusinian mystery
rites because its initiates were sworn to silence. There are some things we
do know, however. We know that men as well as women participated in a
ritualized experience of the myth of Demeter and Kore. In the myth Kore,
the adolescent daughter of Demeter, goddess of the grain, is picking flowers in a meadow with her friends. She is drawn to a particularly beautiful
flower, a narcissus. As she picks it, the earth opens up and Hades, Lord of
the Underworld, seizes her and carries her, crying and protesting, into the
realm of the shades. When her mother, the "awesome goddess with her
beautiful hair," realizes that her daughter has disappeared:

A sharp pain
seized her heart.
With her lovely hands
she tore the headdress
on her immortal hair
she threw off
the dark covering
on her shoulders,
and she shot out,
like a bird,
over dry land
and sea,
searching.[6]

The goddess goes into so deep a state of mourning that her beauty
fades and she looks like "an old woman . . . beyond childbearing, beyond
the gifts of Aphrodite." In her rage and grief she causes the earth not to
take seed, the "white barley" to fall "uselessly upon the earth." So angry
and full of grief was she that "she would have wiped out the whole race of
talking men" if Zeus had not interceded, ordering Hades to return his
bride so that her mother could see her "with her own eyes."
The mother-daughter reunion that follows is ecstatic and fruitful:

"The whole earth was weighted with leaves and flowers." Their joy is marred only by the fact that Hades enticed his bride to eat a pomegranate seed, and this assured her return to the underworld to spend at least one third of the year with him. The race of "talking men" is saved, but must endure a seasonal cycle that includes winter, when Kore goes into the underworld again and the earth bears no fruit.

Clearly, this was a very different psychological time for women, when the mother-daughter relationship was seen as so central that its violent severing endangered human continuity; a time when men as well as women sought spiritual rebirth by becoming one, not with the father or the son, but with the mother! Women in such a time bore no shame for being female. Their gender connected them directly to the life source and the sacred. What was a mystery in those days was the unalterable facts of life: the birth and death of the individual and the sacred continuity of the species. At the end of Homer's "Hymn to Demeter," the goddess teaches the people her rites:

> *and she revealed to them*
> *her beautiful mysteries,*
> *which are impossible*
> *to transgress,*
> *or to pry into,*
> *or to divulge:*
> *for so great*
> *is one's awe*
> *of the gods*
> *that it stops*
> *the tongue.*

Imagine, if you can, a society of men and women so permeated with the inner meaning of the female mysteries that they would hold in silence the secrets of life that were revealed to them. Imagine women and men sharing the rage and grief of the mother whose daughter has been seized by the lord of the underworld. We can understand the agony of the goddess as grief for the loss of her own younger self, or grief for her child, who must go off and live her own fate. All of us who live long enough can identify with such grief. Cast into the emotional void of facing their own mortality, the initiates at Eleusis were offered no way out of their human fate. No promises of eternal life after death, no mastery of the aging body through jogging and lowering cholesterol levels assuaged their pain. The initiates had fasted. They had suffered the agony of the goddess. Their heads had been wrapped in darkness, and they had been forced to surrender all control.[7] In a mysterious moment of illumination, something was revealed—a secret—the essence of the mystery. What could it be?

In silence a mown ear of grain was shown to the assemblage. Eleusinian emotions reflect a religious attitude that is at one with the organic world, with the natural cycles of the grain, of animals, and of human beings. This is in contrast to modern attitudes that split off the body, in which nature is to be mastered, and in which women suffer shame about their bodies' organic processes. In Eleusinian days these processes were seen as a revelation of life's most profound meaning. The seed of grain, buried in the ground, sprouting into new life, was the metaphor for our mortal situation. In the words of mythographer Carl Kerenyi, who has told us much of what we know today about the Eleusinian mysteries, "Every grain of wheat and every maiden contains, as it were, all its descendants and all her descendants—an infinite series of mothers and daughters in one."[8]

I began to understand why I felt so disoriented as a modern mother and daughter. I found little in contemporary psychological or feminist theory that mirrored the depth of my experience of the life cycle. Thinkers such as Carol Gilligan and Emily Hancock influenced me to study other women's lives in order to understand my own. They argued that women's lives do not fit into male theories, and that the psychology of women must be informed by women's descriptions of their own lives. I began talking to women who were both mothers and daughters. I interviewed twenty-five women, all of them mothers and many of them grandmothers. I found, to my amazement, that modern women expressed Eleusinian emotions. Listen, for example, to a woman whom I'll call Carolyn, describing her feelings about her daughter's first menstruation:

> I can remember the date, February 14, Valentine's day! She came in and showed me her underpants and she said: "Have I started menstruating?" And I said yes and I started to cry. I could just feel, it was an incredible experience, that connection, that sense of being in the middle between my mother and my daughter, and that I was the bridge between generations. She said: "Oh Mom, what are you crying for?" But I was so moved by it. It confirmed my womanhood, the woman in me. I was seeing the continuum of the women in the family, the pride of being a woman. I think I had a sense both of my mortality and my immortality.

Carolyn was granted a vision of the continuity of life as manifest in what Nor Hall has called the "inheritance of the body." It is an experience of what Jung described as "her life being spread out over generations." Her daughter begins to menstruate: she has within her the potential to bear a child. Mother and daughter stand outside ordinary time in this moment of sacred recognition: the birth-giving goddess is revealed in a stain on the daughter's underpants.

Carl Kerenyi speaks of the birth-giving goddess as the "principal thing in Eleusis . . . through which the individual's mortality was perpetually counterbalanced, death suspended, and the continuance of the living assured."[9] But the Eleusinian mysteries have not been practiced for over two thousand years. How can modern woman express the religious attitude that was central to the ancient goddess cult?

Carolyn's consciousness dipped into the underworld flow of Motherline consciousness that has coexisted with patriarchal consciousness since Eleusinian days. Consider the story of Adam and Eve, in which a woman emerges out of so physically unlikely a place as a man's rib. While children are learning such Bible stories, they are also hearing the stories of their own births out of the appropriate female orifice, resulting in the peculiar split between patriarchal religious ideas and ordinary life which we all live with.

Thus it is that the human experience expressed in the Demeter cult continues. We may no longer practice these mysterious rites, but women continue to give birth. We continue to experience menstrual cycles, which, like the seasons, move us from times of darkness and bloodletting to times of ripeness and the capacity to bear new life. The feminine myth of mother and daughter and its attendant Eleusinian emotions live on in the worlds of women. Carolyn finds comfort and meaning in her daughter's birth-giving capacity as she comes to the end of her birth-giving time. What she calls her "pride in being a woman" is an Eleusinian emotion that allows her to find her "place and meaning in the life of the generations," to use Jung's phrase.

The Motherline, then, is the embodied experience of the female mysteries. For women it is the living knowledge that we are the "life vessel."[10] For men it is the connection to woman as life vessel. Women are the carriers of the species, the entryway to life. Although a woman may choose not to have children, or be unable to do so, every woman is born of woman and bears the potential to give birth. Every woman alive is connected to all the women before her through the roots of her particular family and culture. We all emerge out of the ancient line of mothers.

The Eleusinian emotions associated with the Motherline are not limited to a particular time and religious practice. They take many other cultural forms: Native American religions value the sacredness of all living things; Asian religions such as Hinduism worship the cyclical nature of life; contemporary ecological thinking integrates rational, scientific thought with a spiritual attitude about the interconnectedness of all things. But for those of us who were raised in a "man's world," which has left our feminine experience so deeply in the shadows, bringing our Motherline stories into consciousness involves a powerful shift in our worldview. It has been hard for us to claim our own lives and speak in our own voices in a world in which history has been written by men about men. Historian Gerda Lerner puts it eloquently:

> We now know that man is not the measure of that which is human, but men and women are. Men are not the center of the world, but men and women are. This insight will transform consciousness as decisively as did Copernicus' discovery that the earth is not the center of the universe.[11]

There is a natural reticence in speaking about the Motherline. After all, the initiates at Eleusis were sworn to silence. But the sacred silence that revered a mystery is shadowed in this culture by the shame many women feel about their bodies. Yet every woman has had times, usually with another woman, when she has found words for the ineffable and those words have been received in the spirit in which they were spoken. The power of the knowledge within, transformed from silence to a mutual understanding, gives validation to the female vision of the world. For a moment our truths are illuminated. We are no longer background figures in our own lives, but full-fleshed beings; we are no longer mothers sitting in the dark, but three-dimensional human beings who are able to give full voice to our meanings.

TIES OF BLOOD

The Motherline and the Eleusinian emotions roused by it are the deep sources of our female power and authority. No matter what the state of our

emotions, lifestyle, values, or gender, we are all children of the Motherline. Those of us who have children and those of us who do not are tied by
blood to the physical source of our lives, tied by powerful emotions to the
woman in whose body our life began. The Motherline ties us to our mortal
bodies, our bloody beginnings and endings, our experience of the blood
mysteries. Every woman who wishes to be her full, female self needs to
know the stories of her Motherline. We all participate in the human drama;
our personal Motherlines connect us to universal myths.

The Motherline is not a straight line, for it is not about abstract ge-
neological diagrams; it is about bodies being born out of bodies. Envision
the word *line* as a cord, a thread, as the yarn emerging from the fingers of
a woman at the spinning wheel. Imagine cords of connection tied over generations. Like weaving or knitting, each thread is tied to others to create
a complex, richly textured cloth connecting the past to the future.

These cords of meaning weave through our birth-giving experiences
like umbilical cords, connecting us through those we bear to those who
bore us and to those who bore our mothers and fathers. Women in their
childbearing years are tied by blood to their potential to give birth. Our
culture is full of informal acknowledgments of the power of blood. In
African-American culture "blood" is an affectionate expression of kinship
between men. The British use "bloody" as an expletive. Menstruating
women are considered dangerously powerful by Orthodox Jews. According
to Simone de Beauvoir, the Christian tradition of churching, in which a
woman is blessed after childbirth, gives modern form to the ancient practice of ritually purifying new mothers to cleanse them of the blood of
birth-giving.[12]

Ambivalence and fear about the female blood mysteries live in the
shadows of our culture. To bleed is to be a woman in the full flower of her
reproductive life. But we have lost the sacred associations to female blood.
We have forgotten the myths that say we were all made of "moon blood"[13]
in the beginning. We have forgotten that in Hebrew the word *blood* also
means mother. A girl beginning her period in our culture is likely to experience herself more as wounded than as flowering. Often she loses a glowing sense of self, which author Emily Hancock calls the "girl within," and
begins to feel uncertain of her competence and self-conscious about her
body. Her cycles of mood, her body's ebbing and flowing, are pathologized, called PMS, instead of being honored as aspects of female experience.

Our cultural ambivalence about blood is associated with our ambivalence about mothers. Blood embodies life's potential and its suffering. So does being a mother. In a culture that constantly seeks hygienic mastery over suffering, we do not want to honor the experience of the mother, knowing what a bloody business it is, physically and emotionally. A woman today whose professional standing is threatened by the baby she has just born; who feels torn by the opposing demands of career and family; who wonders if the "Mommy track" is a wonderful idea or an insult to women; who struggles to hold on to her Motherline connection while taking her place in the "real world," is being ripped apart by this ambivalence about the feminine.

To consider the complex meaning of blood may help us to see that honoring our Motherlines is not to idealize or sentimentalize being a mother. When a woman today comes to understand her life story as a story from the Motherline, she gains female authority in a number of ways. First, her Motherline grounds her in her feminine nature as she struggles with the many options now open to women. Second, she reclaims carnal knowledge of her own body, its blood mysteries and their power. Third, as she makes the journey back to her female roots, she will encounter ancestors who struggled with similar difficulties in different historical times. This provides her with a life-cycle perspective that softens her immediate situation. It reminds her that all things change in time: Babies grow into school-age children; every recent generation has had different ideas about what's good for children; no child is raised in perfect circumstances. Fourth, she uncovers her connection to the archetypal mother and to the wisdom of the ancient worldview, which holds that body and soul are one and all life is interconnected. And, finally, she reclaims her female perspective, from which to consider how men are similar and how they are different.

SONS OF THE MOTHERLINE

Because the Motherline lies in the background of modern, patriarchal consciousness, women are often as unaware of their connection to the Motherline as their sons and fathers are. We typically understand our lineage in patriarchal terms, describing it in terms of a father's or grandfather's standing in the community. ("I am the daughter of a well-known architect." "My father failed in business." "My mother's father was a doctor.")

Men are as much the sons of the Motherline as women are its daughters. A man knows his Motherline through his physical and emotional relationship to his mother and to his kinship web. It is rare, however, to hear a man describe his lineage in Motherline terms: by telling you how long his mother labored at his birth, or how many stillborn children his grandmother had. Our cultural standards of lineage make it difficult for him to feel these human connections.

Patriarchal lineage is quite a different matter than is male participation in the Motherline. It is abstract and cognitive; it is about the handing down of names. It is about legitimacy, inheritance, marriage contracts; all the ways men assure that their seed will fertilize the next generation. On the other hand, the Motherline is a function of what Jungian analyst Erich Neumann has called matriarchal consciousness. He explains the embodied, carnal nature of this feminine mode of cognition:

> It is in the act of "understanding" that the peculiar and specific difference between the processes of matriarchal and patriarchal consciousness first becomes apparent. For matriarchal consciousness, understanding is not an act of the intellect, functioning as an organ for swift registration, development and organization; rather, it has the meaning of a "conception." Whatever is to be understood must first "enter" matriarchal consciousness in the full, sexual, symbolic meaning of a fructification.[14]

This distinction is tied to the difference in the experience of female conceiving and male begetting. No woman has to wonder whether it is her child she is bearing; she has conceived the child. She has carnal self-knowledge of her maternity as the baby develops within her. But a man, leaving his seed in the darkness of a woman, has to assure himself of his claim to the future. So he tags his woman with his name and his status. It has been pointed out that the development of patriarchal civilization began as a way for men to appropriate women's birth-giving capacity, to stake their claim on women's fertility. Psychoanalyst Karen Horney goes so far as to speculate that it is not women who envy men their penises, but men who envy women their wombs and biological creativity.[15] The monuments of patriarchal civilization are sublimations of a womb envy so hidden in our culture that we have spent close to a century arguing about whether women suffer penis envy!

Men and women live, at least partially, in different cultures, because of the difference in attitude of the Motherline and patriarchal consciousness. Men play leading roles in Motherline stories: women give birth to them and they father women. But women often complain about men and find them hard to comprehend. We love them and we fight them. We struggle with their "otherness"; we try to make them more like us, or ourselves more like them. We fear their betrayal and we yearn for their embrace.

It is a little like the difference between soap operas and action shows on TV, between "As the World Turns" and "Miami Vice." On "Miami Vice" the myth is heroic; the hero defeats the villain; right and wrong are clearly defined, courage and strength are virtues. On "As the World Turns" the myth is matriarchal: fate takes a hand with the good as well as the bad; relationships are complex and of central importance; betrayal is an ever-present possibility; miscarriages, deaths, sudden illnesses, axe murderers spring out of the shadows at hapless humans.

The heroic myth is the more valued one in our culture, but it is only one of many ways of understanding our lives. Men, too, live in matriarchal stories, have nonheroic experiences, know themselves as embodied beings who are not in charge of their destinies. It is not only the feminine that is wounded in the patriarchal version of reality; men also suffer from cultural attitudes that split the psyche and body.

There is a Fatherline equivalent of the Motherline in which a man experiences his physical and emotional life as a father and a son. Men are mortal; they experience life-cycle changes, and are physically and emotionally involved in human continuity. In their book on the father, Arthur and Libby Colman argue that the biological aspect of fatherhood is transformative for men.

> Becoming a father can be life-changing all by itself, even if the child is killed or dies in utero, even if the overt parenting responsibility is denied. It is the biological act which sets in motion the forces that will in time alter consciousness, self-perception, and even attitude toward the outside world. The importance of the biological "blood" tie in the father's experience is as uncanny as it is powerful.[16]

The Fatherline is even more unknown in our culture than the Motherline, for, while women's mysteries have been segregated and disenfranchised in the patriarchy, men's mysteries have been either sublimated beyond recognition or obliterated. In the men's movement that has emerged recently, they speak of the total absence of fathers in their emotional and physical development. They speak of how little access they have to their instinctive nature. The fact that many contemporary men today are involved so deeply with their children is, hopefully, the beginning of a compensation for generations of Fatherline deprivation.

The male experience of Fatherline embodiment is, of physical necessity, different from a woman's Motherline experience. Jungian analyst Eugene Monick gives us a glimpse into this male mystery. He describes seeing his father's genitals when he was a child.

> The organs were my father's, and through them I came into being. They were also archetypal in essence—something more, even, than my father. He and I were united within a masculine identity having its roots beyond us both.[17]

This Fatherline experience was a solitary one for the young boy. The father was asleep while the son gazed at his maleness. Such a lonely recognition of male continuity must be typical in our culture, which values male achievement in the outer world so much more than interpersonal connectedness. Few men are aware of their own Fatherline feelings. Instead, they sublimate them into feelings for women and children.

WHERE THE CORD IS BURIED

In its fullest meaning the principle I am calling the Motherline describes a human experience available to everyone. Being a parent is not a prerequisite for experiencing the powerful, Eleusinian emotions about mortality and continuity that are avoided in our culture. Robert Jay Lifton, a well-known psychiatrist, argues for the development of a new psychological paradigm of "biohistorical continuity." Lifton believes that feeling part of a "collective life-continuity is a primal human need." His ideas are informed by his study of the psychology of survivors of the atomic blast at Hiroshima. He writes:

> Immediately after the bomb fell, the most terrifying rumor among the many that swept the city was that trees, grass, and flowers would never again grow in Hiroshima. The image contained in that rumor was of nature drying up altogether, life being extinguished at its source, an ultimate form of desolation that not only encompassed human death but went beyond it. The persistence and continuing

growth of wild "railroad grass" (which, in fact, had to serve as food for many during immediate postbomb days) was perceived as a source of strength. And the subsequent appearance of early spring buds, especially those of the March cherry blossoms, symbolized the detoxification of the city and (in the words of its then mayor) "a new feeling of relief and hope."[18]

For the survivors of Hiroshima, the persistence of the wild grass and the return of the cherry blossoms provided an Eleusinian experience of the rebirth of hope after terrifying loss, mutilation, and devastation. Lifton argues that no human being can face death without access to this principle of continuity. In our culture's denial of death we have lost touch with the sacred fragility of all life. This spiritual imbalance is expressed in the danger our weapons and technologies pose to the continuity of life on the planet. It is fitting that those who survived an atomic bomb would be the ones to remind us of the simple and profound truth that we are children of the earth, participants in seasonal cycles, dependent upon the continuity of plant and animal life for our own lives.

The same paradigm, in a different form, is described by a woman artist as essential for her creativity.

> I have never conceived, but whether or not a woman does conceive, she carries the germinative ocean within her, and the essential eggs. We have a spirituality, full from within. Whether we are weaving tissue in the womb or pictures in the imagination, we create out of our bodies.[19]

These are the words of Meinrad Craighead, a contemporary painter whose work is powerfully evocative of the Motherline. She provides us with an image of a childless woman who lives fully in her bodily cycles, is linked to the generations that precede her, and whose creativity emerges from this life source. She says of her art: "Each painting I make begins from some deep source where my mother and grandmother, and all my fore-mothers, still live; it is as if the line moving from pen or brush coils back to the original Matrix." In telling of her childhood visits to the grandmother she calls "Memaw," she describes a Motherline that is more conscious and more rooted than most.

> Each year in June my mother put me on a train in Chicago and sent me to her parents for the summer. She could not go with me but

she told me that it was good for me to be there where I began. I had
to touch home, and through me she did also. When I was old enough
to understand, she said: "Your flesh is growing there. When you were
born, Memaw buried your cord and membranes in the soil in Little
Rock. You are rooted there like me and Memaw."[20]

I once visited a petroglyph site on the big island of Hawaii. Small
holes, some of them with circles around them, had been dug in the lava
hundreds of years ago by the Polynesian native people. These holes, I
learned, were used to bury the umbilical cords of new babies. Meinrad
Craighead's grandmother and the ancient people of Hawaii, separated by
vast oceans, hundreds of years, and great cultural differences, practiced a
similar Motherline ritual to connect their new babies to the land. It is poignant to imagine these ancient Hawaiian people, whose myths tell of their
long ocean journey by boat to an island that is regularly shaken by volcanic
explosion, symbolically tying their young to the unstable lava that became
their home.

All human beings, whether or not we have children, are children of
the earth, rooted in the Motherline; all of us need access to our biohistorical
sense of continuity to be fully, creatively alive, to face our own mortality
and to honor life in all its forms. It is essential in this historical moment
that we become conscious of our roots in the natural world when so many
species of earth's rich, biological life—including our own—are threatened.

BLAMING MOTHER AS A STAND-IN FOR THE GODS

To conceive the human story from within the mammalian experience of
mothers; to honor the carnal, bury a placenta, speak of blood and of ghosts,
is clearly to commit a heresy in the Judeo-Christian religious tradition. It
is the sort of thing for which witches were persecuted.

It also commits a heresy against twentieth-century psychological
thought. To include our mothers' stories in telling our stories undercuts a
collective fantasy we hold about the perfectibility of childhood. Psychology, in trying to be a science, has created a paradigm of causality for our
human situation. This kills off the gods, who used to hold responsibility
for our fates. We institute mothers in their place, and rage at them for all
the negative things that befall us. But no mother sets out to hurt her children. She has her own limitations, those the culture imposes, and she has

her fate. Today mothers suffer the collective wound of being seen as the perpetrators of all suffering.

Contemporary authors like Alice Miller write eloquently of the power of the mother to skew her child's sense of self because of her own needs. The underlying assumption seems to be that mothers exist for the sole purpose of supporting their children's healthy development. What is forgotten is that mothers are people with their own lives, who are profoundly affected by the experience of having children. Nancy Mairs, in writing of her experience of her daughter Anne's birth and childhood, says: "All the analyses I've read of mother-daughter relationships fail to account for my experience of Anne's power in our mutual life."[21]

It has become a part of our cultural understanding that children are influenced for life by early experiences. According to this view the mother has enormous power in the most formative period of human development. Yet there is little empathy or interest in what this is like for mothers. Instead, she is objectified.

Paula Caplan gives an example of this phenomenon in her book *Don't Blame Mother!*

> Since the 1960s, therapists' attitudes toward mothers have been widely influenced by Margaret Mahler's work on the importance of the child's psychological "separation and individuation" from its mother. . . . Mahler advised therapists to watch carefully when a mother entered the room used for observing the family's dynamics. They were to take note of whether she carried the child "like a part of herself"—which would then brand the mother as being unable to separate from the child—or "like an inanimate object" which would label her as the cold-and-rejecting type. Imagine being a mother observed by a therapist who used such a pigeonholing scheme in which each pigeonhole is a different form of bad mothering![22]

We mothers are seen as all-powerful in psychology, but are personally disempowered. Our subjective experience is unknown and devalued in our own minds, as well as in those of the experts. To quote Mairs again, "we live in a culture of object-mothers. The subject-mothers, culturally silenced for millennia, are only just beginning to speak."[23] Meanwhile we struggle with the guilt we feel for failing to provide perfect childhoods.

In arguing against the objectification of mother I want in no way to minimize what we have learned about the importance of early childhood. Until recently it was not recognized that childhood is a distinctly different time of life, or that children have different needs than do adults. Generations have been damaged emotionally and physically as a result of our ignorance of child development. Recognizing the power of early childhood experience supports those who struggle to free themselves from unhappy childhoods and who hope to raise their children sensitively. But the tendency to focus exclusively on childhood, and the fantasies we hold of the perfectibility of childhood, create cultural attitudes that scapegoat mothers.

In a clever piece in the *New York Times Magazine,* Janna Malamud Smith complains about this idea, declaring that mothers are "tired of taking the rap." She writes:

> If a patient is in trouble, the underlying assumption is that the mother must have done something wrong. Just as strep throat comes from bacteria, other problems come from inadequate mothers. Here is an example from "Psychosomatic Medicine and Contemporary Psychoanalysis" by Dr. Graeme J. Taylor, published in 1987: The "typical 'psychosomatic mother' . . . may be domineering, excessively demanding, and clinging and smothering." Her behavior is said to be an important cause of her offspring's bronchial asthma, ulcerative colitis, anorexia nervosa, peptic ulcers, hyperthyroidism, eczema, and neurodermatitis. While colic apparently no longer makes the list, mothers remain, according to studies cited by writers like Taylor, a convenient missing link in germ theory. If it is not viral or bacterial, it must be maternal.
>
> . . . [T]he indictment of mothers in the psychological literature has historically been so nasty, so massive, so undifferentiated and so oblivious of the actual limits of a mother's power or her context that it precludes a just assessment of real responsibility.[24]

Contemporary psychological thinking suffers from the fallacy that all our troubles have a definable cause—mother. We have great difficulty sorting out the limited human power of an individual mother from the Great Mother archetype because we don't want to believe that much of what happens to us in life is beyond the control of mere mortals. Mothers get blamed because we refuse to face our fates, which must be suffered. Thus mothers are used, indeed abused, as stand-ins for the gods. Human suffering is more than the product of personal parenting. It has cultural, historical, and archetypal derivations. It is only through our suffering that we come to know ourselves and life, when we catch glimpses in the darkness of the powerful mysteries of the Motherline.

LOOPING THROUGH TIME

The concept of the Motherline came to me in the process of interviewing women who had raised daughters to adulthood. These women were telling their stories in the middle of their lives from their considerable experience as both daughters and mothers. I found as I interviewed them about their daughters that they spontaneously referred to their mothers and grand-mothers in the flow of their thought. There was a palpable way in which mothers and grandmothers entered the room as daughters were described.

This all seemed very natural to me. It was how women always talked, especially women in midlife. I might not have given it a second thought had several women not apologized to me. They felt that they were getting off track. Didn't I want them to talk about their daughters? Yet they were weaving back and forth in the generations. It was as though they would suddenly wake up from the familiar flow of "women's talk" and remember that, while I was a woman, I was engaged in that patriarchal task: a re-search project. Were they being linear enough for a "study"? Was it ap-propriate to be thinking "like a woman" in the context of an interview?

I suddenly saw how women's talk recapitulates the experience of women's lives, making loops through time. Let me give you an example. Carolyn told me that her daughter was about to leave the area and go live with her boyfriend in another town. I asked how she felt about this. She said:

> I'm pleased she's going, and I'm glad it's not as far away as the other coast. My mother is in Detroit where I grew up, and I wish we were closer so my mother would not be so alone. When I left at nine-teen, it was the right thing to do. But now it's different. It would be so comforting and grounding for my mother if I were there.

Carolyn's awareness moves rapidly from her twenty-one-year-old daughter, who is leaving home, to her aging mother alone in Detroit. She remembers leaving home as a young woman and uses it as a reference point to help her support her daughter's leaving. I call this phenomenon looping.

Looping is an associative process by which we pass through our own experience to understand that of another. Carolyn understood her mother's feelings by looping through her own feelings about her daughter leaving home, and her fear of being far from her daughter in old age. Looping ties together life stages, roles, and generations. It disregards linear time. It involves a cyclical view of life, it finds meaning in patterns that repeat. We measure our lives in our mother's terms, and in our daughter's terms.

I'm not sure I would have seen the Motherline if I had not been talking to women in the middle of their lives, and if I were not in the middle of my life myself. The view from here encourages looping. You re-experience your past in your children and anticipate your future in your parents, while at the same time your children constellate the future and your parents the past. Carolyn sees her own youthful home-leaving in her daughter leaving home; her own aging in her mother's aging. It is as though she stands in the middle of the symbol of infinity, figure eight, looping to the future and the past as she bridges the generations. She is at once cycling through time and standing still. For at the core of the Motherline is a sense of timelessness.

WHEN THREE WOMEN MENSTRUATE

What makes a Motherline story different from other kinds of stories? I hesitate to define these stories too explicitly because, by its very nature, the Motherline is inclusive as opposed to exclusive. But because women suffer so deeply from a lack of narratives, our lack of history in the formal sense, it seems vital that we learn to recognize the stories we do have, the history that surrounds us in a medium so familiar we don't know we live in it.

A simple old wives' tale from a collection of lore about birth illustrates a number of elements found in stories from the Motherline.

> If there are three women sitting in a room and all three are menstruating, it is the sign that one of them will be pregnant before the year is out. I was sitting in a room with two ladies and all three of us were menstruating. I laughed and said, "It won't be me being pregnant, for I have been married eighteen years and have no children." They had the laugh on me, for before the year was out I was pregnant and the only child I have was born.[25]

Motherline stories are the product of matriarchal consciousness. What is understood is "born" or brought into life. In this story the narrator conceives the meaning of the sign that all three women are menstruating, and bears the fruit of that conception. It is a story about embodied experience, in this case specifically about the blood mysteries and pregnancy. This story, like many stories from the Motherline, illustrates what is known in the Jungian world as synchronicity—that is, a psychologically meaningful coincidence that cannot be explained by ordinary causality. The coincidence of three women menstruating and one getting pregnant is not causal, but meaningful. It is a story about kith and kin and relationships that loop through time. The narrator loops from present time—sitting with two friends who are menstruating, to past time—eighteen years of childless marriage, to the future and the child she will bear, all in three sentences.

Motherline stories describe a world in which the boundaries of fantasy and reality are permeable. In this story the narrator's laugh expresses at once her fantasy that she may bear a child and the reality of her long-established childless state. I am reminded of Sarah's laugh in the Old Testament when she and Abraham are told by God that she will bear a child. Like her modern counterpart, Sarah is amused because she is old and has long been barren. The practical reality of a woman's body and the mystery of generation are intertwined in Motherline stories. From the viewpoint of the Motherline, there is no clear separation of the biological and emotional spheres of life. The manner of a child's birth is connected to the mother's psychological sense of that child throughout life.

In many Motherline stories, though not in this one, the boundaries of life and death are effortlessly crossed. Motherline stories evoke a worldview in which all beings and times are interconnected, a worldview connected to the feminine mysteries of menstruation, birth, and death. They are as common as the repetitive loops made in weaving, crocheting, and knitting. They are as powerful as the memory of touching a grandmother's face in childhood or seeing a daughter suckle her newborn child.

Nobody can choose her Motherline or her fate. We are all born into a lineage, a family, a historical time filled with difficulties over which we have no control. If our female experience is to be meaningful to us, we must awaken to the female depths from whence we come.

In the chapters that follow, the journey to the female source, the Motherline, will be amplified through stories from women's lives. Like the heroine of a myth or a fairy tale, a woman has a series of tasks to perform, aspects of her feminine self she must reclaim, in order to find her feminine soul. To do this she must remember what her culture has forgotten about the feminine. She must pass through the layers of shame, the humiliations caused by the culture's devaluation of the feminine in order to honor what her body knows, to be able to hear her own voice.

She must wrestle with her personal mother, and with her children if she has them, in order to differentiate her own identity and fate. She must honor the life perspective inherent in the mother-daughter loop. She must make a journey into her familial past, sort through the strands of history, culture, and myth, see beyond the particular biases of her historical time and place to conceive the lives of those from whom she is descended. Tracing her line back on her mother's side and on her father's side, looping back into other times and places, she must make her way down into the realm of the dead to find her relation to her ancestors. This is a journey into shadows, into abused and neglected aspects of the feminine, into other countries, ways of life, and states of mind that have been abandoned and devalued. Ultimately, she must grapple with the archetypal feminine in order to find the deepest, most taboo parts of her soul.

The feminine wisdom that is born of this labor knows that all things change in time, but also that they remain the same. The moon waxes and wanes and waxes again. Women's lives cycle, daughters become mothers bearing daughters. And yet each woman is different; each generation is different. We are linked to one another's bodies, throughout time and history, in a female lineage that has carried on the human story, carried the men and the women, given life and suck to all the living, closed the eyes of all the dead.

Maxine Kumin's poem, which opens this chapter, evokes Eleusinian emotions about human continuity in the phrase "may we carry our mothers forth in our bellies." To carry our mothers forth in our bellies is to know them in our own bodies and souls, in the life they gave us and the life they denied us, in their pain, their labor, their love, and their hate. We must face with them the dark passageways through which they passed to bring us here, and which we face again in the end of our days. For the mother in our bellies knows there never is any telling what will happen next, who will be born and who will die. She is our mother and our child, the face of our future, the womb of our past. She loops together all of human life. To honor her is to bring to consciousness the stories she tells, the stories of the Motherline, and to hand them down to our children and our children's children.

CHAPTER TWO

FEMINISM AND THE FORGOTTEN FEMININE:

Mastery versus Mystique

I n 1963, the year my son was born, a new awareness in women was
born as well. Betty Friedan published the *Feminine Mystique,* and
the self-image of millions of women shifted irrevocably. In words
that expressed the suffering of a generation, she spoke to the unspoken
problem that "lay buried in the minds of American women."[1] She described the suffocation of the women of her time, the narrow servitude of
their roles as mothers and housewives. She spoke to the mute stirrings, the
wordless longing of women who yearned to be more than just the caretakers
of others.

THE BIRTH-GIVING GODDESS AND
THE FEMININE MYSTIQUE

The feminine mystique, as Friedan described it, was a patriarchal projection on women—it expressed the way men wanted women to feel. According to this theory espoused by experts on breast-feeding, penis envy,
and marriage, women's true and only fulfillment was in devoting "their
lives from earliest girlhood to finding a husband and bearing children."[2]

Friedan's book made conscious the agony of women who did not find their only fulfillment in others, who struggled throughout the fifties and sixties with a secret appetite: the hunger to become themselves. By giving a name and a voice to the "problem that has no name," she empowered women to see the cruelty of the projection that said that women should be "selfless." We began to understand that lives lived only to meet the expectations of others were hollow and meaningless; such lives robbed us of identity and direction. Like a woman whose breath and life energy are constricted by tight corseting, our true selves we constructed by the psychological girdle Virginia Woolf had named the "Angel in the House."[3] Trapped in the cultural expectation that, to paraphrase Woolf, we become intensely sympathetic, intensely charming, that we sacrifice ourselves daily, that we never have a mind or wish of our own, all that was original, creative, and full of spirit in our natures was crushed.

In the great shift of consciousness whose early stirrings were reflected in Friedan's book, in the rage that developed against the "feminine mystique," a generation of women emerged whose values were formed by *Ms.* magazine, consciousness-raising groups, feminist politics, and the estrangement from mothers expressed by much feminist literature. Many women chose career over children, at least in the early part of their lives.

My coming of age was mirrored in disorientingly different mediums. At the personal level, I became a mother, and my sense of life and its meanings was shaped by that experience. At the cultural level, I came to understand myself in the reflections of feminist writers. I longed for an arena in which to express my creativity and passion, for a life in the outer world of history and action. I felt deep shame in being "just" a housewife and mother. I longed for an illustrious identity, a profession I could name, a way to make a contribution, to be seen and appreciated for work well done. Instead, I changed diapers, which only got soiled and had to be changed again; cooked meals, which were eaten and had to be cooked again; washed dishes, which got dirty and had to be washed again. My husband was out there in the world, advancing toward a goal. I was caught in cycles that repeated themselves. I was a mirror for others, but had no self of my own. I was frustrated and confused.

Yet each time my son woke from his nap, I raced to see his beautiful face. I was in love with the smell of his body, his warm arms around my neck. I remember the day we brought him home from the hospital. His father drove, and I held the precious new life in my arms. I looked out at the familiar landscape, streets I had walked since early adolescence. They looked entirely new now, aglow with a sacred light. I thought: How can these people walk around as though it's just another day? I am bringing my new baby home!

I remember when my son, Jason, was three. I was putting him and Ellie, his little playmate, into the car to go to the park. As I fastened her seat belt, Ellie asked me how I "got" Jason. I gave her a brief description of the process. She looked from me to Jason in amazement and delight and cried: "Just like I came out of my Mommy! Jason, you're a born baby too!" In her shining face I saw mirrored my own feeling of awe and joy at the mystery of the birth-giving goddess.

I could not put the two realities together—the meaningless cycles of diapers and dishes, and the joy of watching my son's development. I identified with them both and felt torn between body and mind, children and ambition, love and rage. I knew the physical and emotional pleasure of responding to a child. I knew the anger of feeling that my life was entirely in the service of others. I looked at myself in the mirror of feminist thought in the 1960s and 1970s and, slowly, began to feel my potential for action and creativity in the outer world.

LIVING OUR FATHERS' LIVES

It was a heady time for women. A woman named Alta founded the "Shameless Hussy Press." The name expressed the ferocity and delight with which women were taking their lives and meanings into their own hands. Poet Judy Grahn evoked in her audiences the growing desire to be women for ourselves, not for others, as she chanted her powerful poem "She Who":

> She Who turns things over.
> She Who marks her own way, gathering.
> She Who makes her own difference.[4]

Nancy Friday, in her enormously successful book *My Mother, My Self*, castigated mothers for imposing culturally held inhibitions about sexuality and self-development on their daughters. A generation of my peers rebelled against the constrictions imposed by our mothers and grandmothers. We did not concern ourselves much with the fact that they, too, had suffered such constriction at the hands of their mothers and grandmothers. Even those of us who were mothers saw ourselves as daughters, and our mothers took the rap for keeping us down. We sought our own voices, our own experiences, our own visions of the world. We rebelled against the maternal expectations that kept us in split-level suburban prisons, isolated from other women and from our own souls.

In a great collective leap we distanced ourselves from the lives of our mothers and grandmothers. We were meant for greater things than what de Beauvoir refers to scathingly as our "misfortune to have been biologically destined for the repetition of Life."[5] "Biology is not destiny" was the battle cry against the great unconscious undertow of pregnancy and nurturing that keeps women in thrall to the needs of others.

I found myself in the grip of a great, pulsing energy that demanded expression. A fiercely female poetry began pushing its way through me. In one long poem, called "It's Her Period!" I "wailed my menstrual rag time blues," expressing the female agony of being torn between childbearing and the wish to "etch my intricate designs upon the world." Feeling as though I had been "kept very well" in Peter's proverbial pumpkin shell, I burst out of the constrictions of the conventional roles I had played, leaving my marriage behind me like a great empty gourd. During that angry time, I wrote in a poem:

> *Today I will grind no man's corn*
> *nor bear his pain nor suckle his child*
> *nor harness my labor to anyone's plow*
> *there is no one to compare me to this day*

I declared my independence from male projections. I did not want to be an unnamed lady in a Shakespearean sonnet, whose anonymous fame came from being compared to a summer's day, only more lovely and more temperate. I was determined to shape my own sense of self. One year I threw out my makeup, cut my hair short, and smoked a pipe. Another year I got a perm and painted my nails. But through it all, I was a mother and a daughter, and usually in love with a man. I read feminist thinkers who devalued mothering and expressed revulsion about the feminine mysteries of gestation and menstruation. In the *Dialectic of Sex,* Shulamith Firestone[6] raged about the cost to women of being solely responsible for the reproduction of the species, and wondered whether we might not be better served by finding artificial means to procreate. "Femininity," it was argued, was basically a product of socialization and we would be better off without it. Pop psychology books scolded women for not being more like men. In her best-selling book, *The Cinderella Complex,* Colette Dowling rebuked women for their affiliative needs, which she condemned as emotionally crippling.

Women seemed to want to live their father's lives. Mother was rejected, looked down upon, left in the dark. In the headlong race to liberate those aspects of ourselves that had been so long denied, we left behind all that women had been. Emily Hancock, author of *The Girl Within,* puts the problem succinctly:

> Both historic and contemporary constructions of femininity thus thrust a woman down a path that has little to do with who and what she really is, impelling her toward a destiny that is hardly her own. Each does so by forcing a single aspect of female identity into the foreground to the exclusion of the whole—the historic by excluding all but servility and nurture, the contemporary by severing the personal from the professional and blocking out all but competence.[7]

Many of us who joyfully accepted the challenge of new opportunities discovered in retrospect that we had cut ourselves off from much of what was meaningful to us as women: our mothers, our collective past, our passion for affiliation and for richness in our personal lives. We felt split between our past and our future.

MOTHERLESS DAUGHTERS

This split created a dangerous situation for women. How dangerous it was for me was expressed in a terrifying dream I had during the early years of the women's movement. I dreamt my three-year-old daughter's head was severed from her body. I could hear my mother's voice saying, "You'll never get her together again." I took the dream literally and thought something terrible was about to happen to my child. I felt haunted.

Synchronistically, a friend invited me to a Jungian weekend workshop called "The Forgotten Feminine." Something about the title tugged at my soul, though I could not then have said what it was.

The workshop was conducted by three vibrant older women, Jungian analysts, who spoke about "the feminine principle" and "women's mysteries."[8] I had never before seen women who were successful in the outer world speaking with reverence and understanding about menstruation and birth-giving. They talked of the patients they worked with in analysis, telling their dreams and showing their artwork. They described the struggle women were having to integrate the forgotten and devalued feminine principle into their sense of self. Like a sudden illumination at the dark core of my being, I understood that my frightening dream was not about my daughter. It was a symbolic statement of my own psychological difficulty. It was I who could not get my head and body together; I who could not integrate my intelligence and ambition with my deeper, instinctual, female life; I who felt split between the feminist and the feminine aspects of my being. That moment made a Jungian of me.

In the years that have followed, I realized that the dream was not only about me; it was also about the collective situation of women. Woman's sense of self lay in fragments throughout our culture. Head was torn from body, womb torn out of the female experience of meaning, nurture from sexuality, intelligence from giving birth, mother from daughter. All of these splits were pre-existent embodiments of patriarchal projections on women. Judeo-Christian culture had long ago cast out female sensuality, allowing the mother of God only her nurturant aspect. It had persecuted intelligent and powerful women as witches. The culture left us motherless, bereft of a heritage of female power and authority.

But in our rush to join history, to be part of the "real world," to be equal to men, we forgot something essential. Our mothers also were women, worthy of our respect. The feminine mystique was more than an idea dreamed up by men. The mysteries of conception, of swelling with new life, of straining to give birth, of breasts filling with milk in response to a baby's cry, of the waning and waxing of body and moods in tune with the menstrual tide, are expressions of a power that runs much deeper than male projection or socialization. For all of us, men and women, are "born babies"; none of us arrives here without first passing through a woman's body.

In the generation that has passed since my son was born and the *Feminine Mystique* was published, I have come to understand that we are living out a cultural split that can be described as the feminist ambivalence about the feminine. Our culture proceeds on two levels that have little to do with each other. One is the realm of history; the other is the realm of mystery, the cyclical nature of life, the realm of women's bodies.

The women's movement launched us into history. Until then women were, with some few exceptions, trapped in the cyclical mysteries in times that either idealized or devalued them. Women gave birth and tended the cycles of life and death. When they asserted their power over these rites, they were called witches. Men, on the other hand, dashed off, swords unsheathed, into history.

Cyclical rounds, as I discovered while washing dishes and changing diapers, are suffocating. Feminists were right to rage that we, too, have intelligence and energy to offer the historical period in which we live. Our culture has for so long devalued the cycles of the natural world that women cannot claim their connection to the life cycle without feeling inferior. A woman who wants her freedom feels she must cut loose from her bodily cycles, cut loose from her mother who wants her to be a mother, cut loose from patriarchal projections on her power and sexuality.

But as many women are beginning to discover, we pay a terrible price for cutting ourselves off from our feminine roots. Betty Friedan spoke to this problem in her later book, *The Second Stage:*

> From these daughters—getting older now, working so hard, determined not to be trapped as their mothers were, and expecting so much, taking for granted the opportunities we had to struggle for— I've begun to hear undertones of pain and puzzlement, a queasiness, an uneasiness, almost a bitterness that they hardly dare admit. As if with all those opportunities that we won for them, and envy them, how can they ask out loud certain questions, talk about certain other needs they aren't supposed to worry about—those old needs which shaped our lives, and trapped us, and against which we rebelled?[9]

Women today, who have spent years working hard on their professional identities, are feeling empty and full of grief for the children they have not born, the relationships they have not had. Women who "have it all," careers and families, feel torn with guilt and confusion about priorities and roles. Mothers and daughters suffer a wrenching distance between them. Women who divorced in order to free themselves from suffocating roles and relationships have come to learn over the years how excruciatingly painful the family breakup has been for their children.

What does all of this mean? Do we have to return to the suffocation of our traditional roles and leave the world of history and action to men? It would be a death blow to women's spirit to do so, and a dangerous loss to the world, which needs to integrate the feminine principle. Our difficulty lies in the fact that in asserting our right to partake in the man's world we have come to identify with the very patriarchal attitudes that devalue our mothers and grandmothers. We are ashamed of our yearnings for connection, our tears, our mothers. We try to live like men: valuing separateness and achievement.

These attitudes split us from our bodies and our past and leave us wandering like motherless daughters in the too bright light of patriarchal consciousness. Our task now is to integrate our feminine and feminist selves. We must connect the historical self that was freed by feminism to live in the "real" world, with the feminine self that binds us to our mothers and grandmothers.

ADULT CHILDREN OF TERRIBLE MOTHERS

To bring mother and daughter, body and soul, head and heart together requires not only assimilating the nurturing and sensual aspects of life, but the terrible aspects as well. This problem is integral to the psychology of women and to the difficult work of integrating feminism and the feminine.

In my psychotherapy practice I find myself involved in the heart rending work of helping daughters differentiate themselves from terrible mothers and suffocating cultural expectations, while at the same time they seek access to their authentic female authority and to their Motherlines. Many enter psychotherapy longing to be mothered, but hating their feminine selves. Many are terrible mothers to themselves, engaging in ferocious battles with their own female flesh. These take the form of eating disorders, compulsive exercising or fighting their menstrual experience. They are an expression of their internalized devaluation of the female self. If these women are not to feel motherless, they must face the terrible mothers in their souls, as well as in their childhoods.

Both men and women spend many hours in my consulting room in psychological battles with their mothers. Every day I hear appalling stories of how mothers have damaged their children. In the sanctuary of the therapeutic relationship, the frightened inner child dares at last to emerge and tell how it was for him or her. Perhaps the mother squelched the child's natural life energy, or neglected the child's need for structure and direction, or failed to protect the child from an abusive father, or abused the child herself.

I find myself in a painful paradox in my dual roles as mother and psychotherapist. Becoming a psychotherapist after years of being a mother had seemed a natural progression to me. After all, as Jean Baker Miller has said, the work of psychotherapy is essentially imitative of "women's work."[10] Psychotherapists, like mothers, are engaged in the work of supporting human development. I had learned most of what I knew about child development from my children. I could feel my way back to the vulnerable young feelings my patients brought me, not only through my own remembered experience, but that of my children.

In my role as a psychotherapist I see myself as a midwife, delivering my patients from the dark constriction of their family's pain. I rage with them at their mothers' failings. I defend them from their internalized mothers' attacks. Again and again I side with them, against their mothers. As a daughter I remember the years I spent in therapy, sorting out my identity from my mother's, determined not to be like her, angry at her for not being all I had needed her to be.

But as a mother, I wonder what my patients' mothers would feel if they could hear their children's rage. What woman could bear to know herself to be the perpetrator of such carnage? What mother could bear to know how ineffective she was? I wonder what my own children might say about me to their psychotherapists. I suffer spasms of maternal guilt. I long to be honored for the difficult work of mothering, and I'm sure the mothers of my patients wish this, too. They, too, had difficult childhoods, negative mothers, unhappy marriages, and raised their children at a time of enormous cultural ambivalence about women's roles.

I hold these feelings in silence, knowing that the mother looms large over her child's development, over her child's inner life as an adult, knowing that it takes enormous psychological courage to see a mother's limitations, to wrestle her down to size. From the mother's point of view this is all very puzzling. She doesn't experience herself as particularly powerful. More likely, she feels caught in circumstances beyond her control. It's hard to wrestle with her because she doesn't have her feet on the ground of her own experience; she doesn't know her own strength. In fact, she may forget that she is a mother and think of herself primarily as a daughter, longing for love and acceptance from her own mother or from her daughter.

But as I sit with the adult children of terrible mothers, angry, intrusive mothers who appear as birds of prey in their daughters' dreams and whose sons refer to them as "battle axes," or profoundly depressed mothers who appear half dead in the psychological landscapes their offspring describe, I feel torn between the mother and the psychotherapist in me. How do we illuminate the mother without casting the daughter into darkness?

How do we name the sacred connection among women without trivializing or denying the pain so many mothers and daughters feel?

When I find myself torn between my role as psychotherapist and mother, between the suffering of a daughter who feels unmothered, and the suffering of the mother who feels dishonored, I am falling into the dualistic dilemma that plagues Western thought. When ideas are framed in polarities, in either/or structures of the mind, we see them as either one way or the other, good or bad, black or white. To honor the mother is to dismiss the daughter who didn't get enough mothering; to embrace the power of birth-giving experiences in women's lives is to belittle women who have had no children; to support the struggle of sons and daughters to see their mother's failures is to deny the love those mothers bear their children. We must wend our way around these opposites, or we will lose the very ground on which we seek our female lineage.

In Jungian and developmental psychology, the ability to transcend dualistic thinking is seen as essential to the adult maturational process. Jungians speak of the "union of opposites." Jane Loevinger, creator of a psychological measure of adult ego development that bears her name, describes people who "construe the world in terms of polar opposites" as being at a lower stage of development than those who can transcend "polarities, seeing reality as complex."[11]

The ability to unite opposites, to understand both the viewpoints of the wounded child and of the mother, who, in most cases, has done her level best, is one that comes with maturity and is, parenthetically, a good outcome of psychotherapy. It is not an easy task. It requires sorting out issues with one's personal mother, from the cultural milieu that devalues female experience, from the generational shifts that make the lives of children so different from those of their mothers, and from the archetypal Great Mother, who stands for our connection to life. It requires looping to our mother's childhood, and understanding her early wounds.

Wounds of the Mother

As I have worked with the concept of the Motherline, taught it to my students, spoken of it to friends and colleagues, I am confronted again and again by a great wash of grief and anger. The very image of female continuity and interrelatedness seems to evoke its absence, its loss, the pain we feel in the feminine. We are all born of deeply wounded mothers, who, in turn, were born into a culture that feared and excoriated the feminine. The face of our mother turned to us in rage or frustration, or away from us in deep depression, is the face of what women have suffered.

In listening to the stories from my patients' Motherlines, I can usually trace the deprivation or anger back for generations. Terrible mothers are usually daughters of terrible mothers. Most have been raised by women with no positive connection to the feminine. Many have mothers who have acted as henchwomen of the conventional. Out of touch with the instinctive nature of mothering, they fed their babies on schedules; denied them baby talk; pushed them to perform feats of precocious cognition, because the conventional ideas of the time told them to do so. They bound their daughters' feet, sexuality, or soul because their own sense of self had been bound.

They look at their daughters with the hatred they feel for their own female selves, and profoundly stunt their daughters' development. The daughter of such a woman has no feminine ground on which to stand. The first woman in her life, mother, is banished from the land except in nightmare form. She has no female lineage in which to root her sense of self. Her mother, in turn, feels cut off from the meaning and feeling for the future that her daughter carries for her.

If we think of our psychological wounds only in terms of the failure of our mothers, we run the risk of furthering our alienation from ourselves as women. Our mothers, and their mothers before them, have been grievously wounded. Go back a few generations and you will find a daughter whose mother died in childbirth, or abandoned her child, or was terrified to present her husband with another girl child. Go back just a few years in this century and hear the stories of generations of women who lived lives much smaller than their potential, whose souls were cramped in interior spaces, who clung to daughters as to companions in misery.

Behind the failure of the personal mother lies our collective fear of the Great Mother. Babies who don't receive "good enough mothering" feel savaged by the archetypal mother. Who dares identify with her bone-crunching power? Who dares look directly at the taboo aspects of the feminine? We would rather see ourselves as eternal daughters than become mothers who can be so terrible.

The Great Mother, in all her aspects, is especially fearful for women who identify with feminism and the women's movement. Many of us broke free of the stranglehold that biology had on our destinies. Surpassing our mothers we charged into the world of achievement and mastery. We want to feel we are living conscious lives directed by muscular egos. The Moth-

erline and matriarchal consciousness are at odds with these goals. The heroism of yin, which opens up the boundaries of the female body to take in
seed, allowing new life to grow within it and be born out of it, is seen as
a frightening swamp of passivity. Female flesh—fat, breasts, hips—become a fearful shadow.

The Virgin Mary on her pedestal looks pale and sweet. Never an angry word crosses her pallid lips; never a sexual feeling parts her thighs. If
it is her slim, lustless body that carries the archetypal feminine in our culture, we are left only with feelings of shame and inferiority for the blood,
sweat, desire, and fury of our female experience.

Integrating feminism and the feminine requires bringing to consciousness the Motherline as it is expressed in the very texture of how
women talk, the looping that ties together life-cycle experiences, the Eleusinian emotions that reflect the sacred nature of organic experience. This
requires honoring the ebb and flow of a woman's body.

A friend once said to me of her vagina: "I feel as though I'm cultivating a small swamp." To honor the swamp of yin, the opening of our
bodies to receive life, to give life, is to know ourselves as part of the natural
world. We must suffer a conception of life in which mastery and mystique
are intertwined; then we participate in women's mysteries as well as in the
history of our times.

A woman who can integrate her hunger for the world with carnal self-
knowledge lives in relation to her body, as well as to her generation. She
can attend to her life's unfolding from the inner whispers of her dreams,
to the interpersonal dialogue with kith and kin, to the collective currents
that sweep her time. She knows who she is, where she comes from, where
she is going, and what her place is among the living and the dead.

CHAPTER THREE

OLD WIVES' TALES:

Relearning the Mother Tongue

Swing a silver needle over the mother to tell if it's a boy or girl.
Swing a golden ring over the mother to tell if it's a boy or girl.
If it spins, it'll be a girl.
If it swings, it'll be a boy.

If you carry the baby low, it'll be a boy.
If you carry the baby high, it'll be a girl.
If you're pointed it's a girl.
If you're round or broad it's a boy.[1]

AMERICAN FOLKLORE

S tories from the Motherline are audible only to those who will listen to old wives' tales and gossip, the spinning of meaning from
the most interior and private realms: the secret darkness of wom-
en's bodies, the intricacies of kinship ties, the complexities of relationship.
They are stories about the uncanny way mothers bond with their children
and children alter their mothers. Educated women may find them difficult
to hear, schooled as we are in rational thought and the scientific method,
which sets itself apart from what it studies. The wisdom of the forgotten
feminine is trivialized, considered irrational and superstitious, as embarrassing as female blood, or the shame we feel about our mothers and our
bodies.

Stories from the Motherline are part of an oral tradition of lore about
conception, pregnancy, birth, and child-rearing that is seldom taken se-

riously as adult conversation. Ursula LeGuin makes a helpful distinction between what she calls the father tongue and the mother tongue:

> Using the father tongue, I can speak of the mother tongue only, inevitably, to distance it—to exclude it. It is the other, inferior. It is primitive: inaccurate, unclear, coarse, limited, trivial, banal. It's repetitive, the same over and over, like the work called women's work; earthbound, housebound. It's vulgar, the vulgar tongue, common, common speech, colloquial, low, ordinary, plebeian, like the work ordinary people do, the lives common people live.[2]

This deep-seated sense of inferiority makes it difficult for us to honor our own lineage. We feel that we are going against the very grain of our intellectual development in paying conscious attention to the looping, meandering mother tongue.

SPEAKING THE MOTHER TONGUE

What does it mean for modern women to speak in the mother tongue, to honor the richness of the Motherline, to hear the voices of the lost women in our souls? It means to sink down into a world outside ordinary time, to sink into what we feel in our bodies and in our emotions, to allow ourselves to see with the inner eye as well as the outer, to delve down into the forbidden areas of our experience, to attend to those things that make us ashamed. I had an experience recently, sitting in a circle of women, of entering into this ancestral female realm.

Most of the women in the circle were professionals. Usually we attend meetings with agendas, speakers, and goals. This meeting had none of those. We sat in a circle to be women together. Each woman had a turn to tell a story from her life: a dream, a moment of illumination. A woman spoke of her mother's death. She had not been with her when she died and felt guilty and disoriented. Her mother's death did not seem real to her. She couldn't grieve.

A few days later, standing at the kitchen sink and looking out her window at the backyard, she noticed that the princess tree in her garden had bloomed suddenly, unseasonably. Her mother had given her this tree, years earlier, as a wedding gift. She stood with her hands in dishwater, seeing the brilliant blooms that her mother had loved, a wild spot of color in her wintry backyard. Her mother's spirit touched her and her tears let down, flowing into the standing water in her sink. Feeling the bond to her mother once more, she could find her orientation in life.

The circle of women was haunted suddenly by all of our mothers. We who were in mid-life and older recounted our struggles, shame, rage, and love for the women who gave us life. Each woman told her version of the story: how ashamed she had been of her mother; how angry she had been at her mother; how hurt she had been by her mother. Some spoke of daughters who were angry or ashamed of them. Some spoke of how, in the process of beginning to accept their own limitations and to see their own lives as shaped by circumstance and historical moment, tempered by failures and burnished by pain, they could begin to accept the limitations of their mothers' lives.

As I looked about the room, I had a split image. I saw us all in our professional personas, hurrying around our busy schedules in cars. Underneath was another image: we sat in this circle throughout time, telling our stories, naming our mothers. In this subterranean world, time is circular instead of linear. We have been meeting thus in kitchens, at baby showers, or bleeding into the ground in the sanctuary of the women's hut, eternally. Rushing around in our everyday lives we forget this other, deeper level of life. Like a spring gone underground, we forget the healing source that we embody: women among women, telling the stories of our lives.

BIRTH MYSTERIES

Among the most powerful and mysterious stories from the Motherline are those of birth, of the bonding between mothers and children. For we are conceived in the context of great mysteries of which we can only be dimly conscious. We are tied to our lives by bonds that we cannot comprehend. What was the field of emotion between our parents when they made love that fateful time? What did it mean to our mother to bear us? Were we conceived in a state of deep sorrow that we will never understand? Are we something sacred and profound to our mother that she could never express? What were her fantasies and wishes? What world of personal and political events did she live in when the news came from within her that she was pregnant?

Our mothers hold the inner knowing. When a woman becomes a mother her world changes from the inside out. She is shaped from within by the child's development. Boundaries between herself and her baby are blurred as her body and awareness shift to embrace the unknown child. Yet the one she is bearing, intimate of intimates, sharer of blood and of bodily secretions, is unknown to her. She may not know its sex or the color of its eyes. Certainly she does not know its personality, its fate, its meaning in her life. In her private musings, she weaves the feelings and fantasies that become her baby's psychological receiving blanket. And yet at the same time, her consciousness is being woven by her experience of the pregnancy. She is creating and being created, forming and being formed.

Inner and outer events, personal and collective meanings, are spun together in the mother's realm during the mysterious beginnings of new life. Feelings about the child in utero, during the birth process, and in the early months of life are intertwined into a woman's sense of who her child is and what kind of mother she will be. These form the first bond between them.

It is not only in biological conception that mother and child shape one another, or that uncanny processes create connection. The bonding experienced by adoptive children and their parents, and by stepchildren and stepparents, create other kinds of Motherlines. My Motherline has been shaped by the son and daughter to whom I gave birth, the daughter I adopted and the three stepchildren brought into my life by marriage. They have taught me how various the bonds of kin can be.

Worlds of Men and War

I have a bodily memory of my first pregnancy and how I was shaped by the worlds of men and war before my son was born. I remember myself sitting with my hand on my belly with that diffuse look of inner listening you see on the faces of women when they are pregnant. I had missed a period. My breasts were sore. The food I used to love now turned my stomach. Who was becoming within me, and who was I becoming? Curled up around the future in my belly, my baby was forming like a dream, a dream that would become as real as I was and change my world. That was one kind of time, Motherline time.

The other kind of time measured external, historical events, and it was a very bad time. It was October, 1962: the Cuban missile crisis. Soviet ships reputedly carrying missiles were advancing toward American ships blocking the way. The fate of the planet and of my unborn child lay in the hands of two men I had never met. Kennedy and Khrushchev eyeballed one another on the covers of national magazines, and I feared for my own young life, for the life of the child I was bearing, for my husband in medical school, for the world. I was at once amazed by the ordinary, underrated miracle of bearing a child and dazed by our collective powerlessness in the world situation.

My father called me up during the height of the crisis to say he hoped I was not planning to get pregnant because this was no world in which to bring a child. Did some part of him know that I was already pregnant, as though the Motherline in him was being tugged? I had not intended to tell my father about my pregnancy so early. But under the circumstances, under the shadow of the end of the world, I did. "Oh Lord," he said. "Well, then we're just going to have to get through this."

During that pregnancy, I found myself compelled to explore organizations about the draft and conscientious objection in the driven way other women describe cravings for certain foods. I would sit with my large belly in meetings made up of troubled-looking young men who were at a loss to understand what I was doing among them. I was filled with thoughts of my paternal grandfather, who had fled Russia in the early years of this century to avoid the twenty-five-year draft then current for Jewish men. I considered becoming a Quaker, so that if I gave birth to a boy, he would be born a conscientious objector.

None of us knew then how we would be affected by the growing involvement of the United States in the Vietnam war. We had no inkling that my husband's future choice of Peace Corps service in India over military service in Vietnam would be influenced by my pregnant attendance at meetings about conscientious objection, or that the resulting logic of events would bring us, five years later, to adopt an Indian child.

Motherline stories are filled with the sense of the future held in the seeds of the past. As I consider my son's life from the middle of mine, I marvel at the connection between his personality, his birth, and the collective events that filled my consciousness during my pregnancy with him. I can still hear his outraged scream as he entered the world, and I recognize that attitude in him today. He is outraged by injustice and political stupidity. He is fascinated with recent American history and can discuss in learned detail the machinations of the superpowers during the terrifying moment in which he was conceived.

The amazement of sons is that they are of us, such intimates, and yet so other. The sorrow of sons is that their young lives are endangered by the large political games of nations or the small political games of the street;

they move in realms in which their mothers have traditionally lacked power. Did my father feel similarly about me, sensing I was entering a world in which he could not follow me, the world of women, of pregnancy and babies, at so dangerous an hour in this century?

A Pregnant Failure

My second pregnancy was filled with entirely different feelings and associations than was my first. World danger, always imminent, did not fill my consciousness. Instead, I found myself filled with a wish to voice the powerful experience of pregnancy and birth. Most of what had been written about women, at that time, had been authored by men. As though some part of me knew I was bearing a girl child, my thoughts had to do with the lack of a literature by women directly out of our lived experience. I thought: here I am, pregnant, having this amazing experience. I need to write about it, give it a voice.

Again, but in a very different form, inner and outer realities seemed to merge. In that historical moment, 1966, the second wave of the women's movement was about to explode. It would affect my entire generation, changing our expectations of ourselves and our relationships. My young self knew only that I was confused about my identity, unable to find my voice, unable to write more than a few paragraphs of a story, a few lines of a poem. I accused myself of being a twenty-three-year-old pregnant failure.

In that feeling of failure lay the seeds of my future development. For the child I was bearing would become a young woman who would help me illuminate the very questions I contemplated while I was pregnant with her. Recently, I showed her an earlier version of this chapter. She was taking a Feminist Studies class in college. She wondered if I had seen Ursula LeGuin's essays, especially her Bryn Mawr commencement address, in which she talks about the differences between the father tongue and the mother tongue. "It's exactly what you need for your book!" she told me.

That is how Ursula LeGuin found her way into the reworking of this chapter, and how she and my daughter helped me understand what had me so tongue-tied during my second pregnancy. I was trying to write about Motherline experience in the father tongue. No wonder I couldn't find my voice!

My daughter's birth is inextricably woven into the women's movement in my psyche. I remember pushing and pushing, face all red, body straining, doctors and nurses and husband about me, like a cheering section: "One more time: Push! Now look!" I saw her wet head emerging out of me in the large, delivery-room mirror. She hardly cried. Instead, with a cool, intelligent gaze, she looked around the delivery room. I thought: "My goodness! A daughter who is going to be looking at me!" I knew then I would have to become true to myself, so I would not be ashamed of what she saw in me.

In her early teens she won a scholarship to an out-of-town prep school and left home much earlier than any of us had planned. I felt a great empty place in my being. It was visceral, an aching hole in my body. I admired her courage, taking on the challenge that life offered her, and I envied her the opportunity to choose her own path over family ties. I myself was newly remarried, negotiating the complex issues of making a step family work. I knew I was in danger of settling for less than I wanted for myself, because I did not want to rock the complex family boat. My daughter's courage challenged me. It sent me back to graduate school for a doctorate, back to the patchwork quilt of this book, which I had begun when I was pregnant with her.

Two Motherlines

My connection to each of my children stands outside ordinary time, a blend of my psyche and theirs, hard to separate into self and other. How and when each came into my life, how each changed me, what images each etched into my sense of who I am forms the bond I feel. When I think of one of my children, a host of associations sends me looping back through my life, to find the pattern of meaning that child evokes in me.

An adopted child, whose life was conceived in another woman's body, evokes a different pattern of imagery. Born to an Indian woman I have never met, my adopted daughter ties me to the body of an unknown woman in mutual motherhood. I think of the moment I first saw this child and conceived that she should be my daughter. She was ten months old, a vibrant, dark-eyed being on the hip of a nurse in a small missionary hospital in southern India. She was irresistible: the kind of child one reaches for, wants to hold, yearns to take home. Yet, because she did not enter life through my body, the process of our bonding was a complex business in which she had much to teach me.

A kaleidoscope of memories resolves into one picture: I see myself in a disorganized apartment, a single mother with three young children. My voice is raised, my face a furrowed fury. I am locked in a power struggle with my Indian daughter. That fierce, little, brown-bodied being once again has found exactly the point in my psyche that makes me lose perspective and turn on her, furious. She is four, a year younger than her sister, and becoming very verbal about what she feels. I can feel the child's tension in my own body, and suddenly the words come to me.

"Look," I find myself saying, "are you trying to see if you can get me to kick you out of the house?" "Yes," she says, not batting an eyelash. I have been trying to understand her behavior for months. Now it is as if the child has planted the words in me, words that are obvious, but difficult for me to say: "It is because you're adopted, because you're different than your brother and your sister, and don't come out of me?" "Yes," she says. "Well," I tell her, "you can get me awful mad at you. But you won't ever get me to kick you out of the house."

In that moment I understood something I hadn't known before. This was not a knowing from the head. I had not yet studied psychology. It was a knowing that began in my body and in my experience of my daughter's body. I ached for her, for my beautiful youngest who had never been inside me, never been nursed by me, whose face I did not see when she first entered this world. I felt grief for the pregnancy I had not experienced with her, grief for her birth and her early months. I felt the empty place in her, left by the birth mother who could not keep her. I understood that my daughter and I needed to feel these things together.

During the next few years I often spoke to her about these feelings of grief and loss. She would climb into my lap and her wiry little body would relax in my arms. We spent many hours like this, mourning together, creating a bond out of our feelings of loss. She never again pushed me with quite that ferocity, and I began feeling the visceral level of my connection to her more consciously.

I marvel, looking back, at how my wise, youngest child found the way to show me what was obvious to her: the bond between adoptive parent and child requires conscious and physical attention. She understood a kind of knowing of the body. Out of such communication she and I have woven our relationship.

I told her the story of her adoption often, like a favorite bedtime story: how her birth mother, a poor village woman from the east coast of India, had traveled a long way on foot to find a good place to leave her child. She was not married to the baby's father, she told the missionaries at the American hospital where she delivered her daughter. In her village she could have been stoned for bearing a child out of wedlock. So, knowing she was pregnant, she told the villagers that she had an illness and had to go to the hospital. She walked for many miles to the best hospital in that part of India, a hospital that would take good care of her baby. That is where, ten months later, when my then husband and I were traveling in that part of India, we met this beautiful child and fell in love with her.

She recently told me that she often thinks of her biological mother, whom she has never met. She was afraid that it would be hurtful to me for her to feel love for her birth mother. I was surprised. After all, I had told her the adoption story again and again because I wanted to connect her to her birth mother and her country of origin. This was the same child who taught me most of what I know about adoption, who taught me to name the painful, obvious truths. Of course, she would have strong feelings for the woman who brought her into this world.

I, too, have strong feelings for her. I wonder what her life is, and what she imagines has become of the child she had to give up. But I realize that the work of one developmental stage must be redone at the next developmental stage. It's a very different thing to deal with your feelings about being adopted when you are four than when you are eighteen—the age her birth mother was when my daughter was born. "It's like I have two motherlines," my daughter said, "one through you and one through my birth mother."

I realized that my daughter was struggling with the same dualistic dilemma I have known in the conception and writing of this book: When honoring a neglected aspect of experience, do we dishonor the rest? As her feelings for her biological Motherline surface, must she minimize her feelings for her adoptive Motherline? If I honor the experience of birth-giving in the psychology of women, do I dishonor women who have not given birth?

My adopted child does not have to choose between her birth mother and her adoptive mother. In order to be fully herself she must claim her relationship to both Motherlines. Both her biological and her adoptive parents are essential parts of her psychological makeup. To say that biology is a potent part of the Motherline does not exclude the power of the non-biological connection. She and I made our bond conscious through the recognition of its nonbiological nature.

Where Family Begins and Ends

Each of my three stepchildren also has taught me something about human bonding, about the creation of kinship ties outside the biological realm.

After nine difficult years as a single parent, after many impossible relationships, I began to think my fate was to remain unmated. To my surprise, I found myself in a relationship with a loving, humorous, mature man. It was clear to both of us that we had each found our life companion. What was wonderful for him and me, feeling deeply at home with one another, recognizing our capacity for a flexible, joyous partnership, was not at first so wonderful for the six children our relationship threw together. They were suddenly forced into a complex new family that altered birth order, and required each child to give up his or her unique position in one family, and take on a different position in a larger, unfamiliar family. Much of the work of bonding with my stepchildren required my recognition that I was not their mother and would not try to be. It was an earth-shaking time for them. They needed their own mother, and they needed to know I respected their strong bond with her.

Over the years I have worked out very different relationships with each of my husband's children. They are a part of me. I dream of them, learn from them, worry about them, love them. But my connection to them lacks the wild irrationality of my connection to my own children. If one is sick or in distress, their father goes through the kind of agonies I know as a mother. It was he who gets obsessed with worry, his heart torn to bits. I am more detached because I know where they end and I begin, something I'm much less clear about with my own children. As a result, I can put things in perspective. I can reassure him, as he can reassure me when I am wild with worry about one of my children. My stepchildren have taught me that strong kinship ties can be woven out of the ambivalent feelings that are natural to step families. And through all the complexities of relationships we have created a family pattern that has rituals, history, conflicts, and jokes.

It is not so clear where family begins and ends, since my children's family extends to their father, his wife and her kin, and my stepchildren's family extends to their mother, her husband and his kin. Unlike the lists of "begets" in the Bible, where son is begotten by father in a clear, linear descent, the Motherline web is raggedly creative, tying in the severed connections of divorces and remarriages, creating new family fabric and inspiring our children to ask endless questions about who is related to whom and how.

Although I pride myself on my personal knowledge of many kinds of Motherlines, there are new variations on the theme that I know only through the experience of colleagues, clients, and friends. A lesbian friend conceived her daughter through artificial insemination. Her partner has legally adopted the child. They have both been powerfully shaped by the experience of becoming parents. My friend's relationship with her mother, once strained, has now blossomed into a mutuality of motherhood.

New developments such as surrogacy and in-vitro fertilization raise ethical and emotional issues of enormous proportions. Women are profoundly shaped by the experience of bearing a child for another woman, or not being able to bear a child, or spending enormous amounts of time and money opening their bodies to fertility experts. All these experiences become part of the psychological field in which mother and child relate.

THE DIALOGUE OF DEVELOPMENT

When mothers speak of child development in the mother tongue, they describe a life in which their children influence them as much as they influence their children. Influences and development loop not only in the direction of parent to child, but back again from child to parent. This experience of being raised by the one you are raising is described by women from their children's first moments in the world: my son's outraged cry after birth; my daughter's cool look around the delivery room.

Some years ago a colleague and I led groups for new mothers. We sat in the circle of mothers and babies, amidst all the familiar sounds and smells—women cooing, absorbed in their babies' every facial movement, babies sucking, whimpering, or sleeping, diapers being changed—and invited the women to speak of their experience.

What never failed to amaze a woman about her baby was how strong a personality her child had from the beginning. No woman found herself with a blank slate to write upon. Babies are relaxed or intense, placid or easily upset, curious or accepting. Each child's temperament raised different issues for the mother; each child took the mother on a developmental journey into unknown aspects of herself and of her connection to life.

A woman told me of the special feeling she has for one of her children:

> You know I love all my children. But there is something very special about Pamela. It's as though all the good fairies were standing around her cradle when she was born and they just gave her everything. She is a life enhancer. She is a window into another world.

When Pamela was in nursery school, she was three and a half, she did a painting. I still have it. It was a square of orange, within it a circle of turquoise, a triangle of orange within that. Below was the exact same thing except smaller and the colors reversed. And the teacher said: "Tell me about this." And Pamela looked at her with a pitying air as though she were thinking: "You poor dumb thing" and said: "It's a mother and child of course!" I think part of the reason that I just stand in awe of her is because I think she is what I might have been if I hadn't had that rigid Catholic education [there are tears in her eyes as she says this].

Pamela taps unknown yearnings in her mother. The daughter's richness of character is transformational for the mother, as though through her child she can experience aspects of her own personality that were repressed in her own childhood. Our different children tug at different aspects of ourselves. Pamela's siblings strike different chords in their mother's soul.

The particular nature of one's children shapes what a mother learns and feels. A woman raising an athletic daughter or a bookish son may find herself experiencing concerns about masculinity and femininity, body image and persona, popularity and introversion, through children who don't fit the gender roles into which her own generation was squeezed.

Sometimes a child will reconnect the mother to forgotten pleasures, lost parts of her personality. Author Angela McBride writes of this:

My daughter reintroduced me to the soothing luxury of a bubble bath and to the charms of reading out loud and pretending. Her expressiveness has encouraged my own. I find the edges of my personality rounding out, not because she has fulfilled me, but because her own sensuous, spontaneous, pleasurable self is a good role model.[3]

As children grow, a mother has the opportunity to relive her own development from the parental perspective. She is also nudged by her child to new stages in her adult development. Many women feel pushed to go back to school by a child's developmental leap. Her child's entrance into kindergarten or college may make the mother realize she is also ready for the next step in her education.

Suzannah told me how her daughter's development spurred her own:

My daughter, Sunny, asked me what I had majored in in college. That stunned me. It made me realize that I had put my intellect in cold storage. And it was just after she went to college that I joined the Women's Study Committee which changed my life. I became aware of women's history and my personal history. I went back to school and reclaimed my mind. It was a difficult time for me, my oldest child going off. A time of opportunity, but also a time when something ends. I struggled with a shifting sense of self. After a long struggle, I began to become myself.

Sometimes it is a daughter's development that inspires the mother's; often it is a child's suffering that forces the mother to look at herself in new ways, to see her limitations, to understand her failures. The pain this causes a woman is visceral, because her bond with her child is experienced at a bodily level.

I can remember, for example, when my son was born. At that time babies and mothers were separated after birth; the babies were kept in nurseries overnight. At midnight on the night of his birth I woke up suddenly from a medicated sleep, knowing something was wrong. I felt a terrible ache in my breasts. Later I learned that feeling was my milk letting down. A minute later the nurse opened the door softly, saw me awake, and said: "Your son is crying. Do you want me to bring him to you?" The bond between my newborn son and me reached through hospital doors and down corridors. The nurse, who, despite her official duties, was also a woman and a mother, brought me my child and I nursed him. She bent the rules for us, letting him stay with me the rest of the night.

When he is unhappy now I feel the ghost of the physical response that woke me on his first night in this world. I am haunted by the need to do something to make it better. But doing anything, even saying anything, seems to be intruding in his life. I long for the time when I could kiss a hurt and make it all better. There are times when I'm convinced that everything he suffers is my fault. I am dazed by a mid-life rush of grief and guilt.

It is clear that my guilt is out of proportion. The guilt of other mothers seems absurd to me. It seems inflated, as though the mother hasn't gotten herself scaled down to human size from being the huge and powerful mother of infants. An older woman, for example, tells me that it's all her fault that her daughter divorced her son-in-law. "How could it possibly be your fault?" I wonder. But there's no shaking her. She feels tugged at by her daughter's suffering, helpless, and believes it's her fault that she can't soothe her child.

A woman of my own generation tells me: "When I call my mother, she often says: 'But you don't sound happy.' As if happiness is required. As if my not sounding happy is a comment on her mothering, instead of on the nature of life."

I know I failed my children in many ways that were beyond my control. I had them too young, I got divorced; my life was chaotic; I was immature. When they were young I was rebelling against my own strict upbringing by having as little visible structure as possible. Now I can see how important supportive structures are for kids.

I remember my mother visiting me when the children were young and gently suggesting that a little more regularity of schedule might not hurt. I thought she was an old bourgeois fuddy-duddy. I thought my children needed freedom because I needed freedom. My son, still raising me, told me recently that he wished I had provided more structure for him when he was small. "I'm different than you. I'm a person who needs a lot of structure, Mom," he said. I knew he was right. I wish I could go back and reshape his childhood with what I know now.

On the telephone with my mother, I repeat what he said, and tell her I realize now that she was right. "Isn't clarity of hindsight awful?" she says. "I see so clearly now the load I put on you. You had too much responsibility for me and for your brothers. How I wish I could give you more of a childhood than you had. But back then, I was just barely surviving."

We sit in silence, on either side of the long, invisible cord between us. It's one thing to face one's own limitations, and quite another to know the impact on one's child. "It's impossible," my mother says, "to be a perfect mother. What matters is that you and he can talk about it."

"It's like a new stage of mothering," I tell her, "when they're young adults and they work over their childhoods with you."

"Yes," she says, "and it never stops. You never stop being a mother. You just become a lot of other things as well."

The Path of Shame

To face one's limitations as a parent is painful and filled with shame. But pain and shame do not rob our mothering experiences of meaning. These are the ways our children teach us about ourselves and about life. Seeing how we have failed as mothers, giving up the grandiose fantasy of maternal perfection, opens the door to our own mothers.

Often we come to this place in the middle of our lives, when our children are old enough to tell us their anger. It is at this stage of maturation that we can feel our way into the suffering of our mothers' and children's lives. For she who cannot sink into the pain of her mother's experience, who cannot imagine her grief, love, bitterness, life's tragedy, life's joy, remains forever a daughter, frozen in her development.

The psychological fantasy that there is some sort of ideal childhood dehumanizes and inflates our mothers. If our mothers were only not so dense, or crazy, or limited, such a childhood could have been ours. It is a defense against confronting the tragic nature of life.

Jung understands this when he says:

> A "complete" life does not consist in a theoretic completeness, but in the fact that one accepts, without reservation, the particular tissue in which one finds oneself embedded, and that one tries to make sense of it or to create a cosmos from the chaotic mess into which one is born.[4]

A child-centered view of life is not sufficient to understand human development. When we integrate the viewpoint of the mother, looping from mother to child and back again, we are able to transcend the dualistic thinking that splits parent from child. A richer view of human development then emerges in which past and present, the experience of being parented and of being a parent, are woven into a single texture of memory and emotion.

When we listen to stories from the Motherline, we hear of no perfection. We don't even hear "good-enough" stories. What is good enough about post-partum depressions, the death of mothers and grandmothers in childbirth, the loss of young children to childhood diseases? Whose Motherline does not contain such tragedy?

In a patriarchal culture the Motherline has been a repressed aspect of experience. Women today run the risk of projecting the tragic side of life onto their own mothers. It is as though the sins of the mother, rather than the nature of life, create life's difficulties. They are ashamed of their mothers and, like Athena, would like to live as if they had jumped out of their fathers' foreheads. Jungian analyst Jean Bolen's description of Athena's geneology is instructive here:

> The goddess did not acknowledge her mother, Metis; in fact, Athena seemed unaware she had a mother. As Hesiod recounts, Metis

was Zeus' first royal consort, an ocean deity who was known for her wisdom. When Metis was pregnant with Athena, Zeus tricked her into becoming small and swallowed her. It was predicted that Metis would have two very special children: a daughter equal to Zeus in courage and wise counsel, and a son, a boy of all conquering heart, who would become king of gods and men. By swallowing Metis, Zeus thwarted fate and took over her attributes as his own.[5]

We live in a culture that has swallowed Metis, the mother. We do not even know that we are born of a lost heritage of female wisdom and power. To find our female ground we must reclaim Metis, and that is no easy task. A dream provided me with an image of what it would mean to reclaim our maternal lineage, to know her nature. I dreamt I was in labor. The woman attending me, my midwife, held a mirror for me. She did not hold it up to let me see the child being born. She held it up to my own face, straining in labor. "You need to see your laboring self as beautiful," she said. "Beautiful?" I thought, ashamed of my unsightly face, all bloated and grimacing with the strain of pushing the new life out.

And then I understood the wisdom of her words. What could be more profound than this beauty of woman, able to immerse herself, body and soul, in the great tide of life bearing life, birthing babies, or books, or institutions, or ideas? She is at once fully herself and fully open to being the channel through which new life can pass; she is at once filled with power and completely vulnerable. She is as common as the everyday miracle of birth. She is the bearer of the ancient ocean tidings of Metis that perpetually change the world.

CHAPTER FOUR

WRESTLING WITH THE MOTHER:

Of Love, Rebellion, and

Our Personal Shadows

*There is nothing in human nature more resonant with charges
than the flow of energy between two biologically alike bodies, one
of which has lain in amniotic bliss inside the other, one of
which has labored to give birth to the other. The materials are
here for the deepest mutuality and the most painful estrangement.*

ADRIENNE RICH[1]

T here is a paradoxical challenge in our development as women. We
need to know our uniqueness, that we are different from our mothers, and we need to know our alikeness. Our mothers represent
our roots and tie us to our Motherlines. Differing from our mothers helps
us find our individual destinies so that we do not blindly repeat our mothers' lives. Identifying with our mothers connects us to our origins.

Mothers and daughters can become painfully polarized in the struggle to honor both sides. From the mother's point of view the process of
differentiation, of sorting out me from thee, tugs at the most primal places
in her nature. She remembers the child she bore in the very cells of her
body. What mother is not wildly subjective about her offspring, driven by

a passionate core connection that is the psychological ghost of her pregnancy, her birth-giving, her breastmilk letting down when her baby cried?

Many mothers identify with their daughters so profoundly that any difference is extremely difficult to navigate, while their daughters insist ferociously that they are absolutely different from their mothers. The image of merger is at the core of the psychology of women: we yearn for mutuality and fear engulfment. Having been within one another's bodies, we know how to get under one another's skin.

A son is different. The identification is at a slight remove, a respect for his otherness informs a mother's fantasies of who her son will be.

But our daughters are our younger selves; our mothers are our older selves. Our daughters were in our bodies as we were in our mothers. We think we know our daughters' experience through our own experience. We identify from the inside out, expecting perfect understanding from our mothers, from our daughters. They are our extension into the past and into the future. As daughters we may have been terrified of being devoured, taken over, sinking into an undifferentiated swamp of yin; we may have fought fiercely to establish our uniqueness. Yet, our daughters' struggle to differentiate from us feels like the torment of sharp objects under the skin.

None of this Motherline wrestling fits with the official version of how a mother should be. We shouldn't "need" our children; we shouldn't "merge" with our children except when they are infants; we shouldn't let our messy feelings leak all over our children's development. We should raise them to become separate individuals. We should have firm boundaries, always know what is them and what is us, and never intrude our personal desires into their lives. The fierceness of maternal feeling is taboo in our culture because it threatens our cultural sacred cow: individuality.

CUTTING THE CORD

Traditional psychological theory was written by men and applied to women. It held that the ability to separate oneself from mother, to have a clearly defined autonomous identity, is essential to emotional health. A male model of development was superimposed on women's lives, leaving the many women who could not recognize themselves in this official description of adulthood feeling inadequate and inferior. Emily Hancock, author of *The Girl Within,* makes this point in her wryly titled chapter "Men's Theories, Women's Lives." She wonders:

How is it that we have polarized the human agenda, lionizing separation and independence, leaving out, entirely, meaningful connections between people and the human capacities for intimacy, empathy, care, and compassion?[2]

Hancock is one of a growing number of psychology writers who question the conventional wisdom about adult development. They argue that the problem is not with women but with a culture that devalues women's natural strengths. They point out that something is missing from our national obsession with the heroic drama of autonomous, usually male, accomplishment. In the background, sorting his papers, bearing his children, rubbing his back, believing in his goals, are the women upon whom the hero depends: his secretary, his wife, his lover, even perish the thought, his mother! The hero hasn't separated. He just ignores the women on whom he depends.

In our new version of development, when women tell the stories of their own lives, we discover that daughters don't usually cut themselves off from their mothers when they reach adulthood. The mother's place in her daughter's life is not superceded by a relationship to a man, as psychoanalytic theory has assumed, but is a continuing and important aspect of adult women's lives. In the words of psychoanalyst Jean Baker Miller, "women stay with, build on, and develop in a context of attachment and affiliation with others."[3]

But ongoing connection does not mean peace and harmony. Many women have painful and volatile relationships with their mothers and daughters. As I have thought about the women I know, the image of wrestling has emerged to describe the differentiation process. In my image each woman stands on her own two feet, fully engaged in a struggle about identity, territory, and power. When the dialogue of development heats up in adolescence and young adulthood, it turns into a wrestling match for renegotiating an intimate relationship. But like a father teaching his son to box, the mother wrestling with her daughter knows she is the older, responsible one, and gives her daughter room to establish her own potency.

Mothers and daughters wrestle with bodily, temperamental, stylistic, generational, and usually very emotional differences between them. It is a great gift to a daughter if her mother can at once be her own authentic self, and honor her daughter's struggle with her. Sometimes it takes a lifetime of misunderstanding for mother and daughter to learn how to have an open dialogue. Nancy Friday, author of the popular book *My Mother,*

My Self, in which she wrestles with her mother's neuroses to find her own identity, comes to a new appreciation of her mother's strengths. She says that it took her the "entire writing of this book to acknowledge in my heart that the qualities I am proudest of in myself I learned from her."

> The more I grow away from her and define myself, the more I see in her this other person she was before she became Nancy Friday's mother. That is the magic: not that we can ever recreate that nirvana of love that may or may not have existed between us as mother-and-child, but that once we have separated we can give each other life, extra life, each out of the abundance of her own.[4]

This is a hopeful image of the richness that is possible when mother and daughter have wrestled with their differences and found their own ground in life to stand on. The tragedy for many women is that their personal mothers are never strong enough to wrestle with them. Many are devastated by their daughter's differentiation struggle. Longing for the affirmation of their motherwork, which the culture denies them, longing for a mirror of their female selves that they never had, envious of opportunities their daughters have that they were denied, these mothers need affirmation from their daughters. In that wish they short-circuit the true developmental work of mother and daughter. To the mother, the daughter's statement of differences between them can feel like a betrayal of all the work of mothering, all the love she's felt for her child. Wounded and enraged, she turns against her daughter, who is then forced to do this work internally, wrestling in her soul or in her psychotherapist's office with her mother's limitations.

But if the mother can stand on the ground of her own lived life and wrestle with her daughter's feelings and her own, she frees them both to create an intimacy that respects differences and is responsive to life-cycle changes. Far from creating separation, this kind of wrestling is the beginning of an authentic relationship. Bonding and differentiation are not separate human endeavors, achieved at different developmental levels. They occur simultaneously and throughout development.

At the moment of birth when the baby is born out of the mother, the cord is cut. This is the first step of differentiation, sorting out one body from the other. At the same time it is a powerful moment of bonding, the first touch of hands and lips, the first eye contact between mother and child. We cannot know the nature of a child held within our bodies or within our psyches. It is only when the baby is born, when the child begins to say "no," when the young adult begins to rebel, that we can know the otherness of our child and begin to form a conscious relationship.

This is the central paradox of human relationship: although connection begins with the umbilical cord, with the looping of identification, the resonance of similarities, only the recognition and working through of difference, of otherness, secures a bond and makes it personal. Mother and child are doomed to a shallow living out of conventional roles, without the real substance of each personality, unless they can wrestle with the terrible angel each is to the other.

WRESTLING WITH THE ANGEL

In the Old Testament story, Jacob wrestles with his angel all night long. Jacob left home in his youth because his brother, Esau, wanted to kill him. Jacob had tricked his father, Isaac, into giving him the blessing of the oldest son, which rightly belonged to Esau. In the middle of his life, with wives and children and herds of cattle, he returns to his homeland to make peace with his brother. During the long night before he is to see his brother again, he wrestles with a shadowy messenger from the divine who wounds him, blesses him, and tells him that his name is now Israel.

Today, Western women are like Jacob, trying to find our way home, wrestling with the terrible angel who knows the shadows of our past and holds the secret of our future. Like Jacob we will be wounded in the struggle—and blessed. As women who seek to be ourselves, as well as to find a conscious relationship with our Motherlines, we find ourselves in fierce internal combat with unwelcome aspects of the feminine self.

The messenger from the divine is almost always first experienced as a devil, an obstruction on one's path, a depression, a negative mother, an illness, or an impossible life situation. In Jungian psychology this struggle is referred to as the confrontation with the shadow, in which one encounters repressed or denied aspects of the self. Jung calls the shadow a "moral problem which challenges the whole ego personality."[5] In order to find our way home to our female roots, we must confront our shadow—or be caught in a life without depth. A life lived afraid of our shadows is only a half life, driven by the constant necessity to prove to ourselves, to our mothers, or to the culture, that we are some sort of ideal selves, instead of fully our-selves. Jungian analyst Esther Harding describes the kind of person who tries to live without a shadow:

> One has the feeling that they do not stand on a substantial foun-dation; consequently their judgement does not inspire confidence, for they do not seem quite real. They are two-dimensional, because they have mislaid, or possibly even lost, their shadows. They never touch the deeper experiences of life but go along on the surface.[6]

To become fully herself, a woman must honor the side of her nature that feels crazy, nasty, devouring, intrusive, passive, angry, depressed—fill in the blank with what you hate most about your mother. In poet Rob-ert Bly's phrase she must "eat her shadow."[7] This means "eating crow" for many women; it means seeing our mother's worst traits in ourselves; it means acknowledging the shame and grief of our lineage.

A woman who confronts her shadow moves beyond victimization. She learns about her own hard edge, her power, the pain she can inflict. Knowing her own shadow as well as her mother's, she can find her way back to feminine ground, the ancient shadow world in which the mothers sit by the river of life washing the world's dirty linen and telling the stories of women's experience, of birth and death and the heartaches of relation-ship.

Sins of the Mother

The confrontation with the shadow requires a mother to face her sins. Our daughters help us in this work when they tell us about the ways we failed them. Were we guilty of sins of omission: not being available or protective enough, neglecting aspects of a daughter's development, not seeing her true self? Were we guilty of sins of commission: being overly involved, critical, or cruel? Are our daughters haunted by our unspoken feelings about love and sex, or by the life potential we never were able to live out?

It is soul-rending work to face such painful truths. We are crippled in it by the cultural lack of empathy for mothers. A mother whose child feels angry, abused or misunderstood by her experiences herself as a failure. She stands accused in the judgmental language of the father tongue: if she had only mastered the tasks of mothering, her children would have grown up happy, well adjusted, successful, and proud of her. But parental failure is built into the Motherline, an unavoidable condition of life, like death. As Jungian analyst Larry Jaffee has written:

> . . . our parents always fail us massively and decisively. Why is this so? Because they are limited human beings; and for the same reason we, too, will fail our children.[8]

The truth is that we are bound to fail our children by our own human limitations. We need to be people as well as mothers; we will always be balancing our own needs against those of others. We are certain to err on the side of too much or too little control, discipline, love, support, attention, money. We are doomed to fail the ones we love the most.

This is why "the terrible" is part of every mother-child relationship. Mothers and children live in different bodies, are born into different families in different historical contexts. They are people in different life stages, usually of different temperaments. Even in the best of circumstances, with the conscious choice of pregnancy and child care, mothers are terrible and children insatiable.

A baby wants to be responded to in the perfect rhythm of her needs. But her mother has different needs. She has just given birth. She is exhausted. She hardly knows her own body, let alone her baby's. Perhaps she is depressed. Undoubtedly she is deeply disoriented. Her baby's cry does not always fall on willing ears. No child can help being an assault on a mother's sense of self. No mother can mother all aspects of her child. And in those moments of feeling overwhelmed, the demons emerge. The mother may wish her child dead because the child is devouring the mother's existence. The child feels the mother's fury and is terrified. Negotiating these differences in the early mother-infant bond is fraught with emotional danger.

The struggle over differences continues as children grow up. Children who dare to be themselves are bound to disappoint their mother's wish for immortality. They are moved by different urges than their mothers. They are influenced by different generational forces. The child also is bound to be disappointed. A daughter longs to be mothered by a mother like the potential woman in her. A son longs for a mother who embodies his internal image of the feminine.

Even under the best of circumstances, when children are welcomed by mothers who want them, there will always be mourning for the mother we didn't have; for the daughter or son we didn't have; and anger about the selves that were sacrificed to the mother or child we did have. Disappointment and anger are givens in any parent-child relationship because what our children mean to us is very different from what we mean to them. A child is only a part of her mother's life, but the mother or caretaking person is the source of all essential supplies for the child. This inevitable inequality of power and needs creates a rich soil in which differences and difficulties grow. Kathy Carlson, author of *In Her Image,* states the problem well:

> The child perspective sees the mother ego-centrically, believing her to be all-powerful and able to fulfill the daughter's needs. The mother is not seen as individual, or as limited by circumstances within and without. The great expectations surrounding her from this perspective are rarely met; this gives rise to the unhealed child full of rage, blame, hurt, and need. Although frustrating and too narrow, the unhealed child is a true inner experience; it is valuable for finding and claiming the importance of oneself.[9]

Further difficulties arise because we mothers also have great expectations of ourselves. Most of us are determined to differentiate from our own mothers by being better mothers. We raise our children as we wish we had been raised; we bring to them the values of the generation that formed our consciousness. We pour our love and our passion into this work, and therein lies the rub. Our children are not impressed. No child is grateful to her mother for not visiting upon her the sins of the mother's mother. The young one simply suffers the empty places left unmothered in her own childhood. She sees the fallacies of her parents' generation. She knows and names the sins of her mother.

It is painful to face the terrible aspects of our own natures. But if we are to understand the experience of our children, to hold a consensual reality with them, we must be able to face the ways in which we failed them. We must release them from our yearning to be affirmed as good mothers and let them be people living in a time we find difficult to comprehend.

The wrestling between mother and daughter takes place in many arenas. Among them are the struggles to differentiate bodies, to differentiate style in clothing, lifestyle, choice of career and mate, to sort through differences in temperament, and to sort out what has been the mother's responsibility for her child's pain. Both mother and daughter must wrestle with the cultural prejudice that at once devalues female experience and projects impossible power on mothers. And they both must wrestle with the real archetypal power of the mother: the power to give birth, to nurture, and to destroy. Having sorted out the archetypal and cultural levels, having sorted out personalities, styles, and bodies, a woman can clarify her authentic connection to her personal mother. But, because every mother is also a daughter, the wrestling goes on and on.

SORTING OUT BODY FROM BODY

The mana of a mother's body is powerful and taboo. In a culture that lacks religious rituals to express these mysteries the daughter is left to grapple with powerful feelings that she assumes are her personal problem. She has no context in which to recognize that the tortured mixture of repugnance and desire with which she regards her mother's body is a response to the archetype of the life source that her mother embodies.

As she enters puberty and her body becomes more like her mother's, she may lose her self-confidence and become depressed and unsure of herself. In *The Girl Within,* Emily Hancock describes the negative transformation of the glowing girl of nine or ten into the sullen, withdrawn, insecure girl of early adolescence. She suffers her identification with her mother because of how it limits her personally and culturally. If she has inherited her mother's body type she may be determined to change her shape. If she has a different body type, she may feel superior or inferior to her mother. She can see in her mother's flesh the imprint of her difficult fate. Writer Connie Zweig, editor of *To Be A Woman,* describes this eloquently in a vignette she calls "Massaging My Mother's Legs."

> My hand on her thigh, thick unmovable flesh, dense to the touch, heavy to the eye. I see her shame as my hand moves deeper into tissue, feeling for the flow of life, reaching for the force in my fingertips. I see the deadness in her eye that lives in this flesh, the unspoken rage, the unshed tears, choked up in her throat and locked into her leg. How did these feelings, denied for so long, suffocated like a child in an airless room, move down her body and lodge in her leg, there to grow heavy with weight, with fear, with immobility? Woven into knots, this tapestry of tension is now visible in my mother's every move, in her reaching gesture, in the turn of her head, the call of her voice, the glance of her eye. I see it—I cannot see her without seeing it—her life story so revealed, so unbidden.
>
> My hands push deeper into the thigh, she breathes with relief, she moans with pain, she wants it worked out by another, from out-

side. She blames it on bread, the food of the great mother. She craves dark bread, full of raisins, light brown bread full of seeds, twisted toasted blond bread with warm butter. She opens her mouth for bread as she does not open for words.

And she believes the bread, like the unbreathed breath, the unspoken rage, the unshed tears, moves through her body like water downstream, to land in the round recesses of flesh, to be dammed up and harden into these thighs, her thighs.

I see the bread and the sorrow and the fear in her legs, my mother's legs. And I see the hidden source of my own allergy to wheat, my inability to take in bread, to digest the nourishment of my mother, the food of the great mother.

I look down at her thighs and I wonder if this is my future.[10]

In this vignette a grown daughter reaches deeply into her mother's body and soul. The powerful resonance between mother and daughter described here is experienced by younger daughters as well. A three-year-old dancing in and out of her mother's presence, asking to be held, dashing off, returning to tug at her mother's skirts, expresses how tuned in she is to her mother's changing moods. Feminist psychologists point out that there is a field of mutual, empathic atunement between mothers and daughters at all levels of development. Daughters feel the unconscious depths of their mothers' feelings.

Writer Nancy Friday, describing how teenage daughters pick up their mother's unspoken attitudes, says:

Nobody knows a mother like her daughter. Mother says sex is beautiful. When her words go in one direction, but the music is going in another, the daughter listens to the music.[11]

Daughters feel their mothers' unspoken fear and grief and often navigate in their own lives to avoid the shoals of pain on which their mothers' lives have beached. A daughter, for example, reading between the lines of her mother's body language or voice tone that she is afraid of sex, may be compelled in her own life to make a full exploration of sexuality. A daughter who feels the grief and disappointment of her mother's marriage is likely to make an internal decision to marry a different kind of man or to live a different kind of life.

Eating disorders are toxic embodiments of this determination not to be like mother. Women wreak havoc on their bodies as though by so doing they can avoid becoming their mothers. Anorexic and bulemic women starve themselves, or force themselves to vomit up their food in a ferocious assault upon their own maturing bodies. A woman told me that her daughter became anorexic after seeing snapshots of her mother that showed her slim in her twenties and matronly in her forties. The daughter swore that this would never happen to her. She began dieting and running obsessively, determined to maintain an athletic body. Her wish to evade the fate of women's bodies was granted in a terrible form: her periods ceased for many years. She could not become a mother.

Another woman, whom I'll call Kate, spoke to me of her feelings about her daughter, Allison, who had been dangerously anorexic.

> When Allison was in high school she went on a diet. And she just kept losing. A friend of mine said: "Gee, she's looking awfully thin. Haven't you ever heard of anorexia nervosa?" It wasn't something people knew about in those days. My friend said: "I think she's got it, she's much too thin." And then I realized it wasn't just that Allison had a lot of will power. She was under the spell of this thing. She wanted to be a dancer and her thighs rubbed together and she couldn't stand that. She got her weight down, down, down, and one day she looked at herself in the mirror and said, "Gee, I look just like a little boy." She didn't want to grow up and be a woman.
>
> I look back on her illness and realize that if she had gotten any thinner she would have had to be hospitalized. She had no flesh on her, not even on her fanny. I saw her getting into the bathtub once, and she looked like a Dachau prisoner.
>
> We got her into therapy and, after a long time, she overcame the anorexia. Only now her problem is that she's overweight. It's harder for me now to see her overweight than it was to see her underweight. I feel guilty about that. I know it's the other side of the same thing. I even talked to a therapist about it. He seemed to think that I identified so much with her that it was as though I were fat. I've always hated being heavy. I feel that I know what she's going through. Only she doesn't seem so unhappy now, or as dissatisfied with her body as I am.

As a young woman Kate told me she was plump and unhappy. Then she met the man she was to marry and lost all the extra weight as she settled into a supportive relationship. She wants the same happiness for Allison and can't bear to see her heavy and alone. Kate struggles with her passionate overidentification, knowing her daughter needs to free herself.

> I think she's changing. She used to call me her best friend. She doesn't do that anymore. She doesn't need me as much. I know that's good. She's gotten critical of me too—of the food I serve. She doesn't believe in white rice or frozen vegetables. She's actually taught me a lot about preparing fresh vegetables. I think she goes overboard though. I can't stand brown rice or tofu.

Kate and her daughter are engaged in sorting out body from body. They wrestle in themselves and with each other about body shape and closeness and food. They are disentangling life histories: Kate's loss of weight early in life is a different story from Allison's anorexia. Both are being retold in their painful exchange.

A HEROIC SEAMSTRESS STORY

Daughters are very aware of how their mothers dress. As little girls we may long to "dress up" in our Mommy's clothes. As we mature into full-bodied women, our feelings about our mothers' clothing become more ambivalent. A woman I know speaks of being repelled by her mother's clothing as a teenager. Recently she found a well-cut 1940s suit in her mother's closet and asked her mother for it. The aura of mother that had earlier made her uneasy in her mother's clothing was now a pleasing identification and she took pleasure in wearing her mother's youthful elegance.

Mothers, on the other hand, often find their esthetic sense challenged as a daughter asserts herself through dress. My own mother likes simple, functional clothes. I love extravagant, beautiful clothes. One of my daughters refused to wear dresses until her late teens, and likes the simple functional lines that her grandmother appreciates.

A woman I call Molly tells a heroic tale about supporting her daughter Mary Lou's self-expression in dress.

> Mary Lou has always, from conception, been my most difficult child. I already had three kids and I was ambivalent about the pregnancy. I had thoughts about going to Puerto Rico for an abortion, which I told no one, not even my husband. I had trouble getting myself to a doctor, which is not like me. And I've had trouble of one sort or another with Mary Lou ever since. She's had a hard time in life.

She is an introvert and has difficulty making friends. She doesn't fit in the family because we're all very political and Mary Lou isn't.

Mary Lou is the family beauty. She went far away from home to San Diego. She didn't like it there, nominally because there weren't any cute guys. But I think she secretly missed me. So she comes back to Berkeley and what does she do but go to rush and join a sorority. Nobody in the family has ever been in a sorority. I was cool. I didn't say anything. That girl is such a clothes horse! She says I'm stingy. I've got money in the bank. She'll take care of me if I need things when I'm old. Money is there to be spent. She needs more sweaters. And why don't I buy her a BMW for her 21st birthday? I never had anything new until I was thirteen years old. That's inconceivable to Mary Lou.

Mary Lou is always chewing me out about my son, Paul, and his wife living with me since my husband died. She says I'm the softest touch in the world and that I shouldn't bend over backwards to be nice to them. You see, they are both consummate slobs. I'm not Miss Prim but I am tidy. However I just ignore their mess. You've got to have your priorities straight: I love having them there. But Mary Lou is young, she hasn't experienced things. She doesn't understand what it means to me not to be alone, and to still feel necessary. She has a way of pushing me, as though to make sure I'm willing to put out for her.

Like the time she needed a dress for her sorority party. This is a major party, a really big deal. A couple of weeks before this party I said to Mary Lou: "If you want me to make a dress you have to let me know so I have time." "Oh no," she said, "I'm going to Macy's." Well, she went to Macy's and she tried things on but she's Miss Picky and she couldn't find anything she liked that she could afford. The party was on a Saturday at five. On Friday evening at supper she says: "Mom, the party is tomorrow. I did go to Macy's and I couldn't find anything, so could we go buy some material?"

Well, I had told her, "I am not going to do this. You are not going to get me under the gun like this." However, she talked me into it. We bought this gorgeous fabric, seventeen dollars a yard. I came home and I cut it out. I had a meeting the following morning. This was the reason I had told her I couldn't do it. I cut the meeting short. I started working at 1:40. It was 95 degrees. I had the fan right on me. This dress was strapless, fully lined, with boning to hold it up—a lace overlay. I didn't make one mistake. I finished the dress at 4:45.

She told me later that some of the girls asked her, "Who did your dress? Bill Blass?" and she said: "My mother made it." She would never have said this a few years ago. She told me her friends said: "Your mother made it? You're kidding. Hey guys, come over and look at Mary Lou's dress. Her mother made it!" They were all saying it in a praising way, whereas earlier she would have felt embarrassed like it was a hick thing. Now she's mature enough to take pride in it.

I am struck by how Molly has put herself out in support of values so different from her own. But Molly sees it differently. Her response is an illustration of how intertwined are the processes of bonding and differentiation.

Actually it's because we are so different that we had to find some common ground. Clothes are it. I love to sew them. She loves to wear them! I'm making up for never having new clothes as a child. My mother sewed for my older sisters, and their clothes were handed down to me. That's what it meant to be the fourth daughter. No wonder I'm so interested in clothes and textiles. My mother didn't sew because she loved it. She sewed because she had to. She taught me, and I love it. So it means a lot to me for Mary Lou to have a beautiful new dress that I sewed. And it means a lot to her. It was an important moment for us, a real feeling of connection. And I feel the connection in both directions: to my mother who taught me to sew; to my daughter who loves what I sew.

THE COLOSSAL SWALLOWING UP

Women who become mothers find that it is often in the crucible of that experience, in what is in so many ways a sacrifice of self, that she touches her deepest experiences of the female self and wrestles with an angel that at once wounds and blesses her. Writer Marguerite Duras argues with those who would protect women from such suffering.

Why discourage women from the colossal swallowing up which is the essence of all motherhood, the mad love (for it is there, the love of a mother for her child), and the madness that maternity represents? For her to feel like a man, free from the consequences of maternity, from the fantastic shackles that it implies? That is probably the reason. But if I answer that men are sick precisely because of this, because they do not have the only opportunity offered a human being to experience a bursting of the ego, how would I be answered? That it was men who made motherhood the monstrous burden it is for sure. But to me the historical reasons for the burden and the drudgery seem the most superficial, because for those there is a remedy. And even if men are responsible for this enslaving form of motherhood, is this enough to condemn maternity itself?[12]

Women who become mothers early in life must differentiate from the personal mother and from the devouring archetype that would gobble up all individual development. The risk for such a woman is to remain stuck in an undifferentiated female identity, living out life stages that are neither illuminated with a collective sense of their sacredness nor with an individual quality belonging fully to her. The danger this represents for a young woman whose personality is yet unformed is expressed in a letter from the poet Charlene Baldridge to her daughter, Lou, in which she wrestles eloquently with the awesome, cellular power of the mother archetype.

> You mustn't allow your ripeness for marriage and motherhood to get in the way of your choice. I think you've reached that dangerous place in the physical development of women like us where every cell is crying out for a mate, for motherhood, to suckle . . .
> You must un-ready *your*self. You're right, you have to put from your mind marriage as a goal unto itself, apply all your energy to your dorm duties and your studies, finish school, and pray for wisdom.
> Maternity and marriage will come, but later. Stall off those cells which cry out. They'll still be there in 3–5 years, and so will all your wonderful qualities.
> I realize that I have unwittingly pressured you. I long for *your* happiness, and I long for your baby. But, I'll still be here, darling. I promise.
> I see myself as a participant in a fertility rite as old as the world, and I can't help myself. The circle must be completed. You are my eternity, womanchild of mine. And I am sorry for this. And this is the sorrow of every woman. And in this knowledge, I forgive my mother, my grandmother, my great-grandmother, my great-great-grandmother . . . it is all I can do.[13]

The "sorrow of every woman" is the terrible loss of self that motherhood necessitates. Even women who have children later in life must wrestle with the "colossal swallowing up."

Women who have followed the path of the hero, who have developed strong egos and good careers, face another kind of suffering when they become mothers. Such a woman finds that her worldly achievements count for nothing as her hour draws near. She must take off her armor of the successful professional and open herself naked to the elements. This requires the bravery of surrender rather than of mastery, the sacrifice of physical and emotional boundaries to allow the new life through. She suffers the loss of her body's integrity and her sense of personal identity. In pregnancy, at birth, in early childhood, to some extent throughout life, the boundaries between mother and child are not clearly defined. How much of the mother must be sacrificed for the sake of the child? How much of the child must be sacrificed for the sake of the mother? The terrible question for a woman giving birth is: What will bearing this new life do to my life? The poet Sharon Olds looks directly into the ambivalent soul of the new mother.

> *Dreading the cry, longing for the cry,*
> *the young mother leads what is called*
> *her own life*
> *while the baby sleeps.*
>
> *Crossing the sill again, she inhales that*
> *peace like ether. Leaving again she*
> *enters the dream of murder, mutilation, her*
> *old self bleeding in pieces on the butcher paper.*[14]

From the moment of conception a mother faces this two-edged threat: that she will be destroyed by having a child; that she will destroy her child.

MY WISDOM CAME TOO LATE

The portrait of a mother wrestling with her shadow is powerfully drawn in Tillie Olsen's classic short story, "I Stand Here Ironing." The story takes the form of the mother's inner dialogue with a school authority who thinks her nineteen-year-old daughter needs help. Sorting through her memories like old photographs, she is "engulfed with all I did or did not do, with what should have been and what cannot be helped."[15]

The mother was nineteen when the child was born. The father left soon after. She had to work. Her baby was a "miracle to me, but when she was eight months old I had to leave her daytimes with the woman downstairs to whom she was no miracle at all."

As she irons, the mother sorts through memories, the painful necessities of poverty, her other children, a second marriage. She is struggling with two lives, two fates—her daughter's and her own. How much damage has she, the mother, done? How much damage was done by life? She remembers the old man who once said to her in his gentle way: "You should smile at Emily more when you look at her." She wonders, "What was in my face when I looked at her? I loved her. There were all the acts of love." Painfully she feels her way though her daughter's life, seeking the truth.

The daughter comes. The mother is relieved to see her looking happy tonight. For a moment she feels relieved until the youngster's light-hearted statement, "in a couple of years . . . we'll all be atom-dead" dredges up the mother's pain again.

> I will never total it all. I will never come in to say: She was a child seldom smiled at. Her father left me before she was a year old. I had to work her first six years when there was work, or I sent her home and to his relatives. There were years she had care she hated. She was dark and thin and foreign-looking in a world where the prestige went to blondeness and curly hair and dimples, she was slow where glibness was prized. She was a child of anxious, not proud, love. We were poor and could not afford for her the soil of easy growth. I was a young mother, I was a distracted mother. There were the other children pushing up, demanding. Her younger sister seemed all that she was not. There were years she did not want me to touch her. She kept too much in herself, her life was such she had had to keep too much in herself. My wisdom came too late. She has much to her and probably little will come of it. She is a child of her age, of depression, of war, of fear.[16]

There are many layers of reality in this beautiful short story. The mother's inner struggle is both culturally overdetermined and psychologically essential. At the cultural level, it seems unbearable that one whose life has been so difficult, who has had so little opportunity herself to bloom, should feel so vulnerable to the criticism that holds her entirely responsible for her child.

At a psychological level, it is the mother's moral problem to sort through her daughter's difficulties and her own sense of responsibility. This process clears the channels of her love for the child. Having done this she will be ready for her daughter's wrestling words, if and when they come. If she were defensive, unable to feel her own guilt and pain, she would alienate her daughter at a critical time. In this story she does her homework. She is ready to wrestle, to stay in contact with her daughter when the time comes for her daughter to seek self-understanding.

At an even deeper psychological level we can hear her identification with her daughter, her struggle to make sense of her own tragic fate as well as that of her child. She is speaking of herself, too, making peace with her own life, when she says: "So all that is in her will not bloom—but in how many does it? There is still enough left to live by." The narrator's tragedy is the tragedy of the human condition, for all of our wisdom comes too late.

A Single Motion of Forgiveness

Some mothers and daughters wrestle for most of a lifetime before coming to a resolution of their differences. Such a Motherline story is told in Kim Chernin's moving book, *In My Mother's House.* It tells the story of the painful, illuminating, and, in the end, transformative struggle between poetic Kim, formed by the sixties and feminism, who seeks a spiritual connection to life, and her mother, Rose, formed by the thirties and communism, who is a political heroine of the left. Kim describes the argument they had again and again over the years, a quarrel over the "fact that we thought different thoughts, and experienced the world differently."[17]

Kim, like many women of her generation, tells her mother that she needs distance in order to become herself. " 'Become your self?' my mother would shout over the telephone. 'Why should you need to become what you already are?' "

Rose Chernin had become herself via the political demonstration, the political platform. She stood before crowds of the disenfranchised with raised fist and urged them to stand up for their rights. She had differentiated herself dramatically from her own dreamy mother, lost in her memories of the old country, whose husband battered her and who could not stand up for herself. Rose had fought her oppressive father, and continued all her life to fight oppression, even when the fight took her to jail, separating her from her young daughter, Kim. She had not accepted conventional notions of who she should be, yet she could not understand her daughter's introspective, psychological way of becoming herself. She was hurt by the distance between them, and by the fact that Kim did not carry on her mother's fight for justice in the external world, choosing instead a study of the matriarchy, "a work of solitary scholarship and poetry she does not understand."

Kim, torn between her desire to connect with her mother and her need to be herself, tries to translate from her mother's world to her own:

> "Mama," I say, throwing my arm around her shoulders with the same conspiratorial appeal she has used in approaching me. "You know what I found out? Marx and Engels, both of them, believed there was once a matriarchal stage of social organization. Yes, I'm serious. I'll tell you where you can read it."
>
> "Marx and Engels?" she says. "You don't say, Marx and Engels?"
>
> But now she sighs, shaking her head. "So all right, I am what I am, we can't be the same person. But I don't like to see you spending your life like this, that much I know."[18]

In Chernin's book a mother who has entered history, who, unlike most mothers of her time, has outwardly affected the course of human events, wants more than an oral tradition to carry the stories of her Motherline. She makes a significant request of her daughter; she asks her to write the story of her life. Kim feels "torn by contradiction." She yearns to give her mother what she asks, and she is afraid.

> This enterprise will take years. It will draw me back into the family, waking its ghosts. It will bring the two of us together to face all the secrets and silences we have kept. The very idea of it changes me. I'm afraid. I fear, as any daughter would, losing myself back into the mother.

Like a woman facing an unwanted pregnancy, Kim's heart sinks at the sacrifice that life is asking of her. Yet it is in the writing of her mother's story, in the illuminating of her mother's life, that Kim and Rose are able to move beyond their struggle to affirmation. Kim finds a way to listen to her mother—and remain herself. It is the work of a lifetime, hers and her mother's, and through it Kim finds the love she has been seeking all her life.

> I look around me in this garden behind my mother's house. It has become a wave of light, an affirmation that rises not only beyond

sorrow, but from a sense of wondering joy. I glance quickly at my mother, who has fallen silent, and I watch with disbelief the way the distance between us, and all separation, heals over. We are touched by a single motion of forgiveness. Her hand touches my cheek, she calls me by my childhood name, she says, "The birds sing louder when you grow old."

. . . It is late. My mother is tired. She reaches over to hold my hand. Suddenly, she speaks familiar words in a voice I have never heard before. It is pure feeling. It says, "I love you more than life, my daughter, I love you more than life."[19]

In the end, the wrestling of this mother and daughter, the sacrifices they have made for one another, and their fierce assertions of self reward them with that longed-for gift between women: a daughter's affirmation of her mother, a mother's affirmation of her daughter.

CHAPTER FIVE

STORIES FROM THE MIDDLE OF OUR LIVES:

The Mother-Daughter Loop

*At Laguna Pueblo in New Mexico, "Who is your mother?" is an
important question. At Laguna, one of several of the ancient
Keres gynocratic societies of the region, your mother's identity is
the key to your own identity. . . . Failure to know your mother,
that is, your position and its attendant traditions, history and
place in the scheme of things, is failure to remember your
significance, your reality, your right relationship to earth and
society. It is the same as being lost — isolated, abandoned, self-
estranged, and alienated from your own life.*

PAULA GUNN ALLEN[1]

I n the middle of my life I began feeling lost. My sense of direction
faltered. I had suddenly become a member of the past generation.
My children and stepchildren were growing up. They had their
own music, their own fashions, their own sense of values. I remembered
myself at their ages. Then *my* life was center stage. My parents were supposed to play walk-on parts, saying hello to my friends, but not embarrassing me further. Was that the role to which I was now relegated?

I looked around at friends who were my age. Many had young children, or no children. They were no help. They seemed to be in a different stage of life. They had not had to suffer the takeover of their adolescence by their child's with alien music, dances, and hairstyles. Though a number of them were parents, they still spoke of their mothers as though of a species apart. A visitation from Mother was a dreaded event. Telling a group of friends that one is expecting such a visitation caused nervous laughter and sympathetic noises. Everyone knows how hard it is when Mother comes to town. The dreaded Mother is experienced as part grand inquisitor, testing one's friends and lovers to see if they achieve impossible standards of virtue, and part female Frankenstein, so embarrassingly monstrous that one hides her from reasonable society. Was I about to become this dreadful creature?

BECOMING THE DREADED MOTHER

I wondered what I could say to a young person who was hanging out with my son or daughter. They talk about their music, their clothes, their complex friendship networks. What is our common ground? I hear myself asking: "What are your plans?" "Are you going to college?" "What do you want to do with your life?" Glazed young eyes look back at me. I've just become the grand inquisitor. From the perspective of my stage of life, those are important questions. I am trying to locate this youngster in a geography I can understand. But the youngster is no youngster to herself, and feels invaded and judged.

I think back to a time in my life when I was embarrassed by my mother. I wanted her to wear flashy clothes and to speak her truth boldly. Looking back, it's clear to me that I was the one who wanted to be flashy and bold. I was provocative when my mother came to visit. It was the sixties. I was newly divorced. I smoked marijuana in my mother's presence. I introduced her to men with wild hair and irreverent attitudes. I wanted her to be like me—and I wanted to prove to us both that I was different from her.

"Mother," I say into the telephone on one of our Sunday long-distance talks, "how was it for you when I was going through all those changes after my divorce, going with that strange guy, wearing wild clothes?"

"It was hard. I was scared for you and for the children. But I felt I had to keep my mouth shut because I didn't want to alienate you. You've changed as you've matured. Now you have more family feeling. You've become more accepting. Life looks very different from the middle, don't you think?"

I feel a familiar shudder of irritation. My mother has always said that when I matured I would have more family feeling. I haven't always been sure I wanted more family feeling. I wanted to explore life, to become my own person. I wrestled with my family-oriented mother to prove I was different. Now, she's saying I'm like her. My young woman self is irritated. But my mid-life self plunges into a much more painful feeling, a feeling aligned with my mother's. I think of my young children and how confused they must have been when their parents separated and their mother suddenly flew into a frenzy of becoming herself, becoming so different from the mother they knew. I think of how chaotic those times were for them.

I am beginning to see what my mother has meant all these years, that life looks different from the middle. I see my mother's side of my childhood, my children's side of my young adulthood. The ties to the past and the future through parents and children seem essential to me. What will happen to these connections, to all my insight and grief? Who will I be, how will I see life when my children are my age and I am my mother's?

I fear the darkness that surrounds the older woman in our culture. I fear becoming the dreaded mother. I am lucky with my personal mother. But I need more than one guide for my future. Where is a cohort of older mothers to show me the way? Where are the wise women of the tribe to teach me the shape and meaning of a woman's life?

And so I begin to talk to women outside my family, to learn their stories, their perspectives. I talk to mature women, generations of women, who have raised children, who have wrestled with their mothers.

Stories from the middle of a life are different from those that begin at the beginning, or begin at the end. From a mid-life perspective something new opens up, a view from a mountain where one can see in all directions, a vantage point from which one can see forward in time while also seeing backward in time. Stories from the middle of a life involve an intense layering of experience that allows us to understand where we are going from looking back at where we have been, and where our mothers have been. That is because in the middle of a woman's life three aspects—child, mother, old woman—meet and need to understand each other.

In the four stories that follow we meet women who have had difficult lives. As each woman loops from daughterly to motherly perspectives, she reveals her unique version of the pattern of a woman's fate—its cycles, its meaning, its tragic and redemptive potentialities.

A BRIDGE BETWEEN GENERATIONS

> It was an incredible experience, that connection, that sense of being in the middle between my mother and my daughter, and that I was the bridge between generations.
>
> *Carolyn*

Carolyn has a glowing presence. Her story of her daughter's first menstruation, quoted in Chapter 1, brought the concept of the Motherline to consciousness for me. Carolyn is in her early fifties and has recently re-married. She speaks of being surprised and warmed, after many years alone raising children, struggling to understand herself, by how good it feels to be in love again. In her resonant voice I hear the authority of a hard-won self-knowledge. All through her childhood and early adulthood she has lived at the edge of a bitter chasm that severed her from her mother. In the middle of her life she has come at last to understand what caused the rift between them. In her story, the nature of a birth, the first days of life, create a Motherline rift that takes most of two lives to untangle.

> I was born prematurely, two months early. I weighed three pounds. My mother had to leave me in the hospital for six weeks. During that whole time she never touched me. In those days they wouldn't let you. I never understood this until recently: I must have bonded to someone else, a nurse in the hospital. And so when I came home there was this stranger, pretending to be my mother. I think our whole life together has been trying to bridge that gap.

I sit looking at her, enjoying her warm presence. I hardly know this woman. She is talking about very painful things. And yet I feel so comfortable with her. It strikes me that my comfort has to do with her comfort. She knows this territory of her life very well. I am a little dazzled by her ability to sum up her life relationship with her mother in one sentence. "How did you bridge that gap?" I ask her.

> By growing up, by bridging the gap within myself. And she's doing the same thing. She's 83. She started therapy when she was 78.

She's a tough Irish lady and her therapist is a tough Irish lady and takes no shit from her, and it's terrific! She says now: 'I wish I had started this thirty years ago.' But she always pooh-poohed it and thought that people should solve their own problems, that they were weak, that sort of thing. Now, because she's not so judgmental toward herself, she's not so judgmental toward me.

There was always grief in me for not feeling close to her. I know she felt it, too. She never understood it. I always had crushes on women teachers to whom I looked for mothering. I didn't look to her for it. Now I realize that was because of those six weeks in the hospital. The gap between us started back then. It was a minor miracle that I survived at all. Also that I wasn't blind. There was a high percentage of blindness among premature babies of that era. I do have damage to one eye, retina damage.

The traumas my mother must have gone through. I didn't have a name on my birth certificate for a year. I recently realized why that happened. I was a seven-month baby. People don't usually pick out names that early. My mother must have been so afraid I would die. There is a terrible fear that as soon as you name the baby, you get attached to it and then it will die. So she didn't get attached. She protected herself. It's taken me most of my life to understand all this.

There has been no knowledge in the therapeutic community about the trauma of being born prematurely. So I looked at myself in terms of the dynamic between my mother and myself. I remember saying to my analyst that I had a memory of being in the incubator. And he laughed. So I dropped it. I never mentioned it again. It never was dealt with in my analysis. That's why I hate overhead lights—I detest them! So it's only recently, after doing therapy with a woman, that I've thought about the distance between my mother and myself as having to do with my premature birth. It made it hard for me to trust her. It's been a mutual growth process for both of us. As we began to feel stronger about ourselves, we could acknowledge more to each other. She finally has some ease about the pain she feels she has inflicted on me.

My mother was a hard-driving person: get ahead, do it, do it right, be the best, constantly be the best. I was more comfortable with my Dad because he was the softer of the two. Since my mother has begun therapy she's told me more about what shaped her. My mother was the youngest in her family. She wasn't wanted. She was an afterthought. The next sister was eight years older. My mother was the only one who was unmarried. She was athletic, which was considered unfeminine, and people in the family were critical of her.

Originally my father was married to my mother's sister, my aunt. And they had three sons. When my aunt died, my father married my mother. So my brothers are actually my cousins and half brothers. And everyone on both sides of the family wondered if she could be a good mother. It was a hard thing to take on. Stepmothers get a bad press anyway. I think there was an unspoken doubt between my parents. Did he love her, or was he just marrying his wife's sister? My poor mother. Again she was an afterthought, not really wanted, a fill-in for her older sister. She could have treated those boys very badly. She didn't, though. My brothers are so loyal to her, so loving. They must have been 11, 9 and 8 when their mother died. It must have been very traumatic for them. You know, I've never talked to them about it; isn't that strange?

When I came along I was a favorite because I was the cute, little red-headed sister. This didn't feel like it was about me. It was about my looks. I identify with my daughter, Susi, in this. She is physically very beautiful. She has red hair, which has been noticed from the day she was born. I've always wanted her not to have the feeling I had, that people only saw my red hair. I felt very alone in my childhood, always.

I think Mom was a real healer and that she worked hard to give all of us a family feeling, at least on a sibling level. You know, I hadn't thought of it till now, but I'm playing the same kind of role with my husband's children. His ex-wife went crazy and insisted on divorcing him. It was so painful for everyone, for him, his children. And I'm now playing the role of healer, like my mother did. To see him happy again, I bring them all together. It's what my mother did. I'll have to call her and tell her that. It will please her.

Carolyn locates herself in relation to her kin in great loops of language that intertwine generations. Here she connects her mother's role as second wife to her own identical role. She connects her daughter's issues to hers as a child. She realizes that she doesn't know what her half brothers experienced when their mother died. She was born into a complex drama that has taken half a lifetime to conceptualize.

It took me years to forgive my mother, to understand her life. I remember when she was in her early fifties and I was in my twenties. She had a severe gallstone attack and was in the hospital. Those attacks are excruciatingly painful. I didn't feel for her then. In fact, I remember wishing she would die. I remember telling her that (she shook her head in disbelief) maybe ten or twelve years later, after I'd gotten over the feeling. It was as though I'd slapped her. I can still see her physical response. It then took another ten or fifteen years for her to believe that I no longer meant it. So she and I have really been through it. It's only in the last ten years that I can say I love her, and fully mean it.

I was determined, because of the pain between my mother and myself, to be a different kind of mother to my children. The gap between my mother and myself was established at the very beginning. And the difference with my daughter is that the gap was never there. I remember when she was six weeks old. It was Thanksgiving. I felt strong, and had prepared dinner for the family. Susi began crying, so I picked her up and nursed her. When I brought her back into the dining room with me and was holding her, she looked me straight in the eye—and she smiled at me. It was incredible! I knew it wasn't gas. It was overt bonding right there. I always felt that with her.

From the vantage point of what I now know about my own birth, I see why that was so powerful, so healing. Because when I was six weeks old I was taken away from whoever it was I had bonded with, and given to a woman who was not attached to me, a stranger, whom I didn't know. I have always had this strange feeling that a part of me died when I was very young, as though I had a twin who died. Now I know it was that nurse. Susi's birth began to heal that wound.

It was different with Tommy. He was my first and I had no confidence in myself as a parent. I was very tense during the pregnancy. And it was a long labor. When he came out he was blue, absolutely blue. They had to give him oxygen. There was trauma at his birth, like there was at mine. I'm sure it made his first months of life more difficult.

I can still remember his father and me at three o'clock in the morning, Tommy screaming bloody murder and we're paging through Spock. Poor Tommy. I was very angry at him for being born. I wanted to put him back in the oven. I felt he was taking my childhood away from me. The night after he was born I found myself standing straight up between the beds in the hospital screaming bloody murder. Nurses, orderlies, everyone came running. I have no memory of what I was dreaming.

I remember my mother calling me up after Tommy's birth and saying: "Oh, my baby has had a baby!" That was the beginning of my mother and I feeling closer. I remember soft moments. I can still see her face the first time she saw him. He had just awakened from a nap and was standing up in his crib. Her whole demeanor was so loving and so beautiful. She gave him some sugar on her finger. Put her finger in his mouth. You have to understand that my mother is a very restrained woman, not warm, not physically affectionate. When I saw her do this, put her finger in Tommy's mouth, it was so sensual. I had never seen that side of her before. It warmed me, touched me deeply.

The view from the middle of her life allows Carolyn to see her mother's life events and her own. Though her son's difficult birth seemed a re-wounding of her own birth trauma, healing began with her mother's sensual response to the baby. Carolyn's embodied experience of bonding with her daughter gave her the connection with her Motherline that she missed in her childhood. Her tie to her daughter enabled her to find the tie to her mother. Now, bridging the generations, she can face the losses of the future because she's at peace with the past.

She sighs, looking at me:

Now it's a rite of passage time. Susi is leaving home, moving away from her boyfriend. My brothers' mother-in-law is very ill and about to die. After her it will be my mother's turn. And then it will be ours, my husband's and mine. [She pauses, lost in her sadness. Then brightens, suddenly.] But I told Susi this morning that I was coming over here to be interviewed and she said: "Tell her you're a wonderful mother!"

And you know, I feel that way about my mother, too, that she's a wonderful mother. I feel very luck, having her, because her struggle has been so poignant, and because in the end, we have grown so close. I think she's going to die with peace.

IN THE WAKE OF LOST MOTHERS

I've heard of people who have gone into these hospitals and never come out. I have this horror when I think I might still be there. Because it's a vicious circle—you can't behave normally. They see everything you do as crazy.

Blanche

Blanche is a tall, elegant woman in her fifties. She wears her graying hair in a bun low on her neck. She is a study in paradoxes: beautiful and unsure, awkward and full of grace. She is the wife of a successful businessman and the mother of four grown children. Her closest relationships are to her daughters and her sister. She has a luminous inner self. But outwardly, she is nervous, uncomfortable, slightly inept. She speaks softly, as though apologizing for herself. She is a woman of the hearth, a keeper of the home fires. Sadly, she muses about how old-fashioned she is, how she knows hardly any women like herself, who tend their house and garden, accompany their husbands on business trips, and have no great designs upon the world.

From the middle of her life, Blanche looks back at a childhood torn by losses. Her mother died when she was ten. Her mother's mother died in childbirth when her mother was thirteen. Her mother's early death is like a refrain in all she tells me, and the satisfaction she takes in her positive connection to her four grown children is palpable. It is as if through her children she heals her childhood wounds.

Blanche's story gives us a glimpse into a terrible aspect of our female lineage—the abuse and pathologizing of women's emotional lives. In her generation it was still common for women to be locked away from family and friends, hospitalized against their will, because they were depressed. Blanche remembers:

> I was very fond of my mother. About a year before she died, I remember thinking to myself that if she died I wouldn't want to live any longer. At the time I had no reason to think she would die.
>
> When my mother got sick, we went over to my aunt's. My mother was taken to the hospital and she was dead within the week. Influenza. All three of us, my sister, my father and I, moved into my aunt's flat where she lived with her son, her second husband, and her father in five rooms. This wouldn't happen nowadays. I don't know why my father didn't do something else. He must have been very distraught.
>
> My aunt had a pact with my mother that if anything happened to either one of them the other would take her children. She was very close to my mother. I think she was so upset by her death that she didn't cope well.
>
> Mother had never talked to us about sex. In fact I later learned that my aunt had been delegated to talk to us about it because my mother didn't want to. My aunt was no more adept. I brought up the subject, shy as I was. She really put me off and finally said one sentence to me that was supposed to explain it all, and then said: "Go

tell your sister." But, meantime, my sister had friends who told her the correct information and my sister explained it to me.

My aunt did take me aside to tell me about menstruation. I guess it scared me because it reminded me of when we were taken aside and told that my mother had died. She didn't mean to do that. She didn't explain it very well, and when she talked about belts and stuff, I thought blood comes out of your skin like perspiration. She did not connect it with childbirth.

"My goodness!" I find myself exclaiming. "What a painful connection! Your mother's death and your aunt's awkward attempt to explain menstruation." My voice sounds loud to me, and Blanche looks startled to hear it. She looks at me wide-eyed, and speaks with sudden intensity.

Yes. You know, I've never thought this before. But maybe all that fear and confusion has something to do with what happened to me later. I had a post-partum depression after the first child. I think it has colored his whole life.

I was scared to death to have a baby. After my mother died, people told me that she was in hard labor for thirty-six hours to produce me. Also, I just couldn't understand how an eight-pound baby could come out of such a small opening.

I was in a room with another woman who was screaming that she would never have any more kids. My son's birth wasn't bad, though it lasted eight hours. I had had such bad menstrual periods that even though it hurt it didn't seem that bad. I was going to breast-feed the baby. They brought me hot cloths that were supposed to reduce the swelling, and I got third-degree burns on my breasts. A nurse came in and quizzed me about whether I hadn't had the burns when I came in, as though I was a bad person, a criminal.

When I came home with the baby my mother-in-law wanted to come to help me; my aunt wanted to come. I didn't want any of them. I know my aunt loved me. But she was never a substitute for my mother. And my mother-in-law was always very critical of me. I think deep down I wanted my mother. I always thought she would have gone to bat for me; she would have taught me to stand up for myself. In order to keep them away, I hired someone whom I didn't want, either. She was just a ball of energy teaching me how to fold this, how to do that. There was all this activity going on—I was just overwhelmed. I wanted her to leave. But I was in such a state that you'd take one look at me and say: "Oh my God, we can't leave her alone. We've got to keep this woman on!"

> For years my husband and I did not talk about this. When we
> finally did, he told me that I looked so withdrawn it scared him. My
> doctor recommended a psychiatrist who made a house call. When I
> think of this, it's like a nightmare. This guy comes in the door. He's
> as big as a mountain—a very frightening looking man. And I'm very
> fragile. He just picked me up. He didn't tell me where I was going.
> I was put into a car. I didn't know why I was there. I was put into
> isolation for ten days. I never agreed to be there. It was the equivalent
> of a state hospital, a room with a peephole. It was winter in Montreal.
> My husband came every Sunday. He left my son with his mother.

I listen to this shocking story and wonder whether Blanche has told
it before, whether she has let herself experience her rage and grief and hu-
miliation. This unbearable experience is not an unusual Motherline story.
The intensity of women's emotions, especially post-partum, has frequently
been pathologized. Unemphatic responses, which don't help a woman find
her way out of the underworld in which she is lost, have left women like
Blanche traumatized and ashamed. As Phyllis Chesler has documented in
Women and Madness, until recently it was common psychiatric practice to
hospitalize women who suffered powerful feeling states, such as depression,
rages or ceaseless mourning.

"Blanche," I say, "I'm just outraged at what happened to you." She
gives me a long look out of wide, gray eyes. Her face softens, and I feel
the sudden sting of tears. Are they my tears? Her tears? The room fills with
sorrow, and I feel the presence of her lost mother, and her lost mother's
lost mother, generations of grief. After a few minutes of silence, heavy
with tears, Blanche continues:

> I think I was angry about getting burned in the hospital and
> then getting blamed for it. But nobody talked to me about what I
> was feeling. When they released me after three months, they said:
> "She's not better but there's nothing we can do for her." As if I was
> terminally insane but I wasn't violent, so they were letting me out.
> Since then I've heard of people who have gone into these hospitals and
> never come out. I have this horror when I think I might still be there,
> because it's a vicious circle—you can't behave normally. They see
> everything you do as crazy.

Blanche had done what women of her generation were supposed to
do. She had "married up" a Yale man from a good family. They have been

married thirty-five years. But Blanche never felt prepared for any of the consequences of marriage. She had no image of herself as a woman, no mother to teach her to stand up for herself. She gave birth to four children in five years. Blanche continues:

> Our children weren't exactly planned. It was just allowing things to happen to you. I had a doctor whom I liked a lot. You get all this attention. It was nice having a girl the second time. Just because I'm female, too, I felt a little more relaxed than I did with a boy. I think having daughters has changed me. They've told me about their lives, their feelings. They've taught me about being a woman.
>
> So many women have painful relationships with their daughters. I think it's because they don't allow them any leeway. They try to tell them how to live. A mother can be jealous and really come down on her daughter. Sometimes I find myself thinking: "I wish I'd had a chance to do that," about something they're telling me. But I would never want to take it away. So I listen. I try to appreciate what they're saying, to understand things from their point of view.
>
> It's not always easy. There was a scene with a boyfriend of my daughter's. I thought I was just talking to him. But to her it looked like flirting. I looked at myself and thought: "I'm her mother, I'm in my fifties, this guy isn't going to look at me like that." But I realized that maybe I was being a little provocative because I didn't value myself enough. It surprised me that my daughter could see me as a threat. I began watching myself more carefully. And I talked to my daughter, told her I was sorry, that I hadn't been aware. I learned a lot about myself from that experience. I'm always learning from my daughters. There are times when my older daughter can explain to me what my husband is thinking. She's closer to how he thinks. She learns from all her relationships. So do I.

Conventional wisdom holds that mothers shouldn't need their daughters, that daughters are the ones to need and mothers the ones to give. That is the perspective of a single generation, a single life. Looked at from the middle of a life, from a Motherline perspective, Blanche's need for her daughters is not pathology. It is the reality of human lives. Blanche's childhood was emotionally deprived by the early loss of her mother. Naturally she is hungry for the stuff of women's lives. Her connection to her daughters feeds this hunger. She does the psychological work of staying connected, knowing the danger of letting envy and jealousy destroy the intimacies her daughters bring her. And she has been willing to look at the ways she herself can be provocative without meaning to be. This is the work of looking at her own shadow so that she can honor her connection to her daughter.

Blanche says:

> You asked me what my life would have been like had I not lost my mother. My younger daughter lives in Seattle. She came for Thanksgiving. She said how nice it was to be home and leave her troubles behind. And I thought that, if my mother had lived, there might have been a family home when I was my daughter's age. How nice that would have been. Maybe I wouldn't have had so much trouble with my mother-in-law, maybe I wouldn't have had that post-partum depression. I've had times of feeling pretty negative about myself. Here I am, in my fifties, and there's no entry-level job I could do. But I realize that I've made a home for my children to return to and that makes me happy. I feel a certain serenity these days. I don't always have it, but these days I have it most of the time.

GUILTY, GUILTY, GUILTY

> Allison's birth was a normal delivery. But I labored for twenty-four hours. I've often felt guilty, guilty, guilty because I was so tired. I pushed and pushed. I've never pushed so hard. And finally I said: "Doctor, please help me." Then he reached for his forceps. And I've often wondered if that damaged her.
>
> *Kate*

Kate is an elegant and dramatic woman. She is an interior designer, and dresses with a flair that borders on the outrageous, wearing vibrant colors and big jewelry. She speaks boldly and minces no words.

We met Kate in the previous chapter, wrestling with her daughter Allison's eating disorder. Her determination to be a perfect parent was a direct response to how deeply rejected she felt by her own mother. In the middle of her life, she has had to come to terms with her own terrible feelings of guilt, and to reassess her rage at her mother.

> Allison has been the greatest joy and the greatest tragedy of my life. She has all my insecurities, and I don't know why because I blame mine on my mother. My mother never listened to me, and my mother

was a prude, and my mother never wanted to have me in the first place. My mother was consumed with the desire to be a lady, to be proper, to do the right thing, to be polite, to never insult anyone, to never let her hair down, to always have the house clean, to always write the thank-you note.

She was a very Victorian lady. My mother told me, with pride, that she had been married 35 years to my father and he never saw her naked. She thought menstruation was dirty. When my period began, I came down into the kitchen and said: "Today I am a woman!" My mother said: "SHHH! Your brother is in the next room!" How do you suppose that made me feel? My mother was a total pill, and I have tried very hard not to be a pill! I am not a Victorian woman. My kids have said every four-letter word in front of me. They've smoked pot in front of me. I've been totally in love with Allison since the day she was born, and still she's insecure. Why is that?

Kate looks at me as though I can answer that guilty question that every mother asks when she feels her child suffering. I can imagine how her daughter's unhappiness churns in her own body. She feels caught in it, helpless. Yet in some dim, larger sense she feels responsible, all powerful, guilty as accused.

Kate continues:

During the time Allison was anorexic, her period stopped for nine years. It worried me to death. I was afraid her little uterus would dry up and she would never be able to have children. When she finally got her period back, we celebrated. We drank champagne. She gained enough weight back so that her body said: "OK, you're big enough now to support a child. Here's your period back again."

Maybe I'm not supposed to feel this way, but I really want Allison to have children. My son has a child, so I'm already a grandmother. And I love my granddaughter. But grandchildren from sons are just not as awe-inspiring as from a daughter: having my little girl have a child as opposed to somebody else's little girl having a child. I know my son's sperm is in there, but it's not the same. The child of my daughter is my way of being eternal I guess, of living past death.

I hope she's one of these women who has children easily. I didn't. I labored with my older son for days before they realized it was a case of placenta previa and that I needed a cesarean. It was terrible. I felt like I was being pushed through a brick wall every time one of these things hit. People say you forget the pain. I never forgot the pain. It was worth it, but it's the worst pain I've ever experienced.

Allison's birth was a normal delivery. But I labored for twenty-four hours. I've often felt guilty, guilty, guilty because I was so tired. I pushed and pushed. Finally I said, "Doctor, please help me." And it was then he reached for his forceps. And I've often wondered if that damaged her.

Listening to Kate I begin to understand some of the complexity of female guilt. In the powerful birth-giving time we are also the most vulnerable. No wonder we get so confused about how much responsibility we carry, and whether we are powerful or powerless.

Kate goes on:

The relationship between a mother and child begins in utero and goes on until death. It changes so much, but some things always remain. My mother didn't want me. She tried to abort me. I always felt that, so, of course, I didn't like her. She made it very clear that my sister, Ernestine, was a little female Jesus. She could do no wrong. She was my mother's helper. She got all As. She cleaned up her room. She didn't waste time reading the funny papers. She didn't wear too much makeup. She cut her hair. She cleaned her fingernails. She was little Miss Priss and I hated her.

My mother never believed what I said. One summer my brother and I were out playing, and I saw a rattlesnake. He didn't even look at the thing; he just jumped up and began running. So I tore home after him. Everybody got in the car. They were going to kill the rattlesnake with the car. But when they got there, no rattlesnake! Why would a rattlesnake want to stick around? So I said: "There *was* a rattlesnake." But they began to doubt that I had seen it.

My mother said, "It probably wasn't a rattlesnake, Kate. You're too dramatic about things." I said, "It was too a rattlesnake!" She said, "How did you know it was a rattlesnake?" I said, "I took the time to look and there were rattles on the end of its tail." Well, Mother knows best. And so it would have ended, except, thank God, the thing decided to cross the road right where my mother stood. That was typical of how my mother didn't believe me. And it was the only time I can remember being proved right.

My mother was a very bossy woman. So was her mother. Very stern. "Get out in the kitchen and help your mother!" My kids tell me I'm bossy, but I'm not half as bossy as my mother was. My son imitates a sound I make when things don't go right, which is very much like a sound my mother made. I tell him, "I do not make that sound!" "Oh yes, you do," he says.

Kate laughs and so do I. "I can think of some moments of truth when I've heard of myself sounding just like my parents," I say. "Awful, isn't it? Why don't our kids appreciate how hard we work not to be our parents!"

"Really!" says Kate.

I deserve an award for how bossy I'm not! People say I should forgive my mother. And I say, "I'll be damned if I'll forgive her." But you know, I think I have. I think I've figured out that she was just an uneducated, pathetic old broad. Why not forgive her? She didn't know any better. I've realized that everything may not entirely be her fault. She had a hard life. My father was sick during most of their marriage. I used to blame her for everything, but now that I'm a mother and Allison has had her difficulties, I realize mothers should not be blamed for everything, because we're not in control of everything!

THE HEROISM OF WOMEN

I learned from my mother that a woman gets an important part of her identity from childbearing. For her it's the heroism of women. My mother didn't lay a trip on me about this. It was through her example, her joy in childbearing that I internalized that value.

Sometimes I feel I'm not being a good feminist in my belief that people who don't have children are missing something. That's a choice, not to have children, and yes, people do have the freedom to make choices. But I'm saying that with some choices, you just miss out.

Molly

Molly has a unusual capacity to describe the heroism of the feminine. In Chapter 4 she told her heroic seamstress tale, describing her support for her daughter Mary Lou's differentiation process through the symbolism of clothes and sorority parties. In this chapter her story illustrates two kinds of female heroism, her mother's and her own, in the face of very different kinds of tragedies of childbirth.

Molly is a well-known community leader. She is esteemed for her eloquent essays, her political work on behalf of women, and her success in combining her career with a long, happy marriage and raising four children. She is a particular hero of mine. I have read her writing, heard her speak, and admired her from a distance. Since I knew her to be a good storyteller I was delighted when she agreed to talk to me about her Motherline.

But the woman I see in my office hardly looks like the one I remember from afar. Her shoulders curve over her chest, her hair has gone white, and her face is shadowed by pain. Her story reminds us that tragedy is a part of even the richest, most fulfilled lives.

> Matt, my husband, died eight months ago. I feel as though I've aged twenty years in that time. For the first four or five months I had a physical pain in my chest. It's so true—what they say about a broken heart. It was just as if I had had a tree, rooted in me, pulled out and the rest of me is all jagged and scarred and incomplete. That acute pain has abated. But it's still terrible. You know how it is, the intimacy, the million little things that you can talk over with your husband, like, "Was I crazy or did that really happen?"
>
> Of course, the kids are there. My son, Paul, and his wife have come to live with me and that helps. After taking care of another person for so many years, it's wonderful to be able to keep taking care. When I could concentrate on nothing after Matt's death, it was so important to do the meals and the grocery shopping. If I had been left to myself, I would have starved to death.
>
> I didn't realize how much Matt really needed me. And you need someone to need you. Right now no one needs me. It's not a question of self-pity. I know I'm doing valuable work, I know people love me, but it's not the same. I think of people who go through this experience who don't have children, and I don't know how they can stand it. You do live on in your children. A friend of mine says the hair rises on the back of his neck whenever Paul walks into the room because he looks so much like Matt.

Molly talks about her mother:

> My mother, Maggie O'Brian, knew how to run things. She would have been fantastic as a hotel manager, she was so competent in managing the household. During the Depression my father made $35 per week. That was considered a good wage. My mother fed all

ten of us on $12 per week, not including the milk bill, which was
separate. And we were well fed. My father got ten cents: five cents for
the Saturday Evening Post and five cents for a sack of Bull Durham.
Another ten cents went for a sack of Necco wafers, which my mother
then sorted into colors, and then sorted into piles to distribute among
the children as our weekly treat out of the paycheck.

She was the real authority in the family. My father was the one
you went to whenever you had an intellectual question, whether it
was about astronomy, economics, geography, anything. He had an
encyclopedic memory. I felt closer to him than to my mother when I
was young, because I was the family intellectual. He worked as a tele-
grapher for the railroad. He died when I was in my twenties, and
never knew my children. That has always been a sadness to me.

I didn't realize, until I had children of my own, how much like
Maggie O'Brian I am. Having children was what meant most to her
in life. She gave birth to ten babies but lost two in early infancy, had
serious congenital problems. We knew it was for the best that the
babies died. But still we cried and cried. In large families there is a
great feeling for life. The two babies who died would have been the
eighth and ninth children in the family.

My mother had to prove, after losing them, that she could have
a healthy baby. At age 45 she got pregnant and gave birth to my
youngest sister. It was a home delivery. I remember hearing the doctor
and nurse saying that they dreaded responding to my father's phone
call announcing that she was in labor. They were afraid of another
damaged child. All this happened at night and I didn't know anything about it. But I remember the next morning, walking into my
mother's room, and there she was in bed with the tears streaming
down her face and in her arms was the most beautiful baby.

I learned from my mother that a woman gets an important part
of her identity through childbearing. For her, it's the heroism of
women. My mother didn't lay a trip on me about this. It was through
her example, her joy in childbearing that I internalized that value.
Raising children is a transforming, transcendental experience. I think
I have grown so much as a person through having children. Sometimes I feel I'm not being a good feminist to feel that people who don't
have children are missing something. That's a choice, not to have children, and yes, people do have the freedom to make choices. But I'm
saying that with some choices you just miss out.

I got married when I was twenty-three but didn't have children
until my early thirties. Matt and I traveled. We lived in Mexico and
in England. They were wonderful years, but I always had some anx-

iety about the fact that I was putting off having children. I was very ready for a child when I first suspected I was pregnant. When I was about six months pregnant, I developed a bladder infection. I was given an examination which included an X-ray. Now I've always been very conscious and assertive about my medical care. I asked if it might be harmful to the fetus to have an X-ray. They said, "No." Of course, now we know differently. We lost the baby.

At the time I had a neighbor who had an infertility problem. She had not been able to get pregnant for seven years. She had a doctor who had a technique of forcing oil through the fallopian tubes, which opened them up for twenty-four hours. It worked. She had four children. Well, for her the sun rose and set on this doctor. I was having trouble getting pregnant and she referred me to him. I called his office and couldn't get an appointment right away. But they told me that he wanted all his patients to keep a basal-temperature chart. I did this, and found out when I ovulated, and by the time I got into his office I was one day pregnant. He didn't even want to examine me, so as not to disturb the pregnancy. But he was a great believer in diethylstilbestrol (DES) as a way to prevent miscarriage. I wanted to have a baby so badly that I took it religiously.

I'll never forget the day, April 23, 1971, when I saw a newspaper story: "Rare Cancer in Daughters Linked to Mother Taking Drug." Monica was 15. I was so upset. I filed it away. I didn't say anything to her because I didn't want to scare her. After reading more stories about DES daughters, I talked to a woman gynecologist. I told her my concern and asked her to examine Monica. I told Monica that part of becoming a young woman was to have a physical exam. The gynecologist didn't find anything. But she didn't know, and neither did I at the time, that you need a special test to detect the effects of DES. A story appeared in *MS* magazine in 1974 that described the special test. I was able to find a doctor who could perform this test. But, of course, I had to tell my daughter and that was very hard. We both cried.

The doctor said that she looked like most of the other DES daughters he had examined—no sign of cancer. But he wanted to examine her every six months. Monica was very relieved. But I couldn't keep from thinking about the people who didn't know, who didn't read the papers so carefully or whatever. The test needed to be publicized and available.

I talked to a local feminist health clinic and they were very interested in providing the test. So I got this doctor, a conservative fatherly man, paternalistic in the best sense of the word, to train these

young women in detecting DES. And that wasn't easy for him. This
was the 1970s and they all had long hair and long skirts and beads.
Monica volunteered to be a teaching patient. That was meaningful
for her because she felt she was doing something about her situation.
And that's how my work to raise consciousness about DES began.
Since then Monica has had an ectopic pregnancy. She didn't want a
child at that point, but we don't know what will happen when she
does want a pregnancy.

Molly's face has opened; light has returned to her eyes and I begin to
see the woman I admire, a woman who can turn the tragedy of having a
DES daughter into community action and good works.

In many ways I had a good childhood. My mother and father
loved each other. They were open-minded, good people. My mother
never fussed at me for marrying a non-Catholic. She had seen misery.
Her mother had been in love with a non-Catholic and her grandfather
had broken that engagement and had then brought around the man
he wanted her to marry. And my grandmother was so brow-beaten
that she married him. This was 1870. Women had no sense of choice.
It was a loveless marriage. My mother used to say to me when I was
in college, "I'd like you to marry Catholic. But only if you love him.
The most important thing is that you follow your heart."

My mother was wise and open-minded. But she was also very
anxious. After I was born, the fourth girl, she had what I suppose you
would now call a post-partum depression. In those days, who knew
from psychiatry? Her doctor told her she had to have complete bed
rest. My three older sisters were sent to her sister and to her mother.
Because I was just six months old, I was put into the nursery in the
hospital where I was born. I was there for six weeks. I think the separation caused considerable psychological stress for my sisters. But my
father came down to the hospital every day to see me. Isn't that amazing?

These were the days of strict schedule feeding. When the nurses
turned me back to my mother, they all cried and said: "Oh, Mrs.
O'Brian, we have spoiled your good baby." She had me on a schedule.
But at the hospital the nurses picked me up and cuddled me all the
time. All the other babies were newborns. I was a healthy six-month-
old baby, what could be cuter?

I think her crisis healed over with scar tissue, but the underlying conflict was never resolved. She developed what she and the fam-

ily thought was heart trouble. I would come home from school and find her on the couch. Now she's ninety-six and healthy as a horse. I think it was psychosomatic. I think she was a very anxious person and it made me an anxious person. However, I had a chance to work it out in therapy, which she never did.

Early in our marriage, when Matt and I were living in Mexico, I had an anxiety attack. I had never had one before. It is the most terrifying thing that can happen. I was conflicted because Matt wanted to keep traveling and that put off our having a family. My two closest friends were both seeing an analyst in Mexico City, so I had access to a very good analyst, a student of Erich Fromm. You have to understand, this was 1951 and not so common in those days. He saw me right away, twice a week.

After me, the fourth girl in a row, my mother had three sons. My brother was twenty-two months younger, and I can remember his birth and people's remarks like: "After all the trying," as though I was a disappointing failure because I wasn't a boy. And then there was my next older sister, who was a beauty. And I wasn't. She was brunette with brown eyes and I was blond with blue eyes. People would say: "You two can't be sisters. You don't look anything like each other!" Well, that was true but to me it had only one connotation: She was pretty and I was not.

I was a very different person from my sister. I wasn't what you call "feminine." I was very forthright. So I figured out that there must be something wrong with Matt for having married me. When I understood this, it was like a glass wall broke between me and the world. I used up a box of Kleenex every time I went to the analyst. I said to him: "You know, I never cry." He said: "That's part of the problem." He also said to me once: "You know, you'll be glad this happened to you someday." And I looked at him and thought: "I'd rather have a broken leg." But of course he was absolutely right—it changed my whole life.

In the end, of course, my so-called "masculine traits" have stood me in good stead. I've been more successful than my sisters and my mother because I've had more of a sense of empowerment. If only the women's movement had been there when we were young women. I always knew the limitations on women were wrong, but in those days you had to seethe by yourself.

My mother and I have had very different lives. Her fulfillment was in her family, in giving birth and raising children and loving her husband. I've had some success in the world, which she never did. But right now what matters most is having children, feeling needed.

You know, Maggie O'Brian is now ninety-six years old and living in a convalescent home. She was my age when my father died. She has now been widowed as many years as she was married. I wonder how she has managed so well.

AN ELEUSINIAN WELL OF MEMORY

They remember what she gave. What she made. What she did. What we were to each other. What she taught me. What I learned at her breast. That she made things. That she made words. That she fed me. Suckled me. Clothed me. Cradled me. Washed me. We remember her labor. She told us how she almost died. How she was weary. How her skin ached. What soreness she felt. What her mother's name was. How her mother made things. What her mother told her. How she was pushed away. How she was hated. How her milk was sour. What she wore at her wedding. Where she had dreamed of going.

Susan Griffin

Carolyn, Blanche, Kate, Molly: their Motherline stories helped me locate myself in mine. As familiar as the sound of women talking in the kitchen, their stories remind me of my own story, my mother's story, my grandmother's story. The problem is not a lack of stories or carriers of female wisdom. The problem is that these stories do not surface into our official versions of the world. The life experience of older women is seldom heard as providing meaning and a sense of how life is shaped. Listened to respectfully, they help us understand how the Motherline is an organizing principle in the psychology of women.

When stories are told from the middle of a life, simplistic psychological causality and easy parental blaming can be avoided. The process of looping through generations serves to tie together human themes. The pain of a woman as daughter is understood at another level as she sees her limitations as mother. A mature woman knows how much her life has been forged in the heat of generational change; how much she has lived in the hands of her fate. As she comes to see her own life in the context of her historical moment, she can see her mother in the context of her time and forgive her, as she forgives herself. A psychology of women needs to begin in this mid-point of life, gathering the viewpoints of mother, maiden, and crone.

A core theme of these stories is the nature of birth—terrible births, heroic births. Although their children are grown and it has been many years since these women actually gave birth, memory lives on in their very cells. They weave the stories of pregnancies, births, and psychological development into one fabric, without separating body and psyche, looping back and forth in the generations. Transformative, terrifying, awe-inspiring, painful, these birth experiences create the psychological landscape on which Motherline stories unfold. The drama of a lifetime is rooted in the feelings surrounding a birth: Carolyn's premature birth and the rift it created between her and her mother; Blanche's childhood loss of her mother and her plunge into darkness after the birth of her first child; Kate's guilt about the use of forceps at Allison's birth; Molly's hunger to bear a child and the consequences of using DES; Maggie O'Brian's heroic last pregnancy.

Such subjective experiences of mothers are unknown in our official version of the world; they are too fearful. Woman as mother is a part of nature. Caught in the awesome jaws of fate in the birth-giving process, her stories clash with our cultural fantasy about mastering the natural world. Each of these women came to the brink of life and death in the process of being born or giving birth. Each has been eaten alive by devouring events: a premature birth, the death of a mother in childhood, a mother's attempt to abort her, a well-meaning medical intervention that turns out to endanger a daughter's fertility.

It takes the maturity of mid-life for a woman to understand how fate and the generations have met in her life drama. Meeting her mother in herself, she can begin a reconciliation of generations that ties together her future and her past.

A forgotten well of Eleusinian memories underlies this pattern of a woman's life, memories as familiar as women's talk and as unknown as earthlight shining on the moon. When we honor these memories, body is not split from mind or spirit; life is cyclical, intertwining generations; birth and death are the central mysteries of life; and the daughter who is brave enough to let new life be born out of her body, and wise enough to learn from being a mother how to find her way back to her mother, to all mothers, leads us to a new experience, an ancient sacred experience, of what it means to be human.

Perhaps, if you ask your mother the right questions, approach your grandmother in the right spirit, you can evoke her Eleusinian memories and find your own roots in the Motherline.

CHAPTER SIX

OUR PLACE AMONG THE GENERATIONS:

How We Are Shaped by Our Times

Although we human beings have our own personal life, we are in large measure the representatives, the victims and promoters of a collective spirit whose years are counted in centuries.

C. G. JUNG[1]

There was a time when the story a great-grandmother told about the shape of her life would be much the same story as the grandmother would tell, and the mother. It would, essentially, be the daughter's story as well. Such a time was described by the anthropologist Alfred Kroeber:

> The house belongs to the women born of the family. There they come into the world, pass their lives, and within the walls they die. As they grow up, their brothers leave them, each to abide in the house of his wife. Each woman, too, has her husband, or succession of husbands, sharing her blankets. So generation succeeds generation, the

97

slow stream of mother and daughters forming a current that carried
with it husbands, sons and grandsons.[2]

In such a time, a woman would know her future by looking at the
faces of the older women. She was reminded of her youth in the faces of
the younger women. She would be the daughter of one, the mother of
another, passing through the stages of her life in a predictable rhythm.
Reciting the names of the women of her line would place her within the
web of life, naming her kin, her culture, her land, her history.

But we live in a generation of change. The word *generation* contains
a paradox. It refers to reproduction. It also refers to a cohort of people
whose differences from their parents' generation is shaped by history. In
one word we name the warp and the woof of life, the archetypal truth of
Motherline continuity and the historical truth of change.

The cyclical nature of life is easily lost in a historical perspective. The
essential myths of the human condition, the motherless child, the child
who dies too young, the wanderer to new lands, the seeker after new meanings, lose their timeless resonance in our modern focus on generational
change. Vast political and economic shifts tear us from our past. Differences in the cultural understanding of what it means to be a woman leave
mothers and daughters on opposing sides of jagged breaks in their common
ground, fighting battles larger than personal lives can contain. Apparently
petty arguments about hemlines and makeup are, in fact, much larger
struggles about the nature of being female at a particular moment in
history.

The sameness between mothers and daughters looping through time
goes underground in a period of rapid intergenerational change, feels oppressive and dangerous to the daughter, who swears at a young age that
she will never be like her mother. The mother, who has lived out the dic-
tates of her generation, finds her values left behind in the dust. She feels
betrayed by her daughter. Wrestling with the mother is not enough to
claim our Motherlines. We must reach beyond our own generation to conceive the lives of our mothers in the context of their time.

Few women in our culture are carried along in the archetypal "slow
stream of mothers and daughters." Most have been caught up in the rip
tides of history, the terrible convulsions of the twentieth century that have
tossed families about like branches torn off trees in a storm, severing generations, altering cultures. We must find our way back to the lost shores
of our Motherlines. Only in this way can we begin to claim our history.

THE MUSIC OF DIFFERENT WORLDS

Finding our connection to the women of our line requires sorting through the generational, cultural, and historical differences that would make strangers of us if we could not bridge them. From my great-grandmother, Babette, who died in childbirth when my grandmother, Emma, was two, to Emma, who lost three of her six children and had to flee her homeland in mid-life (a Jewish refugee from Hitler), to my mother, who married young and twined her life around her husband and children only to find herself a divorced woman in mid-life, to my own complex life journey, which would astonish my grandmother and great-grandmother, the women of my line have lived in entirely divergent realities.

How strange it is, then, that I can set my table with Babette's wedding china. I try to imagine the hopes and dreams of this young woman on her wedding day. Her initials are intertwined in the gold letters she chose for her trousseau. A few years later she was dead, and so were the twins she had labored to bring into the world.

Anyone who has ever been a child can imagine how utterly bereft, how fearfully unprotected, my two-year-old grandmother must have felt at the loss of her mother. Any of us can imgine how she felt toward the woman her father then married, who was critical and cold, a real-life wicked stepmother. My grandmother was Cinderella. When I became a stepmother I remembered my grandmother's childhood and promised her I would be a better stepmother than the one who had made her so unhappy. Stories from the Motherline are as familiar to us as our own lives. But the historical moments in which they take place are worlds apart. I never saw the house my mother grew up in; can't picture how my grandmother lived when she was the age I am now; can't begin to imagine the world in which Babette chose the china I use for special occasions more than a century later. History makes aliens of women in the same family. We belong to the times in which we are born as surely as we belong to our families. We do not leave our families only to cleave to a beloved other, but also to find a connection to our generation, which is often in conflict with our family values.

For a modern woman to root herself in her female lineage, she must honor both the archetypal and historical aspects of her Motherline. She must be able to feel the archetype of continuity, as well as the generational and cultural differences between the women of her line.

Modern family rituals carry these threads of connection and discontinuity. In families we fight out the great shifts in human consciousness as though they were only personal issues, invented by us to torture one another. Consider, for purposes of illustration, the family reunion. The powerful mix of feelings that inevitably occurs is a product of combining generations, life-cycle events, and the archetypal level of life.

Imagine, for example, that all your mother's children, their spouses, and their children, are gathered together to celebrate her birthday. Perhaps you are seeing your brother's child for the first time. He looks just like your brother looked when he was a baby. Your childhood, your brother's childhood, this child's childhood loop together in a blur of love and tears. You are rather too passionate in kissing the child and he pulls back, frightened by your intensity. His look says clearly what a strange large creature he thinks you are. You can remember such feelings about the aunt who kept pinching your cheek, the great-aunt who kept exclaiming how much you looked like your grandmother on your father's side. It has taken you over half a lifetime to understand what they were feeling when they made that fuss about you.

Soon enough conflict begins. Often it is generation vs. generation. You find yourself fighting as though for your life, furious about issues that in other contexts you would shrug off. Some families fight about politics, some about religion, or food, or child-rearing. My family fights about music. Passionately, as though lives are at stake, we struggle over why children are giving up their piano lessons, why the teenagers are allowed to listen to such kitsch. Can't they turn down that awful stuff?

I remember such a reunion some years ago when my mother's children gathered from all the corners of this country to celebrate her 65th birthday by a lake in the mosquito-laden summer heat of the Midwest. All of her four children and most of her eleven grandchildren were there. There was much commotion, laughter, and good feeling. Flashbulbs went off; kids struggled to sit next to their favorite cousins at the long table. We could barely see each other down the long stretch of four combined tables.

I was acutely aware of how differently the three generations experienced the gathering. A rush of energy like a high wind seemed to whip through the youngest generation. It was as though their bodies were receiving the power of the intergenerational connection but they could not have given a name to their excitement. We in the middle generation knew more consciously what we were feeling. We were moved and amused by the delicious ironies of being at once parents and children. The oldest generation sat quietly, observing the rich flow of life that emanated from them. They seemed in a more distant relation to the hubbub of life that carried the younger people along like a strong current in the river.

Soon enough tension emerged. The generations did not understand one another, could not speak the same language. Who was John Lennon and why was it so important for the teenagers to leave after dinner to get his latest album downtown, when grandma and her friend, Sonia, were going to play chamber music in the little auditorium of the resort?

"Because John Lennon is dead!" came the passionate wail from the teenagers. "Don't you even watch the news? He was assassinated last year and "Double Phantasy" is the last album he did and he did it with Yoko and there is even a song about his son on it and we've been planning all day to go out and get it tonight!"

"Who is Yoko?"

"Do you remember when we were kids," the middle generation tries to intervene. "There was a famous rock-and-roll group called the Beatles? Remember when we sat you and Dad down and tried to get you to hear that their music was brilliant? But you were entirely closed-minded. You said popular music is ' kitsch'! John Lennon was a member of the Beatles and Yoko Ono is his wife."

"John Lennon was a Beatle?" Several of the youngsters are totally astonished by this piece of information. The members of the middle generation look at each other in a state of shock. Our own children don't know that John Lennon was a member of the Beatles? "Who did you think he was?"

"A famous rock star. Who's dead now. And we'll never get to hear his album if we have to listen to chamber music tonight."

"There will be plenty of time to hear the John Lennon album. But how often do you get to hear grandma play Beethoven?"

"What's so great about Beethoven? John Lennon's music is as great as Beethoven's!"

"Now wait a little minute!" The members of the middle generation feel suddenly ashamed of their children. "Your ignorance is showing! It's true John Lennon is great, but Beethoven is great in an entirely different way. It's very important for you to hear and appreciate 'good music'!"

"Why is it so important? You never told us we had to come to the concert. We want to go to our room and listen to our kind of music!"

We in the parental generation feel torn between our parents and our children. We feel the unspoken criticism of the older generation and their old-world values. We have failed to educate our children properly. They have no appreciation of Beethoven. Further, we seem incapable of controlling them. On the other hand, we are identified with them against our parents, remembering what it's like to be young and American, struggling to assert or own generational autonomy and our right to enjoy the popular culture our parents abhorred.

Later, in the small concert hall, we listen to my mother and her friend, Sonia, playing an early Beethoven sonata for violin and piano. The teenagers are long gone and we struggle to hold on to restless young ones. My mother and Sonia are passionate about their music. I watch the faces of the members of my mother's generation. The music evokes a set of values, a historical period, memories of a time and a country long gone. Sonia leans her whole body into the keys; my mother's bowing arm reaches for the notes with tender power, her body swaying, her face entirely rapt in the music. "Good music" carries the sense of worth, of values, of culture for this generation in my family. A person's background can be gauged by how much they know about "good music." A lost way of life is reaffirmed in their precise and passionate rendition of a Beethoven sonata.

Suddenly, I feel that we children of these highly educated, musically gifted European refugees have betrayed our family values. We have not insisted on the meaning of "good music" in our children's lives. We have let them give up the piano and flute lessons that we had to take whether we wanted to or not. Nor have we dragged them to the concerts we were dragged to as children. Watching my mother and her old friend in their passion, listening to the beauty of the music, I feel that something precious is being lost. Will my children ever hear a Beethoven sonata with the pleasure I now feel, sitting in the dusky glow of memory?

My mother's playing evokes the most sacred memories of childhood, when my parents were still married, and my father playing Bach fugues in the evening caught us all up in a tender hush. All was well in the frightening world as his sure fingers on the piano keys delineated each elegant enunciation of the fugal theme. Bach was the architect of security in my childhood. In the clean, arching lines of the fugue, in the intense movement of our father's hands over the keyboard, we knew we were loved and that life had great and sacred meanings. The tribal rituals in which small groups of expatriate Europeans gathered in our living room to hear chamber music further consolidated the musical faith. Hiding from parental eyes because we were supposed to be in bed, we would peer through the stairway railings at the transfixed faces of our parents' friends, carried away into another time and place by the resonating strings of a Schubert quartet.

In the middle of my life I begin to understand the pain it caused my parents for me to turn into an American teenager, listening to rock and roll, diffusing the high European culture by which they evoked their most sacred cultural memories. And yet I remember how desperate I felt as a teenager to join my peers, to be part of the culture, to be a member of my generation. It felt like a life-and-death struggle. If my parents didn't let me out of the house to run with my peers, I would suffocate; I would die!

And so, loyal to our remembered teenage struggles, we let the teenagers listen to their own music, create their own generational ritual, while we sit in the midst of the music of our childhood, allowing the archetypal experience of the family reunion to move us. We are transported behind the surface of everyday life to see the eternal patterns of existence. In the face of my brother's child I see the child my brother was, the child I was, the eternal child in us all. In the face of my mother's joy at the gathering of her children and her children's children, I see our family's continuity, our future. For a moment my mother is all grandmothers, I am all mothers, my children are all children, our family is the human family. We are in touch with the generation cord that ties us back to a time before the writing down of history.

A HISTORY OF WOMEN IN THREE GENERATIONS

> I liked history. Not the kind in the textbooks, the treaties and political parties and government shenanigans, all of which gave me a headache. There was more to history than that. There were things hidden in it, mysteries worth going after. I didn't want to know about the Mugwumps or the industries of Japan or fifteen steps in the unification of Germany. I wanted to know, to put it bluntly, the secrets of life. I believed they were to be found in the dusty corners of human history. Human history.
>
> *Josephine Humphries*[3]

Let me introduce three generations of mothers in one family whose attitudes about sexuality illustrate how women's lives have changed. Their differences illustrate a generational imperative that severs daughters from mothers as the times shift human consciousness. Sarah, the great-grandmother, is a strong-minded woman in her eighties. I met her in the company of her daughter, Sally, and her granddaughter, Suzanne, as I was talking to women about generational differences. Suzanne is forty-one, married, and raising an eight-year-old boy and a thirteen-year-old daughter. She recently completed law school. Though she and her mother, Sally, who is sixty-two, fight often about how Suzanne should lead her life, she told me that her mother has inspired her ambition. Sally, who was widowed in mid-life, became a lawyer and is now a judge in family court.

Sarah doesn't understand why her daughter and granddaughter are so obsessed with work. She had to work from the time she was ten, first in her father's store, then in her husband's. The best thing that ever happened to her, she says, was finding out that her husband had left her a wealthy widow and that she didn't have to work. "In my day it was different. Success for a woman meant not having to work."

We are sitting in Sarah's fussy living room, filled with doilies and displays of painted china, drinking tea. Suzanne has been telling us about her thirteen-year-old daughter's questions about sex.

"Mom," Suzanne asks Sally, "when did you first learn about sex?"

"You know," Sally responds, "I don't remember. It's something my mother never discussed with me!" She looks pointedly at her mother as she says this, and I can imagine how provocative she must have been as a child.

"Well," says Sarah, "whatever it was, it worked!" Suzanne and I laugh. Sally looks furious.

"Congratulations," she says. "Bully for that."

Suzanne, clearly fascinated by this intensity between her mother and grandmother, asks: "What does that mean that it worked?"

"That I was a virgin when I got married." There is enormous bitterness in her tone as she says this.

Suzanne pushes further into the secret parts of her mother's life. "You wish you hadn't been a virgin?"

"With all due respect to your father, it was no favor to him or to me that I was so stupid!"

Suzanne is looking at her grandmother now, who is clearly furious. "That's something that has really changed over generations," Suzanne says in a mollifying tone.

"I'll say!" her mother says. "A guy can't find one today!"

"I don't think things have changed for the better!" Sarah says angrily.

"You don't like the changes, grandma?"

"I don't think a woman has anything to gain by it."

"Do you think she has anything to lose by it?"

"Besides her virginity," smart-aleck Sally gets her two cents in again.

"After she goes through it once," says Sarah, "she'll find out what it's all about. I think a young girl cheapens herself. She comes to know that later."

Sally says, "I don't agree with my mother. You know what happens to good girls?"

"What?" says Suzanne.

"Nothing," says Sally. Everyone except Sarah laughs.

"When did you get this attitude?" asks Suzanne. "I don't remember this from my childhood."

"Too late!" says Sally. Again, we of recent generations laugh, and Sarah sits in an angry silence.

"But what do I say to my daughter?" Suzanne looks around at us all. "I'm so afraid she'll get AIDS or Herpes or pregnant!"

"Boy," says Sally, her tough stance softening, "that's a hard one. I don't know the answer to that."

In this emotional interchange, worlds collide. When mothers and daughters were part of the slow stream that Kroeber described at the beginning of this chapter, such a discussion would not be heard.

Sarah's Generation:
A Woman's Reputation Is a Beautiful Jewel

Sarah, Sally, and Suzanne represent powerful generational shifts. Let us consider the historical moment that formed each woman so that we can reach beyond generational differences to claim our female history.

Sarah was born shortly after the turn of the century. Freud had not yet shed light on our dark recesses; sex wasn't talked about out loud, and it was unclear to Sarah whether her mother practiced any form of birth control.

I spoke with a number of women of her generation. Most were uncomfortable talking about sex, and none of them had been openly informed about sexuality as young women. Their mothers gave vague speeches about menstruation and "becoming a woman." Usually they filled in the meanings from talk among peers. They described entering puberty in a world without tampons or Kotex. "We had to wash out rags," I was told by the matriarch of a large Catholic clan, "and that's very disgusting and unsanitary and everything else."

Sarah, brought up as an Orthodox Jew, remembered that women were not allowed near the podium in synagogue when they were menstruating. Though never told directly about sex, her whole life was set up to protect her from its power. "My mother watched me like a dog. She told me that my reputation was like a beautiful jewel and that I had to guard it as one would a valuable object." She described a world in which a woman's sexuality was a property, to be guarded, protected, and eventually traded on the marketplace for a good husband and security.

Sexuality in this world was no ecstatic communion between lovers, but a dangerous business in which women had little control but bore all the consequences. Before marriage it could be fatal for a woman, unless carefully, seductively harnessed. A woman's body was her destiny. She was entirely dependent on her husband for name, identity, security for herself and her children, and for whether or not she could avoid pregnancy. The women of this generation let me know, mostly through euphemistic allusions, that their husbands took care of contraceptive matters. I learned from the daughter of one of them that her mother had had at least six abortions, "of the coathanger type," and that her mother had once sold her engagement ring to purchase an illegal abortion.

Birth-control advocate Margaret Sanger's autobiography gives us a glimpse of women's lives during this historical moment. She writes of the fate of the lower-class woman whose husband seldom assumed responsibility for preventing conception.

> But more and more my calls began to come from the Lower East Side, as though I were being magnetically drawn there by some force outside my control. . . . As soon as the neighbors learned that a nurse was in the building they came in a friendly way to visit, often carrying fruit, jellies or gefilte fish made after a cherished recipe. It was infinitely pathetic to me that they, so poor themselves, should bring me food. Later they drifted in again with the excuse of getting the plate, and sat down for a nice talk; there was no hurry. Always back of the little gift was the question, "I'm pregnant (or my daughter, or my sister is). Tell me something to keep from having another baby. We cannot afford another yet."
>
> I tried to explain the only methods I had ever heard of among the middle classes, both of which were invariably brushed aside as

unacceptable. They were of no certain avail to the wife because they placed the burden of responsibility solely upon the husband—a burden which he seldom assumed. What she was seeking was self-protection she could herself use, and there was none. . . .

Pregnancy was a chronic condition among the women of this class. Suggestions as to what to do for a girl who was "in trouble" or a married woman who was "caught" passed from mouth to mouth—herb teas, turpentine, steaming, rolling downstairs, inserting slippery elm, knitting needles, shoe-hooks. When they had word of a new remedy they hurried to the drugstore, and if the clerk were inclined to be friendly he might say, "Oh, that won't help you, but here's something that may." The younger druggists usually refused to give advice because, if it were to be known, they would come under the law; midwives were even more fearful. . . . They asked everybody and tried anything, but nothing did them any good. On Saturday nights I have seen groups of from fifty to one hundred with their shawls over their heads waiting outside the office of a five-dollar abortionist.[4]

The secret that Margaret Sanger spent a lifetime making available to women was the diaphragm. A woman of Sally's generation told me that she remembered lying in the bathtub as a young mother, reflecting on the fact that her life had been shaped by a piece of rubber. Thanks to the availability of that piece of rubber she was able to plan her family—two children and no abortions. Many of the differences between Sarah and Sally can be understood in terms of which side of that piece of rubber they lived on.

The women of Sarah's generation raised their children during the great depression. Many worked, not by choice, not for self-expression or development, but out of desperate necessity. They have found it strange to hear their granddaughters agonizing over whether to have children or a career, wondering how they will find themselves, how they will choose. Life did most of the choosing for them, and their strength and courage lay in their ability to accept and work with what life gave them.

A woman of Sarah's generation, Doris, told me of being newly married during the Depression. She often wondered where her family's next meal was coming from. There were no food stamps in those days, no welfare.

When I say we didn't have a dime, the kids laugh at me. But we didn't have a dime for weeks on end. I said I would have gone home to mother many a time, but it cost 35 cents to take the bus, and that just wasn't in the picture.

Doris is an unusual women of her generation. She was pleased to talk openly about sexual matters and had been blessed by a loving and egalitarian marriage. She told me that during the Depression she and her husband were so poor they could only afford to have one child. It took them two and a half years to pay the $134 hospital and doctor bill for that birth. They were often so low on funds that they couldn't afford rubbers. They saved them for special occasions. The partnership and open dialogue between Doris and her husband made poverty negotiable for them. But it was far more common that women suffered the terrors of unwanted pregnancies, coathanger abortions and economic deprivation without any marital support.

Sally's Generation: The Second Apple

The women of Sally's generation are at the fulcrum of a powerful, collective change. They have eaten of what Irene de Claremont Castijello calls the "second apple," the apple of contraceptive knowledge.[5] They suffer, as a consequence, a much larger sense of responsibility for their fates and the fates of their children. They were raised in the Depression and know the power of fate to mold a life. But they were young adults during and just after World War II. They saw the new freedom that women had acquired to work in a man's world. But they joined the retreat to domestic femininity and experienced the isolation of the nuclear family when they were raising their children.

Influenced by the permissive and self-conscious ideas about child-rearing propounded by the followers of Freud, they stand in the middle, between mothers of a less ethically confusing time, and daughters who are swept up in the enormous identity problems of the modern woman. Their lives were shaped by Margaret Sanger's piece of rubber. As a result they had much more personal choice, and often painfully, much more personal responsibility, than did their mothers.

Somewhere, in the middle of the lives of many women of Sally's generation, something happened: a marriage failed; a husband died; a way of life fell apart, leaving the woman disoriented and vulnerable. In Sally's case, it was the death of a husband that catapulted her into change.

After my husband died, despite my college background, I was completely helpless, completely dependent and completely insecure. I didn't even think I was employable. I said to my daughter, "What can I do? All I know how to do is bake pies."

This is the same Sally who gives her mother a hard time for not teaching her about sex. It's hard to imagine Sally, a highly intelligent woman, a lawyer, a judge, and a smart-aleck, as a woman who thought all she was capable of was baking pies. Feminist author Adrienne Rich, a woman of Sally's generation, writes:

From the fifties and early sixties I remember a cycle. It began when I had picked up a book or began trying to write a letter, or even found myself on the telephone with someone toward whom my voice betrayed eagerness, a rush of sympathetic energy. The child (or children) might be absorbed in business, in his own dreamworld; but as soon as he felt me gliding into a world which did not include him, he would come to pull at my hand, ask for help, punch at the typewriter keys. And I would feel his wants at such a moment as fraudulent, as an attempt moreover to defraud me of living even for fifteen minutes as myself. My anger would rise; I would feel the futility of any attempt to salvage myself, and also the inequality between us: my needs always balanced against those of a child, and always losing. I could love so much better, I told myself, after even a quarter-hour of selfishness of peace, of detachment from my children. A few minutes!
Like so many women, I waited with impatience for the moment when their father would return from work, when for an hour or two at least the circle drawn around mother and children would grow looser, the intensity between us slacken, because there was another adult in the house.[6]

Sally's daughter, Suzanne, told me how it was when she was a child and her father came home.

I remember my mother going upstairs, putting on lipstick and combing her hair and changing her dress, every night before my father came home. But once he was home the day went downhill. He was tired and he was moody and he didn't really want to communicate and he just kind of wanted to have dinner and read the paper and have a quiet time. He was fairly selfish about his time. He had a tremendous commitment to his profession, and to his golf, and that took up most of his time. I don't think my mother got a whole lot from him. She certainly never got self-confidence from him. She was very beholden to him for decision-making and for being the head of the family.

Sally was born to a mother for whom life was not about choice and individual development, but about survival. Sarah's generation are adherents of what the late Jungian analyst Erich Neumann called the old ethic. By this he means a collective system of values that operates by suppressing negative feelings and behavior and making the needs of the group more important than the need of the individual for self-expression. Sally, too, was living by these standards until her husband died and her world fell apart. Unknown potential stirred her. She went to see her family lawyer for advice during those dark days. He suggested she get a teaching credential. She knew she didn't want to do that. She remembers looking at him, bemusedly, and asking: "How about law school?"

> Well, he looked at me like I was a retarded child with greatly diminished capacity. He didn't even bother to answer. I never forgot that look. But when I finally, years later, passed the bar, he was the first to whom I sent an announcement!

Our life stories are our own, but they are also a manifestation of the collective spirit of our time as it passes through us. Sally's story would have been very different in another historical moment. Her courage would have taken other forms, her intelligence run through different channels. The historical moment at which she spoke to the family lawyer was 1966. The second wave of the women's movement was beginning. Her very question to him was part of a movement she did not know she was in. Moved by larger-than-individual forces, she rode a wave of women's development, leaving her mother bewildered and confused. Their conflict is generational. It is a struggle between external and internal values. For Sarah, people of high character are outwardly recognizable; they are living the good life. Sally struggles with a more psychological and inward sense of ethical dilemmas. Like most modern mothers, she suffers the certainty that she has damaged her children despite her conscious intentions.

> I'm sure I inflicted my own psychological traumas on my children. But you certainly don't do it willingly or maliciously or con-

sciously. And sometimes you do it not by what you do but by what happens to you.

Another aspect of the generational imperative is the difficulty women have imagining themselves in any other generation. Sally said:

> I'll tell you, I really feel sorry for young women today. I've met a lot of young women who have young children, and if they're not out doing anything they feel guilty. Their friends are all out doing exciting things and they say, "What do you do all day?" like they're sitting on a satin cushion eating bon bons. I'm very grateful that while I was raising my children I didn't have a career. I'm glad Suzanne waited until the kids were older to go back to school. But even so she feels torn between her career and her children. I feel sorry for both sides. She feels guilt-ridden and the children feel deprived.

Suzanne's Generation: A Rare Moment in History

Suzanne came of age in the sixties, as did I, in the midst of what was then fervently called the sexual revolution. In our generation, women were shaped by powerful forces such as the women's movement, the politics of the sixties, the hippies, gay and lesbian liberation, the natural childbirth movement, the drug culture, the human-potential movement, the many divorces that resulted from the shifting roles of men and women. Suzanne looks a little wistful when she speaks of her young adulthood. Having married young and stayed married, she "sat out" much of the excitement. She envied some of her friends who experimented with drugs and had wild love affairs. But she feels that her life, conventional as it looks from the outside, was profoundly affected by the greater freedoms possible for women. Suzanne has always had a sense of her own identity and direction. Even when she hasn't worked, she has had her own goals.

She is grateful to her mother for realizing her own ambition. This opened new territory for Suzanne. And she worries about her daughter, coming of age in a difficult time, surrounded by perplexing social problems. Sally and Suzanne fight regularly about politics, about child-rearing, about how they spend their time. But underneath the fighting they respect and admire each other; they have in common that both of their lives were profoundly influenced by the collective shifts in women's consciousness. It is Sarah and Sally whose connection has foundered in the midst of the generational upheaval, who are embittered and estranged, unable to understand what means most to the other. As sometimes happens, it is Suzanne, the granddaughter, who can bridge the gap between her mother and her grandmother, and find the Motherline connection to Sarah.

But the understanding between Suzanne and Sally is not necessarily typical. Vivian Gornick tells a story of the generation-gap phenomenon between members of the sixties generation and their parents. She is describing her mother's response to being proselytized by a guru-struck young Jew:

> "Can you believe this?" she says. "A nice Jewish boy shaves his head and babbles in the street. A world full of crazies. Divorce everywhere, and if not divorce, this. What a generation you all are!"
>
> "Don't start, Ma," I say. "I don't want to hear that bullshit again."
>
> "Bullshit here, bullshit there," she says, "it's still true. Whatever else we did, we didn't fall apart in the streets like you're all doing. We had order, quiet, dignity. Families stayed together, and people lived decent lives."
>
> "That's a crock. They didn't lead decent lives, they lived hidden lives."[7]

In Suzanne's Motherline, the break with traditional women's values occurred in her mother's generation. In Gornick's story, and in many others, it is the daughter who breaks the mold. And yet, even in their generational quarreling mother and daughter seek to understand each other. Gornick's mother, responding to her daughter's question about whether people were happy leading hidden lives, says:

> "No," she capitulates instantly. "I'm not saying that."
>
> "Well, what are you saying?"
>
> She frowns and stops talking. Searches around in her head to find out what she is saying. Ah, she's got it. Triumphant, accusing, she says, "The unhappiness is so alive today."
>
> Her words startle and gratify me. I feel pleasure when she says a true or a clever thing. I come close to loving her.[8]

Reaching across such vast differences, seeking to grasp the issues of another generation, to understand and feel empathic to their struggle, is no easy task. It requires accepting differences, because it is in the nature of generational shifts that one generation will be conscious of the blind spots of the one before.

Gornick and her mother spend a lifetime fighting over generational differences about love. The mother is an idealist, the daughter a cynic. Both are women of their time. The mother gave up work for love. The daughter has work but cannot find a love that lasts. Their connection splinters along the knife edge of a difference they never fully bridge. In that they are like Sarah and Sally.

In the Motherline stories of many modern women we hear of such a generation of change, in which the collective shift that allows a woman to be more than a vessel of life, to have her own identity, is fought out between a mother and daughter. Sarah and Sally fought out one version of the story, freeing Suzanne to experience a fullness of life.

But Suzanne came of age in a rare moment of human history. It is a time that expects mothers to survive childbirth and assumes children have a birthright to full, happy lives. She wonders what lies ahead as she considers the new darkness into which we are currently shifting with AIDS, babies born addicted to drugs, and threats against women's reproductive rights.

Suzanne, meditating upon her daughter, describing to me her beauty, intelligence, and potential, feels a shudder of fear that shadows her joy. She is afraid her daughter's generation will lose the hard-won right to abortion and return to sexual puritanism because of the fear of sexually transmitted diseases.

Dark wings of the future swoop over the middle-aged children of the Aquarian age. Suzanne and I see each other with the shared experience of women of the same generation. In each other's eyes we recognize our mutual fear: that a great sea of change will blow our daughters' lives far from the world in which we raised them; that they will lose access to what their mothers have so recently grasped—full lives of love and work and the freedom to become themselves.

CHAPTER SEVEN

ON MY MOTHER'S SIDE:

The Power of the Grandmother

My grandmother was a storyteller. I remember the telling. Lying in her arms, I heard her voice gather in the rhythm of the front porch swing, the night chorus of cicadas, the flashes of the fireflies in the boxwood hedge. . . . My imagery originates here . . . in the pulse beat I learned from her body and the breath of her dark imagination which I still feel in the wonder of the natural world.

MEINRAD CRAIGHEAD[1]

S tanding at the crossings of family history, generational change, and archetypal meanings, a grandmother locates her grandchild in the life stream of the generations. She is the tie to the subterranean world of the ancestors; she plays a key role in helping a woman reclaim essential aspects of her feminine self. Standing close to death, she remembers the dead. She tells their stories, hands down their meanings and their possessions. Often she is the first to tell her granddaughter the stories from her Motherline. Evoking the Eleusinian emotions of the life cycle, these stories return a woman to her place of emergence, reminding her that she is woman, born of woman. Telling these stories enacts an archetypal healing principle found in tribal cultures and in psychotherapy: the "return to origins."

In Native American healing ceremonies the retelling of the creation myth reorients a sick soul. In psychotherapy the wounded woman touches the child within her, remembering the early experiences that formed her, reclaiming lost aspects of her self.

During the course of her maturation, according to author Emily Hancock, a woman must reconnect to the girl she was in order to access her creative spirit. Often this remembered child sits on her grandmother's lap, holds her grandmother's hand, and listens to stories from her grandmother's life. Finding the "girl within" is not enough to heal a woman's soul; the mother-daughter dyad is not sufficient to locate her in her Motherline. She needs a grandmother, if not a personal, real-life woman, then an archetypal one, to bring her into harmony with her life's unfolding meaning.

RESTORING THE LIVES OF THE ANCESTORS

Grandmothers loom behind parents, casting shadows, evoking the mysteries. Less familiar, less everyday than the mother, a grandmother is a woman of another time, telling stories out of long ago, when she was a child, when mommy or daddy was a child, when we of the present generation had not yet been dreamt of.

When the grandmother enters consciousness, a great archetypal pattern is evoked: the two become three, the mother-child dyad opens to include a third generation. These biological relationships are channels through which symbolic meanings flow. The presence of three generations of women evokes a sacred trinity: the three ages of woman, the three aspects of the goddess—maiden, mother, crone—which have been worshiped in many cultures from earliest times.

The appearance of the grandmother throws the mother into relief. She is seen as one of a long line of mothers, forming a pattern that lives in the female body and is expressed in the meeting of the three. The grandmother holds these three in her body and psyche, the maiden and the mother she was, the crone she has become. The wholeness of the feminine self is evoked, and the granddaughter's potential development is stirred. Someday, perhaps, she too will have a granddaughter to whom she will tell the stories of her female line. Grandmother consciousness opens a woman to images of the past, to the face of the future, and to the symbolic pattern of a woman's life.

The feminine psyche hungers for the grandmother who can link her to her future and her past. Blanche, who told her Motherline story in Chapter 5, lost her mother when she was ten. She told me that her mother's mother also had died when her mother was a child. She described her powerful yearning for her grandmother:

> As a child I longed to see my grandmother's face. I used to pester my mother about it. I just had to know how this woman looked. I said things like: "Couldn't we just go to the cemetery and dig her up?" Looking back I'm impressed that this did not disturb my mother. She seemed to understand what I was feeling.

Blanche's hunger to see the face of her dead grandmother comes from a longing to know "her place and meaning in the life of the generations," the Eleusinian emotion described by C. G. Jung in his essay on Kore.[2] She yearns to see the mother of her mother, her origin, her future. This memory is a painful foreshadowing of a lifetime of maternal deprivation.

But even women whose mothers are alive often suffer maternal deprivation. Many mothers are so out of touch with the sacred aspects of the feminine that they cannot help their daughters. A daughter longs for the intervention of the crone, for the viewpoint of the objective feminine. One generation removed from the heat and passion of mothering, the grandmother can see with the cold eye of the witch, with the irreverent eye of the baud, with the healing vision of the wise woman. When mother and daughter fly into their polarized viewpoints, grandmother consciousness provides the integrating third viewpoint, honoring differences, valuing both sides, seeing the struggle as part of an impersonal pattern of female development.

My feeling for the power of the grandmother is rooted in my childhood. I remember, when my brothers and I were children, how life seemed to shift and deepen when my mother's mother came to visit. It was as though another element, a third perspective, was added to the everyday struggles between parents and children. We called her Oma, the German word for grandmother. She was my only living grandparent, the only link I had to my family's European past.

She told us stories from my mother's childhood. Her eyes were violet, looking inward, looking backward. I remember how the soft folds of skin at her throat shook when she spoke. "Once I told the children that I, too, had had a mother. Your aunt was about four then, your mother three. Do you know what your aunt said to me? She looked me up and down, because of course she was very little, and I was very big, and she said: 'You had a mother? She must have been a giant!!' "

We children all laughed, as we had many times, hearing this familiar tale. But looking back I see that my four-year-old aunt was on to something. Grandmothers do belong to a race of larger beings. They brought those huge creatures, our parents, into this world. The very word *grand* makes the point. A grandmother is grander than a mother; holding on in a wider circle of meanings, a larger perspective, than the tight little everyday intimacy one lives in with a mother, with its irritating ambivalence, its intensity of hope and disappointment.

Often a personal grandmother is not able psychologically to hold this consciousness. The woman who fills the role may not be biologically related, or may be an older woman in one's dreams. A woman needs this third viewpoint to initiate her fully into the Motherline, for guidance into the realm of the mysteries. She needs the grandmother as she ages, as she becomes a crone herself, to integrate this aspect of the feminine, to become whole.

Henchwomen of the Conventional

Women who are out of touch with their Motherlines are lost souls, hungry ghosts inhabiting bodies they do not own, because for them the feminine ground is a foreign place. Often they suffer because their personal mothers or grandmothers are so negative, depressed, or uninspiring that they have no access through them to the Motherline.

In my psychotherapy practice I see many women who feel isolated, abandoned, and self-estranged. Many feel barred from access to their own true natures by a mother's punitive attitude, neglect, or abuse. Some grandmothers provide a sanctuary for their granddaughters, a haven from the mother-daughter storms.

But some are not so helpful. There are negative grandmothers who bind and abuse their daughters' souls. In turn the daughters bind and abuse their daughters' souls. In turn the daughters bind and abuse their daughters. Often I sit with a woman and experience a telescopic experience of generations of pain.

The negative personal mother or grandmother bars a woman's access to her feminine self as long as she is perceived as larger than life. The negativity feels archetypal. But when the older woman is brought down to size, as a suffering being herself, the daughter can sort out her own sense of self from that of her mother and grandmother. She can become the kind of mother and crone it is in her nature to be, instead of reliving the constrictions of generations past.

Because most of our grandmothers came of age in a time that denied the feminine, split it into angels and whores, and tied up women in tight corsets that denied them contact with their bodies, many of our grandmothers became henchwomen of the conventional, denying their daughters' sexuality, teaching them fear of their child-bearing capacity. Like the Chinese mother who binds her daughter's feet, such a woman cripples her daughter so that she may fit into the cultural requirements that have already crippled the mother.

My own grandmother punished my mother severely for a childish game she played with a friend when they were eight or nine. The two friends lay one on top of the other. A baby doll came out from between the legs of one of them. They were enacting the drama of sex and birth. My grandmother found them doing this and was very upset. She talked to the other child's mother, and both children were punished. My mother's natural connection to her sexuality was deeply wounded, she tells me, by this conventional attitude of her mother.

The relationship between grandmother and granddaughter is often easier than that of mother and daughter. My love for my grandmother was not compromised by the difficulties my mother experienced with her.

Sometimes, however, a daughter will be allied with her mother against a powerful, negative grandmother. Such a grandmother casts her shadow over both lives. The mother never fully emerges from her status as a daughter; her daughter tries to protect her mother from her grandmother, and is not mothered herself.

I heard such a story recently from my mother-in-law. She is a tiny woman in her mid-eighties. A brilliant plume of white hair lights up her face and her dark eyes. I watch her with her grandchildren, with the infant great-grandson who is the first of a whole new generation, and marvel at the generations she spans. As we work together in the kitchen, she tells me stories from the Motherline to which I have become attached through marriage. These days most of her stories are about her grandmothers, as though her psyche is reaching for support to the crones of her childhood. They are not happy stories.

She tells me that when she was very young her mother's mother came to live with her family. This was supposed to be a help to her mother, who was "frail." Her mother's first pregnancy had brought triplets who died at birth. "She was torn by that delivery," my mother-in-law says, shaking her head in the way women do about the terrors of childbirth.

She never really regained her strength. After my sisters and I were born, my mother had trouble keeping up with all the work. Her mother came to help, to do the cooking. But this was very hard on my mother because my grandmother took over the kitchen. My mother had three daughters, and she wanted to be the one to teach them how to cook. She felt pushed out of place by her mother, the life squeezed out of her. I remember when I was fifteen, I came into the living room and my mother was lying on the couch, weeping and weeping. "What's the matter Mama?" I asked. "I hate my mother!" she said. I was shocked. We never said such things in our family. That was the beginning of her nervous breakdown. She screamed and cried a lot. Finally her mother died, and then she began to have a life. But by that time I was grown up and out of the house.

Grandmothers in the Underworld

My mother-in-law tells another story. Her father's mother, she tells me, bore ten children and buried six. Cholera, measles, ear infections—these things killed off the children of the poor. When her father was a boy of twelve, his mother fell into a melancholia so deep that she was institutionalized for the rest of her life. The young son had to go to work to help support the family. She remembers going to visit this grandmother at an asylum for the insane. Drained of life energy, the old woman didn't talk or eat much. But when they visited, the grandmother checked the girl's scalp and that of her sisters for some unknown disease she feared they might have. Caught in perpetual mourning for the children she had lost, she reenacted a blind ritual of protection but was lost to real human contact.

"I didn't tell my husband about this grandmother for a long time," my mother-in-law tells me. "I thought these things were inherited, and I was afraid someday I'd lose my mind too."

It's a rare Motherline story that does not contain such terrible suffering. Blanche's grandmother died in her mother's childhood as Blanche's mother died in hers. My own grandmother bore six children and buried three. Her mother died in childbirth when she was two. My grandmother, my mother-in-law's grandmother, Blanche, women transfixed in a terrible

Demeter mourning, remind us that death, loss, and mourning are an inescapable part of life. If you follow many a Motherline back, you'll find a woman like my mother-in-law's grandmother who falls into the underworld and never finds her way back into life. This unredeemed suffering lives on in her children and her children's children like a curse from an angry fairy.

Much of my female identity was shaped by the only grandmother I knew. The terrible losses of her life are my psychological place of origin. When I became a new mother, making her a great-grandmother, it was she who oriented my emerging young female self. Far away from my parents both geographically and emotionally, my contact with her tied us both to a past and a future: I at the beginning, she at the end of our lives.

THE BALLAD OF MY GRANDMOTHER

Once a month as regularly as the waning moon we visited my Oma on Sundays, my first husband, my baby, and I. Oma was the right word for my grandmother. The resonant, round, sound felt ancient in my mouth. Her eyes were so deep you could see eternity in them. She had soft, withering skin and a slow thoughtful walk.

It was the early sixties. I was taking classes at the university; my husband was going to medical school. Life was arranged around mid-terms and finals. Our marriage, our family life was postponed to some day in the future, post degrees. In between reading Virginia Woolf, caring for a baby, and yearning for my husband, who was seldom home, I was disoriented, as chaotic on the inside as was my living room, with its heaps of unfolded laundry on the couch and Woolf's *Mrs. Dalloway* lost somewhere under a pile of rubber baby pants.

It was a chorus in my life, a monthly refrain that took us to a sanitarium in the wine country, where Oma lived. As in a ballad, where each verse tells of events progressing although the chorus is always the same, so this visit was always the same, and that was a comfort. In the midst of studying for exams; the baby getting teeth; the car needing a brake job; and the growing protest about the country's involvement in Vietnam, the visit to Oma was as predictable, as soothing as a lullaby. Her soft, inward melancholy, her hand on my shoulder, were a reassurance and a blessing.

Little happened on our visits. We walked around the grounds. We ate a meal together. She held the baby. We talked in German, our private language. (My husband did not understand it.) She told me again and again the central stories of her life. They were the myths of my development. I never tired of hearing them. The stories were about how her mother had died in childbirth when she was very young and she had been raised by her cruel stepmother, who sent her out to buy sweets and ate them all herself. Or how she had gone to Italy as a young woman to study painting, and how she sat in the great museums painting copies of the masters, Rubens, Van Dyck. Once she had been in love with a young revolutionary, and her father had intervened and sent her away to live with an aunt and get over it. She told me how she had suffered so loudly at the birth of her first child that her husband, who had been pacing the hours of her pain in an adjoining room, came to her after the birth of the child and said: "I'll never put you through that again." There were five more children. She told me of the deaths of three of them: her sons, Walter and Heinz, her daughter, Ruth.

Her sons, she told me, were fine young men in their early twenties, one studying engineering, the other medicine. They went to Austria to ski. There was an avalanche. They didn't return. During the summer, fall and winter of that year the family waited. Only after the snows melted, late the next spring, and the bodies were found, could they begin to try to understand: the sons of the family, the only two sons, were dead.

Oma was in her menopause. She told me she went crazy with grief. The only comfort she found was in painting portraits of those she loved. This is the period of her life in which most of her fine portraits were painted. Two of them hang in my living room. One is of my mother, age nine, a study of a child grieving. The other is Oma's own stark and painful self-portrait, the image of a middle-aged woman, grieving. Her grief was a constant companion. I visited her grief each time I saw her. It is woven into my earliest sense of what life is about.

Seeing Hitler

The death of her sons had another side, a terrible irony that became the avenue of our family's survival. This side of the story opens simply in a restaurant in Berlin. When Oma told this part she spoke in a voice of such horror that even now, remembered years after her death, I can feel the fear at the bottom of my spine. For in that restaurant, in Berlin, she saw Hitler, just a few feet away from her. He looked straight at her and it pierced her being. She knew that he knew she was Jewish. I can see him, looking through her to me—cold terror. She felt that terror and went home and told my grandfather that they had to get out of the country, that this man Hitler would destroy them all.

My grandfather was a successful businessman. Being Jewish was not an important part of his identity. He was an engineer, the manager of a company. He always had been treated with respect. He thought my grand-mother was being hysterical. Hitler would pass, just like other difficult political phases passed. Always, telling this story, Oma would shake her head in wonder at the workings of fate. "We might all have died in con-centration camps. He would never have agreed to leave with one boy in medical school and the other studying engineering. If they had not died we might all have been dead."

And I might never have been born.

Today, a winter afternoon in Northern California, in the late 1980s, there is a chill in the air, but no rain, no snow. It's unseasonably mild. Staring at my computer terminal I feel lost in the layers of time. I see Hitler staring at my grandmother in a hotel in Berlin in the early 1930s. I see Oma telling this story to me; it's the mid-1960s. So much has hap-pened that I could not have foretold. Now, in my mid-forties, divorced, remarried, with children and stepchildren the ages of my grandmother's dead sons, I think of my Oma at the age I am now. Many of the major events of her life had not yet happened. Her sons were still alive. She still lived in the country of her birth. She had not yet painted many of her strongest paintings. I wonder what lies ahead for me and those I love?

Fear flickers and suddenly, like a child, I need my mother's voice. I call her, long distance. I get her answering machine. My mother's voice on tape is reassuring, familiar, embarrassing. I know her every inflection, her edge of anxiety when speaking English, though she has barely an accent, her slightly incorrect usage (after the sound of the "beeper"), her hesitance about her authority, her warmth. I am aware of the many levels on which I hear her voice, my feeling for her complexity, my scanning her for mood.

I see my daughters' faces, their anxious eyes scanning my face when I am sad, exhausted, angry. They read me like I read her.

She calls me back. I hear pleasure in her voice. Concern, too. Did she pick up the flicker of fear, of longing for her in my voice?

I find myself talking to her passionately about Oma; about my need for her to read what I have written about the family, to tell me the stories again, to be sure of the history.

Yes, she says, she will read what I have written, she will tell me the stories. I hear in her voice the dark place that has opened up, the place of the losses, the place of her feelings about her schoolmates who remained in Germany. Will she talk to me out of that place? Can I bear to listen? And then she surprises me. "You know," she says, "it would help you to understand me if you came to Germany with me. Why don't you come with me next summer? I want you to see the landscape of my childhood. I want you to come back behind the Holocaust with me."

In a dream I see the photograph of a tormented young girl. She is eight or nine years old. Her face is twisted with anguish and fear. She could be me as a child, or my mother. I know her anguish has something to do with surviving the death camps. It also has something to do with surviving the deaths of three children, three deeply beloved siblings.

My mother has thrown down an unexpected gauntlet. She says I cannot do justice to my subject without making a journey to my origins. But it's hard to see Germany as my origin: this is Germany before reunification, still in the shadows—Germany the horrible, the taboo, the land Jews never visit. My mother has gone several times, but I've not really listened to her talk about it. Germany is the land of unspeakable horrors, the land of my grandmother's dead children, of the big beautiful house my grandparents owned that was bombed in the war.

Disoriented, afraid, I turn to the grandmother in my soul. I go to stand before her self-portrait, hanging in my living room, painted after the death of her sons. Beside it hangs the portrait of my nine-year-old, grief-stricken mother. I look at my grandmother's eyes, as she saw them with the hard-edge of her painter's focus. There is a horror in them, a bitterness. My poor little mother is the saddest girl in the world. No little girl should have to feel such sorrow. She loved her big brothers passionately, especially Walter, who was studying to become a doctor. She thought she would become a nurse and work with Walter. But Walter died and then everything changed.

Below those two portraits is a third one, a baby picture Oma painted of me when I was two. She was worlds away from the Germany where she mourned her sons. She was in a new land, painting a new generation, but only fourteen years later. What softness and love there was in the hand that traced my round baby cheeks. What amazing sweetness after so much grief.

But the deaths of the boys were not the most important deaths foreshadowing my birth. There was an earlier one, the death of a daughter. That death is most particularly mine to possess: it is part of my origin and part of my name. It is the inner child in me who first understood the power of her Motherline. So I tell you this story in the voice of the girl within me.

Dear Ruth

It is summer vacation and I am nine. Every summer we come to this little town with a lake in Vermont. It is called Crystal Lake because it glistens in the sun and looks like bright crystals are shining on the blue water. We rent a log cabin with whole round logs put together like in the history books about Abraham Lincoln. In the summer everything is different. The air smells different. My mother takes deep breaths and says: Aaaah, here we have room to breathe. What she means is that we can all go out to the beach while Daddy is writing and not be stuck in the house with him when he gets mad.

In the summer I get a feeling in my chest that I never feel during the rest of the year. Especially when we are running out of the house in our swim suits, our towels all rolled up, and we have nothing to do but swim all day. Or walking in the sunlight with the green mountain so high it makes your head go up to see to the top of it. Or walking along the road toward the village and suddenly, around a bend, the sharp little church steeple appears, sticking into the sky. Or the sudden hot, sweet smell of the strawberries Mr. Grodin plants for us in the spring, now ripe in the summer sun. He calls our Dad "Guvna." Our Dad isn't a governor. He's a professor. It makes us all laugh, my Dad and Mom, too. This feeling is sharp, it almost hurts it is so strong, like sun has come into the dark of my chest, like Crystal Lake is shining inside of me.

Most summers Oma comes to visit. She talks to us, and she paints. She gets along better with Daddy than anyone else. He never gets mad at her. She has a way of saying his name, "Eli," like she is singing it. It makes him happy. He likes to make puns about her last name "Kunstler," which means artist. "Grandmother Artist what art art thou making today?" We children groan and he laughs. He's in a very good mood.

Oma sits for hours in a spot in the shade, her easel before her, painting the lake. She can make the crystals shine in her painting. It looks like the real lake and not like the real lake. If you look carefully at the painting she puts in colors, purples and browns and pinks, that I can't see in the water. But it looks like Crystal Lake. When I take out my crayons and draw the greens and blues I see, it never looks right. Sometimes she takes a mirror and looks at what she has painted in it.

"How come you do that, Oma?" She is standing with her back to her painting, looking at it in the mirror.

"When I have been painting for hours I am the same as the painting. I do not feel separate. I cannot anymore see it. But in the mirror everything is the other way around. It looks different. I can again see if the color is right, if the light and the shadows are right, if it all is in balance."

In the evenings, after dinner, we sit together and Oma tells stories. The air is a little cold at night, but when Oma is here it is happy and cold. "Oma, tell the story about Erich," my brothers shout. They always want to hear that story. And so she tells us, for the thousandth time, the story of the old tiger in the Berlin zoo, whose name was Erich. She had painted him when she was a young woman and he was near the end of his life. She couldn't paint very fast yet, because she was just learning, so it was good to paint an old tiger who didn't move around very much. He was dying. But he knew her. Every time she came to paint him he would greet her with a sound, and she would make this sound from the back of her throat, rolling a soft open "aarrrr" like Germans can do, and the soft skin of her throat shook gently.

"And then I would say, 'Guten tag Erich. Wie geht es?' Und Erich would raise his tired old head and say: 'aarrrr, aarrrr.' That is how he said Guten Tag to me." And one day, when she was almost finished painting, she came to the zoo, and Erich was not there. And then she was very sad, because she knew the tiger had died. But she finished the painting. And she let me have it to hang in my bedroom. I like the tiger. I like to look at it, hanging over my bed at home when I am going to sleep. I can hear the "aarrr, aarrr," and see my Oma's crinkled throat shake, and I feel safe in the night.

But the story I like the most is about Ruth. Ruth is my middle name. Like Ruth, I am the oldest child. Like Ruth, I have two younger brothers. Ruth died of diabetes when she was ten. I am nine. I don't have diabetes. But I could die when I'm ten.

Ruth was a remarkable child. She painted and wrote stories and was very creative all her childhood. Also, Oma says, she was wise beyond her years. Am I wise beyond my years? Ruth, she says, with sighs, was able to live a full life in her ten years. She was so special a child, so gifted. I want to be gifted. I want Oma to talk about me the way she talks about Ruth. Only not so sad, because I'm alive.

Oma has a book of poems and stories that were written by Ruth.

After her death her parents published it. They said it was a book for all those who had known and loved their little Ruth. It is sixty-three pages long. How can a ten-year-old girl have written sixty-three pages of stories and poems? I don't even have one page to show for all my nine years. Often she reads us stories Ruth wrote. They are good stories. There is one about a leaf in the fall. It is the first one in the book because Oma says it is about death, that Ruth must have known that she would die soon. In it the leaf tells the story of its life, and it was a happy life, born into so much sunlight, amazed by the beauty of the world and the sunlight. When Oma reads that part, in German, about "sonnenlicht" and "sonnenstrahlen" I feel that sharp bright feeling in my chest, and see the crystals in Crystal Lake. But in Ruth's story the weather changed, and it was fall. And the story ends with this line: "Da zitterte das Blatt und dann kam der Traumwinter." It means the leaf shivered, and then the dreamwinter began. Only it's more beautiful in German. The word *Traumwinter* sounds so deep and full of mystery. Oma says this last line means that Ruth accepted her death and was not afraid. But inside me, where the sun was, it now feels dark and cold. I wonder how Ruth felt, when she died.

I want to be a writer like Ruth. Only I wouldn't die. I'd write beautiful stories and poems and make Oma happy. But here I am nine years old and I have barely started. How can I write sixty-three pages in one year? I have written one poem. I like it and Oma likes it and Daddy likes it. It came to me one day walking on the road and seeing clouds coming over Crystal Lake. It was like a voice in my head. First it was rhythm, then words came, making the sound of how it feels when clouds change the air and the light.

> *Low cower the pine trees*
> *In fear of the wind*
> *The shivering flowers*
> > *pull petals in close*
> *The waters of lakes*
> > *in anger do rise*
> *For a storm is coming from the north*
> *A storm is coming on.*

Later, when I am twelve, someone gives me a diary with a lock and a key. I name my diary Ruth and address my deepest, most private thoughts to her.

Inheriting the Dead

My grandmother's dead children are woven into all that I am, and all that my mother is. And whenever I visited my Oma I visited Ruth, Walter, and Heinz. Woven into the fabric of dead children is all that she taught me about color and shadow and light. These were the things she wanted me to carry on for her: memories of her dead and her vision of the world. We walked on the grounds of the sanitarium, perched on a hill overlooking vineyards. Look, she would say, how green the hills are in winter, how yellow they become in late spring. And as they yellow the vines turn green. And look, she would say, how the light is, changing from morning to early afternoon, changing to early evening. That was her favorite light, beginning about four or five on summer afternoons, the vineyards drenched in gold and the shadows growing dense. She spoke about the color of shadows, purple, blue, and mauve. To this day I see the wine country with her painter's eyes. Our family has paintings looking out of all the windows of my Oma's life, except these final vineyard views. She could paint no longer. She was tired. Her friends, the people of her generation who had fled Germany when she did, were all dying. She hoped she would die soon; she was ready.

I wasn't ready, or so I thought. I needed her to give continuity to my life. When I saw her I no longer felt isolated in my nuclear family cubicle surrounded by dirty diapers. I knew that I came from a history and could move into a future. She, after all, had been an artist as well as a mother. And she had been both for a long lifetime. She had a past that she emerged from so there must be a future for me to move toward. I needed my son to sit on her lap. He would be unusually quiet and contained, as though he understood her frailty and her sacredness to us.

I have a picture of her old face, from more than twenty years ago, gazing down at his young face, with his sweet round cheeks and warm, blue-eyed smile. It's the same smile he has now as a young man. But she, my Oma, is dead. And he has only an unconscious memory, living in his body, to connect him to his mother's mother's mother.

I always told myself that I would get her life story on tape. I never did. She was in her eighties and I was so young, so diffuse. I was pregnant again and then we were off to India, to the Peace Corps. We were living the life of our generation, angry about the Vietnam war, discovering the subtlety of Asian cultures, expanding our consciousness. When I returned home with a five-year-old son, a two-year-old daughter, and my youngest, newly adopted Indian child, I was not prepared to see my Oma dying, inarticulate, bellowing an ancient, wordless agony and wearing diapers. Too late to get her story on a tape recorder. Too late to get her blessing for my daughters.

Do the dead know when they walk with the living? Oma, do you know that you are always with me? Your life work of painting hangs in my home and in my office. Do you remember the watercolor of the living room in Berkeley where I visited you often? You painted the light streaming in through the arched window onto floors and rugs. It is a painting of inner space—one you live in as an old woman and I visited as a girl. You served me tomato soup and crackers in the light from that window, and taught me how to sketch. That painting hangs in my office now, grounding me in my own childhood as I listen to the stories of other people's childhoods.

Do you remember your blue vase? It was one of your favorites, a deep, glowing blue. You painted it often with flowers. I keep the vase in my office and put fresh flowers in it, every week. Strange how objects survive their owners.

Sometimes, Oma, you visit me in dreams. I am grateful for those visits. Just a few nights ago you came to me. You showed me pictures of people I did not know, people who had gone to the concentration camps. Some had survived, some had not. "Remember the dead," you say. "If you don't, who will?"

I stand before your self-portrait in my living room. Facing the terrible grief of the middle of your life I promise you that I will go to Germany, that I will visit the graves of the dead, that I will make the journey to the realm of the ancestors and honor the place of your origin.

ON MY FATHER'S SIDE

In the course of her life, a woman has inner dialogues with many voices from her childhood. Buried memories, especially painful ones, release essential energies when they are uncovered. In psychotherapy, we examine those stories, open our souls to forbidden, repressed stories. We remember the secrets we were told to forget. We open dark chambers in our souls and let the light in. To remember is literally to bring back members of our family, aspects of ourselves, to reclaim the dismembered members of our souls.

During the writing of this book my own stories of origin underwent a revolutionary change. I had always thought of myself, and my work with my Motherline, as primarily descended from my mother's side of the family, from her mother, my Kunstler Oma, with her painter's eyes and her passionate melancholy. The girl within me, who wrote poetry, who wanted to be like the lost ten-year-old aunt for whom I'd been named, is an aspect of my self that is inextricably tied to my maternal grandmother. A fierce love of my Oma and her dead daughter, Ruth, seemed to be my channel to the creative aspects of my nature.

Most of us have forgotten essential parts of our stories, locked them in closets with childhood terrors and childhood taboos. Terrible things had happened before my birth, that I knew. What I did not know, at least consciously, was that the neglected ghost of a paternal grandmother haunted my life.

In conceiving my Motherline I did not think about my father's mother, Clara Vrodsky, who died before I was born. She had always been an indistinct figure to me, lost somewhere in the mass graves of Hitlerian Europe, and in my tumultuous feelings about my father and his sister, Lizaveta. The photo of my Vrodsky grandparents, in a silver frame on the piano, showed a handsome grandfather with high Russian cheekbones, but a grandmother whose face sagged with exhaustion. My father seldom spoke of them. On the few occasions he did, it was to describe his father as a loser, a man without a spine. There was always bile in his words about his father and some sort of painful regret when he spoke of his mother.

Once Oma told me that my brothers looked like her side of the family, but that I looked like my Vrodsky grandmother. I felt hurt. I did not want to look like my father's mother, although I was ashamed of feeling that way. I did not know I had a resistance to the aspect of my female self carried on my father's side until one soft spring day when I received a letter she had written to my parents before I was born. I realized then that the shadow that had been cast on my girlhood when my Aunt Lizaveta came to live with us threw one whole side of my Motherline into darkness. This is the story the girl within me tells.

The Concentration Camp Witch

I am seven years old. We live in a brick row house in Queens. All the houses are alike. But our house is different because it has a fish pond in front. The pond is deep and dark. If you look in it, and hold very still, you can some-

times see the catfish that live under the lily pads like shadows with whis-
kers. Our house is also different on the inside. None of the children I know
have parents like mine. They speak German to each other and sometimes
to us. Often my father gets very angry and makes a dark cloud fill the
house. Then my mother cries, and my brothers and I are afraid to say or
do anything. I have two younger brothers. They share a room and I have
my own room. That is one good thing. My brothers are either fighting or
being silly. When I don't have to take care of them so my mother can type
for my father, I can go in my own room and read.

Lizaveta comes. She is from the concentration camp. They chopped
off her toes one winter when they froze and so she hobbles in great, black,
witch's shoes. She is my father's sister and they fight like brother and sister,
only worse, because they are grown-ups. I have to move in with my brothers and I can hear her through the wall, in my room next door, walking
around. Her walk is uneven, like someone who limps, kadumpf, kadumpf.
There is something wrong with her. Her body is humped and small. She
is as little as I am. They say it is because she had polio when she was a
child. But I know that isn't it. It is the concentration camp. It makes her
sick inside, oozing, like a cut oozes when it's not healing right. A sticky
poison comes out of her when she speaks, which makes people feel weird,
and it is hard to get away from her. You can't tell what is true, and what
is unreal. She was engaged to a handsome count, she tells us. My father
says that is nonsense, she is making it up. Her eyes are luminous and green,
like my father's eyes. They stare into you, beyond you, they look into some
space that is you and isn't you. I don't want to be looked at that way.

She has chocolates in her room, the kind that come in a big box; and
each piece of chocolate is different, cradled in ruffled paper. Some are
wrapped in bright foil. If you study them you can sometimes tell what
each one has in it. The square ones are usually caramel inside. I don't like
that kind. The dark round ones squirt a liqueur when you bite into them.
They are pretty good. My favorite is marzipan. I can't usually tell which
one has the marzipan, and if one of my brothers gets it he'll show me,
laughing, "See what I got?" and then eat it all himself. My brothers don't
even like marzipan.

Chocolate is forbidden in our family. When people come over to dinner they often hand my father big boxes of beautiful chocolates. Flowing
from German to English we children hear them say: "Fur sie, and auch fur
die kinder." Then they wink at us children, who are hanging around shyly.
"You youngsters aren't interested in these are you?" My father laughs his

company laugh, pretending to be just like other parents who indulge their children's sweet tooth just a little. Sometimes, when a guest really insists, we are allowed to choose one little chocolate, to be eaten after dinner. Our father doesn't want his guests to know how strict he is. But as soon as they leave, the chocolates disappear. I've discovered his hiding place in the buffet, in the dining room, in the locked part. I know where they hide the key and sometimes I steal just one chocolate at a time, so they don't notice. I don't tell my brothers because they'll eat too much, and we'll get caught.

But when Lizaveta comes, we can eat lots of chocolate in her room. Somehow it doesn't taste as good, sitting there with Lizaveta's eyes on us, waiting for our father to find us and explode. There he is, knocking at the door. "What's going on in there?" His knock becomes louder and louder. Very slowly Lizaveta limps to the door, unlocks it. "What do you get so upset for? You begrudge me a little time with my niece and my nephews?" Her voice is soft, ingratiating, false. It infuriates my father. "What are you feeding them? I've told you sweets are bad for them!"

By now my father has pushed me out the door, has my brother Leon by the arm, and is reaching for David, the youngest. Lizaveta grabs him, pulls him into her breasts, hunches her whole body around him. All you can see is David's little white face and great green eyes, terrified. "It's not good all the time to deprive children. They want to be like other children. Eli, why are you so dictatorial? A little chocolate gives pleasure and it's not so bad. Isn't that right, children? You like to eat your Aunt Lizaveta's chocolates." I look at my father swelling with rage. Lizaveta seems to be stroking his anger, making it bigger and more ferocious. My father grabs his youngest child. Lizaveta keeps her hold. It is like a tug of war, with David as the rope. Without our father's restraining hands on us, Leon and I flee, leaving behind our sobbing little brother, Lizaveta's sinuous voice, father's crescendoing shouts.

Mother is in the kitchen, making Lizaveta's lunch. I can tell from the back of her neck and the slope of her shoulders that she has heard the whole thing. She has heard it a hundred times. Her tiredness makes gray pools of exhaustion at her feet. She will bring Lizaveta's lunch to her on a tray. Then she will make our lunch, and put my brothers down for a nap, which they think they are too old to take. Then I'll help her fix my father's lunch. I'll serve him his special herring, his pumpernickel bread and Bel Paese cheese, because he needs her to type a manuscript.

My brothers are mad that I don't have to take a nap. But they don't have to cut up cheese and apples, just so. I don't know how Mommy does it when I am in school. She has David, still too young for kindergarten, getting into everything, and my father's lunch and manuscripts, and Lizaveta in her witch shoes. She doesn't laugh much these days, our mother who can be as silly as a child. And when we crawl to her for comfort, she has none left to give. Lizaveta's concentration-camp poison fills the house. It makes my father shout like Hitler. And it makes my mother gray and tired. I think that Lizaveta must be a witch who has put a curse on us all, especially me, because I am a young girl, without deformity. She puts the concentration-camp thing in me. It makes me feel sick. One day I throw up again and again. Inside me it is dark blue, like a flickering flame. The flame goes out.

Then I am flung over my father's shoulder. I remember feeling the urgency, the love in his frightened hands. They take me in a taxi to the hospital. I have intravenous feeding because I am dehydrated. No one knows why I am sick. Suddenly all the juice of life has gone out of me. They have to pour it back in through long, clear tubes and a needle in my arm. They say it is sugar water. The doctors are feeding me sugar, even though my father always says sugar is bad for children. I never point this out to my father. I think it would make him mad. When I get back home, Lizaveta has gone to live with my Oma in California. I have my room back and I think how strange it is, lying in my bed, that just a little while ago I was on the other side of that wall, hearing the big black witch shoes going kadumpf, kadumpf, in the night.

A Letter from Before My Birth

Thirty-five years later Lizaveta has been dead for years, and it's my father's funeral. He died between summer and fall, devoured rapidly by a stomach cancer. We line up, my brothers and I, even my mother, long divorced from my father, to put shovels of dirt on his coffin. It is a profoundly ambivalent custom. We bury our dead. This makes it unbearably real: ashes to ashes, dust to dust. We enact the finality of it, putting familiar flesh into the earth. And we the living separate ourselves from the dead. There he lies, covered by earth we have shoveled, while we continue to live, and walk on the earth.

Winter comes, and then spring. On a sunny day in my forty-second year, a day I have set aside for writing and reflection, I receive a letter written before my birth. It is from my father's mother, Lizaveta's mother, my grandmother, Clara. It was addressed to my mother and father and found in my father's safe deposit box, labeled "Mother's farewell letter." Because I am the executor of my father's estate, I received a copy of the letter, among other documents. The letter is in German. I understand much of it. The letter begins:

> "Dearest Giesele, dear Eli:
> If you receive this, understand that it is a farewell letter. If, however, God lets me live until there is peace, then this letter will be superfluous. Then I can straighten everything out myself."

Clara was dying of cancer in a concentration camp in Holland. Lizaveta was with her, having given up an opportunity to escape the Nazis because she refused to leave her mother alone. The purpose of the letter was to convey her last wish to my parents: that they do for Lizaveta what they would have wanted to do for her, Clara, had she lived. She says to my father, and I can see her motherly forefinger pointing at him through the years: "Elias, God has blessed you with an open hand, taken you out of Europe, given you a wife and a job. God expects you to do something in return. Do for Lizaveta whatever is necessary without hurting her. She is my most urgent concern. She has suffered the most terrible inhumanity because of me. Remember that with my death the last spiritual bond is cut."

I can hear an edge to her voice in the letter, the edge of the fearful mother, asking her son to do something she knows he won't want to do, calling up all her maternal authority, calling up the power of the last request, to make him obey.

Suddenly I understand that Lizaveta came to live with us in my childhood because my parents were trying to fulfill Clara's last wish. It didn't work out. Even the voice of my grandmother from the grave could not make Eli and Lizaveta get along. I think of my father, of what ate away at him, of what must have driven him crazy. He had left his mother and sister in Europe. He knew that terrible things were happening to the Jews. Safe with my mother's family, my mother told me that there was one long night when my father wept and wept. He could not stop crying. He never told her what it was, but she knew he was crying about his mother, that he sensed she was dying. After that, my mother said, he never cried again. He shut it all down.

Not entirely true, I told her. There was once, after you were divorced, that I went with him to see the movie *Judgment at Nuremberg*. There was footage in that movie of the concentration camps, of how people looked when they were liberated. Like walking skeletons, like the living dead, how Lizaveta must have looked when the Russians set her free. My father sobbed in the movie theatre. For me it was like catching a glimpse of him naked. I did not ask him about it. He never referred to it. But I have never forgotten the wrenching sobs that tore up from the bottom of his being.

My father carried unbearable pain in him, unbearable guilt. I know he was not responsible for any of what happened. I think he did not know that. The guilt was so deep he could not bring it up to sort through what was his and what was not. So he swallowed it, and lived his life about his work, honed his scholarly craft to a fine, diamond edge. He was a superb scholar, a crafter of words and of thoughts. But it was impossible ever to be entirely with him because of that terrible guilt that he swallowed every day of his life, that sat in the middle of his body, blocking his innermost truth. I wonder if it was that which devoured him in the end?

What mysteries our parents are. We spend our lives trying to imagine what it was like to be them.

As I read my grandmother Clara's letter, her fervent wish for her daughter's safety, her concern that there be a reconciliation between brother and sister, I remember my last visit with my father, before we knew he was dying. I knew something was wrong with him. A white luminescence glowed under his skin, had been with him the last few times I saw him. I asked him if I could bring a tape recorder, have him tell us about his life. I wanted to feel close to him, to understand how he saw himself. He resisted. No tape recorder. But one evening, when my children and youngest brother were with us, he summoned us in that king-of-the-mountain way of his: we were to gather around him; his wife was to serve us her fresh apple juice, healthy for the digestive system. Wasn't it delicious? My children, hiding their grimaces, nodded obediently. He told us the story of his mother's last days, and of his sister Lizaveta's courage and loyalty. Never before had I heard this story.

In all the family stories we had heard my father tell, he had been the hero. In one story my father made the family's exodus from Germany possible by writing his doctoral dissertation at the University of Heidelberg in a dizzying thirty days. It was a brilliant piece of work, launching a distinguished career at the worst possible time for a young Jewish scholar. After it was signed he and his family fled to Holland across borders in the night. They were illegal aliens.

In another story the family is threatened by Dutch immigration officials. Unless they could legitimize their status in the country, they would be taken to the borders and released. Since they had no country to return to, this meant they would be shot by border patrols. My father saved the day. He knew the violin teacher of the Dutch royal family. At my father's request, this music teacher told the Queen and the Princess about the plight of a young musician who had written a famous dissertation about a Dutch composer. The subject of my father's doctoral dissertation saved the family. The royal family intervened in the fate of the Vrodskys, and their legal status was achieved.

Such were the stories I grew up with. The point of them was usually my father's brilliance, his ability to prevent disasters or to make miracles. If it hadn't been for his foresightful intervention I would have fallen off tables as a baby, my brother's hernia would never have been diagnosed, the Vrodsky family would not have been able to stay in Holland.

But this summer, with children and grandchildren gathered around him, my father told another kind of story, betraying an attitude I'd never heard from him before, about the courage of others, the courage of women. He was not center stage because the story took place after he had left Europe, leaving his parents and Lizaveta behind. His parents were separated and his mother was ill with cancer. The Germans had invaded Holland, and all Jews were in danger.

His father, who was still protective of his estranged wife, sold the family silver to raise money. He used the money to buy protection for mother and daughter in a convent. For some time they were safe in the convent. But then the mother grew so ill she had to be hospitalized. Lizaveta was terrified for her mother, knowing that if she were taken to the hospital the Nazis would find her. But there was no option; Clara was too sick, the nuns could not care for her. Clara begged Lizaveta to stay in the convent, where she was safe. But Lizaveta would not be separated from her mother, would not let her mother be alone. She stayed with her in the hospital. And when the Nazis came to take them both away, Lizaveta stayed at her mother's side. "My Mother, Gott sei dank, died soon after the Nazis took them." My father sat on the couch, tears streaming down his face. "But Lizaveta, that dear brave girl, had to go through it all. She would not let our mother die alone. And then she was alone. And she survived, even Bergen Belsen."

A MESSAGE FROM THE BOOK OF JOB

I remember being in Lizaveta's house in California after her death. My father was with me. I held in my hands a beautiful Jewish bible with silver plates on which were carved the seven branched candlelabra. I showed it to my father, who asked if I wanted it. "Yes," I said. I held it in my hands, knowing I would open it to a message from her. The bible opened to the book of Job.

>   Ch. III. v.20 Wherefore is light given to him that is in misery
> and life to the bitter in soul?
>   v.25 For the thing which I greatly feared is come upon me and
> that which I was afraid of is come unto me.

I felt humbled, taken to task for the years of anger at my difficult aunt. Who would I be had I had polio as a child, had I been a prisoner in Bergen Belsen? Who can presume to make judgments on the sufferings of others? In life I feared her power and stayed away from her. In her death I could reclaim her, marvel that she stayed with her mother in such terrifying circumstances, that she wrote poetry in Bergen Belsen, that she had the courage to survive.

My father finally made his peace with her before he died, by telling the story of her heroism. I can see his face, his not-yet-conscious death gleaming through thin skin, the tears flowing, as I read the letter from my grandmother Clara.

What complexity of relationship lies behind the subtleties of this letter? Why is it that my mother is called dearest, "liebste Giesele," while my father only rates a dear? Was there tension between mother and son? Great love between Clara and her daughter-in-law? My father is dead. But even in life there was no talking to him about such matters. Lizaveta, were she alive, would have told me her own heavily embroidered version of the story in which her magic and clairvoyance would have played a major role. I would have had difficulty sorting out the truth. My father still has sisters who live in Israel. I've never visited them there. My mother, as usual, is my only source of family history.

"Your grandmother Vrodsky," she tells me, "was a very fine woman. She was kind, intelligent, even-tempered, loving."

"Then how did she get two such crazy children?" I ask, miserable that I have so long misjudged this unknown grandmother by the personalities of two of her children, and because of that misjudgment, never claimed her. My mother, with her considerable training in early childhood development and family therapy, believes as strongly as do I in our modern psychological paradigm, that early childhood and parental influence are powerful molders of human personality. But childhood doesn't explain everything.

"I don't know," she says, "how they got so crazy. Their lives were very hard. And the war did terrible things to people. Clara was a good mother. But her life was full of suffering. If anything, she was too indulgent, too permissive."

"You know," I say, "she sounds like the kind of mother you are, the kind of mother I am." Suddenly, I find I can identify with my paternal grandmother and can imagine how Clara Vrodsky felt about her brilliant, arrogant only son. She had indulged him and set no limits with him and, in the end, this plagued her. Her last request is written in the torment of not trusting him to listen to her. I can imagine her frantic concern for her crippled child, for the child she fears will not be able to survive on her own. In the letter, Clara's love and warm feelings flow toward my mother who was much more capable of receiving them than my father was.

She had known my mother since my mother was thirteen. My father was the piano teacher in my mother's family. My mother and her sister, knowing that Clara and Lizaveta were sick and poor, had helped them out by cleaning house. Here is Clara's voice, speaking to her daughter-in-law. "Dearest Giesele, how shortly I knew you. I wanted so much to see you develop. You are only a child yourself. I wanted so much to know your child. Who knows, maybe you're expecting?"

"You know," my mother says, "the time in which she wrote that letter was the time in which you were conceived. Nine months later you were born and she was dead."

The fog lifts from an unknown place in my soul. And on this soft spring day, forty-three years after Clara Vrodsky's death, I learn that I am not only descended, spiritually and psychologically, from my mother's side of the family. I am also descended from the mother of my father whose voice is so familiar, speaking from a time before my birth. She values development, she values continuity, she fears for her children, she greets the grandchildren who will never know her, and she bargains with God for a sense of meaning. "May God take all I have suffered," she writes at the end of her letter, "as a sacrifice for all of you, that your lives should be better. Then this will have had some meaning."

I realize that this unknown grandmother has been speaking through me for many years: demanding a voice for the mothers of mothers, requiring of me that I attend to the lived experience of women. Although I did not know this until halfway through the writing, this book is most importantly for her.

One soft spring day, in the late 1980s, reading a letter from before I was born, I decided I would go to Israel and meet my unknown aunts, Tania and Esther, Clara's daughters. I would go to Israel to remember my father's side of the Motherline. And I would go to Germany to remember my mother's side.

We never got to bury you, Clara. My father never threw his shovelful of dirt upon your grave. A restless ghost, you have haunted me without my knowing you. Can you rest in peace now, knowing that Giesele's daughter knows you in herself? Knowing that your difficult son came around to an appreciation of your daughter's courage? Knowing that your great grandchildren have been told your story, have read your letter, have been given your blessing from the suffering of your life? We understand the subtle gift your letter gives us. We are not to feel guilty for what happened to you. That was my father's great mistake. We are to care for the living, to develop into who we are capable of being, knowing that in doing so, and in remembering you, we honor you and the bargain you made with your God.

CHAPTER EIGHT

GHOST STORIES:
Entering the Realm
of the Ancestors

*Even as a young child I could sense the unspoken terrors that
surrounded our house, the ones that chased my mother until she
hid in a secret, dark corner of her mind. And still they found
her. I watched, over the years, as they devoured her, piece by
piece, until she disappeared and became a ghost.*

AMY TAN[1]

Motherline stories are haunted by ghosts. The unredeemed grief and
suffering of generations of women stalk us. Those who were stillborn and those who died in childbirth, those who were orphaned,
abandoned, murdered, and abused, live on past their lives in the nightmares of their descendants. Women whose ties to life and family were dis-
rupted by the wild tides of history—natural disasters, human cruelty in
war, slavery, genocide, and political oppression—cast shadows upon our
souls.

Their stories have seldom been told from a woman's point of view.
But in the inspired voices of contemporary writers like Amy Tan (*The Joy
Luck Club*) and Toni Morrison (*Beloved*), we are hearing Motherline stories
filled with the power of ghosts, stories that ground us in our ancestral
roots.

HONORED GUESTS FROM THE UNDERWORLD

The word *ghost* is derived from the German word *Geist*, which means both spirit and guest. In pre-Christian Europe the relationship between the living and the dead was hospitable. Ghosts were honored guests, especially at certain sacred times of the year such as Halloween, which was seen as a "crucial joint between the seasons . . . allowing contact between the ghost-world and the mortal one."[2]

Contemporary North American culture operates under the illusion that we have escaped the ghosts of the Old World. We pour ourselves into concrete, materialistic, modern shapes and deny the power of our ancestors. We don't identify with the myth-bearing cultures out of which we have sprung. Amy Tan evokes the gap between the worlds of mothers and daughters in *The Joy Luck Club*:

> All these years I kept my mouth closed so selfish desires would not fall out. And because I remained quiet for so long now my daughter does not hear me. She sits by her fancy swimming pool and hears only her Sony Walkman, her cordless phone, her big, important husband asking her why they have charcoal and no lighter fluid.
>
> All these years I kept my true nature hidden, running along like a small shadow so nobody could catch me. And because I moved so secretly now my daughter does not see me. She sees a list of things to buy, her checkbook out of balance, her ashtray sitting crooked on a straight table.
>
> And I want to tell her this: We are lost, she and I, unseen and not seeing, unheard and not hearing, unknown by others.[3]

We have lost our souls in the world of objects and prestige, lost our mothers and what they know of the deep, painful truths of life. We have forgotten the meaning of the underworld, the ancient Eleusinian imagery of the mown ear of grain, the cycle of death and rebirth. We have forgotten that we are animals, entirely dependent on the earth and what it produces for our existence.

The search for the Motherline requires a downward journey into the realm of the ancestors. Here one discovers lost meanings, forgotten lives, generations of grief; here one begins to feel the power of the ghosts one has feared to acknowledge.

Many kinds of ghosts have their way with us. Those we have buried consciously, whose lives have been full and whose deaths have been timely, leave us with shivers of guilt about our unfinished business with them. Eventually we make our peace with them. Sometimes they become guides or mentors in our inner lives. They remind us that we are mortal and connected to those who came before us. These are the ghosts of lives fully lived. My mother's mother, my Oma, is such a ghost for me, inspiring and guiding the work of this book.

There are also ghosts who are not dead, those impossible relations we prefer to forget: the difficult mother we swear we will never again speak to, the prodigal daughter gone astray whose family pretends she never existed. My father's provocative survivor sister, Lizaveta, exiled from my childhood, was a ghost of this sort in my life.

There is such a living ghost in *The Joy Luck Club*.

> When I was a young girl in China, my grandmother told me my mother was a ghost. This did not mean my mother was dead. In those days, a ghost was anything we were forbidden to talk about. So I knew Popo wanted me to forget my mother on purpose, and this is how I came to remember nothing of her.[4]

Such a ghost is a part of life that is denied, sent into exile because she represents what cannot be integrated, or because she has broken cultural taboos. She is the living dead. Her repressed life makes itself felt in psychological blocks and family dysfunction. Novels such as Amy Tan's begin the enormous work of reclaiming discarded women, reconnecting us all to the forgotten and forbidden aspects of the feminine self.

In a powerful scene where the grandmother, Popo, is dying, the young daughter of the woman who is a ghost grows to see beyond her grandmother's prohibition. She comes to love her mother, to see in her "my own true nature. What was beneath my skin. Inside my bones."

> I saw my mother on the other side of the room. Quiet and sad. She was cooking a soup, pouring herbs and medicines into the steaming pot. And then I saw her pull up her sleeve and pull out a sharp knife. She put this knife on the softest part of her arm. I tried to close my eyes, but could not.
>
> And then my mother cut a piece of meat from her arm. Tears poured from her face and blood spilled to the floor.
>
> My mother took her flesh and put it in the soup. She cooked magic in the ancient tradition to try to cure her mother this one last time. She opened Popo's mouth, already too tight from trying to keep

her spirit in. She fed her this soup, but that night Popo flew away with her illness.

Even though I was young, I could see the pain of the flesh and the worth of the pain.

This is how a daughter honors her mother. It is *shou* so deep it is in your bones. The pain of the flesh is nothing. The pain you must forget. Because sometimes that is the only way to remember what is in your bones. You must peel off your skin, and that of your mother, and her mother before her.[5]

Motherline stories are not for the faint of heart. They tear us out of our skin deep images of life; they take us down to the terrible bones of the human condition. They are not tales of heroism or of the conquest of new frontiers. They are about gathering together the pieces of what has been broken or rent. Merlin Stone, author of *When God was a Woman*, tells us that in the myths of many cultures the goddess journeys not to "find an answer or seek a source of wisdom." Rather she journeys to "gather something together."

Isis traveled throughout Egypt to gather the scattered body parts of her brother/consort Osiris, whom She reassembled. Tara travels in Her Boat of Salvation to rescue souls shipwrecked on the Ocean of Life and brings them back to safe shores. The Shekhina travels about the lands to gather up the Jewish souls in exile and helps to bring them home. Nu Kwa traveled throughout the world after a universal holocaust, repairing and restoring the shattered columns that hold up heaven; She then patched the torn heavens together again. Demeter searched far and wide for Her daughter Kore/Persephone, to reunite her family.[6]

On her journey to make sense of her female lineage, a daughter is forced to confront what haunts her mother and her grandmothers. Often these are restless ghosts, the discordant souls of those who died violently, ripped out of their lives before their time. We fear their terrible fates. Understanding their power reorients us in our lives.

In Toni Morrison's profound novel, *Beloved*, the ghost of the baby daughter of a runaway slave woman springs into terrifying clarity. Her death was the unbearable solution to the unbearable situation of slavery. *Beloved* haunts us with the suffering, the wrenching separations that African-American women endured for centuries in our land. Here is the situation of a slave mother:

Seven times she had done that: held a little foot; examined the fat fingertips with her own—fingers she never saw become the male or female hands a mother would recognize anywhere. She didn't know to this day what their permanent teeth looked like; or how they held their heads when they walked. Did Patty lose her lisp? What color did Famous' skin finally take? Was that a cleft in Johnny's chin or just a dimple that would disappear soon's his jawbone changed? Four girls, and the last time she saw them there was no hair under their arms. Does Ardelia still love the burned bottom of bread? All seven gone or dead.[7]

The dialogue of development between a mother and her children was brutally interrupted, the looping of intergenerational connections butchered, the mother left with only grief "at her center, the desolated center where the self that was no self made its home."[8] Morrison tells a Motherline story that takes us down to the primal depths. A slave mother has no power over the lives of her children; she can't even protect them. Her only power is death. She can kill her children at birth because they are the product of her violation at the hands of white men. In the case of Beloved, the runaway slave mother slits her baby daughter's throat rather than let the white men recapture her.

Anybody white could take your whole self for anything that came to mind. Not just work, kill, or maim you, but dirty you. Dirty you so bad you couldn't like yourself anymore. Dirty you so bad you forgot who you were and couldn't think it up. And though she and others lived through and got over it, she could never let it happen to her own. The best thing she was, was her children. Whites might dirty her all right, but not her best thing, her beautiful, magical best thing—the part of her that was clean. No undreamable dreams about whether the headless, feetless torso hanging in the tree with a sign on it was her husband or Paul A; whether the bubbling-hot girls in the colored-school fire set by patriots included her daughter; whether a gang of whites invaded her daughter's private parts, soiled her daughter's thighs and threw her daughter out of the wagon.[9]

Beloved, the furious, seductive, mother-hungry ghost of the baby whose mother slit her throat to save her, devours her mother's life. Her sister, Denver, who has lived in the narrow confines of her dependency on her mother, finds herself abandoned by her mother's mad passion for a ghost. It is quiet, understated Denver who, in the end, carries the reader's hope for healing the ruptured feminine self. Denver has to piece together the story of her birth, her sister's death, her mother's life. She must comprehend Beloved's insatiability in the context of her mother's unredeemable guilt. The terrible dance of this mother/ghost-daughter couple forces Denver into what she fears the most—the world of whitemen. Hers is the heroism of the feminine, the unsung power of loyalty, devotion, and the determination to keep life going.

Amy Tan and Toni Morrison both have entered the ancestral underworlds of their cultures with open eyes, daring to see the terrible realities of the Motherline. My own work on this book, too, has required a journey to piece together my Motherline, so that the stories of the restless ghosts of my family may be told, and the bones of the ancestors remembered.

THE PROMISED LAND

> It's too late to change you, but I'm telling you this because I worry about your baby. I worry that someday she will say, "Thank you, Grandmother, for the gold bracelet. I'll never forget you." But later, she will forget her promise. She will forget she had a grandmother.
>
> *Amy Tan*[10]

In our mature development there are moments which require that the entire narrative of our lives be transformed, memory reconsidered, life reevaluated. The death of a parent is often such a moment, arousing the ghosts of a life. When my father died the ghost of his mother leapt out of the crack between the upper and lower worlds. She demanded a hearing. She required of me another part of the journey to my ancestral underworld: I had to meet her daughters in the Promised Land.

I am sitting on a couch in Manhattan discussing God and witches with my five-year-old niece. Here I am the aunt and this dark-eyed child with the fiercely questing spirit is the niece. Who will she be when she's my age?

The next day I am squeezed into a narrow airplane seat in mid-air. We are about to descend upon the Promised Land. In a matter of hours, I will be the niece and my aunts will be strangers. Aunt Esther. Aunt Tania. The names do not roll over the tongue with childhood ease. These sisters of my father didn't know me when I was five. I didn't know them when they were in the middle of their lives. I have never heard their stories from the Motherline.

We have flown from midnight at Kennedy Airport into the next day. My watch says 8:30 A.M. New York time. My husband's watch says 3:30 P.M. Tel Aviv time. This great, humming vessel, this huge bird of the night, is carrying over 400 Jews to the Promised Land. Old ghetto voices tug at me. I am haunted by ancient Jewish fears. My inner voice takes on a Yiddish lilt: Why crowd so many Jews in one place? You want to make a target for all the anti-Semites in the world?

It is a difficult journey, swimming upstream in time, against our bodily cycles, against our orientation in time and space. We get there fast—in just one night. No journey by ship or camel for weeks or months. And yet, getting off and on planes, I see the bone-tired faces of the crowd; they look ancient to me. So have travelers always looked. Suffering the difficulty of the journey because the idea of the destination looms larger than the pain of the moment. Squeezing past half-asleep Jews to get to the bathroom, standing in line, walking up and down the aisle, drinking water, waking up a seat mate in order to return to a seat. Bagels for breakfast, or is it dinner, or lunch?

What joy when we arrive. Illuminated faces. Clapping. Tears in the eyes of the dark-haired woman in front of us, who reaches across her daughter and takes her husband's hand. Even I, who needed a demanding ghost to send me on this journey, can feel it now: the sacred moment of return to the collective home, to the land of our history, of our fierce Jewish soul.

It is 1987, before the intifada, the Arab revolt that changed Israeli consciousness. In the limousine to Jerusalem, the man beside us—born in Poland, raised in Israel, gone to America, home to visit his parents—explains the history of the land we pass through, telling the events of 1948 and of Samson and Delilah and the Philistines in one sweep of his language.

We drive up ancient hills where David fought, pass rusting hulks of tanks from 1948, left by the state to remind us of our history, up, up to the glowing city of Jerusalem. *"Yerushalayim,"* our self-appointed guide says, stroking each syllable like a lover's name.

What Kind of a God?

We are touring Jerusalem under the auspices of my aunt and uncle. My uncle is driving and pointing: "There, m'dears, Mt. Zion. And there, Mt.

Scopus. Down there, d'ya see those walls? With the young soldiers in front? The Old City. Enter there and it will be as it was a thousand years ago. Two thousand years ago when Christ died. Asses and mules. Ancient people living as they've always lived. The Stations of the Cross. The Via Dolorosa. Smells and sounds and colors. And then the Jewish Quarter—the Cardo—brand new! Unbelievable! In minutes you walk centuries. From the Wailing Wall, our little corner of the old temple, where they will be davening as they have been davening since biblical times. To the Dome of the Rock. Muslim. Where Isaac barely escaped having his neck slit by his Dad. A bit ironic don't you think? Both Jews and Muslims take this as a first principle: Do not sacrifice your son! And here we are, sacrificing our sons to one another! Walk a bit further to the Cardo and, were you as rich as some who come to this city, you could buy furs in a store that also has branches in Los Angeles and Beverly Hills!"

My uncle's speech and manners are very British. He has lived here all his life, much of it under British rule. My aunt has the sultry Vrodsky manner, very Russian. She has dark, smouldering eyes that draw me in. I see something of Lizaveta in her, and of my father: intensity, sensuality, seductiveness. I sense the secret Vrodsky attitude which, if articulated, would sound like this: "Actually we are royalty, traveling incognito through this world. Those who do not recognize us are beneath our contempt."

Esther sits in the front seat. She twists herself back toward us so that we can see her face, her round smooth cheeks, her eyes. At 67 she is a beautiful and compelling woman. She says, "Henry! Don't bother them with all your lecturing about Jerusalem. They have come here to learn about the family. They don't need a geography lesson."

"They must know about Jerusalem," says Henry. "They're here for so few days. I would be derelict if I did not tell them about Jerusalem."

We seem to be in the middle of a fight as old as their marriage, the fight between Henry's facts and Esther's feelings. I can hear my father's voice: "We Vrodskys have the Russian temperament. Passionate. Emotional." Esther's feelings are full of loss. Often they are bitter.

She is bitter about the encroachment of the ultra-religious Jews in Jerusalem. All over Jerusalem, in the hottest summer in thirty years, we saw them in their 18th-century black wool suits and black hats. They move into neighborhoods, gain political power, demand that everything be shut on the Sabbath. They stone people who drive on the Sabbath. They demand that women not be allowed in the swimming pool.

"Can you imagine," says my Aunt Esther, "what kind of men these are? They say a woman in a bathing suit distracts them from thinking about God. They must have nothing but sex on the mind all the time. It must be so because their women are always pregnant. All they do is go to *schul* and make their women pregnant. Can you believe last week they burned down a bus depot because it had on the wall an advertisement with a woman in a bikini bathing suit? So this is what happens to our Zionist vision! It is very terrible for us. What kind of a God do they pray to? My people left the ghettos of Russia and Poland to get away from that kind of a God. We did not make the state of Israel for such a God. I came to Palestine out of Europe when I was sixteen. I was a socialist. An agnostic. Maybe I am no longer a socialist. But a secular Jew, I am. I don't want to be ruled by religious fanatics. You know they are no different than those fanatical Muslims who cover their women in black.

"But do you know what is the worst? The very worst? Worse than stoning on the Sabbath? Worse than burning bus depots? This is what it is: I have two grandsons in the army. They are 18 and 19. You Americans cannot know how this is. Babies they are, carrying rifles, standing on the border, protecting us all. Everyday I worry are they all right. For their mother, your cousin Davida, it is such a torment. And these Jews, with their Torah and their Shabbat and their black coats from two hundred years ago in Russia, do you think they send their sons to protect this land? No! What do you think they do? They go to the chief rabbi and get special dispensation so their sons shouldn't be soldiers for religious reasons! Religious reasons! They are nothing but parasites upon our land, eating from our hard work, from the danger to our children. And it is you American Jews who make this happen. You don't want to be religious yourself. You want us to be religious in Israel. So you send money for them to live and they contribute nothing except trouble. It is very terrible for us."

"Esther," says Henry, "your charming niece and her intelligent husband have, I am sure, never contributed money to the ultra-orthodox."

"Henry, you know very well these Americans give money even to the United Jewish Appeal and do not know how it gets spent!"

"Now Esther," soothes Henry. "Actually," he says over his shoulder to us, "your Aunt Esther loves your country. Isn't that so, Esther?"

"In America one can get everything," she says. "It is much easier there. But I cannot leave here now, all my children and grandchildren are here. I think sometimes if I had gone to America like your father did, my grandsons would not be standing on the border now, every day, risking their lives. You cannot imagine how terrible that is. We were very idealistic when we came here. And we have had no peace."

I found myself feeling a new kind of guilt, a guilt that I grew up in America, that my family has been blessed with a generation of peace, while the rest of the family went to Israel and has had no peace.

"I have a friend," Esther tells me, "who was in the camps in Europe. Her whole family was wiped out, mother, father, sisters, cousins, aunts, and uncles. Only she and her husband and brother survived. They came to Palestine. The first year they were here her husband died of leukemia. In 1948 her brother walked out of the house one morning and was never heard from again. Still no one knows what happened to him. A few years ago her daughter, her only child, died of a rare incurable disease." Esther tells this story of unbearable losses as a kind of litany. "You cannot imagine what it is to lose everything, everyone, and come to Israel, and then lose everyone again."

We arrive at the house that Henry's father had built and that Henry and Esther live in now, in the flat on the top floor. They rent out the lower floors. We sit on the veranda under the shade of the tree Henry's father had planted, now so much taller than the house. And I try to draw from Esther her story. She gives me snatches of it. But there is a great core of pain that I cannot get near, a center out of which she cannot speak; she has been too unspeakably bereft.

"When your father died," she asks, "did he leave anything from our family home?" Her voice sounds young, querulous.

"I don't know," I say. "My father's wife would know." I hadn't gotten anything.

"You know," she says, "when I left at sixteen, I never thought that I wouldn't be back, that I wouldn't see my parents, that I'd never get any memento of that house." I thought of her, a sixteen-year-old, leaving Holland on a boat for an unknown land, never to see her mother or father again. She must have built up strong walls against acknowledging that agony. But I could hear its resonance in many of the things she said. She spoke of my father. She said he was able to finish everything. Meaning his education. Meaning his growing up. He was twelve years older than she.

It has been a great sorrow to her, she tells me that all of her life she wanted to study and she never could. Always she had to work, she had to support the family. Now finally, at 67, she is retired, and can study. She is taking classes at the University of Jerusalem, where she worked as a tour guide for so many years.

She tells me her mother had a beautiful voice. She sang in the synagogue choir. We never belonged to synagogues, she says. My mother did not find her connection to God in the synagogue. But she went there to sing. And sometimes we went to listen.

"My mother did not find her connection to God in the synagogue." The words sing in my mind like a blessing. I have never felt my spiritual nature reflected in a synagogue, either. Now there is a heritage for this feeling. I feel located, rooted in my family, accepted and accepting of the struggle I have had about religious feeling and being a secular Jew. I come from generations of secular Jews. Among them were many who helped to build the state of Israel.

I feel grateful to Esther. She is now talking about her father. She tells me he was a loving, child-oriented man. I tell her that surprises me, that my father has always portrayed him as a weak man, a man who failed in business, who had betrayed his wife. Her face goes white. I realize I have made a mistake.

"That was a terrible thing your father said." Her voice is shaking. "It was a terrible thing. And not true." But she will talk to me about it no further. Talk to Tania, she says. Tania is ten years older. She can explain these things better. I feel the hurt child in my aunt, and that I have hurt her yet again. She was so young when she left her parents. She was snatched out of the context of her development by the Holocaust. An avalanche of pain stands between her and working out her connection to her parents. I have poked where it hurts. She withdraws from me. I stop asking questions about the family past. And when Henry and Esther drive us back to our hotel, she gives me a long, hard look and says, "Ask Tania to tell you about your grandfather Leontov Vrodsky."

We Have No Survivors Here

Yad Vashem, the memorial to the Holocaust in Jerusalem, drenches those who go there seeking knowledge of their ancestors in the terrible imagery of recent Jewish history. There are large exhibition halls that tell the story of European Jewry in the mid-twentieth century. It is our last stop in Jerusalem, before going on to visit my Aunt Tania in her small village in the southern part of Israel. My husband and I wander amidst crowds of other Jews in a darkened hall; the lighted cases display information and photos. It is the kind of exhibit I have shunned in the past. Too many years of my life have been spent running in terror from Nazis in my dreams. Too many

years of my early life were spent identifying with Anne Frank and wondering why I had been chosen to have a life when she, whose adolescent
first love I so identified with, had never been allowed to grow into adulthood. I have learned not to read the books about the Holocaust, not to go
to the exhibits.

But now in Jerusalem, seeking a grandmother I never knew, I know
that I must look again at the shattering past to find her face. By this time
I am also looking for my grandfather, whom my Aunt Esther loved so
deeply, and whom my father never appreciated.

My husband and I walk together through the nightmarish images.
Hitler's rise to power is described in logical words that are hard for me to
follow. The photographs are much more powerful: a bearded old Jew being
tormented by grinning young German soldiers; the terrified eyes of young
children; the soft, plump nakedness of a young woman falling, shot in the
back in a mass execution. This image stays with me. She has the kind of
soft, voluptuous body that Rubens would paint. In this image of horror,
I am struck by her beauty. How her husband must have loved her nakedness; how her children must have loved to burrow into her soft breast.
There she remains in my consciousness, always falling, among others falling. All that was beloved and soft and secret and sweet denied in her. She
is cattle herded to slaughter. So, the text informs us, are her children, her
husband, her parents.

We walk through the Museum of the Holocaust to the exhibits on
the resistance of the Jews in the Warsaw Ghetto. I feel the hot rage flame
in me, and the relief at armed resistance. I feel in my body the warrior
instinct, and understand, as I had not before, why Israel is a warrior nation.

We come to the Hall of Names, established to commemorate those
who died cruelly before their time, those who were not buried, those who
have no tombstones, those restless dead who have no continuity, whose
children's children have no place on this earth to honor them. I lost a grandmother and a grandfather who could have enriched my life and given me
a wider identity. Entering the Hall of Names I am filled with the need to
find them there, as though finding their names written down on paper can
locate them in time and space and give them reality for me.

The Hall of Names is a dimly lit hall. There is no access to the records themselves. Near the front one may ask if a loved one's name is among
the records. There is a microfiche machine tended by a bristling man whose
bushy, white hair makes a circle around a sun-browned pate. He is small,
with a round little belly and ferocious blue eyes.

We stand before him, we who have re-experienced our worst nightmare, each with our private version of the horror, as well as the collective experience. We are drained. We want to find our fathers, our mothers, our sacred dead. We come to this man with the name of such a one on our lips. The couple beside me speak in Hebrew. They are asking for the name Schlomo Levin. And this pushy old man is arguing with them in Hebrew. What could he be arguing about a name? He is running the microfiche machine and we see the records of ten, twenty Schlomo Levins. They come from different towns and villages. Their wives have different names. They have different numbers of children. They died at different places—Auschwitz, Dachau, Tieresenstadt. Different people have submitted their names for commemoration. How many Schlomo Levins could there be, killed by the Nazis? Still this bushy-headed man is arguing with the couple in Hebrew. They keep shaking their heads as he runs the microfiche past record after record. With a plaintive question in their voices they say the name Joseph Levin. More arguing. Again he runs the microfiche and again there are ten, twenty, thirty Joseph Levins. The couple keeps shaking their heads. None of them is their Joseph or Schlomo Levin. At last the bushy-haired man hands them a form. Apparently their relative's name is not in the records. They will submit his name. Another dead Jew, unearthed after forty-some years, to be remembered on paper with ink.

It is my turn. Vrodsky, I say. Clara and Leo Vrodsky.

"You speak English?" he demands. "Americans?" He is clearly contemptuous. "What makes you think these names are here?"

"I think my Israeli relatives may have given them."

"Brodsky?" he says, "B, R, O?"

"Vrodsky," I say. "V, R, O."

"What do you mean "V?" he says. "In America there are no Vrodskys, only Brodskys."

"The name," I say, "is Vrodsky, with a V!" He is running the machine now. Past hundreds of names, hundreds of lost lives, lost stories, lost souls. "Why do you say V, R, O, D? Why not V, R, O, N? Vronsky! There is something funny about V, R, O, D. It doesn't sound right."

He wants to argue with me, this old Jew, about my own name, my family name?

"Many Americans changed their names," he informs me. He thinks he is telling me something new? He thinks if my family were going to change its name it would change an "n" to a "d"?

"Ah," he says, "Bella Vrodski from Lodz. So there are Vrodskis." If

I tell him it's not "i" but "y," he'll argue with me also, so I hold my tongue. We go through Bella Vrodski's huge family. "See," he says, "this is all one family. One person put in all those names." He's still trying to convince me that I don't have the name that I have or the relatives I have.

Clara Vrodsky—it says on the microfiche—Clara Vrodsky with a "y." The name cuts through me like a hot knife. My grandmother. My beloved, unknown grandmother.

"That's my name!" I say, feeling vindicated, feeling found in some strange way.

"That's your name?" he says, swiveling around in his chair, giving me a look of utter contempt. "If that is your name, then what are you doing standing there?" He is angry at me, that I have found my lost grandmother's name? He is angry at me, that I am not dead in the Holocaust?

Tears rush to my eyes unbidden. He is tormenting me. That is what I have wondered all my life, what am I doing standing here over the ashes of six million dead? My husband, feeling my distress, puts a hand on me and a firm voice into the fray.

"Clara Vrodsky is my wife's grandmother," he says. "See, there it says, born in 1883 in Odessa, died at Lag Westerbourg in 1943. My wife's aunt, Tania Blumen, born Vrodsky, submitted that name. It says so at the bottom of the page. Go further. We are also looking for her husband, Leo, or Leontov."

"Leo," says the fierce old man with bushy hair, "is already past. We don't use your *goyishe* spelling. Be ashamed!"

We stand there confused. Where is my grandfather? A crowd has gathered behind us, all seeking names. A woman pushes through to make herself heard. "I am looking for my father," she says. "Is this where I can find him?"

"You can't find your father here," says the fierce old man, playing once again with the difference between symbol and reality. "This," he says angrily, "is a graveyard of names, only of names. You find no real dead here, only names."

A man pushes in from the back of the crowd, looking urgent. "I am looking for two brothers who survived. Ten died, two survived. In all there were twelve brothers," he says. His speech is filled with the meaning of these brothers to him, to his sense of family. He is an American. Perhaps he has heard since he was a very small boy about these twelve brothers. Now he is here in Israel, in the Hall of Names, looking for them. "Survivors?" the old man says, shaking his head in outrage. "Survivors you are looking for? You are looking in the wrong place. We have no survivors here!"

We are left with a mystery. Why isn't my grandfather's name among the dead at Yad Vashem? Clara's name is there. Why not Leontov's?

My Father Would Be 104 Today

"Do you remember," I would say to my children later, "how your grandfather's eyes would hold you, seem to look through you, pull you to him, get things out of you you didn't want to say?" "Yes," they all nodded. "And my Aunt Lizaveta's eyes were even more intense, hypnotic, seductive. Can you imagine eyes of that power that are simply present, watching you, reading you, but not trying to seduce or entrap?"

That is how familiar Tania is to me when I meet her, and yet how different from those of her siblings who shaped my life. Tania is a slight, dark-eyed woman standing on the path to her little house. She is graceful, very feminine. Clearly she was a beauty. But there is nothing of the coquette in her. I feel a silence at the center of her that resounds in mine. For long moments we look deep into each other's eyes. There is no tug there, as from my father or Lizaveta. No demand, no seduction. Only the deep, clear seeing.

"Naomi," she says. "All my life I have wanted to see your face. You are a Vrodsky, you know. You look like my mother. You have the face of your grandmother, Clara." And she walks us up the path to her house and into the dark room within, curtains drawn to keep out the heat of the day.

"I have always wanted to write a book about my mother. But whenever I would sit down, I would start to cry. So, I never wrote. It is good you are doing it. Sit down, both of you. Please have some food. I have here fruit from the orchard and cake from my neighbor who bakes very well."

"Now," she says, looking at me intently. "I hear from Esther that your father said bad things about our father. You are here so short a time, with me only one day. We must speak the truth to one another, no?"

"Yes," I say, feeling relieved and moved. Many members of my family have said that Tania is the one to talk to. I see they are right. Here is a woman with whom I do not have to be careful, with whom I can be real. "I'm afraid I hurt Aunt Esther when I told her that. She told me to ask you about your father, my grandfather."

"My father," says Tania, "was a wonderful man. Always he brought home something special for us children. He was a wonderful father. And he was so handsome, see?" She showed us the photograph that I had known from my childhood, deep-set, dark eyes, high Russian forehead, high cheekbones. Suddenly it is no longer the familiar old photo on the bookshelf of my youth. It is the picture of a vital, handsome man. Tania sighs. "He was so full of life. I never thought they would get him.

"I want to tell a story about my father," she said, "what kind of man he was. It was wintertime. And this professor of music, his name was Stresser, was old already.

"Please, you must eat. Here is bread, cheese, another cheese. And here is coffee." She has remembered her role as our hostess. "Please. This is very good apple cake. And here a cheese cake. And fruit. Avi's peaches. Avi, you know, is my son-in-law, married to my daughter, Daniella."

"So," I say, eating a sun-ripened peach from her son-in-law's orchard, grown on the land she has spent her life cultivating, "there was the music professor." We are in a dark room filled with ghosts, on a hot day, in the Promised Land. Outside the sun is bright on the bougainvillea embracing her little house. A cow moos. The air is heavy with manure. My Aunt Tania's eyes deepen. She has returned to the cobblestone streets of the Stuttgart of her childhood.

> Yes. It was winter time. My father was in town. And he saw Professor Stresser. It was very cold. And my father asked him how he was. And he said, "Oh it's not so easy. I'm old already. I have not so many pupils anymore." He was not wearing a coat. He was an old man, and he was shivering. My father took his own coat, and gave it to him and went away.
>
> My father came home, It was cold. And my mother said, "Lova, where is your coat?" I can see the coat now. It was beautiful and warm. It had a big collar with fur. And my mother said, "Where did you leave your coat?" And my father said, "I saw Professor Stresser and he had no coat, and he was so down, so I gave it to him." That's my father. Always he had some little gift to bring us children. Some sweets. Some fruit. A toy. He was so full of life. He could dance like a Cossack. You know how I mean? Kicking his legs out? And he laughed. And sang. How we loved him. He always could work things out with people, he could always make a deal. That's why I never thought the Nazis would get him because he always could work something out.

How different, I think, from the image of my grandfather that I gleaned from my father. He did not speak of him often. But when he did it was without respect. He was a cigarette roller working in a factory, in my father's version. That's why my father had always hated cigarettes and smoking. He was a failure in business. He betrayed his wife, my father's mother. He left her for another woman.

Tania must be reading my mind. "And what did your father say about my father?"

"That he was a failure in business. That he betrayed his wife, and left her for another woman."

"My father did not deserve that from Eli," says Tania, her voice shaking with anger. "My father did everything for Eli. In 1933 when Eli had not finished his doctorate, and things were very bad for the Jews in Germany, my father sold all the silver we had at home so Eli would have enough money to finish. But they were never very close, Eli and my father. Because, I don't know, Eli did all with his head and my father did all with his heart."

"I can well imagine that," I say, thinking of the lifelong fight between my father and my brother Leon, named appropriately in memory of his big-hearted grandfather. Leon leads with his heart and my father led with his mind. But Tania is speaking to me.

"I knew that my mother died. But I never thought my father was dead. Always I thought he would come some day, to Eretz Yisroel, to my door. I never heard any news about him.

"I had a dream. Over and over again this dream would wake me in the night. I would be in terror. In the dream there is a knock at my door in the middle of the night. I go and I open it. It is my father. In his arms he is carrying a dead child. He says, 'I have carried it all the way from Russia.' Always I woke from this dream terrified.

"One day, many years after the war, I thought to myself: I have to know what happened with my father. I hired a lawyer to trace him. The Germans have such records for all the horrors they did; you can trace such things. My father was put on a train to Auschwitz in 1943. The train never got to Auschwitz. Who knows what happened? It could have been bombed by the Americans. Still, I thought, he can't be dead. Somehow, he survived.

"By now my father would be 104. I think he is no longer alive."

A Broken Agreement

Sitting in her kitchen, watching her prepare a meal, the child in me longs for this woman; the young woman in me longs for her. This is the older woman I have needed all my life. She has grace, deep femininity, and strength. Had she been a presence in my childhood perhaps I could have imagined myself whole and female at a younger age. Now, at this mid-point of my life, she seems to know exactly what I need. She requires little prompting. She peels potatoes and tells me the stories of my Motherline:

"My mother came from a very good family in Odessa, in Russia. Her uncle was Avram Sussman. Everyone knew him. A respected man. She had an older brother. He studied to become an opera singer. But once when he was singing he had an attack of angina and died. My mother's mother would not let her study music. She though if her son had not studied opera he would not have died. But my mother had a beautiful singing voice. And she loved music.

"Her father left the family when she was very young. He had lent money to someone without asking his wife. He was to get the money back the next day. He never got it back. He was ashamed to face his wife so he just ran away. My mother never saw him again. Some say he went to America.

"My father was from a little town called Kishnev. There was no work there, so he came to Odessa. There he saw my mother and fell in love. They were young. My mother was just twenty. He was five years older. There was not really a family. Only my grandmother and the uncle. The uncle made the marriage. He gave my mother to my father. They didn't know my father's family. But they were in love and what could they do?

"They married in 1904 and the Russian-Japanese war broke out. My father had to go. In those days all the Jews had to go to the war. My mother said if he is going she will die. You know when you are young that is how it is. And the love between my mother and my father was very strong. And so, my mother always told me, with only such a little baggage they ran away. They bought tickets and without telling anyone they went to Munchen, Germany. They said nothing to anyone because the police would catch my father. He would have to go to prison.

"They came to Munchen, and my mother was already pregnant with Lizaveta. And my father searched for work. Lizaveta was ill when she was a little baby, maybe one and half years old. Polio. And then started all the troubles. In Munchen there was not a good doctor. They came to Stuttgart because they heard there would be a good doctor there. And all their money was spent because of searching for a good doctor for Lizaveta.

"In Russia my father had already learned the, how you say, *Ta-*

bak business, tobacco. Cigarettes. Cigars. But in those days a Russian could not own a business in Germany. So he had to find a German partner. This partner did not know anything about the business. It was just for the legal reasons, he had to have this partner. When my father had made the business and it was good, it made money, his partner came to him one day and said: 'I want you out of the business. And if you won't go, I will turn you over to the German authorities.' This broke my father's heart. This he could not stand. So, because of this betrayal, he lost his business.

"But even with all this trouble we had a very good family. Even with little money they always spent money for education.

"Eli and I were very close, in age but also in feeling. He loved me. I also loved him, but I knew him. He was not the kind of man my father was. Generous he could be, but only so people would see how generous he was. My father, it did not matter if anyone saw it, he was generous.

"What your father did, do you know? He and I had an agreement. There was not money in the family for education. So we said, one year he will study and I will work, one year I will study and he will work. So one year he studied, and I worked. I wanted to study medicine. But your father never stopped his studies. He never gave me my time to study. And I never learned medicine, I have never been able to study.

"Each of my daughters has studied. And all have studied medicine. Each one is a nurse.

"When I came to see him in Chicago, it was maybe a year before he died, he said, 'Tania, I am sorry you did not have your chance to study. But you see how far I have come? You would not have wanted to prevent that.'

"He was very intelligent, your father. But what he did was not right."

Life Happens

"What went wrong in your parents' marriage?" I ask, a bit fearfully, since this had been so painful a subject for my Aunt Esther. But Tania is different. She gives me her deep, sad look.

"What happens to people who love each other? Life happens. My mother and father had a great love. But they were very different people. My mother was very intelligent, very cultured. My father loved to joke, to laugh, to have fun. My mother was more serious. She cared very much about the education of her children. She understood each child had a different nature. And so she did different things for each. One went to a Rudolf Steiner school. Another to the gymnasium. She knew my sister Maya was not very interested in school. But Maya loved animals. So my mother got little cats for her. She understood what music was to your father. So when he played the piano, we all had to be quiet.

"Then Maya would come, full of laughter and song, and play, you know, folk music, popular music, music for dancing. Your father would be angry. 'That is schmalz,' he would say, 'kitsch, not real music.' And my mother would come and say, 'Eli, leave Maya alone. She, too, must have her time to play the piano.' She was a very good mother. But she had one child after the other. Six children. And she suffered very much about Lizaveta. Since Lizaveta got sick as a baby, things were not good for my mother. And my father lost his business. It was very difficult. She did not have her mother to help her. Her mother was still in Odessa. She became old and tired. And Lova was so full of life, always, you cannot imagine.

"And then there was the problem of Maya, my mother's second child. Beautiful, you cannot imagine how beautiful she was, and full of life. She married in Germany, a religious Jew, and this was a great mistake. My parents knew it would be a mistake. Because Maya loved to dance and sing and this was not permitted by the religious. But what can you say when young people are in love?

"There was dancing at a certain place in the park. And Maya went there to dance. And her mother-in-law saw her dancing with another man. This caused much trouble in the family.

"Maya had two children already and she was feeling not very good. She came to my mother and said, 'Mother, I don't know what is the trouble. But I feel so weak, so faint.' And my mother said, 'Come, we'll go to the doctor.' The doctor told her the pregnancies had weakened her and she must have no more children. But her husband was religious. He did not believe in, how you say, contraception? So Maya became pregnant with another child. This was after 1933 and my parents had already left for Holland. My mother got a letter saying, 'Come, Maya is sick.' She knew already what she would find when she went there. She went and it was very dangerous to travel then. But she came to the house and already Maya was dead.

"It broke her heart. She got old. She had no energy for my father. And where he worked in a tobacco shop there was an unmarried woman who fell in love with him. Who can blame him? She paid him so much attention. She would do anything for him. She was an older woman. She was lonely. He was so handsome. Who can blame her?

"My father did not desert my mother. He always came over. He always helped. He was always involved. But my mother took it very hard. Her heart, once again, was broken."

My Mother Did Not Need to Die

"My mother did not need to die. She was, how you say, in Krankenhaus, in the hospital. She had had an operation and the Nazis came to her while she lay in bed. Lizaveta was at her bedside.

"The Nazi said, 'Where were you born?' 'In Russia,' my mother said. 'Then you can stay here,' said the Nazi, 'because we are on the same side fighting with the Russians.' 'And she?' he looked at Lizaveta, 'where was she born?'

"My mother was not thinking very well. She was just out from the surgery. She just said, 'She was born in Munchen.'

'Then she is from Germany and she must come with me,' said the Nazi.

'She will not go alone,' my mother said. 'She is my daughter.'

"And so they were taken to Lag Westerbourg, to be shipped then later to Bergen Belsen. I always say, thank God my mother died in Westerbourg. She did not have to suffer Bergen Belson.

"And Lizaveta, how did she survive? She had those eyes, you know. Men always liked her. The Jewish commandant liked her. He gave her always a little more bread than the others. So she survived. That was Lizaveta.

This is a different version of the story of my grandmother's death than the story my father told at the end of his life. In his version Lizaveta is the hero, the one who did not have to die, who stayed with her mother to the bitter end and beyond. I think of saying: "But Tante Tania, my father told it differently. My father said it was Lizaveta who sacrificed her life." But then I think, what does it matter? Do I want to create an argument between a dead brother and his living sister on the only day I have with her? This is the story she has lived with for more than forty years. Let it be. There are so many truths and so many agonies in such a story.

Tania's agony is this: When she left Holland her mother told her:

"When you are in Eretz Yisroel, find Avram Sussman. He is my uncle. He gave me away in marriage. He is an important man with much influence. He will get me out."

When she and her husband came to Palestine they worked for a farmer. They asked this man if he knew Avram Sussman. "Yes," he said, "but he died many years ago." So they did not look for him, believing he was dead.

Years later Tania saw in a newspaper that Avram Sussman had just died. It was the same Avram Sussman who was her mother's uncle from Odessa. She could have found him had she known he was alive. He could have brought my mother out. You must remember, in those days it was Palestine under the British. It was not yet Israel with the right of return. The British did not want so many Jews here. So it was very difficult to get in. My husband and I were young. We had to get a certificate in Holland from two years of studying agriculture. Then we came in 1936. My mother was already old. She could not do hard work. It would have taken a powerful person to get her into Palestine. Avram Sussman could have done it. That man lied to us because he did not want to lose us as workers. Had we found Avram Sussman we would have come under his influence, he would have helped us. We would have left that farmer, and that he did not want. So he lied. My mother did not need to die. I could have saved her, if only that man had not lied.

"Please, you are eating nothing. Here, I have made potatoes just as my mother made them. Russian style. Have a little more meat. Ah! Here are Daniella and Avi. They want we should have dessert at their house."

Daniella, Tania's youngest, is a beauty. Great, dark eyes. Long, black hair. A shy, sweet manner. She works as a midwife in a hospital a few miles away. She married a man of the same village and they have built their house behind Tania's. This, Aunt Esther had told me, was a great blessing for Tania. Since her husband died ten years ago, she has been lonely and has lost much weight. She is totally immersed in her grandchildren now, who somersault around the house, while Daniella presses more cake and coffee upon us.

What a beautiful house Avi has built for his wife and children, made of stucco and stone. He shows us the exquisite woodwork detailing on the windows. This tanned, muscular warrior man, who built his own house, grows beautiful peaches, flies a plane for the air force, and in his spare time is studying computer programming, is certainly a new breed of Jew. None of the men on the American side of the Vrodsky family has ever been good with his hands, or fought in wars, or farmed, or done technical work. They are men of books, of the arts, of ideas.

Avi and Daniella seem to glow with the energy of the frontier. They are building a new land and beside them we feel flabby and gray. Is it this glow that draws American Jews to Israel?

It has been dark for hours when we say good-bye. My Aunt Tania and I look long at each other, knowing we may never see each other again. I give her some chapters of this book, wanting her to understand what this search for my lineage means to me.

The Light Is Different in Israel

Next day we drive north from Tel Aviv to Haifa. My mother's sister, Leni, lives in a village nearby. Leni is a familiar figure from my childhood. She has often come to visit. She looks like a peasant, big-boned, strong. She has spent most of her life as a farmer. I know her to have a questioning, vital, intelligence. I have sent her some chapters of my book. Her response will be important to me.

The Mediterranean Sea is a vivid blue on our left. I remember my grandmother's paintings of Israel. She went to Israel often when I was a child to visit Leni and her family, and returned with watercolor paintings of the blue Mediterranean. The light is different in Israel, she told me. Here we are, driving in the brightness of the Mediterranean light, talking about the Vrodsky side of the family.

With the blue blur of the sea beside us, I see my Aunt Tania's dark eyes looking into mine. My mother and Leni are so down to earth, so practical. With Tania I feel my connection to the mysteries, to a passionate vision of life full of stories of love and of tragedy. In just one day I feel so close to her, so much warmth from her. I imagine my grandmother Clara and long for the intensity of feeling she would have for me, that she would evoke in me.

There they all were in Holland in the 1930s: the Vrodskys and the Kunstlers. My grandmother Clara was in her forties, as I am now, when the families first met. My father, Elias, gave piano lessons to the Kunstler girls. The Vrodskys were poor. Clara's heart had already been broken by Maya's death and the many losses of her life. By that time Leo was involved with the other woman. The Kunstlers had money, a fine house, an upstairs maid. And they were reserved, elitist German Jews. In Israel, Tania and Leni spoke often by phone, and sometimes saw each other, but I had the sense that much of Tania's feeling about my mother's family came from that time in Holland.

How amazing it is when disparate families are brought together by marriage. The issues that emerge can resonate for generations. I wonder how my grandparents, Emma and Simon Kunstler, saw the Vrodskys.

I ask Leni that question a short time later, sitting in the "music room" of her small house. Leni suffers much from the heat and this room is air conditioned. It is a respite from the sounds and smells of the chickens Leni raises on her little farm—a far cry from the house in Holland with the upstairs maid. In it is a piano, a couch, and chairs, music stands, a cello, and many of my grandmother's paintings and sketches. There is one wonderful sketch of my mother, Leni, and Dotti as long-legged, adolescent girls. Dotti sits at the piano, Leni has her legs wrapped around a cello, and my little mother stands with her violin and bow. "That was in Holland," Leni tells me. "Your mother was perhaps 14, Dotti was 16, and I was 19. Your father was the music teacher, you know." Her eyes sparkle at me, full of life's ironies.

Being with Leni is familiar and reassuring. I tell her that Tania has described the Kunstlers as cold, and wonder how Simon and Emma had seen the Vrodskys.

"Well, you know how taken my mother was with your father. Your father was full of intensity, creativity. My mother was drawn to that. My father was more private. I remember him saying that Clara Vrodsky complained too much. I think he saw her as someone who whined about life, and that he could not abide.

"I must tell you, Naomi, that I have read your chapters, and I am very impressed. I think it is very good, what you are doing. But I must also tell you that Tania called me this morning after she read your work, and she took it very ill that you wrote about Lizaveta as you did."

"What was it she took ill?" I ask, my stomach sinking.

"She said Lizaveta suffered enough in her life, she should not be criticized. She did not like how you wrote about her when you were a child. I said to her: 'Tania, Naomi is describing a child's perspective. Later she develops an understanding of what Lizaveta suffered. That is the point. That is what makes this sound true.' But I think Tania wants only that you should write good things about the dead."

The light in the land of Israel darkens. On Leni's farm near the blue Mediterranean, Simon Kunstler's granddaughter shifts family allegiance. Suddenly the Vrodskys seem undeveloped, naive. I feel betrayed. I longed for an aunt and a grandmother who prefigured my own nature, whose psychological heir I was.

"I am surprised," I say to Leni, "that Tania seems unable to think psychologically. I had a different impression of her yesterday. I thought she and my grandmother, Clara, understood development."

"I think Tania has handled her suffering by looking only at the good side of things. For years she would hear nothing bad about your father. Esther or I would speak of difficulties with him and she would insist that we be quiet. He was her beloved Elias. So gifted a man that he could be forgiven anything. Finally, when she visited him, she saw what we meant and changed her view. But you know, she never saw Lizaveta after the camps. She has held on to her image of her sister and does not want it to be disturbed."

"Do you think I should change what I have written about Lizaveta?"

"Absolutely not. I think it is very good. Only change the names."

Leni's down-to-earth manner settles into me like the comfort of home. And I think about betrayal. Is there any story of love that does not include betrayal? I can well imagine how Tania feels. Here she has trusted me with the family lore, the sacred family stories she wanted to write herself. And I turn out to be the kind of younger woman who writes terrible things about the dead, even about those who have suffered unbearably in the Holocaust. What will I do with the stories she told me?

I, too, feel betrayed. I thought I had found the channel to the deep parts of my father's line, and it turns out to be shallow. My Aunt Tania is worried about how things will look, what people will think, instead of about the truth.

I look at my mother's sister. In my heart I have betrayed her, too, joining the Vrodsky critique of the Kunstlers, longing for the women of the other side of the family. But in the end it is Leni who stands up for me, who argues my cause with Tania, who supports my writing, who understands what I am doing.

"You know," Leni says, "I understand why you need to know about the Vrodsky side of the family. It is important for you to know them, even if they are not all you wish them to be. Did you know that it was your father who inspired us all to come to Palestine? He had a Zionist vision before any of us did. He understood the importance of a homeland for the Jews."

"Why didn't he come here, then?" I ask.

"Ah, Naomi, there would have been nothing for him here. There were no universities, there was no musicology. At best he could have played piano in a restaurant." We both shake our heads, imagining Elias Vrodsky in a piano bar. "He had to go to America to become who he was. He was right to do so. There has been much I have been angry about with your father in my lifetime. But he is still the one who inspired me. I will always be grateful. Tania is perhaps not all you had thought she was. But I think she has inspired you, and that is what matters. You are right to look for your grandmother Clara in her, because Tania, of all the Vrodskys, is most like her mother. You can see your grandmother's face in hers."

Leni's words bring the Vrodskys and the Kunstlers together in my heart, and I feel at peace. After all, does it really matter if my grandmother Clara is not the perfect puzzle piece of my psyche, the longed-for voice of wisdom and depth that could explain me to myself? Whose grandmother ever is? Had Clara survived, she might well have been the kind of grandmother who wanted me to be "nice." I would have wrestled with her about it.

Clara, at last count, has fifteen grandchildren and twenty-six great grandchildren! A vital clan has sprung out of her body, whose burial place we do not know! We met some of my first cousins and their children. I remember especially the beautiful young soldier, home on leave, who is stationed at the Golan Heights. His mother fears for his safety. He is idealistic and impassioned. He and his mother fight about the Israeli invasion of Lebanon.

He says, "If a young child comes to throw a bomb at a tank, how can we not shoot him? Even if he is ten?"

She says, "We did not build the state of Israel to kill children!"

He feels frustrated that she is trying to limit his young male glory. I know she is terrified of a world that endangers her son, and the ten-year-old bomb-throwing son of some Lebanese mother.

Clara, who died before seeing the Promised Land, before seeing the strength and continuity of her line, never knew that there has been no end to the turmoil and the suffering, no peace and no sanctuary in Eretz Yisroel. Perhaps that is a mercy.

CHAPTER NINE

ASHES TO ASHES:
A Mother's Childhood Landscape

Bella came from Over There, a place you weren't supposed to talk about too much, only think about in your heart and sigh with a drawn-out krechtz, oyyy. . . . She did drop hints about her parents' home Over There, and it was from her that Momik first heard about the Nazi Beast.

DAVID GROSSMAN[1]

The El Al airplane that carried us from Tel Aviv to Frankfurt is taxiing to a stop under a threatening sky. Despite the comfort of knowing that my mother will meet us at the gate, I feel myself entering the zone of my worst childhood nightmares. An indescribably horrible Nazi beast had lived in our family, frightening us children and making our parents overprotective, haunted and fearful. The beast springs out at me now, filling my soul with the terrible images of an earlier time. Holocaust survivor Zdena Berger tells this story:

> Below the hill the cattle cars are linked together. The cars have small windows, high and barred. A hand under each elbow boosts us up into our car, our bundles and bags are thrown in after us. I see Eva being pushed into another car. The doors roll together and a piece of wood is nailed over the window.
>
> Soon the car jolts, the wheels grind, the couplings squeal and

strain, and the long train pulls taut and carries us away. I sit very close to Father, who has one arm around me, the other around Mother. With the slow movement of the train we lean together, our shoulders touching. Some light comes in through the cracks in the wood, and the edges of wind.

Now there is only now. There is the train, there is the motion, there is the dry tongue swelling in my mouth. I am not thirsty but my mouth is dry. I would like to say something, but there is nothing to say. There is only the feeling: Something is wrong, a mistake has been made.[2]

Now. Any moment you are in is now. And now is constantly changing, altered by seasons, life stage, historical moment. Now is the summer of 1987. Forty-four years ago, in the now of my birth, was the now of the death trains. Now, almost two generations later, an airplane filled with Jews from Eretz Yisroel has landed in Germany. Around the plane are several armored tanks, green-clad German soldiers standing up in them, rifles in hand. A new moment in time. Another now. Terror pitches my stomach. Why should this time be different from then? What keeps them from turning on us now as they did then? This is a relatively civilized time. There are laws, international agreements. The Aryan men in green are here to protect us. From what? Their guilt? Our memory? Our ghosts? Their ghosts?

Why is the plane standing out here in the middle of the landing strip? Why aren't we taxiing in to the gate? This is the now of terrorists. Has someone placed a bomb? The civilized voice of the pilot in German, Hebrew, and English addresses us over the loudspeaker system. We are to disembark and get on the bus. People arise; they follow directions. The doors of the plane open. As we disembark, a sudden downpour causes us to run to the bus. More and more people enter the bus. Thunder in the sky, and then a great clap that shakes us all. And lightning. Outside the windows we see the armored tank still standing, the soldier erect in it, holding his gun as the rain pours down on his helmeted head. A young girl, perhaps thirteen, throws up her airplane food. People move away from her, hand her tissues. Embarrassed, she cleans the vomit from the floor, from her clothes. A sour smell fills the air. So many Jewish bodies pushed together.

Still the bus does not move. Still we are watched by the soldiers and the armored tank, waiting for who knows what, in the hands of authorities over whom we have no control. I think of other vehicles full of Jews, not so very long ago, only the span of my lifetime, my grandfather on the train to Auschwitz that never arrived. In the now of my grandfather, the beloved Russian Jew who could dance like a Cossack, in the now of him pressed against others in the dark of a train, in the unknown now of his last moments forty-four years ago, what role was played by that young, helmeted soldier's grandfather?

They give us no trouble at customs. And when at last we emerge into the well-lit arrival area my mother greets us, violin in hand. She has let her hair, which she has colored for years, grow out white. It is as if some sudden sorrow has whitened her head all at once. I think it's beautiful and poignant to see her white hair for the first time in Germany.

"Your flight was never announced," she tells us. "Arriving on El Al in Frankfurt you are a target. They kept it very quiet, to protect you."

She had flown first to Amsterdam from home. As the plane descended, she told us, they entered the top of a rainbow, and underneath it she saw the city of her adolescent exile, bathed in the yellow light of Rembrandt. Later, from the window of a bed and breakfast near her childhood home, we see another rainbow—a great arc of colors from the thousand-year-old town of Kassel.

AN ELEGANT LIFE AMONG GHOSTS

Wilhelmshöhe is an elegant suburb of Kassel, above the town. It is a great, green park with beautiful mansions and a lake. At the highest point stands the impressive castle, a monument to eighteenth-century rationality expressed in perfectly symmetrical fountains and waterflows. We are staying at a small inn near my mother's birthplace.

The landscape of her childhood descends upon my mother and she exclaims, signs, laughs, and points. The reserve of her adult persona fades, and I can see the exuberant little girl in her. "Ach!" she exclaims, here was the school she loved. Here they walked after school. Here is where her friend, Ursula, still lives, and their dog played with the dog who lived around the corner.

"Here is the wall around the house!" She shows us a stone and iron wall. "This is the original wall! Here we hung over the edge with our bowl of cherries, spitting the pits directly into the open windows of passing buses. I was good at it, too!"

Like curious children we peer through the large iron gate at the house behind. It is a low, modern-looking, 1950s-style house. As though on a dare, my mother looks at me, then at my husband, Dan, and grins. She rings the bell. "Let's find out who lives here now," she says. "Yah?" We hear a woman's voice through the loudspeaker. In German my mother says that she lived here in her childhood before the war, and that she would be very grateful if she could look at the property now to see if she could recognize anything. "Ein moment." The voice sounds irritated.

A blond woman appears behind the iron bars with a large Doberman pinscher. She is slim and elegant, wearing loose, tunic-style pants and a fashionable T-shirt-style top. She peers at us through the bars for a moment, then sighs, and opens the gate. "Bitte, come in. I am sorry to be so cautious, but you know, today, one can't be too careful." "Yes, of course," we agree.

As we walk around the grounds, my mother trying to place her ghost house, the elegant, blond woman with her hand on her tall Doberman begins to understand the nature of our journey. Who is she? I wonder. What were her parents doing in 1933? Can she tell we're Jewish? She seems to warm to us, telling us what little she knows of the history of the house that she and her husband bought recently. It was built by important people, the physician to Konrad Adenauer. She had no idea there had been a house here before, though when she thinks about it, the old houses in the neighborhood and the old wall and gate, she wonders why it didn't occur to her.

"Hah!" my mother says, "this tree I remember." We look up at a tall, swaying larch. "No wonder I've always loved this kind of tree. Now I understand why they are so magical to me. And here is where we used to stand and spit cherry pits!" She rushes to the place from inside the wall, a small parapet, just high enough for seven- or eight-year-olds to hang onto the top. My mother is shy about the excited girl within her, before this elegant woman whose parents may have been Nazis. But she can't seem to keep her internal child down.

"Look!" she cries, "here are the old cobblestones. And this is where the coal man came to bring the coal every Friday. He'd shovel it into the side of the house. Right here. So this must be where the house began." She paces off a spot far from the present house, where there is now only well-manicured, green lawn. "There was a big cellar here where the chauffeur and his whole family lived."

The elegant woman sighs. "I have been living among such ghosts.

And I never knew it. I suppose one can never know what pain and loss one's life will bring, can one?" She looks at my mother, tears in her eyes. "So, one must live one's life to the full while one can, is it not?" She shows us around the rest of the grounds, the indoor swimming pool, the patio area with chairs, her small collections of shells. The place is a mansion. She and my mother discuss my grandfather's company, of which the elegant woman has heard. Her husband is the vice president of a modern engineering firm. He, too, travels a great deal, like my grandfather did. It shocks me to realize that my mother, who has always been frugal, who is uncomfortable when things are too "fancy," was born into the same class as this elegant, gracious, German lady. "Won't you come in? Can I offer you a drink?" We thank her but decline. We are due at my mother's friend Ursula's house for tea.

MY MOTHER, THE RING LEADER

Ursula lives in the beautiful house of her grandmother. Her house dates back to the late nineteenth century, probably built during the same period as the house in which my mother was born. When Ursula was growing up the family had two houses in Wilhelmshohe, her grandmother's and her parents'. Her parents' house was bombed. Ursula now lives on the top floor of her grandmother's house and rents out the other two floors. She is a big-boned woman, with an old-fashioned bun at the back of her neck. She has never married.

My mother's two other school friends are there, Ula and Rony. Rony is seven days younger than Ula, and her aunt. They giggle as they explain that Rony's mother is Ula's grandmother, and Ula's mother is Rony's big sister, and mother and daughter were pregnant at the same time. These two women have gone through life together as friends and almost siblings, explaining their complex, intergenerational connection for more than sixty years, back to my mother's childhood. Now both women are widowed. Their families lost their houses during the war. The bombing of Kassel was relentless because there were munitions factories here. Of a population of two hundred thousand, they tell us, sixty thousand civilians were killed in the war.

Ula, Rony, Ursula, and my mother had been friends at Fraulein Sumpf's progressive school in Wilhelmshohe. The three German women are glad to see my mother, glad to meet my husband and me. But, like old school friends everywhere, they dash off quickly to the territory of their own memories, remembering this friend, that family, that event. Four 67-year-old ladies divided by a terrible war reconnect to giggle about the mischief they made as girls.

They all agree that my mother was the ring leader. And I, who had always been the good girl, take secret pleasure in my mother's early wildness. I, who had stepped carefully around my mother's gray depression during my early years, find a source of life and energy in the image of her mischievous, young nature. There was the time mother and Ula crept into the school and locked it in the early morning, so that students and teachers could not enter. There was the time they put ice on the teacher's chair. How surprised she had looked, leaping up from her seat, clutching her wet, cold bottom. Harmless, they say, those pranks. And there was the time that they crept through the sewers under the streets and saw the blue flame of a gas light. That, they all agree now, was dangerous.

They speak of the dissolution of Fraulein Sumpf's little school. And how they all had to go to the big awful public high school with the Nazi principal. "Why did the little school dissolve?" I ask. As part of the Third Reich, they say, all the schools were state controlled. Small private schools were abolished. Fraulein Sumpf was quite a radical for those days. People said she slept in the nude. That was considered very wild behavior. "We heard," said Ula, "that Fraulein Sumpf died in a concentration camp. She was not Jewish, but the Nazis did not like people with free ideas either."

There sits my little, dark-eyed mother with the fairy-tale name, Giesele. She looks half-child, half-elf in the landscape of her childhood, skipping back from Ursula's house, showing us around the lake where her older sister, Leni, studied bird life for her biology project. The most gifted student, her teacher said, before the Nazis ended it all.

"See, there are the ducks," she says. "But where are the swans? There used to be swans." We walk by the edge of the charming lake, over tree trunks, under trees. My husband walks ahead of us. "Swans!" he shouts. "I found the swans!" Another loop woven in my life. My husband, who hates being in Germany, who is haunted by the restless ghosts of six million dead, is the one who sights my mother's sacred childhood memory— the swans. He is as excited as she to see the large, beautiful birds, with their long necks twisted around into their own feathers, fast asleep. He takes a picture and with the camera's click something falls into place for us all.

"It looked just like this," my mother says. "Just like this. There wasn't any difference."

AMONG GRAVESTONES

Friedl has agreed to take us to the Jewish cemetery. Friedl is ten years older than my mother. Her father was the chauffeur to my mother's family. Her family lived in the basement apartment of my mother's house. It was such a big house, Friedl and my mother tell us, that there was a whole apartment in the cellar, as well as storage areas for fruits, vegetables, and preserves. It smelled so good in there, the two women remember, inhaling their memories of the apples and preserves in the cool, musty dark, and of my grandfather's wine cellar. "No wonder I like good wine," I tell my husband; the connection feels important. "My grandfather loved good wine!"

"You think love of good wine is a genetic trait?" he teases. I'm reaching back to my German-Austrian grandfather and finding precious pieces of myself. I want him to feel the full import of this for me. But for my husband this is the Germany of concentration camps and relentless murder. He has no living roots to reach back to in this soil. Only the horror, remembered from childhood, when Jewish families followed each step of the war, and slowly began to understand what atrocities had been committed to their fellow Jews.

We are driving through the streets of Kassel. The way is mysterious to my mother, who spent little time in Kassel itself. Her memories are all of Wilhelmshohe. Friedl knows the town well but has not been to the Jewish cemetery in more than fifty years. She and my mother sit in the back seat of the car. My husband is driving. I am beside him. Friedl gives directions in rapid German. My mother and I translate when we remember to. But we both get caught up in the family lore Friedl is telling. Time and again my husband is left out, begging, "Which way now? Right or left?"

Friedl had been half-playmate, half-baby-sitter for my mother and her sisters. My mother remembers her excitement when Friedl got married and little Dieter Hanschen was born. "He was so sweet and so little. He smelled so good. He was the first baby I'd ever known. I wanted to have a baby right away."

"I think we've gone wrong," Friedl says to me in German, and I realize with a start that I've once again been neglecting my job of translating directions. It makes my head spin, going from language to language, from my mother's childhood to the present moment. We should have veered right instead of left at the last intersection. Our driver lets out a small, explosive sign of irritation. He's feeling frustrated. Dependent on my translation of directions, he keeps losing my attention as I strain to hear what Mother and Friedl are saying in the back seat.

He turns the car around. Friedl and I are now focused on finding the right way. But my mother is musing about the effect little Dieter Hanschen's birth had on her. "I think that was when I got into trouble for playing sexual games," she says. "No wonder! I was so impressed that you could produce that little Dieter Hanschen. I wasn't so interested in the sex part. I was interested in the baby!" Her voice is excited. She has put another piece of the puzzle of her childhood together.

"We are here," says Friedl. "Here is the Jewish cemetery."

The Jewish cemetery is on one side of the road; the Christian cemetery on the other. The contrast is striking. The Christian dead are protected by an attractive wooden fence through which one can see well-tended, manicured grave sites, recent graves. The Jewish cemetery is behind a great brick wall. "To protect it," Friedl says. Her kind, broad face creases in pain. She tells us there was a big commotion in the newspapers a few years ago when hooligans knocked down Jewish graves. A collection was taken up in the town to build a brick wall to protect the graves. There are very few Jews left in Kassel. So this collection was done by the good people of the town. There are good people and bad people, Friedl says, on the issue of how the Jewish past was treated.

The cemetery is full of ivy-covered graves, tombstones and monuments that have been knocked down. It is clear that recently there has been an effort to clean up a number of graves, to mow the lawn around them. A large monument near the entrance has been placed there by the citizens of Kassel. It commemorates the suffering and death of Jews during "Die Schreckenjahre: 1933–1945," the Years of Terror.

Near the brick wall is a well-kept tomb, surrounded by a small hedge, which creates a private little chamber in which to stand and read the inscriptions:

Ruth Hoffman
b. 2.10.1914
d. 1924
Da Zitterte das blatt
und dann kam der traumwinter

"The leaf trembled and then came the dream winter."

Heinz Hoffman
b. 10.31.1907

Walter Hoffman
b. 10.26.1911

Sie fanden gemeinsam am Aug. 8 1930 den tod in den Bergen.

"They were found together, dead in the mountains, having died on
August 8, 1930."

Three tall evergreens ring the graves, planted at the times of their deaths.

It's one thing to be told all the days of your life that the beautiful
words that ended Ruth's story about the life of a leaf also are inscribed on
her tomb. It's quite another to stand before her tomb and see it.

It's one thing to hear all the days of your life about two lost uncles,
lost in the snows of Austria one summer day. It's quite another to stand
before the double headstone and feel the generations of grief.

I have heard the story of my uncles' deaths many times, from my
mother, from my grandmother. But to hear yet a different version, told by
a stranger, one whose youthful memory contains my family's loss, burns
the old horror deeper into my being.

They were hiking. It was August. In a sudden snowstorm, their
guide was killed by an avalanche. They could not find their way. They sat
down in the snow. Heinz was already asleep. Walter, with the foresight
that was typical of him, took a notepad and wrote down: "Aug. 8, 1930.
Heinz und Walter Hoffman, Wilhelmshohe, Kassel. A snowstorm. We
lost our guide."

For a year their bodies were not found. The truth that they were dead,
though suspected, was not certain. The parents, Emma and Simon, not
wanting to be questioned, to be seen, stayed indoors during the day and
took walks only at night.

In six years they lost three children. Now it is August 7, 1987. Tomorrow will be the 57th anniversary of their deaths. August 8, Friedl says, is also Simon Hoffman's birthday. His two sons died on his 54th birthday.

The graves are well-tended. Simon Hoffman has left money for that. He bought an entire family plot, Friedl says. He expected to be buried here with his three children. Not in Kensington, California, so far away. And yet only 14 years later I was born. A new generation began. My grandfather, aged 65, had a heart attack and died. My grandmother lived on alone for more than a quarter of a century. Similar stories are told by many of these headstones. The men died twenty, thirty years before the women did. But not all the women were allowed, as was my grandmother, to die a natural death.

The gravestones tell the stories of a rich and varied Jewish people. There are gravestones that are over two hundred years old. They tell stories of babies that died after just a few months of life and of full long lives mourned in their season. Too many, however, died in 1933. Headstone after headstone bears that date, as though the elderly let go the ghost in that first year of the Schreckenjahre. And then there are the unnatural deaths, the headstones indicating deportations and deaths in concentration camps:

Bernard Mosbacher
d. 1929

Clara Mosbacher
d. 1942 in Thieresenstadt.

She would have been 83. "Oh," said Friedl, "I know that name. They were business people. They did very well. You know," she says, "in that terrible time we had no idea what was happening in the camps."

Later, pressing photographs upon my mother and me of my mother's father, of the boys, of Ruth, of my mother holding her infant son, Dieter Hanschen, of the house itself—ghosts, all ghosts of what is no more, she says: "Who will value these or understand them when I am gone? Give them to your children, and when you think of us, think well of us."

Across the chasm of the dead, of the horrors of the camps, of all that came between a childhood in which my mother and Friedl ran free and happy, Friedl looks at my mother, presses her hand and says: "Das war unsere Schönste zeit, die Wilhelmshohe ziet." (Those were our best years, the Wilhelmshohe years.) Her family had to leave Wilhelmshohe, of course, when my family did. And so she bundled up her losses and my mother's into one great sadness, one lost beautiful childhood.

Across the chasm she reaches for my hand and asks to be remembered positively. "Your grandparents were good, generous people. They gave to the poor. They always were concerned about those who had less than they did. And not only Jews. They helped all kinds of people. And look how they were rewarded."

I go to join my husband, who has left the Hoffman grave site and is going from grave to grave, weeping. He wants to lay eyes on every gravestone in that cemetery, he tells me, to bear winess to the dead, of natural and unnatural causes, to stand in for all the Jews who cannot visit their dead. Walking with him I see my mother and Friedl from a distance, among ivy-covered headstones, both mothers, both grandmothers, swapping stories of their children and their grandchildren, bragging, showing photos. Dieter Hanschen is a successful businessman. Married, with children. There among the gravestones, two women whose childhoods are joined and whose adult lives are severed, come together in stories of continuity.

Friedl's mother, my mother learns, died in 1945, after learning of the death of her son in the war. What was worse for her, Friedl says, was that she had no grave to bury him in, no remains to bury. He was an unknown soldier.

In the cemetery a monument commemorates the Jewish boys who died in World War I. Another grave bears this message:

Wer im Gedachtnis seiner Lieben lebt
Der ist nicht Tod, der ist nur Fern.

"He who lives in the memory of those who loved him
Is not really dead, just far away."

Later, wandering through exhibits and displays of books in Kassel, after Friedl has left us to run her downtown errands, we find a book about the Jews of Kassel. It is an inventory of the names and fates of Kassel's Jews. It has been printed very recently, in 1986. Looking through it my mother learns the fate of her brother Walter's friend, Hans Wolfgang Lewandowski.

He was born in Kassel on October 2, 1911. He was deported to the concentration camp Auschwitz and died there on January 12, 1941. He got nine and a half more years of life than did my mother's brother, Walter.

"Oh, Hans Lewandowski," says my mother. "He was always at our house. I can still see his face." She is quiet for a moment. And then she says, "It was probably better to die in the snow than to die in Auschwitz."

CHAPTER TEN

THE FORBIDDEN
FEMININE:

Finding Our Spiritual Roots

*A straight track is gaping open before me. An underground
hollow is gaping before me. A cavernous pathway is gaping before
me. An underground pathway is gaping before me. Red I am
like the heart of a flame of fire. Red, too, is the hollow in which I
am resting.*

ABORIGINAL CHANT[1]

T he search for feminine soul requires us to seek a source that runs
deeper than our personal Motherline stories, deeper even than our
ancestral, cultural roots—that takes us down to our primordial
origins in the Great Mother. This is at once the easiest and the hardest part
of the journey. For the Great Mother is all about us, always with us; her
nature is expressed in our female bodies, the food-yielding earth, and our
myth-making cultures. We live in her embrace and she lives through us.
She bears us, feeds us, and buries us. Our Motherline stories are manifestations of her life force. Yet we have lost our orientation to her.

She cycles through our bodies, bleeding and passionate, fecund and
rageful. We are born of her, we become her, we give birth to her so that
she may carry on the life cycle. Yet, consciously, we do not know her in
ourselves. She confronts us with the beginning and the ending of our lives;
yet we deny her. The aboriginal people of Australia face her at a sacred

place they call Ankota, the "vulva of the earth."[2] Though she is the flesh and blood of our instincts, the living myth that gives form and meaning to our stories, our bodily cycles, our dreams, our place on this earth, we have driven her out of our consciousness.

We need the archetypal mother to reclaim the forbidden fruit of our wholeness. She comes to us in dreams and visions, in our relationship to the natural world and to our bodies, and in the shadow realms of what we most fear in ourselves.

THE THIRTEENTH FAIRY

On my journey to reclaim ancestral aspects of my Motherline, I was initiated by a dream and a vision into this archetypal level of my quest. The dream came as I parted with my mother in Germany. I had been filled with the terrible grief of my family and my people, and yet I felt full of new life and pleasure. In Israel and in Germany I had gathered up lost pieces of myself. I thought of this knowledge as having the power of the thirteenth fairy in fairy tales, the one who is not invited to the birth of the new child. It is she, the neglected one, who makes trouble for the little princess when she grows up. I could describe the thirteenth fairy in my psyche as my father's side of the Motherline, which I had neglected until I received the letter his mother had written before my birth. I could also call my mother's German heritage the thirteenth fairy, split off because of the terrible fate of German Jews. On my journey I had reclaimed these previously denied aspects of myself, and I felt new energy flow through me from my Israeli relatives and my European cultural heritage.

And then I had the following dream: My mother led me deep into the European woods to a little glade. There I drank water from a small stream and rested. Then she handed me over to another woman, who was larger than life, red-haired and fair-skinned, slightly eerie, very powerful, who would take me deeper into the woods.

On awakening I realized that because a personal mother can be only a partial channel for the archetype, my mother had handed me over to the guidance of the old fairy goddess of the ancient European pagan rituals. She is truly the thirteenth fairy in our culture, the neglected one who was once worshipped and now is lost and forgotten.

The dream foreshadowed a vision. Soon thereafter I visited Glastonbury Tor in England. It is an ancient sacred mound, said to have been an island once. It is supposed to be the place to which Joseph of Arimathea took the Holy Grail and from which it disappeared. It is also said to have been a labyrinth used for processional dances in the old religion. I looked at the soft green of the English countryside as I sat on the ancient mound, and closed my eyes. I felt my body connected to the earth as to mother. Mother was not only my personal mother, nor was it my mother's mother, nor my father's mother whom I had so recently reclaimed from her mass grave. I sat on the lap of English earth from whence I claim no forebears, and felt the earth as mother.

Then the clear image of a grinning, naked goddess appeared to my inner eye. She was in a semi-squat, using her hands to display her open vulva in a fierce and blatant sexual gesture. I had no memory of ever having seen such an image before. Something in the intensity of her eyes reminded me of Aztec images, but I could not place her. I looked at her for a long time. Then I shook my head, opened my eyes, and got up. Walking back down the Tor with my husband I found myself ashamed of her outrageous pose. I didn't speak of it as we wandered around the Chalice Well, a sacred spring, said to be the womb opening of the goddess of the old religion, whose waters ran rusty as menstrual blood. At the nearby souvenir shop I was drawn to a book called *Celtic Mysteries*. I opened it to find the shameless female image I had just seen on the Tor.

She is Sheela-na-gig, Celtic goddess of creation and destruction. She appears in England and Ireland on medieval churches and castles. She is described as the "repellent Kali-aspect of the goddess" whose usual characteristics are "an ugly, mask-like skull-face with a huge scowling mouth, skeletal ribs, huge genitalia held apart with both hands, and bent legs. . . ." She offers both "a fantasy of unlimited sexual license" and shows off her female vulva as it looks just after giving birth, thus presenting us with the "intimate and awesome sight of the birth mystery and symbolizing the moment when the bloody placenta is severed and new life released."[3] Sexuality, birth, and death are all combined and confused in this powerful, archetypal image of the forbidden feminine who appeared to me on a summer afternoon, demanding that I honor the wholeness of the female experience.

Sheela-na-gig is not an easy goddess to acknowledge. She requires that we honor the comingling of spirit and body, that birth and death are bloody and are always with us; that our existence is structured on the bones of our mortality; and that even the milk of our mother's breast is laced with ambivalence. Her bawdy statement of our human origin is every woman's Motherline truth, yet our access to her has been denied by the Judeo-Christian ethic. This vengeful, neglected goddess appears in various manifestations in many times and cultures.

In the Jewish myth her name is Lilith; she was driven out of the Old Testament as the forbidden side of feminine nature: sexually aggressive, fierce, associated with the bloody side of the female cycle. In the Bible her name is Asherath and she is the mother of the gods in the Canaanite pantheon. She was worshipped by the tribes of Israel for centuries until her "graven images" were driven from the land and from our consciousness.[4] Reviled as the "whore of Babylon" she was the goddess who knew her sexuality was sacred. In the Gnostic Gospels of Christian mysticism her name is Mary Magdelene; she was told to leave the disciples because "women are not worthy of life."[5] She has been disrespected, dismembered, burnt at the stake, forbidden, sent into exile, made taboo.

In a great cultural shift, which took different forms all over the world, the old goddess-worshipping religion was forgotten and reviled; the gods became masculine. We women have learned shame about our bodies and our passions. We have learned a creation myth that splits us from our carnal self knowledge, in which woman is created by a transcendent, disembodied god out of the body of a man: a myth that dissociates us from our mammalian roots and the sacredness of our birth-giving capacity. The too-bright light of patriarchal consciousness, with its emphasis on spirit over matter, has blinded us to the true depths of our own natures.

Elaine Pagels quotes a gospel in which Jesus offers to guide Mary Magdalene in order to "make her male." Jesus says, "For every woman who will make herself male will enter the Kingdom of Heaven."[6] Women have been making themselves male for thousands of years in the hope of feeling acceptable to the powers that reign in heaven, on earth, and in their own souls. The reclamation of our female souls requires facing what we have been forbidden to know in ourselves and in the world—the primal feminine principle.

THE OLD RELIGION

Religions and gods that are repressed often find their way back into the culture that excluded them. Pagan holidays like Halloween have survived centuries of Christianity, and Native American religious practices are resurfacing in our own culture. The sacred feminine emerges in diverse manifestations throughout history. All over the world in Eastern cultures and native societies, there are monuments, carvings, frescoes, underground kivas, temples in the shape of the female body, mounds in the shape of the pregnant goddess, and sacred springs. These holy places and objects express reverence to the birth-giving, death-dealing Great Mother. In Pueblo Indian cultures the kiva, a sacred place under the earth, represents the womb of mother earth and the place of human origin. Silbury Hill in England represents the pregnant belly of the Great Goddess.[7]

Recent archaeological discoveries have unearthed evidence of goddess-worshipping cultures that existed for 25,000 years from Paleolithic to Neolithic times, in modern-day Turkey, Iran, Iraq, and Eastern Europe. From both an archaeological and psychological viewpoint, human culture is based on what Jungian analyst Joseph Henderson calls "an older layer of the mind."[8] "Goddesses," as anthropologist Raphael Patai has observed, "are ubiquitous."[9] They are manifestations of the old religion referred to by indigenous people all over the world. Betty Meador, a Jungian analyst, notes that for most of our cultural evolution, human beings organized their sense of the sacred around the goddess. Meador writes:

> The reality of the goddess religions gives to woman a fully realized matrix in which her intuitive searching can now come to rest. No longer must she settle for an adaptation to the father, that identity which is forever secondary, forever unsatisfactory. She now stands with the mother on female ground.[10]

But it is not just in archaeological excavations or ancient ruins that we find evidence of this female layer of human consciousness. It emerges in the sacred texts and imagery of patriarchal religion as well. In the Old Testament we find a hymn of praise to the female body in the middle of a book that Penelope Shuttle and Peter Redgrove point out is "dedicated to the exclusive supremacy of a male God."[11] That hymn, "The Song of Songs," is a series of passionate love poems in alternating male and female voices.

> I am black but comely, oh ye daughters of Jerusalem. . . .
> I am the rose of Sharon
> And the lily of the valleys. . . .
> I am come into my garden, my sister, my spouse
> I have gathered my myrrh with my spice

> I have eaten my honeycomb with my honey
> I have drunk my wine with my milk. . . .
>
> How beautiful are thy feet with shoes, O prince's daughter!
> The joints of thy thighs are like jewels
> The work of the hands of a cunning workman
> Thy navel is like a round goblet, which wanteth not liquor
> Thy belly is like a heap of wheat set about with lilies.

Shuttle and Redgrove argue that the navel referred to in the "Song of Songs" is a wrong translation. What is in fact being praised is the lady's vulva! The voice of the old religion's eroticism is manifest in this "anti-bible within the Bible."[12] The lover who drinks the wine with the milk is mixing blood and milk, thus violating menstrual taboos and Jewish dietary laws. He is referring to the sacred traditions of many old religions in which the menstrual blood of the goddess, the "blood of Isis," Queen Mab's red mead, Lakshmi's mystic drink called Soma, has the power to immortalize kings and pharoahs and give male gods the wisdom of the feminine.[13]

In Christian myth we find the resurrection of the sacred aspects of the female body in the form of the Holy Grail, said to be the chalice used by Christ at the Last Supper. The Grail myth took on a life of its own, emerging in Europe as the Christianized version of the Celts' holy cauldron of regeneration, a "womb symbol meaning rebirth."[14] The earthy nature of the archetypal feminine made its way into medieval Christianity in the form of the Black Madonna, and into medieval Judaism as the fierce aspect of the Shekina whose feet "go down to death."[15]

We can also catch glimpses of this older layer of human consciousness through cultures less rigidly patriarchal than our own. In these traditions the strength and fertility of the female is honored. In India the young girl is said to have "born the flower" when she begins to menstruate, and is then wrapped in her first sari.[16] In many American Indian traditions, there is an initiation ceremony for the young woman who has begun to menstruate that celebrates her beauty, her strength, and her potential fertility. Unlike the boy who must struggle with his instinctual, biological nature and master it, whose initiation molds him into "the kind of man his culture determines him to be,"[17] a young woman's first period is in itself her initiation into adulthood. The boy's coming of age is outwardly determined, while his sister's is an inward, organic process.

Among the Indians of the Northwest the menstruating girl is celebrated with singing, dancing, and food, and then is taken out to sea in a dugout. To prove her strength she has to swim back to the village alone. Among other Indians, the physical ordeal might involve dancing or running. Although she has to demonstrate her strength, anthropologist Claire Farrar writes that the girl "is said to be a woman immediately upon menstruation. She does not become a woman through the Ceremony; she already is one. Girls become women whether or not they have a Ceremony." The girls' puberty ceremony is a "rite of confirmation and a rite of intensification."[18]

In her beautiful collection of Indian lore and myth, *Daughters of Copper Woman,* Anne Cameron describes the old religion's attitude toward menstruation in the words of a grandmother talking to a young girl:

> "Every month, when the moon time came for you, you'd go to the waitin' house and have a four day holiday, or a party. Most of the women had their moon time at about the same time of the month, and you'd sit on a special moss paddin' and give the blood of your body back to the Earth Mother, and you'd play games, and talk, and if you were havin' cramps there was a special tea you could drink and they'd go away, and the other sisters would rub your back. We'd play Frog if the cramps were a bother. You scrunch down, like this," and Granny dropped to the ground to demonstrate, "tuck your knees up under your belly, and put your head down with your forehead on the ground, and then you'd curl your back like a cat, like this, and breathe in deep, and then straighten your back. Looks funny, but it works. It's good when you first start havin' your baby, too, makes everythin' shift into the right place."
>
> Liniculla dropped to the ground beside Granny and tried the position, and Suzie and I watched, looking at each other with quick looks, both of us blinking to keep from getting all watery-eyed as the girl who was years away from starting her menstrual cycle, and the woman who had finished hers years before, practiced the cramp-stopping position.[19]

Peering past the patriarchal structures that have imprisoned our feminine development, we can imagine the embodied experience of female wholeness in this ancient layer of consciousness, when living the life cycle of a woman—becoming maiden, mother, and crone—was carnal knowledge of the triple goddess in oneself. A woman's life unfolded in harmony with her biological rhythm; it was divided into the time before she menstruated, during her menstruation, and after she ceased to menstruate. Her period defined her place in life; it was the mystery of mysteries, the most sacred of the sacred, the life essence itself. It is woman's relation to this life essence that has been severed in patriarchal times.

BAD BLOOD

What has been forbidden and repressed is the bloody side of women's nature, the fierceness associated with being "on the rag," the wild, undomesticated, sexually aggressive, instinctive, "bitchy" aspects of being female. The witchy power of the old woman, who has ceased to menstruate, who is beyond mothering, whose "wise blood" is said to gather within her for the sole purpose of increasing her wisdom, who has access to a fierce female authority that men fear, and whose aging body brings us up hard against the white bones of our mortality, is hated and feared. Our bloody, organic, wild nature, we have learned, is bad.

Ursula LeGuin writes:

> But the experience of women as women, their experience unshared with men, that experience is the wilderness or the wildness that is utterly other—that is in fact, to man, unnatural. That is what civilization has left out, what culture excludes, what the Dominants call animal, bestial, primitive, undeveloped, unauthentic—what has not been spoken, and when spoken has not been heard—what we are just beginning to find words for, our words not their words: the experience of women.[20]

A man I know told me that as a child he referred to his mother's genitals as the "African jungle." Identifying with the mother I felt a hot flash of shame. Then, recovering, I thought: what a strong statement of the wildness of the female body! We all emerge from that jungle, and we all fear and deny it in the split world in which we are caught.

It seems the only wild place our culture recognizes in a woman's soul is the "girl within," the wild horse or Indian or sleuth of an eight-year-old's fantasy play. The wild aspects of the mature woman and the old woman have been cast out of our culture and into the shadows of our self-perception along with Lilith, witches, and menstrual rags.

How does a woman begin to reclaim these core aspects of her nature? We need to ride our own wildness of thought and feeling to the edges of the culture we've inherited, to see beyond it to our own embodied world. We must find our way past a patriarchal view that separates the maternal and the sexual, the Virgin and Mary Magdalene, Eve and Lilith, body and spirit, the birth-giving and the death-dealing aspects of the feminine.

The habit of thought that splits body and spirit goes back to the days in which Hebrew monotheism struggled with the ancient-mother religions of the Near East for the loyalty of the people, a struggle described by Michael Fishbane as between the "high God of Heaven and history" and "the near gods of nature and cosmos."[21] Worship of the "near gods" was the natural province of the women of Israel, whose worship of the old Canaanite pantheon and the Hebrew goddess Asherath expressed a worldview in which nature was "perceived as an unbroken continuum pulsating with divine life." Fishbane describes the cosmos according to the pagan religions of the ancient Near East: "The same energies flow through all beings. . . . all is linked and every level of being . . . 'mirrors' all others." For generations the women of Israel grounded their sense of the sacred in these Eleusinian emotions, found within their own bodily cycles the same sacred fertility principle that they worshipped as idols and pillars to Asherath, and even brought the image of their goddess into the temple itself.

But eventually masculine consciousness, which placed God and man above nature, became the dominant theology. Fishbane describes the process:

> It was against this awesome insight into the teeming vastness and unity of natural life that ancient Israel made its leap of consciousness. The concordance of all-in-all was ruptured; a hierarchy of natural differentiations, separated and ordered in accordance with a supernatural divine will, was spoken. . . . Elohim is unengendered. . . . Such a god is distinct from nature, which neither contains him nor exhausts his power. It is "will" which characterizes such a god. Such a one . . . is a Father-beneficent perhaps—but not a Mother.[22]

As a consequence of the change in patriarchal consciousness, we rise above the state of nature in which human life is, in the famous words of Thomas Hobbes, "nasty, brutish and short."

But at what great cost this leap is achieved, opening an "awesome abyss between God and man-world/nature,"[23] demeaning and denying the body and the mother, creating a language which splits the world. In Ursula LeGuin's words:

White man speak with forked tongue; white man speak di-
chotomy. His language expresses the values of the split world, valuing the positive and devaluing the negative in each redivision: sub-
ject/object, self/other, mind/body, dominant/submissive, active/
passive, man/nature, man/woman, and so on. The father tongue is
spoken from above. It goes one way.[24]

Author and feminist Deena Metzger writes:

> All the practices that honored the way of the woman ceased.
> The Eleusinian mysteries, which had provided immortality, were sup-
> pressed; the mysteries of the Cabeiri, designed specifically to redeem
> those with blood on their hands, were suppressed; procreation was
> infused with anxiety and guilt, fertility festivals that had provided a
> link between earth and spirit were condemned. When the priests sep-
> arated the body from the gods, they separated the divine from nature
> and thereby created the mind-body split.[25]

Demonizing the Feminine

The development of this split world has cost women dearly. We have lost
our identification with our own cyclical experience. Our bodies no longer
seem like the real world to us. We objectify our own physical beings as
inferior and shameful and try to live like men. In the Orthodox Jewish
tradition, men thank God in their morning prayers that they were not born
heathen, slaves, or women. But every day in a woman's life she betrays her
own full nature, sending her wildness, her fierce Sheela-na-gig birth-
giving sexuality, her rage, and her passion off alone to live by the Red Sea,
as did Lilith according to Jewish lore. There is a tradition in which Lilith
spends the holiest day in the Jewish calendar, The Day of Atonement, in
a screeching battle with another female spirit. As Jungian analyst Barbara
Koltuv comments, this is one of her many attempts to be heard by the
God of the Jews.[26]

But the God of the Jews does not hear her, nor do his people understand her, for the red, fiery, passionate, bloody aspects of our nature, and
the black, death-dealing, underworld aspects of women have been demon-
ized. Only the white, benevolent, receptive, and passive aspects are valued.
Menstrual taboos are an expression of this demonization. The Old Testament declares a woman unclean during her period, and "everything she
lieth upon . . . everything also she sitteth upon." Shuttle and Redgrove
write:

To the Rabbis, sex at the period when the blood is flowing was most strictly taboo. It made monsters, they said. It attracted Adam's other dark bride, Lilith. However, sex at the time when children could be conceived was quite acceptable, as if woman were breeding-stock. This is only one instance of a taboo against sex at menstruation which is spread throughout all cultures dominated by men, both historically and at the present time. It is a taboo which approves only that half of woman's nature which is concerned with childbirth and pregnancy.[27]

Susan Griffin writes of the Christian version of this demonization of the feminine:

And it is decided that the angels live above the moon and aid God in the movement of celestial spheres. "The good angels," it is said, "hold cheap all the knowledge of material and temporal matters which inflates the demon with pride."

And the demon resides in the earth, it is decided, in Hell, under our feet.

It is observed that women are closer to the earth.

That women lead to man's corruption. Women are "the Devil's Gateway."[28]

Women's bodies, especially "down there," our genitals, are the "devil's gateway," associated with hell in a tradition that has forgotten the transformational mysteries of descent into the underworld. That is why women suffer such deep shame about natural bodily functions. We pathologize our powerful menstrual experience, and call it PMS. We take pills to rid ourselves of the red and black, witchy and bitchy aspects of our nature. LeGuin explains the psychological function of this dissociation from our bodies: "People crave objectivity because to be subjective is to be embodied, to be a body, vulnerable, violable."[29] The function of the split world then, is to prevent the overwhelming experience of our human vulnerability, especially at the hands of our mothers. We do this in our culture by separating aspects of the feminine so that we women are divided against ourselves.

The Jewish dietary law, *kashrut* (the practice of keeping kosher), reveals how ancient and deep-seated this process is in Western consciousness.

The separation of dairy foods from meat, of blood from milk, is a Jewish Orthodox practice that goes back to the Old Testament commandment, "Thou shalt not seeth a kid in its mother's milk."[30] This law was seen as so essential that it was actually one of the original Ten Commandments.

Why should this be so central a tenet in the development of patriarchal consciousness? Seething a kid in its mother's milk was part of an ancient Canaanite ritual involving the death of the underworld god Mot, who is "winnowed and enters the earth like seeds for new life."[31] Certainly in establishing new religious practices and rituals the old forms had to be forbidden.

But there is something deeper at work here. The "eternal round of birth and death"[32] worshipped in the cult of the goddess is being divided into manageable categories. Hierarchies are being created by patriarchal thought patterns that divide things from one another. The biblical book of Leviticus, for example, is filled with compulsive instructions about the difference between holy and unholy sacrificial offerings, clean and unclean foods, clean and unclean times in a woman's cycle. Human consciousness was engaged in a process of mastering nature and disidentifying with the power of the biological cycle. In *The Fear of Women,* Freudian analyst Wolfgang Lederer writes:

> Why must man continue to soak the earth with his blood, an anonymous agent of nature? He, son of the god in heaven and a creature of the spirit, why should he have to die? If he were to abjure the flesh and its pleasures, could he not escape its pains and its death— and be himself: unique and individual and immortal? . . . The price of such immortality was fearful: it meant surrender of sexuality, of woman, of family, of children. . . .
>
> But of all the demons bent on deflecting man's glance from heaven, woman, the temptress, is the most effective, and thus the most feared and assailed. World-loathing, wherever it appears, is woman-loathing. The cult of sexual immortality worships woman. The cult of individual immortality, wherever it is found, despises woman.[33]

In separating the blood and the milk, the Jewish patriarchs embarked on the process that all patriarchal religions pursued, separating body and spirit, disempowering sexual immortality, cutting the cord of the Motherline with its roots in the underworld, denying the embodied fact of mortality. They created a religious vision in which no woman could recognize her full self, in which she would have to experience herself as loathsome, fearful, or unclean. The Blessed Mother Mary, "uncontaminated by the darker principle,"[34] is all we get of the feminine principle in this split world.

When the goddess appears in her dark manifestations, as the Black Madonna, or the fierce aspect of the Shekina, or the Celtic Sheela-na-gig who confronted me in England, our Western minds find her overwhelming to face, impossible to fathom. Thus author John Sharkey refers to her "repellent Kali-aspect." He has to summon the feminine power of the non-Western Hindu mind to describe her impact.

> When Raphael Patai, in his important work on the Hebrew Goddess, describes the terrible, death-bringing aspect of the Shekhina of Jewish mysticism, his words move swiftly to a discussion of the connection between the Kabbala and Hinduism, and to a consideration of the monstrous and beautiful goddess Kali. In his consideration of the Black Madonna of Europe, Fred Gustafson compares her darkness to that of Kali.[35]

In Shuttle and Redgrove's work on menstruation, *The Wise Wound*, in which they seek to reclaim woman's red, taboo power, they turn to Hinduism and a description of the worship of Kali as a menstrual cult to ground their argument. The Western mind requires the vastness of the Asian image of the feminine in order to move beyond our own split vision.

The Pot of Blood in the Hand of Kali

Kali, be with us.
Violence, destruction, receive our homage.
Help us to bring darkness into the light,
To lift out the pain, the anger,
Where it can be seen for what it is —
The balance-wheel for our vulnerable, aching love.
Put the wild hunger where it belongs,
Within the act of creation,
Crude power that forges a balance
Between hate and love.
May Sarton[36]

In India the terrible aspects of life and of the mother are worshipped. Every corner of that great suffering city, Calcutta, has its altar to Kali. She is blue. Her tongue drips with human blood. She wears a necklace of skulls and dances on the bodies of the dead. Her name means time, which brings all beings forth and presently destroys them. Her breasts are full of milk. She gives birth unceasingly and suckles the young. People bring her flowers and food offerings. It is difficult for the Western mind to fathom this chaotic image of life-giving and life-taking, this terrible mixture of blood and milk.

Carl Jung, who was not generally squeamish about life's negative aspects, spoke of finding the image of Kali unbearable when he visited her temple at Kalighat in Calcutta.[37] Animals are brought to this temple for slaughter. The head of the animal is given as an offering to Kali, and its blood flows in her honor. But the flesh belongs to those who perform the sacrifice. In this "bloodiest temple on earth,"[38] butchery, blood, and spiritual practice are inseparable, expressing the Hindu worldview that embraces suffering and makes no distinction between the material, corruptible world and the divine.

Although there is discrimination against women in Indian culture, and the Brahmin codes have menstrual taboos that are as rigid as those of Jewish orthodoxy, the old religion has not been entirely lost to the Indian psyche. The esoteric, erotic practices of Tantra honor the energizing, red, menstrual side of a woman's cycle. Yoni worship, honoring the female genitals, includes drinking the "divine essence" from the vulva of the goddess. The Indian writer Ajit Mookerjee tells us that "India is the only country where the goddess is still widely worshipped today, in a tradition that dates to the Harappan culture of c. 3000 BC and earlier."[39]

A twist of fate took me to India as a young mother, where I accompanied my first husband in his position as a doctor with the Peace Corps. Early exposure to Kali powerfully shook my cultural attitudes. I remember a conversation I had with an Indian woman friend about the state of the world. It was 1968. My young American consciousness was formed by the Vietnam war, by the cold war, by the nuclear terror in which I thought everyone in the world lived. What did she do with those feelings, I wondered. My friend looked puzzled. She smiled gently. "But it is the time of Kali," she said. "This has happened before and it will happen again. The world is destroyed and then it returns when Brahma awakes from his lotus dream." Her acceptance of the inevitable cycles was terrifying to me, and yet I envied her comfort with them. She had no illusions about being the master of her fate, and she did not feel guilty for things over which she had no control.

I also remember, during that youthful time, sitting on the eastern shore of India and being suddenly overtaken by the terrible, chaotic power of the Hindu view of life. My first husband and I were taking a trip without our children—a rare pleasure. We had come to see the great stone carvings of the south of India. One huge carving depicts the descent of the sacred river Ganges from heaven to earth. In another, the great mother, Durga, who is both nurturer and warrior, is riding her lion in pursuit of the buffalo demon. These carvings are more than a thousand years old, overwhelming in their complexity and beauty. I remember feeling hot and exhausted. I couldn't possibly comprehend all I was seeing. I was relieved when we were given directions to a government bungalow near Mahabalipuram, just up the beach from a famous shore temple.

We arrived after dinner in the last gleam of twilight. The bungalow was simple: beds with knotted string instead of a mattress, stone floors, no electricity. The shore temple was a glowering of two dark pyramids, mysterious in the dying light. My husband said he was ready for bed. Nothing to do without light, he said. I said I wanted to sit on the beach and watch the night. It took a long time for the light to fade from the huge stretch of sea and sky. I got restless and cold, but I stayed out. I had a point to prove. I was irritated about his lack of imagination. Hadn't most people in most times lived without electric light? Surely I could enjoy one night without the aid of artificial light.

As the night darkened, the stars increased. Far from cities, far from artificial light, their multitude and brightness overwhelmed me. I felt as I had at the Descent of the Ganges, overwhelmed by the smallness of individual human beings in the vastness of the cosmos. India teemed with life, suffering, beauty, history. The sky, though full of light, seemed unbearably far away to me. I was filled with a harsh truth—the stars did not care about me or my small life.

Looking at the vague shape of the shore temple, like a ghost of itself in starlight, I remembered being told that there had once been four more temples, even more exquisitely carved than the one that was left. They had all been washed away by the relentless sea.

I had left my hot little life with children and husband and come out into the night, to the edge of the universe. It was a great black hole that devoured us all, humans and stone carvings and temples and epochs. An icy blade of terror cut into my hot, beating heart. How could one withstand so terrible a vision? By finding the shapes of gods and goddesses among the stars? By carving our sense of meaning into the cold stone? Even such memorials to human immortality were swept away by the endless sea, by the devouring mouth of Kali, who masticates on our meanings and makes dead meat of our love.

More than a year in India should have prepared me for this, I thought. Unthinkable suffering was an everyday sight. I had been to Calcutta, where people live on the streets in their own excrement, bone thin, full of running sores. With every step you take a beggar comes after you pleading: "Amah, Amah, paise amah!"

In the town where I lived there was a gang of beggars. The king of this gang was a man with foreshortened arms and legs. They had been broken, he told me, by the beggars to whom his parents sold him. "No one will give money if there is no deformity," he told me, smiling. He had an open, intelligent face, and pranced around on his tiny broken legs. He barely came up to my waist. That he was doing well was evidenced not only by his clear rulership over the other beggars in his area, but by the crisp Dacron shirts he wore, which only the monied could afford in India.

He and I had worked out an arrangement whereby he would watch my children, who I left in the car, while I ran a few errands. He delighted them by jumping so that his face would appear in the car window, and then disappear. When I came back with my groceries I would find the kids in gales of laughter. For this I paid him 50 *paise*, a few pennies in American money, a generous amount in Indian currency. The first time I saw him I could not bear the sight of his deformed arms and legs. I turned away from him. After some time in India, I could look at him and see the beauty of his face, distinguish him from the faceless mass of suffering, see his competence and power. I never could bear to imagine the story of his mutilation. In a country that adores children, in which the child is divine, how could a child be so abused?

In the dark of that night near Mahabalipuram and the last shore temple, some protective human fabric in my consciousness ripped. The great chaotic terror of the cosmos flowed in. It was not only that human beings were unbearably cruel to one another. If that were all, one could imagine a good god who would inspire us to behave ourselves. Indeed, that was a goal of Hebraic law and its separation of blood and milk, requiring that we separate a sense of ethics from the great cyclical round of life. But the requirement that we make ethical decisions about our own behavior does not save us from Kali. No matter how good we are, she will have her way with us in the end. No matter how obsessive we are about separating the pure and the impure, we must face our shadows or be overcome by them.

What I glimpsed on that cold night illuminated by distant stars is that death and destruction, the loss of four intricately carved shore temples, are just as much part of the nature of being as birth, hope, and progress. My Western consciousness was ripped open by the power of the Indian cosmos, and I understood something that is natural to the Indian mind, natural to the female experience, natural to the Motherline. Kali is part of our nature and part of the natural world. She is the spirit in matter, the great mix of blood, milk and bones, the triple goddess who lives in us all. She is the female religious attitude that hovers at the corners of our Western consciousness, waiting to be reborn. She represents a worldview that does not separate the material, embodied experience of being female as thousands of years of Western culture have done.

I was too young then to know my own Kali nature, but she stayed with me until I began to comprehend her. It is no accident that the Western mind keeps turning to Kali to understand the archetypal power of the feminine. As May Sarton says, we need to bring her darkness into the light. We need Kali with us in order to know the full female experience, to know the hate and violence in our own souls.

My Self the Murderer

Every woman has a Kali side; every mother has a secret devourer, a baby killer in her soul. When contemporary women write honestly out of their own lived lives, they wrestle with the shadows of their actions and their fates. They wrestle with their Kali natures; they dare to name the terrible taboos of motherhood. Some write about their murderous impulses toward their own children. Julie Olsen Edwards writes of wanting to kill her baby, who "woke every other hour around the clock, day and night, for four long months, and slept only two hours at a time for the next six."

> I do not know how I survived that sleepless time. . . . I moved with constant aching bones, could stand no closed doors or shut-in spaces, lost track of days or weeks and wrote long lists of things to do—which turned out to be, on later reading, totally unintelligible. . . .[40]

In a crisis of exhaustion, her baby wakes her once too often. She imagines herself hurling the child's perfect body through the window onto the pavement three stories below. Somehow she manages to protect the baby from her murderous impulse, finally wrapping it in a blanket and riding the bus through the night.

Some women write of the children they refused to bear. In a courageous book about her own abortion, Sue Nathanson writes of the dark night of the soul she suffered as she wrestled with the life she had denied.

> I can find no resting place. I have no inner center of peace and calm to which I can retreat from the pressure and stress of the external world. There is only the anguish, the torment, the shredded remains of my annihilated child, my Self the murderer, confronting me like the garish, alarmingly bright figures that pop up unexpectedly in the horror rides at amusement parks. But rides last only a few minutes, and people choose them for the moments of thrill and excitement they provide. My ride is endless, a hell I can't escape.[42]

In the course of a painful psychological journey, Nathanson comes to understand the damage that is done to women in our culture by our refusal to honor the terrible aspect of the Great Mother. She writes:

> I meditate again upon what a different world it would be if we could each become aware of and take responsibility for our capacity to annihilate others! In such a world we would be less likely to judge women for making the impossible choice between the life of an unborn child, her own life, and that of other family members. . . .
>
> Alone with these thoughts, I begin to cry. I am crying because I have become aware of yet another facet of the loss of my unborn child. I wish now that my fourth child could have been sacrificed with my love and tears, even with my own hands, in the circle of a family or a community of women, in the circle of a compassionate and loving community of men and women who might be able to perceive my vulnerability as a mirror of their own, and not as it was, in a cold and lonely hospital room with instruments of steel.[43]

At a psychological level the abortion issue is about our capacity to confront Kali consciously. Those who would deny women the right to choose abortion seek to control Kali by forcing women to bear children. Kali will then take other forms: ruined lives, neglected and abused children, women maimed or killed in illegal, back-alley abortions. However, those who support a woman's right to choose abortion also need to face the truth that Nathanson's book addresses. Abortion is not merely a medical procedure. It is the tearing from the womb of our own flesh and blood. It is a sacrifice of life, hopefully for life.

Those in the so-called pro-life movement seem to think that people are entitled to be born. This attitude denies another terrible Kali truth: we are all the products of random twists and turns in the life journeys of our ancestors. We could just as well not exist as exist. Gloria Steinem faces the possibility of her own nonexistence in wrestling with the painful story of her mother's broken life.

> She was a loving, intelligent, terrorized woman who tried hard to clean our littered house whenever she emerged from her private world, but who could rarely be counted on to finish one task. In many ways our roles were reversed: I was the mother and she was the child. Yet that didn't help her, for she still worried about me with all the intensity of a frightened mother, plus the special fears of her own world full of threats and hostile voices.[44]

Steinem calls her essay "Ruth's Song (Because She Could Not Sing It)." She engages her mother in dialogue to get behind the frightened face of the mental patient Ruth has been all Gloria's life to an earlier Ruth, a gifted, spirited Ruth, with brown eyes "much like my own." She is struggling to find a mother with whom she can identify. Listening to her mother's stories she finds a thread of meaning that takes her back before her own birth to a time before her mother's first nervous breakdown. She hears about the roads not taken, the roads that might have led her mother to a richer life and asks:

> "But why didn't you leave? Why didn't you take the job? Why didn't you marry the other man?" She would always insist it didn't matter, she was lucky to have my sister and me. If I pressed hard enough, she would add, "If I'd left you never would have been born."
> I always thought but never had the courage to say: But you might have been born instead.[45]

Steinem's question in telling her mother's story is: Was it my birth that destroyed my mother's life? She is looking straight into the terrible eyes of the fate that did her mother in, and gave Steinem a surpassingly rich and successful life.

Struggling to understand her mother's life, Steinem contemplates the sacrifice of her own existence, so that her mother might have had one. We cannot consider the struggle between mothers and daughters without seeing this terrible truth: below the level of our complaints and deprivations is the nightmare world of murderous feelings and nonexistence: mothers whose lives have been devoured by children; children whose lives have been destroyed by mothers; mothers who died in childbirth or whose own potential ended with the birth of children; children who were killed before or after birth, or killed psychologically by their mother's venom.

There is a story from my Motherline that forces me to look into the face of my own nonexistence. It is the story of my grandmother's failed abortion, her attempt to murder my mother in her womb.

I imagine going back in time, looking into her younger face, a face I've only seen in photographs. It is 1919, in Germany. She is almost forty. She has five children, the last of whom was born just last year. Now she is pregnant again. I can imagine how she feels, how her spirits sink: yet another pregnancy. So soon? Isn't there some way to stop this endless stream of babies?

She does not know the fate that lies in store for her, the terrible things that will happen. What mother of young children could face such Kali knowledge? In a few years her oldest daughter will die of diabetes at age ten. One summer, a decade hence, her two grown sons will be killed on a ski trip by an unseasonable avalanche. Soon thereafter Hitler will come to power and her family will flee this beautiful suburb of a gracious, old, German town.

Today, all she knows is that she cannot bear the thought of yet another pregnancy, another child. Even in imagination it is hard for me to look into the eyes of the terrible fate that binds us, she and I, with my mother as the bridge. In her rage, her willfulness, she tries to refuse the new life. She does not get her murderous way, that furious day in late winter, hurling her body down the stairs of her home. Few women of her time did. And so one late summer day she bore my mother; not knowing that in her failure to miscarry lay the continuity of her biological line; not knowing that she would feel a special bond with my mother; not knowing that after all the deaths and all the losses, the birth of my mother's first child would bring a sense of meaning back to her life. I am that child.

It is difficult to look straight into the face of the fate that bore us and so easily might not have. No matter how attached we may be to our lives, none of us knows why one is born and another is not. Every fateful twist in the Motherline affects the future, and a woman's power to bear or not to bear life shapes the generations to come.

So Much Blood

To see a myth in everyday life is to see the river bottom as the water runs over it. Ordinary lives are ever-changing. The myth holds and shapes the flow of water, gives direction and meaning to the life experience. In the writing of this book, I have sought the forms of the old feminine myth in ordinary lives, my own, the women in my family, and women I have interviewed. I have focused primarily on women because it is we who have been left out of history.

But my son challenged me not to leave men out of the telling of Motherline stories. "If it's been a loss for women to be disconnected from their origins, how about for men?" he said. As though my psyche were responding to my son's question, I had a dream: A woman gave birth, sitting on her husband's lap, leaning against him for support and encouragement, covering him with blood. He was entirely engaged with her and comfortable in the red bath of birth. The following story includes a man's Motherline experience.

Some friends of mine had just had a new baby, Lila. Annie gave birth squatting, her feet firmly rooted to the earth. Her husband, Leonard, and Annie's children from her previous marriage, Peter and Sasha, were with her. Hearing the story of Lila's birth, I saw the forms of the old religion re-emerging in everyday life.

I had met Annie when I bought one of her paintings. She had done a series of paintings on cloth. The dominant color was blood red. A simple stick figure, bone white in the middle of a field of red, arms uplifted, legs open as in a squat, seemed to reach down to some primitive core in me. My husband, too, was riveted by the image. He knew it expressed something awesome and ancient, but he could not identify it. Neither could Annie, until after Lila was born.

Through the purchase of her painting a friendship developed with Annie and her husband, Leonard. It was her second marriage, his first. She had brought two children into their relationship, and we often traded stories of the joys and the difficulties of step-parenting. Leonard spoke of how much he longed for a child of his own. Annie told us she wasn't at all sure she could bear another child, physically or emotionally. She told us of almost dying in an automobile accident ten years before. Internally and externally, her body was lacerated and scarred. She wasn't even sure her arms would be strong enough to pick up a baby.

Annie is a vibrant, lively woman. Energy pours out of her face, which is full of light, into the springy curls of hair that frame her face. It would be hard to know how wounded she had been had she not described it in detail. This is the story she told me:

The accident happened at the end of my first marriage. A group of us, including my kids, Peter and Sasha, had been driving down that winding mountain road from Topanga Canyon toward the beach in L.A. Joe, who was then my husband, was driving. A man driving in the other direction fell asleep at the wheel and headed into our lane. Joe swerved the car and the man swerved back into his own lane and hit us broadside on the passenger side. It went right into me.

I woke up in intensive care three days after the accident. I had eight crushed ribs, a broken collar bone, a punctured lung and a tracheotomy so I couldn't speak. I had to mouth my words. When I began to understand what had happened to me, I wanted to know where my children were.

A little boy, Peter's friend, who had been in the car with us, was in the bed next to me. So I figured if he was there why weren't my children there? I was on morphine and things were very hazy. I wasn't thinking clearly. But it meant to me if Peter and Sasha weren't there that they must have died.

Joe came in to see me. My parents were there. Every time I asked the nurses where my children were, their eyes filled with tears because they were touched. They understood my feelings. They were the same age as I was, late twenties. They had children. They knew I thought the children were dead. I'd mouth the words: Are my children dead? They'd say, "No, your children are fine." "Why can't I see them?" They couldn't explain to me why I couldn't see them. They couldn't bring the children into intensive care. It was a rule.

I remember making a promise to myself at that point, believing I had lost my children, that I would never have another child. I couldn't take the pain. I couldn't replace Peter and Sasha. I missed them too much. The thought of ever being so vulnerable again to the loss of a child was unbearable.

Finally, the doctor saw that I wasn't getting better. He understood that I needed to see my children. He got two nurses, because there was all this equipment to carry. And they shot me full of morphine because they were worried about the pain I would be in from being moved. I had eight tubes coming out of me, and two nurses carrying the heart monitor and the lung thing. They wheeled me out into the hallway into a little room next to the nurses' station. And Peter and Sasha came in to see me. I remember seeing those two little people and all of us were crying, everybody was crying. It was so stupid of them not to let the children in the room. After that my body rejected the tracheotomy but I was fine. They were worried. But I could breathe. My life energy took over.

Peter had a little scratch, that was all. And somehow I had thrown Sasha, who was two and in my arms, to the person next to me. Nothing happened to her at all.

I lost about five pints of blood after the accident. They had to give me five pints of some stranger's blood. That event, and losing three days of my life, were the hardest things for me to cope with. I don't know why it was such a big thing that I had someone else's blood in me, but it was. I couldn't believe that someone could do that to another person, take away so much. Take away the blood.

Some years after the accident, I was meditating and a voice came to me and said: There's so much blood with a birth. I didn't know what it meant, but it was very important: there's so much blood with a birth.

You see, I had had a death experience. My heart had stopped. I had gone through the darkness into the light. There was no pain. It was pure bliss and beautiful colors, the other side of life. I had the choice to die or to return to life and I chose to live. I knew I had unfinished business with Peter and Sasha and Joe. I must have taken a deep breath because the most excruciating pain that I've ever felt came into my body. I thought, why am I going back? What do I need this for?

And then I thought, no, this is my first conscious decision. I understood that I wasn't afraid of death, I was afraid of life. Now I was ready to take responsibility for my life. And it all had to do with the blood: my heart stopping and suddenly starting, the blood starting to flow again.

Leonard is a man with a dark, brooding presence. He and Annie met at a conference on death and dying. Like many of his generation he had joined the Peace Corps after college. Two years in India had opened his consciousness to Kali and the dark side of life. Though he was never drafted, he found himself drawn to Vietnam as the war expanded.

After my two years in India, I went to Vietnam with AID. I didn't have to go to Vietnam. I chose to. I had the feeling that this was the experience of my generation, this war. I wanted to know what it was all about. I had seen a great deal of death in Calcutta. But in Vietnam it was more intense of course, being a war zone. I saw many terrible things. The conference on death and dying was part of the exploration I went through later, trying to understand what I had experienced. And so when Annie spoke of her experience, of dying and returning to life, I didn't think she was crazy. It drew me to her.

The story Leonard told me makes my son's point. It is the story of a man who grew up feeling unmothered by his mother, estranged from her body. His connection to his wife's body and his daughter's birth weave him back into a Motherline from which his mother was profoundly alienated. Leonard told me:

Growing up I had a huge amount of anger toward my mother. She really was not a mother. She just was incapable of doing anything motherly. I had nurses from the time I was born. And my birth was bizarre.

She told me this story maybe ten years ago and I still have trouble believing it. Apparently she had a terrible time with the birth of my sister. It was a Cesarean and the doctors did a bad job. She was sewn up so badly that she was in constant pain in her abdomen. Later she had a miscarriage. She's squeamish to begin with. She just can't deal with fleshly issues. When she was pregnant with me, she was afraid I would be stillborn. So she had herself blindfolded and her ears stuffed up at my delivery. That way, she said, if I was born dead she wouldn't have to see me. I think that's typical of the connection between us. It's a symbol of our relationship. I don't have that fleshly fear. I could see dead bodies in Vietnam and handle that. When Annie was in pain during her pregnancy because of scar tissue from her accident, I massaged her stomach almost every day. It was a really direct connection to her body. I'd rub her stomach and five minutes later she'd be in the bathroom.

But when my mother was here recently she picked up Lila and it was as though she had never picked up a baby. She didn't know how to do it. I don't think she ever cooked a meal for me, for anyone. She didn't know how to cook. If I ever got sick she went as far as she could in the other direction. And most disturbing to me, emotionally, she simply was not there. She had no understanding. It was not a happy growing up that I went through.

About two weeks after I met Annie, she said she didn't want any more babies and I got really depressed. I didn't know where it came from but I just knew I wanted to have a baby. I always had this idea that that's what a family is. I wanted to be part of a family and a family has kids. That was one of the biggest issues that Annie and I had to work out. She would say to me at times of greatest frustration: "Well, then just forget it. I'm not going to have a baby." She knew she could really get me with that.

The fact that she had two kids I considered an impediment in some ways but an asset in others. There was a part of me that wanted to get to know them. And there was another part of me that wished I could spend much more time alone with Annie. As time went on and I became a stepfather, I found that I was good at it, that somehow I knew what to do. I don't know where that knowledge came from. Certainly not from my parents. In fact, one of the things that first brought Annie and me close was that she was in constant conflict with her son, Peter. And I could see what he was going through. It reminded me of my own childhood and my dealings with my mother. So I'd tell her to back off a little, to leave him alone. I could tell he was feeling smothered. And she'd listen to me. I was used to not being listened to by my mother at all. So this was quite a different experience. Here was a woman, a mother, listening to me. I liked that. My childhood was so difficult that it was healing for me to be accepted by Peter and Sasha.

When Annie and Leonard got married, Annie agreed to "do her best" to bear another child. She spent years healing herself to make this birth possible. Yoga, running, acupuncture, swimming, meditation and psychotherapy were all part of rebuilding her body and soul. When she learned she had conceived, she started walking every day for exercise.

I was walking four and a half miles a day. That was the most important thing for my body—keeping the blood circulating. The blood in this birth was such an important thing for me. I had promised Peter and Sasha that there wouldn't be much blood. There hadn't been at their births. I had been so afraid of blood when they were little. When they had a cut or put their tooth through their lip like every child will, I would panic.

Annie told me her story with Lila in her arms. Both of them looked beautiful. Annie was more relaxed than I'd ever seen her, her face open and soft, like a woman in love. And certainly she was in love with this calm baby, Lila, her moon face shining and sweet. She told me how different this birth was from her other births.

When Peter was born I felt very alone. His father wasn't allowed into the delivery room and I knew he was terrified during the labor. There was some other woman screaming down the hall and he thought any minute I would let loose. Then in the delivery room there were all those men, no women, giving me support. I think everyone wore masks. I didn't see any faces. But when he was born it was wonderful. I saw his birth through a mirror. I cried, I was so happy. They held him up. I looked at him. I don't remember blood or anything. Then they took him away and worked on him. I just thought, that's how they do it.

When I had Sasha three years later it was much the same experience. I did have the support of a Lamaze group. Again, my husband was not in the delivery room. This time he could have been. He was so afraid. I've never understood what it was he was afraid of, he couldn't articulate it. Whether it was the blood, or my pain. It was a very solitary experience.

Lila's birth was another story. I stayed standing up. I'd put my arms around Leonard for support or around my birthing coach, facing them, just hugging. I also kept my knees bent, that was really important. There was so much blood with this birth and I loved it. Every time I went to the bathroom during my labor there was blood. Because I was standing up for the labor, the blood just seemed to pour out of me. And I was barefoot. I remember once, I know it sounds crazy, walking into the bathroom and there was so much blood that I could see my footprints. I loved it. It was like a painting, like the one I did that you bought. I understand now what that figure is—a birth figure. It was the squatting position in which I gave birth. That blood was healing for me. It was the right blood.

I remember when I was pushing the baby out I got so hot I ripped my clothes off. I had promised the kids I would be dressed. I remember opening my eyes and looking at the doctor. I said: "Tom, I'm so hot." And he said, "Annie, take off your clothes." And I just ripped off the gown that I had on and I stood there naked. It makes me laugh looking back. I felt so rooted, so alive.

I had to push for fifteen or twenty minutes but it felt like forever. Where was that baby? She was so big. There were four or five pushes when I had to really work hard until the doctor, who was squatting on the ground, said: "That baby's there. I saw her head and she's coming!" And I got all my energy together and I pushed and out came that baby! It was just wonderful, that moment. And there was blood everywhere and then she shit. I thought—there it is, that's the metaphor for life. And they were cleaning off the blood and they were cleaning off the shit and I was holding her, putting her to my breasts.

And Peter and Sasha were fine with it. Because the whole thing was so big, it just took over. They saw that I wasn't suffering, that it was all very natural. I kept thinking, God, they are so lucky, they're seeing where they came from. Whereas I have no idea what it was like for my mother. I think she got medication. She never nursed. I was separated from her from the time I was born. I had thrush, so they took me away. She didn't see me for the first few days. Talk about being deprived right from the start.

I asked Leonard how it was to be present at his daughter's birth. He said:

The birth was so elemental. Annie stood up for it and gave birth squatting, and it was very short, three hours. For me it was easy. I like intensity. I also felt deeply connected to Annie's body because I had massaged her every day during her pregnancy. There were many things like this that we did, healing things. It was as though we were given esoteric knowledge that made the pregnancy easier.

I think I felt a little disappointed not to feel more elation when Lila was born. It wasn't the excitement Annie felt. I have a certain distance, which Annie doesn't. It's liberating, freeing me to think about and do other things. But it's certainly not as intense to watch the baby being born as it is to be giving birth to the baby. I could step back from it, and I certainly couldn't feel the pain.

When I found out she was a girl, I was disappointed. It surprised me that I was disappointed. I had thought I didn't care. There went my visions of teaching this kid how to play baseball. Of course, she can play baseball, but she won't be in the major leagues. Now that she's born I'm happier that she's a girl. I'm just charmed by her. I guess it's the opposite sex attraction.

While Annie was pregnant I was scared about my ability to be a good parent. Annie had talked so much about how difficult it was to have a baby and to raise a child, and certainly that was all my mother ever talked about. I was really frightened that I wouldn't have the energy, that I wouldn't have what it takes, that I wouldn't have time for myself. But soon after her birth, it was clear that it just wasn't going to be a problem. Annie was so ecstatic about her. And my connection with her is so easy and sweet.

Right after she was born, she looked at each one of us, straight in our eyes. She was so alert and aware. What I most remember is after everyone left and there were just the three of us in that room, we got into bed with her. She just lay there and looked at us in our arms. She had a real presence about her. I fell asleep with the baby right next to me. I think it was eighteen hours before she ever cried.

For Leonard, whose mother stayed so remote from his own birth, there was powerful Motherline healing in his experience of his daughter's birth. And for Annie there was a recovery of her circulatory system, so wounded in her near-death experience, in the healthy blood she shed in giving birth.

Soon after Lila's birth I discovered the image that had gripped me in Annie's painting in the form of a line drawing in Marija Gimbutas' book about the artifacts of the old religion, *Gods and Goddesses of Old Europe*. It is an ancient image of the "birth-giving Goddess," engraved on a potsherd from sixth-century B.C. Hungary.[46] Annie's psyche had reached into the depths of our human racial memories, forseeing the bloody nature of the birth she was to give, recalling the old religion's worship of the birth-giving goddess. She bore her daughter in the red heat of Kali's power, having known her own death, having claimed a fully embodied birth.

Kali Be with Us

To bear her children, her mother, her life, in the presence of Kali and Sheela-na-gig, requires that a woman know her carnal self, bear her mother's pain and limitations, face the bones of her ancestors and the bloody truth that she has no control over what she is born into, or what she gives birth to. What did it mean in her mother's life when she was born? What familial story, and historical moment, encircles her birth? As she pushes her baby out of her body into the hands of the world, what fate is foretold in the child's first look, first cry? What power has she unleashed that will forever shape her life? What sleepless nights, what laughter and delight, what terror when her child is in danger, what estrangement when the daughter sees her mother as a demon, what agony about an illness or a death, what marvel when her baby has a baby?

A woman needs Kali and Sheela-na-gig to bear all this, to know that though we have our human responsibility, we are not in charge of destiny.

Kali allows us to understand that our personal mothers are not to blame for what is in the nature of human life. She links us to the blood and bones of our female knowledge, to our mothers' suffering as well as our own. She tells us that we are flesh and blood; that we give life and take life, nurture and destroy, suckle and poison; that these are in the very nature of existence, not the terrible fault of women. She knows that it is in the very corruptibility of our flesh that our human souls bloom. She knows that we live in the great hands of history, which can tear our small lives to shreds.

The soul of the woman who has faced the terrible goddess, who has born her mother, and known the carnal wildness of her own bloody nature, has a powerful female ground in which to live. Caught in the relentless flow of time, conceived by a woman she did not choose, and conceiving children she does not know, if she reclaims her Motherline down to the bones of her ancestors, she partakes of the sacred essence of female wholeness, the mixture of the blood and the milk. The wisdom of the old religion takes new form within her. Listen to her story, for she will help you find your way.

RECLAIMING OUR FEMININE SOULS

In an old song the Mother sings: "My sleeping is my dreaming, my dreaming is my thinking, my thinking is my wisdom." She is the bed we are born in, in which we sleep and dream, where we are healed, love and die. In her wisdom we remember day's broken images and carry them down into dreams where their motions roll into shadows and root, growing into stories.

MEINRAD CRAIGHEAD[1]

How does a woman go about finding her feminine soul, honoring her female lineage, learning the stories of her Motherline? How does she make manifest in her own life those aspects of the feminine self this book addresses?

The following pages offer practical suggestions for women who want to know their own Motherlines. The suggestions are keyed to the chapters of the book and to the specific aspects of the feminine self that each chapter addresses.

Finding the Motherline is not a linear process. It is entirely individualistic, and you may begin at any point in the process. It is the work of most of a lifetime. I only suggest places to begin your exploration; remember that every woman's journey takes a different form and that your own life direction will carry you on. There is no right or wrong way to find your Motherline—there is only your way.

RECLAIMING OUR STORIES

Motherline stories are as common as gossip, as ordinary as women's talk while cooking or washing dishes, as easy to come by as are the moon and the tides and the uterine blood we shed each month. They are stories of being female, of being mothers and daughters. They tell of our carnal knowledge of life's mysteries.

At lunch with a friend you may suddenly hear her feelings, emotional and physical, just before her period begins. Perhaps she refers to her mother's attitude about menstruation and remembers, laughing, the atmosphere in her family when she and her sister were teenagers and all the women in the household went "on the rag" at the same time. This is a Motherline story. If you can shift your attitude from culturally induced feelings of shame and let yourself experience the power of what she describes, you can both begin to reclaim the sacredness of menstruation.

At a family gathering your grandmother may bring out the photo album for the umpteenth time. If you can get beyond your generational prejudices and whatever personal struggles you and she have, and listen to the stories that are evoked by the old photographs, you may find yourself the recipient of a rich vein of Motherline lore. We modern women don't have the old female rituals to lean on. We have to be open to the sources of Motherline knowledge as they come to us. A woman can seek her motherline through her female relatives, through imaginal work in her own psyche, or through group work in circles of women.

Mothers, grandmothers, daughters, granddaughters are the most obvious sources of our stories and Motherline meanings. Whether a woman has access to this source depends on the nature of her relationship to the women of her line. Often, mothers and grandmothers are no longer alive by the time we are ready to hear their stories. Or, as is the case for many modern women, the relationships are filled with so much pain and rage that communication is bound to be wounding. In these situations a woman must find other sources. Sometimes a friend, an aunt, or a grandmother can orient a woman in her Motherline when she is unable to talk to her mother.

If you can't talk to your female relatives or you are temperamentally more comfortable with inner work, you can go within yourself. You can use techniques of active imagination, journal writing, painting, or drawing to activate the Motherline sources in your psyche. You can go into a state of deep relaxation and evoke your mother or grandmother. Ask her the questions you would ask in an external conversation. Write in your journal from your mother's perspective. Draw your mother holding you as a child and imagine your mother's experience. It is always amazing to me how much we know of our foremothers' experience. Whenever I have invited women to embark on this inner journey, they surprise themselves and me with how much they know.

Women who gather in support groups, recovery groups, spiritual groups, study groups, professional groups, writing or painting groups can deepen their experience of the feminine soul by evoking the Motherline source. A simple way to begin this process is for the members of the circle to introduce themselves by naming their mothers and grandmothers, and their country or state of origin. For example, I would say: I am Naomi of California, daughter of Giesele of Germany, granddaughter of Emma of Germany and Clara of Russia. I have often used this method when teaching or doing workshops. A rich tapestry of origins emerges; the complex subsoil of our Motherline sources becomes manifest.

These approaches, whether explored with relatives, in solitude, or in circles of women, can evoke powerful emotions of sorrow and loss, fear and rage, love and longing. They require us to work with our grief and to work with our shadows. In seeking soul we must be prepared to suffer deep feelings. I don't suggest undertaking any Motherline work lightly. For many, it will be important to be in therapy while doing this work.

RECLAIMING MASTERY AND/OR MYSTIQUE

The women's movement has been a crucible for our sense of self in this century. It has thrown mothers, daughters, and grandmothers onto opposite sides of the generation gap it created. We fight the mastery vs. mystique fight in our personal lives: Daughters whose mothers stayed home are going to do it "right" by becoming professional; daughters whose mothers worked are going to do it "right" by staying home with their children.

Whether you approach your mother in person, in imagination, or in the context of a circle of women, you can move beyond this cultural split to claim her as an orienting principle in your life. This requires sorting out her archetypal function as life-giver and first nourisher from her life as a woman in a particular moment in the culture. A way to do this is to ask her how her sense of self and meaning was affected by the women's movement. Don't forget that, if you are talking to an old woman, the first wave of the movement came in the early part of this century and culminated in women's right to vote in 1920. She may have memories and feelings about that tumultuous time. Middle-aged women will chart the course of the second wave of the women's movement through their lives and histories.

Those doing imaginal work may want to imagine or paint the feeling tone of their mother's or grandmother's experience of the women's movement. For some it was a wildly exhilarating burst into new life. For others it was a dark diminishment of a sense of self and worth. In circles of women, each can share her experience of the movement. Given enough divergence in ages and points of view, the voices of many perspectives will evoke a complex collective image of this sea change in women's lives.

RECLAIMING THE MOTHER TONGUE

The simple act of consciously creating a space to hear your mother's or grandmother's story, from her point of view, can have a transformative effect on your relationship. Many women go through life without ever being asked how it was for them, what the meaning of their life experience has been. When you ask for your mother's story you are making her the heroine of the drama. You may be surprised at how moved she is, and how willing to share her life experience. Both of you may need to do some work on the grief you feel about not having been able to talk this way before. The central question to ask is: "What was it like for you?" Asking your mother what it was like for her when you were born will elicit an image of who you are to her, what your birth meant in her life.

Another approach is to ask your mother to make you a photograph album that tells the story of her marriage, your birth, and your childhood. The process will call up strong memories for her; ask her to share them with you.

RECLAIMING LOVE, REBELLION, AND
OUR PERSONAL SHADOWS

It can be a relief to learn that our mothers and grandmothers had struggles with their own mothers. Ask your mother what she and her mother fought about, what she disliked about her mother, how she wished her mother had been different. Ask your grandmother how your mother dressed and acted when she was a teenager.

An interesting journal exercise is to write about those aspects of your mother's body and personality that are most revolting to you. In writing, claim them. For example, I have my mother's heavy thighs, or her bad temper, or her trouble meeting strangers. Will her heavy thighs drag you down into the shame she feels about her body? Will her rage alienate you from friends and family? Will her fearfulness about strangers limit your life? In writing from the inside of her heavy thighs, her rage, her timidity, you humanize her limitations and potentially develop empathy for her experience.

RECLAIMING THE MOTHER-DAUGHTER LOOP

How has being *your* mother changed her? How has her experience of being both mother and daughter matured and enriched her sense of life's meanings? Some questions to ask her are: How was your childhood different from mine? How was your mother different from you as a mother? How was I different as a daughter than you were *as a daughter?* Have there been surprises, disappointments, unexpected pleasures in raising me? If you are in mid-life and have raised children, you may want to ask yourself these questions as well.

Photo albums showing baby pictures of mother, daughter, and grandmother can elicit feelings and memories about the mother-daughter loop. Another technique that can be done alone or in circles of women involves imagining the loop with mother in the middle, grandmother on one side, and daughter on the other, and drawing it.

RECLAIMING THE CULTURE THAT SHAPED OUR MOTHERS

How many of us have flinched when an older woman says: in *my* day. We resent her critique of our modern ways from her old-fashioned perspective. Yet she is naming a part of our roots; much of our past is locked into the attitudes of earlier times. Unless we understand the power of the zeitgeist we cannot connect to our origins.

To uncover the cultural attitudes that shaped your mother or grandmother, ask her questions about the values she was raised with concerning sexuality, birth, menstruation, and child-rearing. Most mothers and grandmothers find it so refreshing to be asked about their "old-fashioned" values, instead of having to defend them, that new channels of communication can be opened between generations.

Your feeling for the power of cultural change also can be enhanced by reading books about women's issues in other times. For example, Margaret Sanger's autobiography opens a window into the sexual lives of women in the early part of this century when many of our grandmothers and great grandmothers were growing up. Kim Chernin's brilliant book, *In My Mother's House,* illuminates the entirely different generations, cultures, and sets of political values that influenced a Russian-born mother and her American daughter.

RECLAIMING THE POWER OF THE GRANDMOTHER

There is a powerful affinity in most women between the inner child and the grandmother. Evoking the crones of your Motherline is most easily done by inviting the girl within you, in your mother or grandmother, to tell stories about grandma. Ask yourself, your mother, or grandmother, what it was like when you were little and you visited your grandmother, or she visited you. If you have no living grandmothers, try to remember the stories you heard in your childhood about your grandmother and who you imagined her to be.

Photographs and heirlooms are also stimuli for grandmother stories. Often our mothers have jewelry, china, or patchwork quilts from their mothers and grandmothers. Ask about them: when they were worn, how they were used, when they were made. It is amazing how an old tea cup, a wedding band worn thin from years of use, or a tattered quilt can uncork a fountain of Motherline stories.

In circles of women, it is powerful for every member of the circle to tell a grandmother story. The circle is enhanced by the calling up of so many women from another time. The collective grandmotherly presence shifts and deepens the experience of women sitting together.

RECLAIMING THE REALM OF THE ANCESTORS

What do you know about the dead in your Motherline? What stories do you remember about mothers who died in childbirth, children who died

too young, husbands who left young widows, great grandparents left behind in the Old Country who died unvisited by children or grandchildren?
Life's tragic dimension, the source of much of the pain and depression in
women's lives, begins to be revealed when we ask mothers and grandmothers to tell us who died and how it affected them. Sometimes we bring
to consciousness a grief that has been repressed for generations.

In circles of women, the naming of the dead and the circumstances
of their dying can evoke the context of ghosts we all move among in our
everyday life. Commemorating the dead with our female relatives, in solitude, or in circles of women, gives us psychological access to the grave-
yards of our forebears.

RECLAIMING OUR MOTHER'S CHILDHOOD LANDSCAPES

We are a nation of immigrants. Our people come from faraway lands, usually from terrible circumstances: famine, war, political and religious per-
secution, the slave trade. Those who are of Native American extraction also
live with the devastating loss of lands and traditions. Sooner or later in any
American Motherline story, you learn of some terrible fate.

If you are a first- or second-generation American, your mother or
grandmother grew up in another world. Traveling together to the landscape of her childhood may be a very meaningful journey for both of you.
If such a journey is not possible, you can make it in your imagination, by
listening to the stories of her childhood, reading books about her country
of origin, painting or visualizing the place and the people in your mind's
eye.

If your people have been in this country for generations, a journey to
your mother's birthplace will evoke her memories and ground your sense
of your origins. Ask her to show you the house she grew up in, the school
she went to, where her best friend lived, and where she played after school.

In circles of women, each can take a turn telling where her people
come from, what the circumstances were of their leaving, what they had
to leave behind. This evokes a female version of the Great American myth
of the new world and the frontier.

RECLAIMING OUR SPIRITUAL ROOTS

The Great Mother can be found in many places and cultures. How a woman
seeks her has to do with her religious orientation, cultural roots, and per-

sonality style. Some are drawn to her manifestation in their own cultural context; others seek her in the many forms she takes in other cultures. Finding her may be as simple as spending time communing with the Virgin Mary in your local Catholic church or lighting the Sabbath candles in a Jewish home to evoke the Sabbath bride. Seeking her may be as exotic as bringing wreaths of flowers to the many-armed blue images of Kali in Calcutta, or performing a drumming ritual at the full moon.

For some a descent into the darkness of a kiva in the Southwest, representing the female source for the Pueblo Indians, will evoke a primordial experience of the feminine. Others will seek knowledge of the many manifestations of the goddess in prehistory by reading some of the books now available on the subject. Some may find it meaningful to set up an altar in their home to a favorite goddess. Others evoke the goddess in active imagination or join a circle of women involved in spiritual practices. Spiritual preferences are profoundly individual, and each woman must honor her own deepest truth.

What is most important is cultivating a feeling for the sacred in our everyday lives and listening to our dreams. The goddess comes to us in many ordinary forms: in stories, memories, hand-me-downs, and grief, in the first blood of a daughter's menarche, the last breath of a mother's life, in the dream you remembered this morning in the first light of the day.

Our feminine souls are rooted in the Motherline. As we reclaim these aspects of the female self, we bind ourselves to the mysteries and honor the goddess as she manifests in our lives. She brings us carnal knowledge of our bodies; orients us in the narrative of generations; gives meaning to our suffering and that of our mothers before us; and helps us remember what we have forgotten—the ancient female wisdom that lives in the depths of our stories and our dreams.

NOTES

INTRODUCTION

1. Alice Walker, *In Search of My Mother's Garden* (San Diego: Harcourt, Brace, Jovanovitch, 1983), p. 240.

2. Naomi Ruth Lowinsky "The Generation Cord: A Hand-Me-Down of Mothering in Four Families and a Changing Culture," (Master's thesis, Lone Mountain College, 1977). "All the Days of Her Life: A Study of Adult Development and the Motherline in Modern Women," (Ph.D. diss., Center for Psychological Studies, 1985).

3. Andrew Samuels, *Jung and the Post-Jungians* (London: Routledge and Kegan Paul, 1985), p. 91.

4. James Hillman, *Re-Visioning Psychology* (New York: Harper Colophon, 1975), p. xiii.

5. Joseph Henderson, *Shadow and Self* (Wilmette, Ill: Chiron, 1990), p. 54.

CHAPTER ONE

1. Maxine Kumin, *Tangled Vines; A Collection of Mother and Daughter Poems,* ed. Lyn Lifshin (Boston: Beacon Press, 1978), p. 85.

2. Kim Chernin, *The Hungry Self* (New York: Times Books, 1985), p. 74.

3. Myra Glazer Schotz, "Mothers and Daughters in Shakespeare" in *The Lost Tradition: Mothers and Daughters in Literature,* eds. Cathy Davidson and E. M. Broner (New York: Frederick Ungar Publishing Co., 1980), p. 45.

4. Nikki Giovanni, *Tangled Vines,* p. 79.

5. C. G. Jung, "The Psychological Aspects of the Kore," in *Essays on a Science of Mythology* (Princeton, N.J.: Princeton University Press, Bollingen Series XXII, 1959), p. 162.

6. Homer, *Hymn to Demeter,* trans. C. Boer (Dallas: Spring Publications, 1970), pp. 92–3.

7. C. Kerenyi, "Kore," in *Essays on a Science of Mythology,* p. 139.

8. Ibid., p. 153.

9. Ibid., pp. 144–5.

10. Erich Neumann, *The Great Mother* (Princeton, N.J.: Princeton University Press, 1963), p. 43.

11. Gerda Lerner, *The Creation of Patriarchy* (New York: Oxford University Press, 1986), p. 13.

12. Simone de Beauvoir, *The Second Sex* (New York: Vintage Books, 1974), p. 165.

13. Barbara Walker, *Woman's Encyclopedia of Myths and Secrets* (San Francisco: Harper and Row, 1983).

14. Erich Neumann, "On the Moon and Matriarchal Consciousness," in *Fathers and Mothers,* ed. Patricia Berry (New York: Spring Publications), p. 47.

15. Karen Horney, "The Distrust between the Sexes," in *Feminine Psychology,* ed. Harold Kelman (New York: Norton and Co., 1967), p. 115.

16. Arthur and Libby Colman, *The Father* (Wilmette, Ill.: Chiron, 1988), p. 13.

17. Eugene Monick, *Phallos* (Toronto: Inner City Books, 1987), p. 13.

18. Robert Lifton, *The Broken Connection* (New York: Basic Books, 1979), p. 23.

19. Meinrad Craighead, *The Mother's Songs: Images of God the Mother* (New York: Paulist Press, 1986), p. 7.

20. Ibid., p. 11.

21. Nancy Mairs, *Plaintext: Essays* (Tucson: The University of Arizona Press, 1986), p. 64.

22. Paula Caplan, *Don't Blame Mother!* (New York: Harper and Row, 1989), p. 52.

23. Mairs, *Plaintext,* p. 65.

24. Janna Malamud Smith, *New York Times Magazine,* June 10, 1990.

25. David Meltzer, ed., *Birth: An Anthology of Ancient Texts, Songs, Prayer and Stories* (San Francisco: North Point Press, 1981), p. 76.

CHAPTER TWO

1. Betty Friedan, *The Feminine Mystique* (New York: Dell, 1983), p. 15.

2. Ibid., p. 16.

3. Quoted in *Between Ourselves,* Karen Payne ed. (Boston: Houghton Mifflin, 1983), p. 3.

4. Judy Grahn, "She Who," in *The Work of a Common Woman* (Trumansberg, N.Y.: The Crossing Press, 1978), p. 78.

5. de Beauvoir, *Second Sex,* p. 72.

6. Shulamith Firestone, "The Dialectic of Sex," in *Feminist Frameworks,* eds. Alison M. Jagger and Paula S. Rothenberg (New York: McGraw-Hill, 1978), p. 132.

7. Emily Hancock, *The Girl Within* (New York: E.P. Dutton, 1989), p. 32.

8. The women Jungian analysts were Elizabeth Osterman, Kay Bradway, and Bertha Mason.

9. Betty Friedan, *The Second Stage* (New York: Summit Books, 1981), p. 16.

10. Jean Miller, *Toward a New Psychology of Women* (Boston: Beacon Press), p. 2.

11. Jean Loevinger, *Ego Development* (San Francisco: Jossey-Bass, 1976), p. 23.

CHAPTER THREE

1. Meltzer, *Birth*, pp. 73–74.

2. Ursula Le Guin, *Dancing at the Edge of the World* (New York: Harper and Row, 1989), p. 149.

3. Angela McBride, *The Growth and Development of Mothers* (New York: Harper and Row, 1973), p. 90.

4. C. G. Jung, "A 'complete' life," *in Letters,* vol. 2, (Princeton: Princeton University Press, Bollingen Series XCV, 1973), p. 171.

5. Jean Bolen, *Goddesses in Everywoman: A New Psychology of Women* (New York: Harper and Row, 1984), p. 76.

CHAPTER FOUR

1. Adrienne Rich, *Of Woman Born* (New York: W.W. Norton, 1976), p. 225.

2. Hancock, *Girl,* p. 21.

3. Miller, *Toward a New Psychology of Women,* p. 83.

4. Nancy Friday, *My Mother, My Self* (New York: Dell, 1977), pp. 461–2.

5. C. G. Jung, *Shadow, Animus, and Anima* (Analytical Psychology Club of New York, 1951), p. 1.

6. Esther Harding, *The Shadow,* (Spring, 1945), p. 16.

7. Robert Bly, *A Little Book On The Human Shadow* (New York: Harper and Row, 1988).

8. Larry Jaffee, *Liberating the Heart,* p. 70.

9. Kathy Carlson, *In Her Image: The Unhealed Daughter's Search for Her Mother* (Boston: Shambhala, 1989), p. 11.

10. Connie Zweig, Unpublished vignette.

11. Friday, *My Mother.*

12. Tillie Olsen, *Mother to Daughter, Daughter to Mother* (Old Westbury, N.Y.: Feminist Press, 1984), p. 132.

13. Charlene Balridge, *Between Ourselves,* ed. Payne, pp. 42–43.

14. Sharon Olds, Young Mothers V, *Satan Says* (Pittsburgh: University of Pittsburgh Press, 1980), p. 43.

15. Tillie Olsen, *Tell Me a Riddle* (New York: Laurel, 1981), p. 9.

16. Ibid., pp. 20–21.

17. Kim Chernin, *In My Mother's House* (New York: Harper and Row, 1983), pp. 281–2.

18. Ibid., p. 8.

19. Ibid., pp. 306–7.

CHAPTER FIVE

1. Paula Gunn Allen, *The Sacred Hoop* (Boston: Beacon Press, 1986), p. 210.

2. Susan Griffin, *Woman and Nature* (New York: Harper and Row, 1978), pp. 210–211.

CHAPTER SIX

1. C. G. Jung, *Memories, Dreams and Reflections* (New York: Vintage Books, 1961), p. 91.

2. Evelyn Reed, *Woman's Evolution: From Matriarchal Clan to Patriarchal Family* (New York: Pathfinder Press, 1975), p. 308.

3. Josephine Humphries, *Rich in Love* (New York: Penguin Books, 1987), p. 46.

4. Margaret Sanger, *An Autobiography* (New York: Dover Publications, 1971), pp. 86–88.

5. Irene de Claremont Castillejo, *Knowing Woman: A Feminine Psychology* (New York: Harper Colophon Books, 1974).

6. Rich, *Woman*, p. 23.

7. Vivian Gornick, *Fierce Attachments* (New York: Farrar Straus Giroux, 1987), pp. 31–32.

8. Ibid., p. 32.

CHAPTER SEVEN

1. Craighead, *Mother's Songs*.

2. Jung, "Kore."

CHAPTER EIGHT

1. Amy Tan, *The Joy Luck Club* (New York: G.P. Putnam's Sons, 1989), p. 103.

2. Barbara Walker, *The Woman's Encyclopedia of Myths and Secrets* (San Francisco: Harper and Row, 1983), p. 372.

3. Tan, *Joy Luck Club*, p. 67.

4. Ibid., p. 42.

5. Ibid., p. 48.

6. Merlin Stone, "The Gifts From Reclaiming Goddess History," in *To Be A Woman*, ed. Connie Zweig (Los Angeles: Jeremy P. Tarcher, 1990), p. 215.

7. Toni Morrison, *Beloved* (New York: A Plume Book, 1987), p. 139.

8. Ibid., p. 140.

9. Ibid., p. 251.

10. Tan, *Joy Luck Club*, p. 49.

CHAPTER NINE

1. *See: Under Love*, trans. Betsy Rosenberg (New York: Washington Square Press, 1989), p. 13.

2. Zdena Berger, *Tell Me Another Morning*, p. 53.

CHAPTER TEN

1. Walker, *Woman's Encyclopedia*, p. 639.

2. Ibid.

3. John Sharkey, *Celtic Mysteries* (New York: Thames and Hudson, 1984), p. 8.

4. Raphael Patai, *The Hebrew Goddess* (Detroit: Wayne State University Press, 1978).

5. Elaine Pagels, *The Gnostic Gospels* (New York: Vintage Books, 1979), p. 49.

6. Ibid.

7. Elinor Gadon, *The Once and Future Goddess* (New York: Harper and Row, 1989).

8. *Man and His Symbols,* ed. Carl Jung, (New York: Doubleday, 1964).

9. Patai, *Hebrew,* p. 23.

10. Betty Meador, (Paper given at Ghost Ranch Conference, 1988).

11. Penelope Shutte and Peter Redgrove, *The Wise Wound: Myths, Realities and Meanings of Menstruation* (New York: Bantam Books, 1990), p. 11.

12. Ibid., p. 9.

13. Walker, *Woman's Encyclopedia,* pp. 636–7.

14. Ibid., p. 352.

15. Patai, *Hebrew,* p. 150.

16. Walker, *Woman's Encyclopedia,* p. 638.

17. Don Sandner in *Betwixt and Between,* eds. Louise Carus Mahei, Steven Foster, and Meredith Little (La Salle, Illinois: Open Court, 1987) p. 177.

18. Ibid., p. 258.

19. Anne Cameron, *Daughters of Copper Woman* (Vancouver, B.C.: Press Gang Publishers, 1986).

20. LeGuin, *Dancing,* p. 163.

21. Michael Fishbane, *The Other Side of God,* ed. P. L. Berger (Garden City, N.Y.: Anchor Books, 1981),p. 43.

22. Ibid., pp. 32–33.

23. Ibid.

24. LeGuin, *Dancing,* p. 149.

25. Deena Metzger, "Revamping the World: On the Return of the Holy Prostitute," in *To Be a Woman,* ed. Connie Zweig, p. 184.

26. Barbara Koltuz, *The Book of Lilith* (York Beach, Maine: Nicolas-Hays, 1986), p. 27.

27. Shuttle and Redgrave, *Myths, Realities,* p. 11.

28. Griffin, *Woman and Nature,* pp. 7–8.

29. LeGuin, *Dancing,* p. 151.

30. J. G. Frazer, *Folklore in the Old Testament* (New York: Tudor Publishing Co., 1923), p. 360.

31. Fishbane, *Other Side of God,* p. 32.

32. Wolfgang Lederer, *The Fear of Women* (New York: Harcourt, Brace, Jovanovich, 1968), p. 165.

33. Ibid., pp. 167–8.

34. Heinrich Zimmer, *Myths and Symbols in Indian Art and Civilization* (New York: Pantheon Books, Bollingen Series XXXIX, 1960), p. 215.

35. *The Black Madonna* (Boston: Sigo Press, 1990), p. 79.

36. *Collected Poems* (New York: W.W. Norton and Co., 1974).

37. Conversation with Joseph Henderson.

38. Erich Neumann, *The Great Mother* (Princeton, N.J.: Princeton University Press, Bollingen Series XLVII, 1974), p. 152.

39. *Kali the Feminine Force* (New York: Destiny Books, 1988), p. 11.

40. Olsen, *Mother to Daughter; Daughter to Mother,* pp. 130–131.

41. Elsie Adams and Mary Louise Briscoe, eds., *Up Against the Wall, Mother* (Beverly Hills, CA: Glencoe Press), p. 334.

42. *Soul Crisis* (New York: New American Library, 1989), pp. 149–50.

43. Ibid., pp. 217–218.

44. *Outrageous Acts and Everyday Rebellions* (New York: New American Library, 1983), p. 130.

45. Ibid., p. 139.

46. Marija Gimbutas, *The Goddesses and Gods of Old Europe,* (Berkeley, CA: University of California Press, 1982), p. 131.

EPILOGUE

1. Craighead, *Images of God,* p. 13.

BIBLIOGRAPHY

MOTHERLINE STORIES

Cameron, Anne. *Daughters of Copper Woman.* Vancouver, B.C.: Press Gang Publishers, 1986.

Chernin, Kim. *In My Mother's House.* New York: Harper and Row, 1983.

Davidson, Cathy, and Broner, E. M. *The Lost Tradition: Mothers and Daughters in Literature.* New York: Frederick Ungar Publishing, 1980.

Fastman, Raisa. *A Portrait of American Mothers and Daughters: Photographs.* Pasadena, CA: New Sage Press, 1987.

Gornick, Vivian. *Fierce Attachments.* New York: Farrar Straus Giroux, 1987.

Gunn Allen, Paula. *The Woman Who Owned the Shadows.* San Francisco: Spinsters, Inc., 1983.

Koppelman, Susan, ed. *Between Mothers and Daughters: Stories Across a Generation.* Old Westbury, New York: Feminist Press, 1985.

Lifshin, Lyn, ed. *Tangled Vines: A Collection of Mother and Daughter Poems.* Boston: Beacon Press, 1978.

Mairs, Nancy. *Plaintext: Essays.* Tucson, AZ: The University of Arizona Press, 1986.

Mead, Margaret. *Blackberry Winter: My Earlier Years.* New York: A Touchstone Book, 1972.

Morrison, Toni. *Beloved.* New York: A Plume Book, 1988.

Nathanson, Sue. *Soul Crisis: One Woman's Journey Through Abortion to Renewal.* New York: New American Library.

Olsen, Tillie. *Tell Me a Riddle.* New York: Laurel, 1981.

Tan, Amy. *The Joy Luck Club.* New York: G.P. Putnam's Sons, 1989.

Walker, Alice. *In Search of My Mother's Garden.* San Diego, Calif.: Harcourt, Brace, Jovanovich, 1983.

ON SHADOW, SOUL, AND SELF

Bly, Robert. *A Little Book on the Human Shadow.* New York: Harper and Row, 1988.

Campbell, Joseph, ed. *The Portable Jung.* Middlesex, England: Penguin Books, 1978.

Chernin, Kim. *The Hungry Self: Women, Eating and Identity.* New York: Time Books, 1985.

Edinger, Edward. *Ego and Archetype.* Baltimore, Maryland: Penguin Books, 1974.

Henderson, Joseph. *Shadow and Self.* Wilmette, Illinois: Chiron, 1990.

Hillman, James. *The Dream and the Underworld.* New York: Harper and Row, 1979.

————. *Re-Visioning Psychology.* New York: Harper Colophon Books, 1975.

Jaffe, Aniela. *The Myth of Meaning. Jung and the Expansion of Consciousness.* New York: Penguin Books, 1975.

Jung, Carl G., ed. *Man and His Symbols.* Garden City, New York: Doubleday and Co., 1964.

Jung, Carl G. *Memories, Dreams and Reflections.* New York: Vintage Books, 1965.

Perera, Sylvia B. *The Scapegoat Complex: Toward a Mythology of Shadow and Guilt.* Toronto: Inner City Books, 1986.

Signell, Karen. *Wisdom of the Heart: Working with Women's Dreams.* New York: Bantam Books, 1990.

Whitmont, Edward. *The Symbolic Quest: Basic Concepts of Analytical Psychology.* Princeton, New Jersey: Princeton University Press, 1978.

Zweig, Connie, and Abrams, Jeremiah. *Meeting the Shadow: The Hidden Power of the Dark Side of Human Nature.* Los Angeles: Jeremy P. Tarcher, 1991.

ON FEMINISM AND THE FEMININE

Carlson, Kathie. *In Her Image: The Unhealed Daughter's Search for Her Mother.* Boston: Shambhala, 1989.

Claremont de Castillejo, Irene. *Knowing Woman: A Feminine Psychology.* New York: Harper Colophon Books, 1974.

Dinnerstein, Dorothy. *The Mermaid and the Minotaur: Sexual Arrangements and Human Malaise.* New York: Harper Colophon, 1977.

Douglas, Claire. *The Woman in the Mirror: Analytical Psychology and the Feminine*. Boston: Sigo Press, 1990.

Friedan, Betty. *The Second Stage*. New York: Summit Books, 1981.

Gilligan, Carol. *In a Different Voice: Psychological Theory and Women's Development*. Cambridge, Mass.: Harvard University Press, 1982.

Grahn, Judy. *Another Mother Tongue: Gay Words, Gay Worlds*. Boston: Beacon Press, 1984.

Greer, Germaine. *The Female Eunuch*. New York: McGraw-Hill, 1971.

Hall, Nor. *The Moon and the Virgin: Reflections on the Archetypal Feminine*. New York: Harper Colophon, 1980.

Hancock, Emily. *The Girl Within: Recapture the Childhood Self, the Key to Female Identity*. New York: E.P. Dutton, 1989.

Harding, Esther. *The Way of All Women*. Harper Colophon, 1975.

———. *Woman's Mysteries: Ancient and Modern*. New York: G.P. Putnam's Sons, 1971.

Heilbrun, Carolyn G. *Writing A Woman's Life*. New York: Ballantine Books, 1988.

Horney, Karen. *Feminine Psychology*. New York: W.W. Norton and Co., 1973.

Lerner, Gerda. *The Creation of Patriarchy*. New York: Oxford University Press, 1986.

Miller, Jean Baker. *Toward a New Psychology of Women*. Boston: Beacon Press, 1976.

Rich, Adrienne. *Of Woman Born*. New York: W.W. Norton & Co., 1976.

Shuttle, Penelope, and Redgrove, Peter. *The Wise Wound: Myths, Realities and Meanings of Menstruation*. New York: Bantam, 1986.

Sullivan, Barbara. *Psychotherapy Grounded in the Feminine Principle*. Wilmette, Ill.: Chiron Publications, 1989.

Woodman, Marion. *The Pregnant Virgin: A Process of Psychological Transformation*. Toronto: Inner City Books, 1985.

———. *Addiction to Perfection: The Still Unravished Bride*. Toronto: Inner City Books, 1982.

Woolf, Virginia. *A Room of One's Own*. San Diego, CA: Harcourt, Brace, Jovanovich, 1957.

Zweig, Connie, ed. *To Be A Woman: The Birth of the Conscious Feminine*. Los Angeles: Jeremy P. Tarcher, 1990.

ON OUR SPIRITUAL ROOTS

Bolen, Jean. *Goddesses in Everywoman: A New Psychology of Women.* San Francisco: Harper and Row, 1984.

Brindel, June Rachuy. *Ariadne: A Novel of Ancient Crete.* New York: St. Martin's Press, 1980.

Canan, Janine, ed. *She Rises Like the Sun: Invocations of the Goddess by Contemporary American Women Poets.* Freedom, California: The Crossing Press, 1989.

Craighead, Meinrad. *The Mother's Songs: Images of God The Mother.* New York: Paulist Press, 1986.

Eisler, Riane. *The Chalice and the Blade: Our History, Our Future.* San Francisco: Harper and Row, 1988.

Gadon, Elinor. *The Once and Future Goddess: A Symbol for Our Time.* San Francisco: Harper and Row, 1989.

Gimbutas, Marija. *The Language of the Goddess.* San Francisco: Harper and Row, 1989.

Gunn Allen, Paula. *The Sacred Hoop: Recovering the Feminine in American Indian Traditions.* Boston: Beacon Press, 1986.

Henderson, Joseph, and Oakes, Maude. *The Wisdom of the Serpent: The Myths of Death, Rebirth and Resurrection.* Princeton, New Jersey: Princeton University Press, 1990.

Koltuv, Barbara. *The Book of Lilith.* York Beach, Maine: Nicolas-Hays, Inc., 1986.

Lerner, Gerda. *The Creation of Patriarchy.* New York: Oxford University Press, 1986.

Mookerjee, Ajit. *Kali: The Feminine Force.* New York: Destiny Books, 1988.

Neumann, Erich. *The Great Mother: An Analysis of an Archetype.* Princeton, New Jersey: Princeton University Press, Bollingen Series XLVII, 1974.

Patai, Raphael. *The Hebrew Goddess.* Detroit: Wayne University Press, 1990.

Perera, Sylvia. *Descent to the Goddess: A Way of Initiation for Women.* Toronto: Inner City Books, 1981.

Stone, Merlin. *Ancient Mirrors of Womanhood: A Treasury of Goddess and Heroine Lore from Around the World.* Boston: Beacon Press, 1979.

———. *When God was a Woman.* San Diego, CA. Harcourt, Brace, Jovanovich, 1976.

Walker, Barbara. *The Woman's Encyclopedia of Myths and Secrets.* San Francisco: Harper and Row, 1983.

Whitmont, Edward. *Return of the Goddess.* New York: Crossroad, 1984.

ABOUT THE AUTHOR

N aomi Ruth Lowinsky has published poetry and prose expressive of feminine soul since the early 1970s. She has taught and lectured extensively about Jungian psychology and women's lives.

She is currently on the faculty of the Pacifica Graduate Institute in Santa Barbara, California, an analyst in training at the San Francisco Jung Institute, Assistant Editor of the San Francisco Jung Institute Library Journal, and has a private practice in Berkeley. She has three children and three stepchildren, all now grown, and lives with her husband, Dan Safran.